TO MY OWN DESIRE

Recent Titles by Harriet Hudson from Severn House

TO MY OWN DESIRE

Harriet Hudson

This first world edition published in Great Britain 2000 by
SEVERN HOUSE PUBLISHERS LTD of
9–15 High Street, Sutton, Surrey SM1 1DF.
This first world edition published in the USA 2000 by
SEVERN HOUSE PUBLISHERS INC of
595 Madison Avenue, New York, N.Y. 10022.

British Library Cataloguing in Publication Data

Hudson, Harriet
     To my own desire
     1.   Love stories
     I.   Title
     823.9'14 [F]

     ISBN 0-7278-5589-1

Typeset by Palimpsest Book Production Ltd.,
Polmont, Stirlingshire, Scotland.
Printed and bound in Great Britain by
MPG Books Ltd., Bodmin, Cornwall.

Acknowledgements

Lucky the author who treads the minefield of publishing a novel with two such guides as I had: my editor Marisa McGreevy at Severn House, and my agent Dorothy Lumley of the Dorian Literary Agency. To them both my gratitude for their encouragement and care, and my thanks to Emily Brewer of Severn House for her eagle-eyed copy-editing. I would also like to thank Claire Wood for her help with the world of ballet, my husband for his indefatigable hunt for unicorns in New York, and Ellie Palmer whose enthusiasm for unicorns spurred me onwards.

Amongst the many books and contemporary newspapers I consulted, *Diaghilev* by Richard Buckle (Weidenfield & Nicholson, 1979) and *The Choreographic Art* by Peggy van Praagh and Peter Brinson (A&C Black, 1963) were particularly helpful.

H.H.

It is sayd that Unicorns above all other creatures doe reverence Virgines and young Maides, and that many times at the sight of them they growe tame and come and sleepe beside them, for there is in their nature a certain savour wherewithal the Unicornes are allured and delighted: for which occasion the Indian and Ethiopian hunters use . . . strategem to take the beast . . .

Edward Topsell in *Historie of Four-Footed Beastes*, 1607

One

Tara was impatient to be gone, but for some reason she lingered. Perhaps it was merely the flying feet, the strange intricacy of the dance and the haunting music from the tinny cassette player, or perhaps it was the mesmerising intensity of the dancer, his black hair flying wildly with the passion of his movements. Her rational self informed her that the spring sunshine was good after the whole morning closeted in the conference room, and that the Pompidou Centre exhibition she had intended to see could wait until tomorrow. She was uneasily aware, however, that there *was* no rational reason.

When the young man finished, ousted from his prime spot outside the Centre by an eager juggler, she remained while he took round the hat, surprised at his lack of worldliness in not coming accompanied by someone to do this for him while he was performing. At the sight of the hat the tourist crowd was fast melting away to other distractions, leaving Tara unavoidably conspicuous. She wouldn't usually have minded this, so why did her desire to leave conflict with a feeling that her feet were as rooted to the ground as the Pompidou itself?

The ancient panama – where had he dug that up from? – was duly thrust before her; she dropped in a twenty-franc coin, searching for something to say, which again surprised her. She wasn't usually at a loss for words.

The dancer forestalled her. "I don't do it for the money."

"What, then?" Her expression on seeing the virtually empty hat must have made her thoughts obvious.

"Pleasure, probably. Who knows?"

Ah, a dreamer, an idealist, said her rational self, but it was another Tara that blurted out: "What was that dance you were performing? It was unusual."

Hovering somewhere was a memory she could not pin down.

1

No, not quite a memory, but a sensation, of being lifted into another plane where music, light and colour enveloped her. Even as she snatched at it, it fled tantalisingly out of reach.

He looked at her fully for the first time, disconcerting her with astonishingly blue eyes for the dark hair. Moreover, his grin was too intimate for the level she had unconsciously aimed at; it broke down normal barriers, ignoring her carefully nurtured image of an "in-control" Tara Maitland. That was what she got for stepping out of her appointed line.

" 'The Unicorn'," he answered.

Deep inside that memory-sensation stirred again, a sleeping dragon – or beauty – coming to life. "Of course." She remembered the jumps and twirls and the strange movements of the head. "Did you create the dance?"

He frowned. "I don't know."

She relaxed in relief. His daft reply had given her just the opportunity she needed. She glanced at her watch. Conversation over. She just had time to make the start of the cross-border charity tax session. William would be there; he was most definitely not a dreamer, and even if he had once been a penniless student, he certainly was not now. William represented firm ground – no jumps and twirls for him – and she loved him for it. She did, didn't she? After all, she'd been living with him for two years.

The sudden doubt crystallised her determination to get back to the safe territory of the conference, where the mere sight of William would make her forget this entire incident. She nodded in farewell, but the young man grabbed her arm.

"I mean, I *really* don't know. Where do ideas come from? Our genes, acquired knowledge or products of ourselves alone? Or is there no such thing as oneself alone?"

She laughed, amused at his earnestness. Her days of midnight discussions on the meaning of life were past, and so were snatches of yesteryear. "Now that *I* don't know."

"Josh Santine." He removed his hand from her arm at last, but was looking at her so inquiringly that she was obliged to answer.

"Tara Maitland."

"Do you dance, Tara?"

Her answer came out pat, produced by her adult self. "I lumbered around at ballet classes with all the other five-year-olds in the world, but since then I've stuck to jigging up and down to pop music. You don't meet too many unicorns that way."

Even as she spoke, however, she thought involuntarily of the glory of the dance, the music to which she had fondly believed she was floating in harmony, the colour of her beloved tutu and ballet shoes – and the yawning disappointment when the teacher had told her mother she had no real talent. Tara had not been meant to overhear, of course, but she had done, and the magic of the dance of life had slipped through her fingers like a dying butterfly. Every child faces that moment, consciously or unconsciously, with the coming of adolescence, but for Tara it had been conscious – and too early.

It had caused a hurt that had set her on a different path to achievement, suppressing all thoughts and memories of expression through dance. Perhaps not every child lost the magic, however. There was something about Josh – something indefinable – that suggested it lingered in him, and that in his dance he lived in the magic still.

"Do you lumber around with painting instead?"

"No." Why on earth should she? She came down to earth, realising such an inappropriate question must simply be part of a routine pick-up. She was annoyed with herself, and it was high time to put an end to this, however intriguingly fanciable Josh looked. "I'm a tax lawyer with Pitkin, Watts Hargreaves, and that doesn't give me a lot of scope for dancing off into the sunset."

Josh looked blank, which was hardly any wonder. In the circles in which she moved everyone would know Pitkin, Watts & Hargreaves, and for her to be a senior manager at only twenty-five pinpointed the direction in which she intended to go. Upwards. But Josh didn't know those circles, and at the moment she was a lone trespasser on his pitch.

"I can't believe you're a tax lawyer. You said 'of course' immediately when I told you the dance's name."

That really annoyed her. "Don't assume tax lawyers are programmed never to understand the arts." She tried to make it sound light, but even to herself it sounded defensive.

"I'm sorry." The light went out of Josh's eyes, and from being arresting to look at, he changed to the unremarkable. Tara relaxed again. She could put down all her weird thoughts to the fine spring

3

day. However talented a dancer, he was merely one more student in a world of hopefuls. Tara excused herself and walked briskly away. If she hurried she could still make the first session.

What then made her want to turn round? Some primeval instinct that she was being watched? Something that still puzzled her about their encounter? She had a faint memory of reading that the famous dancer Nijinsky was magic on stage but off stage looked quite ordinary. Good though Josh was, however, he was hardly in Nijinsky's class, and she was, she told herself, quite happy with William, thanks all the same. Why waste more time? She did glance back, though, and sure enough, Josh was still staring at her.

So what? She tried to shrug off her uneasiness. Men did stare at her. One didn't have to be vain to acknowledge the fact, and Tara was aware that the graceful figure, delicate features, and honey-coloured hair she had inherited from her mother rendered her at least passably attractive. If she was to rise in her profession, however, it was important to be seen to do so by ability not beauty, and she wore her severe black suit like a regimental uniform.

She was damned if she was going to walk back to him, however curious she might still be about the unicorn dance, for that too seemed to bring back some fleeting memory of childhood. But in the end it was settled for her, as Josh came strolling up to her. She had no option but to stand her ground. She could hardly take to her heels, and his approach wasn't exactly the usual come-on. For a moment she fancied he looked as puzzled as she did that they were once again face to face.

She realised when he reached her that she had been guilty of theorising too soon, a crime she never committed professionally. He might be dressed casually but he was too old to be a student, certainly in his mid-twenties, and his clothes were not those of a student. The jeans were well cut, as was the French *blouson*-style jacket. All the more reason for her to attempt at least to take command of the situation, even though this meant seizing on the very reason for her disquiet.

"Why choose the unicorn?" she asked. Perhaps her logical sense was just puzzled as to why he had chosen such a fanciful and complicated theme for an outdoor display.

"Just my own desire. What makes you so curious?"

Control whistled down the wind. "There were a lot of unicorns around at home." The sheer fatuousness of her reply made her giggle.

"Now that," Josh replied seriously, "could be dangerous."

"I thought unicorns were emblems of peace."

"Wrong. They are the fiercest of animals, unless tamed by a pure virgin of course."

Tara hovered between yesterday's fantasies and today's reality, waiting suspiciously for the usual nudge-nudge comment or look. He remained straight-faced, and, won over, she commented, "You said *are*. Aren't you rather old to believe in legendary monsters?"

Josh looked hurt. "Unicorns aren't legendary, they're real. You should know. You apparently grew up with a menagerie full of them. Any lamias around?"

"No, but there be dragons. I was fascinated as a child by a series of needlecases with tapestry covers, each showing a unicorn and a lady. There were five of them—"

She broke off. Where the hell had all that come from? Up to a few seconds ago she hadn't thought of those unicorns at home for years. Come to that, what had happened to them?

"Not sight, sound, taste, smell, touch, by any chance? If so, there would be a sixth."

She stared at him, half mesmerised, half scared. She remembered now.

"Oddly enough, there might have been a sixth once," she replied slowly, "but it's been lost." She had a sudden memory of her mother telling her that far too off-handedly, and she supposed it was the sense of mystery that had made it lodge in her subconscious memory. She had found the needlecases in the back of a drawer in a boxroom with a few – very few – other family heirlooms. She hadn't been meant to see them, for her mother had been annoyed when Tara, entranced at her find, had produced them and demanded to know about unicorns. When she next went to the drawer, they and all the other family effects had vanished. This in itself was strange, for in her parents' cheerful, cluttered home, tidying out drawers was at the bottom of the priority list.

Tara pondered now on whether the needlecases she recalled could indeed have illustrated the five senses. "How did you guess?" she asked Josh abruptly, aware that he was staring at her appraisingly. It wasn't the usual lecherous going-over, more a look of inquiry, as if he too were taking a step back to work out why they were both suddenly surrounded by unicorns.

Whatever he saw must have reassured him, for he looked pleased at her question.

"I'll show you. It won't take long to walk there. It's only just over the river in the Latin Quarter."

He took her hand without even waiting for her agreement. Immediately she felt herself mentally recoiling, feeling like Gretel lost in the forest with Hansel. Only mentally, however, for physically it felt like an electric current shooting through her. The gesture was not in the least a brotherly one, and she looked down at her hand clasped in his as though it were on some erratic mission of its own.

"No way, Josh. I'm sorry, but I'm already late for my conference, so if you could kindly return my hand to me, I'll be off." Whatever unicorns the mysterious forest ahead might hold, she didn't want to be in it. It was one step too far.

"Conference on what?"

"The new charity tax rules and the role of 501 CO3s in planned giving."

"On a day like this in Paris?"

"Look," Tara replied patiently, trying to bring some reason back to the situation, even though his thumb, perhaps unconsciously, was performing a gentle dance of its own upon her wrist. "Dancing is what you do. Tax is what I do. Right?"

"Wrong. Unicorns is what you do."

That did it. She had to get away, *now*. "Goodbye, Josh, and I mean it." She marched briskly off towards the Boulevard de Sebastopol to put an end to this craziness, relieved that at last she had had the strength to do so. Ten to one he was a nutter, she told herself, and this time she should not look back. He was pleasant enough, but not for her, either as friend or—

She pulled her thoughts away from Josh Santine, as amid the smartly dressed Parisian crowd she began to calm down, back among her own. Just a short walk north and she could slip into normality again.

By the time she reached the hotel where the conference was being held, she had almost succeeded in fixing her thoughts on tax and planned giving – until, to her amazement and horror, she saw Josh, dancing in front of the hotel entrance to the irritation of the uniformed doorman. Immediately she was thrown back into yesterday's world. Deep down, she was aware that she was dancing too, and not with Josh's strange modern movements, but struggling on *demi-pointe*, a seven-year-old trying so hard to make her feet obey the music inside her. They never did, but inside her the music must still be playing on.

Uncomfortably aware that there were tears on her face, she asked, "How did you do that? You couldn't have overtaken me. Are you a leprechaun in your spare time?"

"Mere illusion, Tara. Please come with me to the Left Bank and I'll explain."

"Absolutely not, Josh." Firmness was essential – both towards him and herself – especially when he was looking at her in such appeal. It was not unknown to slip out of a conference, but those who wished to climb the ladder had to take every chance of being counted among the faithful. Furthermore, she convinced herself, going AWOL with an attractive young man you'd just met belonged to student days, not her life with William.

He hesitated, and for a moment she thought she'd won – if that was the right word. She was wrong, in any case.

"Sorry, but I think you have to. I'm as put out as you are, because I had no plans when I got up this morning to drag a buttoned-up lawyer off to the Cluny, but God moves in mysterious ways."

"Highly mysterious if he managed to get you here ahead of me." Buttoned up? Was that how he saw her? Tara was infuriated now, wanting to shout out, I'm not, I'm not! There's music inside me! For all her dedication to her career, she was as fun-loving and lively off duty as he. "How did you know I was coming for a start?"

"I'll tell you on our way, Tara. Let's go."

His blithe assurance that she had to come with him made her waver. She glanced inside the conference building. Out here it was a sunny spring afternoon. In there was the cool, dark entrance hall. On the lower ground floor, the room she should be heading for was shut off from all natural light and air in the interests of video screens and computers. It was true, she admitted to herself, this afternoon's agenda wasn't really her speciality. She could take time off, and William would not be surprised at her absence, for they often attended different sessions. The problem was Josh himself. Much as Tara longed to prove she didn't fit Josh's stereotype, she should be hesitant about getting into a situation from which he might well read – and take – more than she intended.

To her surprise, she realised her decision was already made, however. She *would* go. What was one afternoon, after all? When doubt returned, it brought compromise with it. She ignored the proffered hand.

It was not until they were crossing the Pont St Michel to the Left Bank that Josh finally explained how his "miracle" had been achieved.

"Strictly against the Magic Circle rules to reveal my secrets, but as I promised, here goes." He struck an elegant pose, straight out of classical ballet, if she remembered correctly. At any rate, it impressed the passers-by, and amused her. "I read the hotel name on the conference book you are still using as an armoured breastplate, and leapt on a passing bus," he explained.

Tara was curiously disappointed. "Not so mysterious," she said sadly.

He glanced at her oddly as they began their trek once more, and when he spoke, he was so quiet that she hardly caught the words.

"Perhaps, Tara, that's still to come. The unicorns are gathering."

The Musée du Moyen Age was housed in the splendid medieval building of Cluny, and so far Tara had been unable to understand why Josh had brought her. She had half expected a whimsical toy collection, but there was nothing to suggest a unicorn might suddenly thrust its horn round a corner. Then Josh led the way into a semi-circular room, and in a moment she realised why they had come. Despite the low level of light she was consumed by colour as five huge tapestries, towering above her, drew her into their glory. The warm red backgrounds set off the central figures of the richly dressed lady and the attendant unicorn, and were admirably dotted with a wealth of colours depicting flowers, animals and birds. Tara recognised them all. Across the years the small child trotted back, clutching five needlecases in her hand, wondering what these strange white animals were, and why they were at the lady's side? These were the same designs, save that on the small needlecases, so far as she recalled, the weaver had concentrated on the lady and the unicorn alone. Certainly Tara had only had eyes for the unicorn. Seeing them here, full size and in their entirety, there was no doubt that they represented sight, hearing, taste, smell and touch.

She had to find something to say, to cover up the depth of emotion they raised in her, even though Josh seemed as rapt as she was.

"The museum calls the series 'The Lady and the Unicorn', but the maid and the lion are almost as prominent. Why is it always the unicorn who gets the best of the deal?" she asked him lightly, trying to ignore the tremor in her voice.

"Because it represents love, passion and instinct, whereas the poor old lion is only might, power and reason. Look behind you, Tara."

She turned round, and there was the sixth tapestry, the crowning glory – so different to the other five, and yet drawing them together perfectly. "It's the most beautiful of them all." Her remark was trite and obvious, for here the lady was shown canopied by a tent over which was emblazoned "*À mon seul désir*".

"My only desire," she translated.

"More probably, to my *own* desire. Free will," Josh corrected her.

"Like your dancing?" The remark came unbidden, and once it had been voiced she needed to know more. "And are these tapestries the reason you created your unicorn dance?"

"It's not so simple. Do you really want to know?"

"Yes." She was certain of it, and moreover, she was sure he was going to tell her anyway. Now that these sensations of her childhood had been stirred, she wanted to know more about the tapestries, more about his dance. Only in that way could she lay the memories back where they belonged, and wipe Josh Santine from her mind. It would, she argued to herself, be a perfectly ordinary story, and there was nothing like reality for dispelling mysterious puzzles, especially unwelcome ones.

But – unwelcome? Why should they be? She wrestled to throw off this image of forbidding forests ahead. She was on good terms with her parents, and had enjoyed a normal childhood, so why should delving back into the past bring present-day problems other than taking her mind away from tax? Neither she nor her parents had been much concerned with history, neither family ancestry nor any other aspect. They were all too busy living in the present, her father in the City until he retired, her mother running a garden centre. As a result, she knew very little save the bare essentials about her forebears beyond her parents, but it had never bothered her. Or had it? Was that, she wondered uneasily, why the disappearance of those family mementoes still obviously troubled her? After all, there couldn't be any great mystery hidden there, and if so she had no need to fear untrodden forests.

"Tell me the story, Josh."

Outside in the fresh air she might not have felt this way, but in here, closeted with Josh in the semi-darkness with the tapestries around them, it suddenly seemed to her she had cast some die of fate, and there would be no going back.

"No plans to rush back to your conference half-way through?" he asked cautiously.

"No."

"Then I tell you by your own desire, madame."

"Unfair," she protested at his teasing.

"Pray sit yourself down." Josh gestured at the bench facing the sixth tapestry. His archaic choice of words rang a bell but she could not identify them, and forgot them as he sat down close to her, taking off his jacket. She felt her body immediately grow tense. Every part of her was as conscious of his nearness as if he were touching her in love. Yet at the same time, there was an elusiveness about him, as in a ballet *pas de deux*. As she mentally leaned towards him, he arched gracefully back. How *ridiculous*. There could be nothing elusive about Josh Santine.

"It all stems," he told her, "from the fact that my great-grandfather way back in the mists of time was a famous dancer and choreographer."

"How famous?" Tara was immediately interested, and not merely because to speak was to divert her thoughts from their previous direction. She was no specialist in ballet, but had a fair general knowledge, yet the name Santine rang no immediate bell – or did it? Was there another faint memory eluding her?

"Enough to dance and choreograph for Diaghilev's Russian Ballet in Europe. You've heard of Fokine?"

"Of course. Diaghilev's choreographer-in-chief."

"They had a major parting of the ways, but in late 1913

10

Diaghilev had to come crawling to Fokine to plead with him to return. He came back briefly as director of choreography, and one of the conditions of the hard bargaining that took place was that other young choreographers could continue to be employed. One of them was François Santine, who in the summer of the 1913 London season choreographed a one-act ballet, and for the 1914 programme a three-act ballet called *The Unicorn and the Nightingale.*"

"I don't think I've heard of it."

"It disappeared from the repertoire, as so many ballets did, for so many reasons – usually the inadequate methods of recording the choreography. It could only be done if careful notations and sketches of groupings were taken by the choreographer, and by relying on the memories of those who had danced in the original productions. In this case, war broke out a few days after its first performance at the end of the season. François went on to choreograph one or two more, which are still occasionally revived, but his major work vanished. If it wasn't that it was in the programme, you wouldn't know it had existed."

"Who danced it for Diaghilev? Karsavina?"

"You do know your ballet," Josh said approvingly, "even though your lumbering days are over. Though I can't imagine you lumbering, Tara. You're too willowy." He laid his hand lightly on her arm, and she had to make an effort to concentrate on his story, not on the long creative fingers and the way that his soft touch seemed the loveline through which, even as they spoke, their bodies were communicating. Back to the story, Tara, she ordered herself, horrified at where her thoughts were running.

"No, it wasn't Karsavina," Josh continued. "It was Arabelle Petrovna. Another condition for Fokine's return was that his wife Vera should be allowed to dance some of the leading roles. Petrovna also was permitted to dance – notably in this one, at Santine's insistence. He was partnering her in it, as well as choreographing."

"Do you have François Santine's notes?"

"I have some of them. There's a problem, though. The music. There was a body of classical established ballets, of course, but new ballets often used music already written. However, Diaghilev began to commission musical scores to be specially written to a scenario, because Fokine's mantra was that the choreography

11

was inspired, or limited by, the music. The music wasn't simply to provide the background for technical virtuosity; it had itself to be inspired by the scenario. *The Unicorn and the Nightingale* was one of the new scores. Unfortunately the score too has disappeared."

"So what was that haunting music you were dancing to?"

"Thanks for the compliment. I wrote it."

"I don't understand. You composed the music merely to dance outside the Pompidou?"

He laughed aloud, drawing disapproving glances from the other visitors. "Let's go," he said, releasing her arm. As they walked from the room, however, he took her hand again, and this time she did not ignore it.

Tara wasn't sorry to be away from the intimacy of the tapestries. Some day, she decided, she would return alone to study them in detail without the disconcerting presence of Josh Santine. Even though he still kept hold of her hand, she felt safer once they were in the fresh air, not because she thought by now there was anything to fear from Josh, but because it gave her a degree of control once more. With no unicorns to prance between them, they were man and woman, who might part – or stay together.

Immediately Tara was once again horrified at herself. *Stay together*? She was beginning to feel all too comfortable with Josh – though she wasn't sure that that was the right word for the almost frightening sense of belonging. Belonging was a safe word too, so that wasn't right either. What then? Sexual attraction? If so, it was an inevitable one, as though her hand had slipped into a velvet skin-tight glove that had been made for it.

Nonsense! Nothing was inevitable, if you had free will.

"I should return to my conference." She tried to sound brisk, but it came out as an uncertain question.

Josh glanced at his watch, and then at her. "I reckon it's teatime there, so you might just as well have tea here and then we'll go to Neuilly."

"What's at Neuilly?" Fatal question. Pleasure at Josh's assumption that their acquaintance was not yet over was taking precedence over all common sense. She couldn't be *that* buttoned up, then. "A live unicorn in a zoo?"

"My grandfather's house. I want you to see it. He's away at the moment, but that's where I'm staying."

Her antennae instantly kicked in. Caution here, Tara. She'd been on the wrong wavelength. After tea, a polite farewell and *off*!

"You're on holiday?" she asked as casually as she could, while they chose a café pavement table and took their places. It was time to establish polite distance.

"Working holiday. I'm part of a company called Music and Mime, which tours during the summer. I design and compose for it, and I need to do some research."

"Don't tell me. On unicorns?"

"Don't mock, lady. Unicorns are serious business. *And* nightingales."

"What's the story of *The Unicorn and the Nightingale*?" She concentrated on removing the tea-bag from the lemon tea, to avoid the intimacy of Josh's probing stare across the table. "That hasn't gone missing too, has it? It was presumably something to do with the five senses."

"Far from it. It was set at King Arthur's court in Camelot. One of the knights falls in love with a Lady Lilith, who is afraid of earthly love. The witch Morgana fancies the knight and when he spurns her she turns the poor chap into a unicorn, and challenges him to track down his beloved, whom she tells him she's imprisoned in the statutory tower in the middle of a forest. Being a first-class chump, he believes her, and horns his way through the forest, hotly pursued by a pack of game hunters, to find Lilith. A nightingale, Lilith, also bewitched by Morgana, comes to his rescue by singing to him of the true path out of danger, but he doesn't listen. When he gets to the tower, he finds it is Morgana there, and she's all set for wedding bells."

"And what happens then?"

"The ballet begins with the revelries at Camelot, and the first act ends with Morgana's spell. The second act is the hunt."

"And the ending?" she asked again.

"I've no idea. The third act has completely disappeared."

"But that's ridiculous. Surely François couldn't just have left notes on two acts. Maybe there *was* no third act."

"Oh, there was. His notes end with a slash of the pen in yellow ink obviously done later. It reads: 'And the third act was Armageddon'. Can you make anything of that? I can't."

"Plans not fulfilled? He never wrote it and the performance was cancelled?"

"You're not even trying."

"I am," she hit back indignantly.

He smiled sweetly. "Then let's go to Neuilly and you can try some more."

She gazed at him in disbelief at his assumption of her *naïveté*. "Just why are you so eager for me to see this empty house?"

"It isn't empty in any sense. There's a room I want to show you, and in case you're thinking my bed is in it, think again. Grandfather may be away, but your maidenly screams would undoubtedly have his housekeeper and her six-foot coal-heaver husband in with their blunderbusses."

"To shoot you?"

"No. *You.* They're very fond of—"

"Poking their noses in?" she finished idly, when he hesitated.

"Quite. *And* there are other members of Music and Mime staying over."

That convinced her, and a fleeting fantasy of what it might be like to be in bed with Josh was firmly dispelled. Housekeepers could be a fiction, but to add another element was over-egging the pudding.

This pudding was beginning to intrigue her, and that, Tara told herself, was why she would go to Neuilly. It had nothing to do with the pudding's chef, Josh. And, she appeased her conscience, William was set on his usual networking routine this evening, and since one of his less endearing qualities was to avoid all public display of their relationship at such conferences, he wouldn't miss her if she were late back. She'd been even crosser than usual at his solo plans for the evening, for night-time Paris, even conference Paris, was surely for lovers.

"My grandfather calls it the Unicorn Room," Josh said, as, less than an hour later, Tara gazed in combined enchantment and bewilderment at her extraordinary surroundings. The house itself had been interesting enough, but this room was completely unexpected. The compact grey stone mini-château, with green shutters at the beautifully proportioned windows, was set back from the road in a garden filled with the promise of colour to come. Plants sprawled from stone pots set on the gravel, trees coming into leaf screened the house from the curious.

"Can you wonder I grew up being fascinated by the beast?" Josh continued. "If I had lived here all the time, I might have been put off. I hope you're not. As it was a holiday treat for me to come here – and still is – it grew in my fevered imagination while I was away from it. Do you sense unfinished business about it? That's what I said to my grandfather, and when he told me shortly afterwards he'd be leaving me this house in his will, I guessed I was right. It's what spurred me on to create my act."

Tara looked around her once again. The room was dark but not gloomy, and painted the same basic colour as the Cluny tapestries, a mellow red. Most of it was covered with photographs and drawings – many not with the unicorn images she was used to seeing, but depicting a one-horned beast of antiquity that offered nothing to sentimentality. There were woven reproductions of the Cluny tapestries and, facing them, of another set of unicorn pictures. Here the lady had no such gentle face, however. It was sly, cunning, and secretive. Tara shivered, despite the warmth of the room.

"That's the series in New York," Josh explained. "The Hunt of the Unicorn."

"Then presumably this is what your great-grandfather based his ballet on."

"Yes; the ballet like these tapestries carries a dual symbolism. The unicorn is the lover, the lady his beloved, even though in this series" – he pointed – "she is luring the unicorn in order to trap him. The only way, folklore has it, that the fierce unicorn can be taken is when he is tamed by laying his head in a virgin's lap. Hence hunters employing young ladies for this very purpose. Woman, the betrayer."

He stopped abruptly, as if uncertain that he still had his audience.

"And what of the Cluny tapestries?" she asked. "The lady's not betraying the unicorn then."

"No. They show the pure virgin, true love. Medieval symbolism took over the virgin and the unicorn lore to represent Christ being born into the world through the Virgin Mary. And there's another obvious Christian parallel in the New York series, in which the unicorn story depicts the hunting down of Christ, the

15

Passion, and his Resurrection. In fact, religion laid its claim to the unicorn at a very early stage, way back in the Old Testament, as a symbol of strength and the power of God, and by New Testament days it was the one faith, the Trinity made one. Hence François's ballet, which was set at Camelot, symbolised not only the lover and beloved, but also the search for the Holy Grail."

"And what of the Nightingale in the Santine ballet? She doesn't seem to get much of a look-in in these tapestries."

"There's one." He pointed to one of the New York pictures. "You can't see it very well because it's camouflaged against the bush. The old name for the nightingale, Philomena, comes from two Greek words meaning sweet and love, but like the unicorn, the bird is not all sweetness and light. Do you know the old Cornish song, 'Sweet Nightingale'?"

That was the bell his earlier words had rung. The old song she used to sing at primary school: "You shall hear the fond tale, Of the sweet nightingale . . ."

"Yes," she replied reluctantly, for this was yet one more uncomfortable coincidence. It had haunted her as a child. "It was an odd song. I never understood it. Why on earth wouldn't the girl, Pretty Betty, stop to listen to the bird's song? And doesn't it end up, 'No more is she afraid to walk in the shade'? Why be afraid of a nightingale?"

"The nightingale is love, and love is an unknown country. It's terrifying to some" – he paused – "like Lady Lilith in François' ballet."

Why the pause? Immediately she felt defensive. Surely he couldn't be thinking of her? If so, he need not bother. The one thing Tara was sure of was her own attitude towards sex. She and William had been partners for two years now, and sooner or later would get married. It was understood, and she was sure that her occasional doubts that this was how she wanted to spend the rest of her life were merely normal in a relationship. Overall, they suited each other.

It occurred to her that William would strongly disapprove of her whereabouts, even though she could say she was on a family quest, which was true in a way. This talk of unicorns seemed to have prompted a curiosity about her own family as well as François Santine's.

It then occurred to her that William would disapprove even

16

more if he could read her mind on the question of Josh. It wasn't just François making his presence felt in this room. It was Josh, with his taut dancer's body, his sparkling eyes and intensity for life.

"As in this pose of Petrovna and Santine." Josh pointed out a photograph of two dancers, not touching, not embracing, but their bodies complementing each other in their poses, the man yearning, the woman poised for flight. Even with the old-fashioned photography, the emotion came over. What were they thinking, those two, as they danced so close together?

"There are plenty of other photographs," Josh said, "but this is the only one of Petrovna."

"Don't you have *any* idea what happened in the third act?" Tara asked huskily.

"Nothing. Not even reviews." He wandered away from her, gazing at the photographs. "I didn't explain fully. There *was* only one performance of the ballet, and that wasn't the public première, which was to take place the next evening, but the dress rehearsal. Even that wasn't complete. It ended before the third act when Arabelle Petrovna fell and broke her ankle."

"It can't have *ended*," she said incredulously. "Didn't she have an understudy?"

"For some reason Diaghilev chose to put on *Le Coq D'Or* and *Schéhérazade* instead. It was almost the end of the season, and François' ballet just disappeared."

"But how could the *music* just disappear? The orchestra must have had copies."

"The composer suppressed it."

Unicorns seemed to leap at her from every direction; she felt sick, trapped within these four walls. The hunt was after her, and soon she would fall to it. Tara desperately tried to pull herself together. What on earth was wrong with her? Josh had made a straightforward statement. Why did she have this terrible feeling there was more here than her chosen rational way of life could cope with? She wanted to run from the room in panic, but Josh was between her and the door.

She licked dry lips as she asked the inevitable question. "Who *was* the composer?"

"Arnold Prince."

The trap snapped fast and terror surged up within her. She must leave, go *now*, back to William, to safety and terra firma, away from imaginary worlds of unicorns and nightingales. Away from Josh's suddenly suffocating presence. She turned to run, but he blocked her way. "I'm sorry, I have to leave!" she blurted out, pushing him aside.

His eyes glinted in the gloom. "Running from an unknown country?"

"*No!*" Couldn't he see? He had it all wrong. "But even supposing I was, would you blame me? There are too many damned coincidences about all this."

"What coincidences?"

"You *knew*, didn't you?" she shouted. "*That's* why you wanted me to come here."

"Knew what, for heaven's sake?" Josh was putting on a good show of bewilderment, she gave him that.

"That Arnold Prince was my great-grandfather."

"*What?*" Josh let out a whoop of joy. "I didn't know, Tara. Honestly. But it's fantastic. I've been waiting all my life to know how the unicorn story ends, and, my beautiful Tara" – he seized her in his arms and hugged her – "you are one whacking great piece of jigsaw."

"I am *not*, Josh," Tara said savagely, fighting herself free. "I know nothing about *anything*, unless it's taxed. I know nothing of my forefathers, save their names; my mother isn't interested in family history, and nor am I. All I know is Arnold Prince's name and that only by chance."

"I don't believe you, Tara," he replied more calmly. "But whether you're speaking the truth or not, you must see, I *have* to pursue it."

"Not with my help, you don't." She was almost crying.

"But, darling Tara, even you wanted to know what happened in the third act. We can write our own ending, my sweet." He looked at her very seriously, then took her hands in his, and she allowed him to do so. She tried to tell herself that Josh was charming her for his own ends, but she could not believe it. It seemed they were being drawn to each other like pins to a magnet. Was Josh the magnet, or a pin like herself drawn by a force between them and in them? The thought of his arms around her, of his making love to her, was blanketing out all else. Her black suit was no protection now, no remedy against the desire that ran through her as he cupped her face between his hands and kissed her on the lips.

"Unfinished business," he whispered. "You know where it will finish, don't you?"

Of her own free will. Her own desire. "Yes."

"If not now, then soon?"

"Now, oh, *now*."

*   *   *

Arabella obediently practised her *fouettés* in accordance with Maître Cecchetti's strictures, but she was not thinking of them. Exercises, whether at the *barre* or of *adage*, *pirouettes* or *batterie*, were routine. She would never manage the thirty-two *fouettés* achieved by the great Legnani in *The Tulip of Harlem* at the Maryinsky, but she did not care. That was a mere bravura exhibition of technique, not of the spirit. Last night she had, as so often, watched Pavlova dance from the wings of the Palace Theatre music hall, where Madame's small company, of which she herself was now a ballerina, had a season this summer, just as Diaghilev's Russian Ballet had taken London by storm at Covent Garden. Arabella's thoughts were soaring into the sunlight with Anna Pavlova's Butterfly, surely greater even than her Dying Swan. Pavlova was all lightness and melody, all spirit and flowing harmony. *The Times* had said that when Pavlova danced, the whole of her danced, and that was what ballet meant, surely. Not just the feet, but the soul. Maître Cecchetti had told Arabella that she could be another Pavlova after he saw her *La Rose Mourante*, but that had not pleased her. She wanted to be herself, to dance with body and spirit united, one melting into the other; her steps must capture the emotions and floating wisps of beauty that she saw in her imagination. The dancer and the dance should be one and the one was her.

The door of the rehearsal room in Shaftesbury Avenue opened, and the maître himself entered, beaming. With him to her surprise was Madame Pavlova, a rare honour. There was someone else too.

"Ah, dear Arabelle," Madame said, "here is someone who greatly admires your art. He is a dancer with the Ballets Russes, but for a few performances Monsieur Diaghilev has given permission for him to partner you. I thought perhaps *Coppélia*, third act, or *Le Corsaire*."

Arabella saw a dark-haired slender man, a year or two older than herself, with dark hair and blue eyes. His fine features were tense, and the bright eager eyes were fixed on her almost in reverence. It disconcerted her.

François Santine bowed low over her hand. "Enchanté, mademoiselle."

*   *   *

Nightingales sing at night, but with the dawn comes the harsh whisper of everyday life. The songs of starlings and sparrows are no match for night-time melodies. The light was flooding in through the shutters, which they had omitted to close, and the cool white painted walls around her, decorated only with the few Monet reproductions which had seemed so welcoming last evening, now made Tara feel an intruder.

She had been crazy, out of her mind. Josh stirred in his peaceful sleep at her side, his hair dark against the lavender-scented pillow, his face ironed of expression. Instinctively, she put out a hand to touch him lightly, as if by so doing she could bring back the tenderness of her lover of the night. If she woke him, she could, but the light of day reminded her that in three hours' time the conference would be starting again and William—

William! Sick horror flooded through her. For once, his infuriating insistence that they should not share a room at professional conferences had proved a blessing, but he would most certainly expect to see her at breakfast. With luck, she calculated, if she could get back to the hotel quickly and change, William would not have noticed her absence, and she would have to deal with guilt as best she could. After all, she had been right. Paris in springtime *was* for lovers. What was networking, compared with the intimate meal she and Josh had shared in the rue St Benoit last evening?

There was also the problem of deciding towards whom she ought to feel guilt. At her side was Josh. The sweetness of the night, the bliss of their love-making could not simply be ignored, even in these days when sex could, in theory at least, be separated from love. This was no one-night stand, an unfortunate and very temporary betrayal by her body. Even by the harsh light of day she recognised there had been more to it than that.

Or had there? Unwillingly Tara forced herself to admit that Josh needed her help. He'd made no bones about that. How could she be sure that he had not used the best means at his disposal to ensure he got it? Sickness at the realisation of her predicament threatened her again. She forced herself to give Josh the benefit of the doubt. He could charm the birds off the trees, but that did not mean he had an ulterior motive, and how could she even think such things of Josh as she lay naked in bed next to him?

But how could she not, when there was William to consider? They'd had, and still had, their ups and downs, but he'd been loyal to her for two years, and didn't deserve this. However much she wanted to stay, go she must and make an effort to put this behind her, for his sake, if not for hers.

In the context of her current life there was no contest; bills had to be paid, commitments honoured. Rationally she would be doing the only thing possible by leaving immediately, yet she felt she was betraying not only Josh but herself by stealing away without a word. Did the fear of drowning in uncharted waters if she continued to help Josh with the unicorn ballet play a part in her decision? It couldn't, for objective reflection would surely prove that there was no mystery about it. Somewhere the answer to the mystery of the ballet would lie on record.

How could she convey to Josh, though, that she *wanted* to remain here, not flee away in the half-light? She must leave some token, some gesture of farewell. She broke off a tiny artificial rose on her brooch and left it on her pillow; the rose must say what she could not.

The early-morning air was cool as she half ran through the small front garden to the main gate, torn by the anguish of knowing she had burnt her boats. She realised she was shivering. She had made her choice, as she had been forced to, and if her heart or body or both still lingered with Josh, she must live with it. The house was silent; if it was peopled by housekeepers and Josh's colleagues there was no noise, no sign of any other living presence save her memory of Josh, peacefully sleeping.

A taxi was just drawing up and Tara hurried to commandeer

it as its passenger, an attractive dark-haired woman in her late twenties, stepped out. She eyed Tara and smiled, holding the door open for her to enter. As Tara sat down, she watched the woman walking through the gate and briskly up the path to the Santine residence.

Two

"This is the Round Pond, François. Children come here to sail their boats."

The information was superfluous, for the pool was full of sailing vessels steering their paths to unknown adventure. Arabella felt stiff in her long tweed coat and felt hat, fearing she was boring François and that he regretted having suggested this February Sunday afternoon walk. When they danced together either in performance or practice dress they were at one with each other, her body moulding to his in their joint quest to fulfil the choreographer's inspiration. But here she was shy, as though she was with some stranger. She wondered if he was feeling the same, if he was disappointed that the dancer who soared with him on stage into such golden realms had proved to have such dull earthbound feet.

It had been six months now since they had met, but apart from the few occasions they had danced together, she had seen little of François. It had not been possible, since he was touring Europe with Diaghilev's Ballets Russes, and she with Madame Pavlova's small company. For 1913, however, the Ballets Russes had planned two London seasons, the first of which had just begun; and now that Madame Pavlova had a home in London, where she trained her company, she was more frequently in England.

Arabella had been sick with pleasure at the thought of this afternoon walk, but now it was happening she could think of nothing to say.

"Did you sail boats when you were a child, François?" she continued in desperation, when he made no answer to her comment.

"Yes." He politely studied a small red-sailed craft that was just being launched at their side.

"Where is it going, do you think?" she faltered, feeling foolish, for how could he understand what she meant?

Perhaps he did, though, for he turned to her eagerly. "To Never-Never Land, mademoiselle. To the land all children fly to in their dreams."

"You know *Peter Pan*?"

"Of course. I saw Miss Pauline Chase in the first production. I was already fourteen, already a dancer, but still I was enraptured – and disappointed."

"Oh!" Arabella cried. "How could anyone not like *anything* about it?"

"They flew on *wires*," François answered simply. "I saw them, and I vowed that one day I would see a dance *without* wires, so beautiful that those who watched would fly to Never-Never Land themselves."

"I hope I shall see it," Arabella said wistfully.

"Mademoiselle, you shall, for I will create it for you, only you. Monsieur Diaghilev has asked me to choreograph two one-act ballets for him, and dance in them too. It is a great honour. The first will be presented this summer, but the second – ah, until I met you that was only a dream that floated in my mind. Now you have lit the spark to give it life."

The children's shouts of mingled laughter and tears intensified. Arabella could not speak, and yet was fearful that if she did not he would never realise how deeply she was moved. What words could she find? None came, and yet he seemed to understand, for he said gently, "If you would take my arm, mademoiselle, we could wander through these gardens. They are, it seems, a place where two is the perfect number."

"It is for dancers." Arabella was already drifting in the clouds of her imagination, and his answer came so low she could not be certain of it.

"And sweethearts, also."

*   *   *

Tara wrestled once more with her conscience. To tell William what had happened would be to upset him unnecessarily. What had happened in Paris, she had managed to convince herself, was a blip in life, one of those terrible mistakes that have to be reckoned with and forgotten. An interesting new concept had emerged from the conference, and she had been asked to speak at a roundtable held by a new organisation on European planned giving. Heaven knows, it was needed.

Back in London in their Notting Hill flat, Paris had receded – during the daytime at least. And if her dreams were troubled (an inappropriate word, she acknowledged) by tortuous labyrinths of dancers and unicorns, these could only be manifestations of her guilt, which somehow she must reckon with. Real life was *here*.

William, ambling around their living room in search of the newspaper, was wearing his usual deceptively unstressed expression. Nevertheless, it was high time their holiday plans were settled. It was nearly May, after all. Perhaps a holiday would chase away the last romantic cobwebs that lingered in her mind about Josh.

"You've still kept those two weeks in June free, haven't you?" Tara asked suspiciously, when he showed little interest in the brochures she piled on him.

"Ah. Well, in fact, we may have to change our plans. Tokyo calls."

Tara groaned. "I don't fancy a holiday in Tokyo. Full stop."

"No chance anyway. Three major clients, all leading to possible further contacts, and three conferences."

"How about two weeks in the Pyrenees instead?"

"I wish." William read her face correctly – he'd had enough practice – and grinned. "Rules, my beloved, rules. You work by them too. It's why you're so understanding."

"Don't mock me. I'm furious. I was really looking forward to the break." Why couldn't William at least *look* sorry? OK, those *were* the rules, but a little wistful longing for more of her company might not come amiss.

"Me too. September?"

"If you hear gnashing of teeth, they're mine. I'm booked in for the Big Apple for a week. I get back mid-month, but I'm pretty sure I've accepted at least two speaking engagements later in the month. There's August—" No, there wasn't, judging by his face.

"We'll make it sometime, sweetheart, but we'll have to play it by ear, I'm afraid."

"It seems to me," she said crossly, "your ear is growing increasingly deaf."

"Tell you what, why don't you give up your career and become a *hausfrau*? We could have a cottage in the country, and you could potter about having a perpetual – *ouch*! Cushions hurt!" William emerged from behind the two she had hurled at him.

"Be glad it wasn't tonight's spaghetti."

Tara felt hard done by. It was the price they paid for high-powered jobs, and usually she paid it willingly. It was hard work, but the travelling, the important clients, the power and the sheer necessary organisation of life were fun, even though she and William popped in and out like weatherhouse figures, often missing each other for days. Such disappointments over free time were a necessary evil and yet the next morning – William having departed early for Heathrow – she found herself resenting it.

Life with William wasn't going to change – ever. William wouldn't want it to change. His life was ruthlessly running forwards like a trolley-bus on set lines, and he wasn't going to switch off the power. It seemed to her that his love for her was popped into his private safe while he was away riding his trolley-bus. This had suited Tara up till now, for she had her own career, and she had pushed to the back of her mind all thoughts of their future life. Now she was beginning to realise that it would never occur to William, for all his jokes, that his plans might sway to accommodate hers. Compromise was not in William's vocabulary, and for him the end *always* justified the means.

Slightly early for her lunch appointment, she wandered over to St Paul's in Covent Garden, where entertainers were busy attracting crowds, just as at the Pompidou Centre.

Watching a Punch and Judy show, she didn't notice the new arrival until his act had started. Then a movement caught the corner of her eye, and as she turned to see the familiar dance and dancer, her stomach lunged.

What the hell was Josh doing here? Didn't he say his company toured? He should be safely down in deepest Muckshire performing, not prancing around in London – especially on her turf.

He raised his eyes, mid-twirl, and looked straight at her. Tara felt her legs trembling. Surely she was too far to the back of the crowd for him to recognise her?

Whether she was or not, she found herself in full flight. How could she stay; what would she say to him? In her mind's eye she saw Odette, the Swan Queen, fluttering away from Siegfried in terror on their first meeting. Here was she doing effectively the same, even if not *en pointe*, but in solid block-heeled shoes. That was a weird image, for she had only seen the ballet once. It must be all the recent talk of ballet reviving her early memories, she reasoned.

"Tara!"

He was calling after her, but she ignored him. Stupid, stupid, *stupid* to turn and run, she told herself, as a few minutes later she reached the restaurant. What on earth had made her do it? Fear of unfinished business? If only she could see Josh and explain . . . She was tempted to rush back, but as she rose to do so her client arrived. When, the lunch over, she returned to Covent Garden, he had gone.

The next day she passed through the piazza again, but to her mixed relief and disappointment she saw no sign of Josh. Not in Covent Garden, at least. As she turned down the road to her office, however, she saw that, with a kind of inevitability, he was dancing on the Embankment. He was too far away for her to accuse him of stalking her, near enough for a reminder of unfinished business.

Should she go down to have it out with him? She hovered indecisively, as she reached the doorway of Pitkin, Watts & Hargreaves. Inside it was dark, cool and familiar, and this time she took the refuge it offered gratefully. She settled down to planning her presentation for the roundtable, but her mind was full of music and movement, strange unfamiliar sounds and gestures that bore no relation to anything she had seen or heard recently, not even Josh's dance. And there was even a scent of roses. It was ridiculous, she told herself. How could music have a *smell*? Even if it were her imagination, however, it lingered.

Why did her parents still live in deepest Sussex? While she had been growing up, Tara had longed for the wider world, but had thought she would enjoy Sussex all the more for simply being a visitor. Wrong. She enjoyed seeing her parents, but as for the country, she could take it or leave it. William might tease her with his secret fantasies of rural life, but Notting Hill suited her much better.

Her parents still lived in the same old farmhouse on the

outskirts of Lewes. Most of the farmland had been sold separately when they bought it, but enough remained for her mother to run her thriving nursery and garden centre, in which her father now helped. Her mother was the one who had green fingers, so Tara had clearly inherited her staid white ones from her father.

Her enjoyment of the day was marred, however, since she was aware she was here to make amends to Josh for having fled from him not once, but three times. This visit would be in *final* payment of her debt. Perhaps, once paid, these disturbing images of music, unicorns and dance would vanish too.

She found her father first, absorbed in removing side shoots from tomatoes in one of the greenhouses.

"I didn't realise you were hands-on too, Dad," she greeted him cheerfully, with a rush of affection for the mild, deceptively bland parent who provided a comfortably solid balance to her whirlwind mother. "I thought you were the financial wizard at the till. You must miss the power, surely." This was the first time she'd seen him since his retirement.

"Not a bit. Besides, working the till *is* power." He came across to kiss her, and she was forced to admit he looked a lot younger than when she'd last seen him at his firm's farewell party.

"I'd miss it, if I were you." Or would she? Tara firmly banished sudden doubt.

"Ah, but it depends what you put in its place. The smaller your surroundings, the more you can make a difference and *see* it."

Tara was about to take up familiar arms by pointing out her one-to-one relationship with clients when Margaret Maitland hurtled in. If ever there was a prototype for the White Queen, Mother was it. Always in a rush, always with life's hairpins scattering around her. "Darling, you're early. I haven't even put lunch on yet."

Her father cast his eyes to heaven. "When have you, Margaret?"

"It won't take a minute."

"I'll help," Tara offered, and followed her mother into the house, through the flagged corridor from the garden and into the big roomy kitchen. She had accepted it all her life with unseeing eyes, preferring the order and convenience of her modern flat, though admittedly that order was masterminded by William. Now the familiar old gas stove, the somewhat rickety chairs round the table and the numerous jars, bottles and pots that her mother found indispensable on the worktops touched something deep within her as though they were threatened in some way. Perhaps it was because of the slight mystery about her family that still had to be cleared up.

And that should be cleared up *now*. She excused herself to run upstairs to the bathroom, but after she left it, she did not return downstairs immediately. As fearfully as though she were a small child again, she found herself creeping into the boxroom.

It was all changed. Tension subsided as with relief she saw that the chest was no longer there. No – she was wrong, it *was* here! With a lurch of her stomach she recognised it, covered with an old plush cloth bearing a potted plant on its top.

She rushed to it, throwing open the drawer she now remembered so clearly, only to find it full of tablecloths. She should have been relieved, yet her heart pounded as she tried to close it. It stuck as she did so. Too full as usual. Tara took the drawer out to remove whatever was wedged above it, and a small piece of tapestry, grimy with years, eventually responded to her tug.

She should have known better, kept away from here. She was staring at the unicorn and the lady. Behind them, emblazoned on the text, was lettering so small she could hardly make it out. She did not need to; this was the sixth needlecase, and she knew what the words were: "*A mon seul désir*".

Put it back, Tara, forget it, was her first panicky, illogical decision. She pushed it back in the drawer and rushed downstairs, common sense battling with second thoughts. So what, Tara? You've found it. So bloody *what*?

"Ma, I heard an interesting story the other day," she plunged in, as soon as she was back in the kitchen and before she could chicken out.

"Really? Put the grill on for the chops, darling."

Tara obeyed. "You remember I once asked you about your grandfather, Arnold Prince?" There was no going back.

"Yes." The answer seemed guarded, but since her mother was busy peeling onions and garlic, Tara decided she was mistaken.

"Here, let me do that. William likes nothing more than garlic on my fingers." Tara took the knife, and continued, as casually as she could, "When I was in Paris last month I came across someone" – what a word for Josh, who immediately danced across her mind – "who told me Prince wrote the music to a ballet

29

called *The Unicorn and the Nightingale* but then suppressed it. Does that mean anything to you? Why suppress it? Wasn't it a good enough score? I know you're not much interested in family history, but—"

"Just what's your interest in it, Tara?" her mother cut sharply across her.

"I want to help him." Shaken by her mother's reaction, Tara said the first thing that came into her head. To her horror she realised it was true, whatever her misgivings about delving into the past. "He's a descendant of the choreographer and wants to revive it."

The grill was smoking, perhaps because of crumbs from the morning toast, but her mother ignored it. "I ask you again, darling. What's your interest? In the ballet or Santine's descendant?"

"So you do know about it. I didn't mention his name."

A pause. "You haven't answered my question."

"Very well. I don't know which it is."

"Come off it, Tara. You *always* know. You're just like your father. It's a good trait to have inherited."

"You sound almost bitter," Tara remarked curiously.

"Nonsense. Which is it?"

Tara surrendered. "Both, but . . ."

Her mother sighed. "I took you to ballet classes but you didn't show any aptitude for it, or for music," she said defensively. "I might have told you, if so. As it is—"

"What?"

The grill was crying out for attention, the onions seemed to be taking an inordinate amount of time, and her mother's eyes looked as if they would be streaming any moment. It *was* the onions, wasn't it? For a moment Tara had her doubts, as Margaret muttered, "I never seemed to get round to it. Blotting out my childhood rather too effectively, probably. There's not much I can tell you, Tara. It's time you went to see your grandmother."

Josh took some tracking down, even with Tara's professional experience of hunting those who would not be found. Neither Covent Garden nor the Embankment proved fruitful. Eventually, after the phone books failed to reveal a Santine, J, she tracked Music and Mime down – with the help of a theatrical agency – to an address in Richmond, with no phone number.

Ten to one there'd be no one there, she thought gloomily as she arrived on the doorstep, for their summer season must at least be in rehearsal, and this house was in a residential street. There was precious little reason to come anyway. She had failed to shake her mother into any further discussion of Arnold Prince. She could not bring herself to mention the needlecases, and when she asked for family papers or photographs, Margaret merely said vaguely: "I expect your grandmother has them, darling."

Always "your grandmother". Never "my mother".

There *was* someone in the Richmond house, however, and it was someone Tara recognised. It was the dark-haired woman who had stepped out of the taxi at Neuilly. Damn, Tara thought as she summoned up a smile, now she'd look like a besotted rejected lover. "We meet again. I was looking for Josh, actually."

"Doesn't live here, more's the pity," the woman said cheerfully. "Anything I can do? I'm Sybille Patterson. I co-run the company with Josh." She looked like a dancer as well as a manager, with her petite neat figure, short dark hair, and fine features.

"It's about a ballet he's interested in." Tara was surprised how reluctant she was to say more, though there could hardly be a secret about it, as Sybille had been staying in the Santine house.

"Unicorns? He *will* be pleased. You'll find him at the Round. Do you know it? It's a small theatre in Kensington where we rehearse."

By the time Tara arrived at the oddly named Round – it was not round at all but a rectangular purpose-built hall – it was already eight o'clock, and the light was fading fast. The air was warm, though, for May, and a rose outside the theatre was tentatively experimenting with buds.

Josh didn't even look surprised to see her, which irritated her. Nor did he show any pleasure, which irritated her even more. The irritation remained as they went to the pub next door, where he left her at one of the two outside benches and disappeared inside to fetch the drinks. He was a long time returning, and she fought her annoyance, which she knew was irrational, managing to subdue it just in time. It would do her no good in the talk to come.

"Tell me why you bothered to seek me out," Josh asked, as he put down the drinks on the table. "I can hardly assume it's for the charms of my person." His voice was neutral, his expression was cool, to say the least, and defensiveness now took over from

31

Tara's irritation. She had not behaved well in France, and the knowledge made her brittle.

"I should have told you. I'm sorry. I'm in a long-term relationship."

"You fooled me very well. Are you going on to explain that you just got carried away?" he asked politely.

She had been, but not now, damn him. "I'm twenty-five. You could hardly have expected me to be baggage-free. Anyway, you aren't either."

He looked puzzled.

"Sybille was staying with you," she continued.

"Yes." If she'd thought he would explain Sybille's role in his life, she was thwarted, for he continued blandly, "Yet as you may have noticed, *I* was not the one to do a runner."

"We'd only just met. I couldn't judge whether you were taking this seriously, or even if I was."

"Oh yes you could."

There was no answering that quiet statement. Tara had known it, and had chosen to ignore it, rightly or wrongly. She had to try to make amends – but words were hard to find. When they came, they were stilted. "I came to tell you I'm going to see my grandmother."

His lips began to twitch. "I am deeply grateful, though this is hardly earth-shattering news."

"It may be. She is Arnold Prince's daughter, she has all the family papers and there is some mystery my mother doesn't want to talk about."

In a second his eyes were sparking fire, and his body had tensed as though he needed only scant encouragement to leap on to the table and perform the unicorn dance. "Oh, joy," he whispered. "When do we leave?"

"Not so fast. She lives in Brittany."

"So what? The company can do without me for a few days."

"No, Josh," she said gently.

A silence, then: "Brittany isn't an unknown country."

"It isn't that. It's *my* family, and I need to find out alone."

Was that the truth, or was it that with Josh at her side once more, she feared her own reactions? Tokyo and William would be a long way away during the nights of June, and temptation, even if resistible, should be avoided.

Resistible? Who was she kidding? If Josh came with her, the nightingale would sing as sweetly as she had done that first night.

Josh fiddled with his glass, his face expressionless. "You'll tell me what happens?"

"Of course. *Everything.* I promise."

"No, I'll leave how much to you, provided you tell me the story whether good or bad. Don't pull punches and don't—" He stopped.

"Let the cock crow thrice?"

He grinned at last. "St Peter regretted it. Could you have a better role model?"

There was another reason that Tara wanted to go alone to Brittany – family pride. Margaret Maitland adamantly refused to see more of her mother than the strict minimum required for keeping in contact, and now that Tara and her brother were adults, the visits had ceased altogether, on the pretext that she couldn't leave the garden centre. As a youngster, Tara had not questioned their relationship, much as she was fascinated by her "French" grannie. She had bearded her mother on the question when she was eighteen, however, and finally her mother had told her the truth.

Giselle Lefevre had run away with her lover shortly after the end of the Second World War when her daughter was only six. Margaret had been left with her father, whom she had dearly loved, and did not see her mother again for over ten years. By that time, she explained briefly, they had nothing in common. That Tara could understand. Margaret's skills and interests hardly coincided with her grandmother's.

Even so, her mother's explanation had puzzled Tara, who had taken to her grandmother although she had established no close relationship. She had only seen her once or twice since she was eighteen, and now she wondered why that should have been. It was true that her father's mother had filled the role of grannie amply for she had been a formidably strong woman and had only recently died. Then there had been university, followed by the heady excitement of becoming established at work. A bright white future blinded one to the past.

Tara enjoyed driving in France, and she took the opportunity

33

to visit a client in Rouen on the way. She had used the Shuttle rather than take a ferry passage, which would, she felt, have been Josh's preferred route.

Her grandmother had aged since she had last seen her. It was hardly surprising, since her husband Antoine – or rather, partner, since there had never been a divorce – had died last year. Tara had wanted to go to see her then, for she had been fond of Antoine, but her grandmother had dissuaded her. "This is not yet the time," she had said, which was odd, but then her grandmother *was* odd, so Tara had thought little of it.

She lived on the outskirts of Josselin, an old medieval town in central Brittany, whose architecture contrasted oddly with much of the Breton scene. Brittany was Cornwall, her grandmother maintained, but Josselin was Normandy. Her own stone house, however, had more of Cornwall in it, grey stone mellowing into bright flowered gardens.

Giselle Lefevre was tiny compared with her daughter, and even with Tara. She could only be five foot one or two, and age had little to do with that. Tara, at five foot five, felt she was towering over her.

"You said you wanted to talk to me about my father," she said briskly, as soon as Tara appeared for the ritual tea. It was one of the few signs of Englishness remaining in her grandmother; having danced through most of her life with a Frenchman, she informed Tara, she had no intention of reverting to former habits.

"Yes. I met someone in Paris who wants to revive a ballet whose score he wrote and then suppressed, *The Unicorn and the Nightingale*."

"And who is this someone?" Her grandmother calmly poured the tea on to the slice of lemon adorning each bone china cup.

"He's descended from François Santine, one of Diaghilev's choreographers, and works in the field himself."

"He's a dancer?" Her grandmother looked at her with suddenly sparkling eyes, and for the first time Tara wondered why the name Giselle had been bestowed on her. Coincidence, or had she been a dancer too?

"Yes; he's not in ballet, though. Modern dance and mime. He designs and composes too."

"And your interest is in him or the ballet?"

34

"Mother asked that. Does it matter?"

"Oh, it matters, Tara. To an old lady like myself it matters very much." She didn't look old now. She was suddenly ablaze with zest for life.

Tara looked at her in amazement. Her earlier impressions of her grandmother had been that she was not remotely interested in her granddaughter or her family, or anybody save her precious Antoine. She was lovely to look at, with her white hair, dark eyes, and petite figure, and fun to be with, but somehow Grandmother had not *related* to her when Tara was with her. Now all was changed. Her face, once distant, was alive and eager. From the entertaining wax doll Coppélia, she had become the woman Swanilda. That was another strange thought, Tara realised uneasily. *Coppélia* was a ballet, and she had never seen it. She had a dim recollection of having had a record of the mazurka, or of having heard it on Classic FM, but where did the names come from? They could – they had to – have come from her early ballet classes. There was no other rational explanation.

"Let's say I owe a debt to Josh Santine – and I *am* interested in ballet," Tara answered her.

"You never were. You were set on the law."

"Of course, and that's the path I follow. But that doesn't stop me being interested in other things, does it?"

All the same, she felt her bright answer had disappointed, that she had failed some test, for her grandmother had withdrawn again.

"You said you wished to know about my father, Tara. He is hard to talk about in isolation. What of my mother?"

"Well yes, she too, if she's relevant to the story of the ballet. And, of course, any family—"

She broke off. Her grandmother was looking appalled. She set her teacup down with a trembling hand and seemed on the verge of tears. Tara didn't understand. What had she said to upset her so?

"How can you ask that, Tara? Arabelle Petrovna is the whole story."

The ballerina of *The Unicorn and the Nightingale* had been *married* to Arnold Prince? That meant Arabelle was her own great-grandmother! "You mean *she* was your mother? No wonder I didn't know," she cried. "*Why* didn't I know? Why didn't my mother tell me?" Her mind was whirling like the inside of a kaleidoscope, trying to absorb the implications of this.

Her grandmother relented, seeing Tara's bewilderment. "Your mother decided to wipe the dust of my family off her feet, I'm afraid, though she was conscientious enough to take you to ballet lessons when you were small. There were, however, no signs of a second Petrovna."

Might there have been? Regret for lost opportunity seized her. The music began to play within her once more, as she danced into *Coppélia*, saw herself dancing *Swan Lake, Le Spectre de la Rose* – and what on earth was that? Again the name was unfamiliar, yet it had performed a *grand jété* into her head with no difficulty at all.

Tara tried to force herself out of the land of make-believe and face facts. She had the figure, but not the looks of a classical ballet dancer. No almond-shaped face, no dark hair to contrast with pale skin, no dark eyes. Moreover, if she had inherited her great-grandmother's talent it would have manifested itself clearly at the age of five. No, the interesting question was why her mother had not at least referred to having had a ballet dancer as a grandmother.

Inexplicably Tara was relieved that Arabelle Petrovna had married Arnold Prince, not François Santine. She had imagined many scenarios – that Arabelle and François were lovers, or that Josh was descended from both Arabelle and Santine. The truth was always more prosaic, she thought, and when she went to bed that night she dreamed not of Josh Santine, but of William. This, when she awoke, might have relieved her greatly – had it not been for the fact that William was hunting a unicorn.

Today, her grandmother had promised she would talk about her father, even show Tara his papers and other mementoes. She might perhaps find some clue to the ballet score, even if her grandmother knew nothing of it. If she could hand that to Josh, it would absolve all debts; they would, in the words of the poet, be able to shake hands for ever, cancel all their vows—

She stopped herself. There had *been* no vows, save in Josh's head perhaps. "Come let us kiss and part", the poem continued. Kiss? Her body stiffened, and the turmoil began again. The sooner she made a start on those papers the better.

"Here it is, my dear."

Her grandmother's voice was matter of fact as after breakfast she opened the door to the large airy attic room – so matter of fact that the shock was even greater than it could have been. Everywhere were unicorns, everywhere huge pictures of a dancing couple, everywhere books, papers, dainty tapestries, stools, cushions, embossed furniture. But it was one photograph above all that drew Tara's attention. The male dancer, all in white, a single, delicate soft horn on his cap, had been caught poised as the soft brown-clad birdlike ballerina nestling at his side tried to dissuade him from his reckless course.

"Did the nightingale ever win him in the ballet?" Tara whispered, drinking in the beauty and sensuousness of the pose. What had happened in the lost third act?

"I have been waiting for you, Tara," her grandmother said quietly. "Sometimes I did not even dare to hope, but here you are: the present. The past is here, an open book to those who are ready to open its covers – as I believe you are. Do you agree?"

"Yes." One word uttered instinctively, without considering all its implications. At the moment Tara did not care. Here was the world she'd sensed in her own ballet days. Here was the music, the melody; here were the smells and scents, the passion and emotion that she'd snatched at in vain when she was a child. "Oh Gran, Arabelle was beautiful. When did she marry your father?"

"Just after the war's end in 1918, by which time she'd ceased to be Arabelle Petrovna, and reverted to her real name, Arabella Peters."

"Josh said she broke her ankle and could never dance again."

"Not professionally. But here, in this room – yes, for this house was theirs, where we would come each summer for many years – here she danced for me. He let her have this room at least."

"You mean your father disapproved of her dancing?" Tara asked incredulously.

"My father believed it upset her to dwell on the past, once she could no longer dance on stage."

"Is that why he suppressed the score of the ballet?"

"It would have upset her to see others dancing it."

"Not because she loved François Santine?" Too late Tara realised she was going too far, but her grandmother seemed amused.

"Where did you get that idea? No, he married someone else,

and in any case, he was killed in the First World War. My father loved her, and she him."

"What happened to the music?" Tara could wait no longer. "Did he destroy it?"

"He may have told my mother he did. But no artist destroys his work, even if it is substandard. It can be useful to avoid pitfalls in the future. Not that *The Unicorn* was below par; it was his masterpiece."

"So where is it?" Tara asked excitedly.

"I have it, my dear. It is here safely."

"Would you let Josh see it?" Tara held her breath. That would be something she could offer him, at least.

"Of course. That is what it has been held for. Waiting."

"To be revived?"

"Something like that. Is this young man *worthy* of the music, Tara? I should like to meet him, and then I will hand it over."

"It's complete – all three acts?"

"Ah, no. The first two only."

"But what of the third?" Disappointment hit her like a physical blow.

"It disappeared. The score was never heard of again after the dress rehearsal which, as young Josh Santine has no doubt told you, was the only performance ever given. My father died in 1939, when I was nineteen, and never mentioned the ballet to me. He was much older than my mother, of course. As was my husband."

"Antoine?"

"You are tactful, Tara. I meant my husband Peter Thompkins. He would never divorce me, and I did not mind. Antoine in any case was a Roman Catholic, and took such matters very seriously." She paused, then said, "I assume Margaret still resents my leaving her with him? Did she suffer terribly over it?"

Tread carefully here, Tara. "She told me she adored her father."

"My dear, she never knew him. She always refused to meet Antoine."

"I don't understand." Tara stared at her blankly.

"I'm sure you do. I am not proud of myself, but it happened. Legally Antoine was not her father of course; Peter was. He married me knowing I was pregnant with Antoine's child, and he was a good man. I had nothing to complain of. He loved Margaret as his own, especially since we had no more children."

She sighed. "Antoine was my great love. We were to be married, and then came the war. Antoine went into the army, and I was told that he died with the Free French forces trying to escape from Dunkirk. Those were very different days to these, and there was no chance for a woman to bring up a child alone. So I married."

"What happened?" So this was the story. This was the reason for the lack of contact. Poor, poor Mother. Never knowing her true father. Tara was filled with a sense of her own inadequacy. *Why* had she never asked these questions of her mother?

"After the war Antoine returned. He had evaded escape, and joined the Maquis in the south. He was betrayed, taken prisoner, and sent to a concentration camp, since by that time there was no proof he had been a soldier. I met him again in 1946. It was not an easy decision then, though it may seem so now. I left, but I could not take Margaret from Peter as well. It would have broken his heart."

Tara had a sudden doubt. "Does my mother know?" Surely she could not, or she would have wanted to meet Antoine.

"Oh yes. I am afraid Margaret has never forgiven me. She told me so far as she was concerned Peter was her father and that was that. She did not even want to meet Antoine. When she brought you here, Antoine had to go away. I have felt it badly. I thought that at least when Antoine died, she would have come to me."

"I wanted to, but you wouldn't let me." Tara realised now how hurt she had been.

"No. And now you know why. So many secrets."

Secrets, family secrets. A shattering day of sure ground slipping from under her feet. During childhood one looked at one's parents through a funnel, with all shut off save what related to oneself. And then, in adult life, came the reckoning. The funnel was gone; one's parents were revealed as having lives and emotions of their own. One could ignore it, or one could face it. How had her mother suffered all those years, needlessly, and without a hint to Tara of what she was going through? Or had her mother been the one to inflict the suffering? Secrets. Sometimes there were answers and sometimes there were not.

What further secrets might still lie buried in the Unicorn room?

Three

Arabella spread out the rug, carefully placed the picnic hamper in the centre and sat down to one side of it, automatically smoothing her muslin skirts. Considering how much of her body was on display on stage, however, such modesty was hardly necessary. Perhaps François shared her thoughts, for he gave her a smile of warmth and intimacy, although all he said was: "In France, young ladies, particularly ballet dancers, would demand a table, chair and a parasol before they entrusted their complexions to the terrors of fresh air."

"This," Arabella laughed up at him, "is an *English* picnic. That means one must eat in as much discomfort as possible. If you want a chair and table, you must dance them."

It was fortunate that the spot they had chosen in Richmond Park was secluded, for François promptly proceeded to do just that.

"*Voilà!*" he cried, black hair flying, in a *pas de bourrée grand jeté en tournant.* "Here is your table, madame."

Arabella rose gracefully to her feet and curtsyed. "Thank you, but sir, pray where is my Louis Quinze chair?"

"Here!" Eyes twinkling, he sank to extend one bent knee, on which she placed herself, his arm holding her. In her light dress, it felt quite different from being on stage for there she was the character or mood she was performing. Now Arabelle Petrovna had been banished, and Arabella Peters was conscious only of François.

His arms grew tighter, and she rose to her feet, whereupon he lifted her off them once more into his arms and deposited her on the mat.

"That," she pouted, "hurt."

"Then I must dance my contrition. Also, I shall dance this splendid picnic of yours. Perhaps I could choreograph a picnic for Pavlova. How would one present the sandwich which you

40

English love so much? Sandwiches are like English girls. Some look dull and insipid but taste divine, others—" He broke off.

"Others?" she prompted.

He grinned. "Others are stuffed with fine feathers—"

"Very unpalatable in a sandwich."

"And others still are exquisite outside and in." He swooped on her, pulling her to her feet again, and twirling her round. "Now pay attention. This is my sandwich dance; please to applaud. First, I close my eyes to get the *idea* of the sandwich, to feel at one with it, and slowly, gently, I become it. See—" His grey flannelled legs spun round in a square from an *arabesque* with four perfectly executed broken movements.

"Bravo!" She clapped.

"I require some salmon paste," François called plaintively. "A *pas de deux*, if you please."

"There are two sides of a sandwich and only one filling," Arabella objected. "It is a *pas de trois*."

"My arms are two," he said as he enfolded them round her. "Petrovna," he whispered, holding her close, "one day we will dance together, just ourselves alone. And it will not be to create a sandwich." His hands were very warm around her waist. "Come, my sandwich filling, dance. Let us shock these trees by dancing a tango." He twirled her round to dance face to face, and galloped her up and down until she moaned for mercy.

"Even sandwiches must eat," she pleaded.

The birds' far-off cries, the stillness of François sitting at her side on the rug and the feeling of the sun warming her arms through the flimsy muslin etched themselves on her memory. No matter what happened in the future, the summer of 1913 would be there for ever, sacrosanct and unchangeable.

Arabella feared François might be bored, because he did not speak, but when he did, her happiness was complete.

"I would like you, Arabella, to come to meet Diaghilev. He has asked to see you. My first ballet, *The Frog Prince*, is to be staged next week. Are you dancing on Tuesday?"

The second Diaghilev season at Covent Garden and Madame Pavlova's at the Palace had coincided this summer, and many said not by chance.

"No," she cried with relief. "Oh no!" Then she remembered that it would be an evening performance, and her face fell. "But you will be dancing and my parents will not allow me to come unescorted." Her parents lived in Kensington, and one of the conditions under which she had been permitted to join Pavlova's company was that she should continue to live there unless on tour. It was strange, to earn her own salary and yet still be controlled by her parents, although as Madame guarded the virtue of her girls on tour even more strictly than did her parents, there was hardly any difference. Madame believed that art and marriage did not mix, and would never encourage friendships between her dancers. Arabella was torn, during her meetings with François, between guilt, the excitement of secrecy, and the disloyal thought that Madame herself was married – or, if not married, at least lived with Monsieur Dandré, and furthermore, she sometimes showed little sign of letting this inhibit her from friendships with other gentlemen. In private, of course, never in public, but the signs were noticeable, and Arabella's fellow dancers gossiped in the dressing room.

"Then your parents must come also," François said, taking her hand, "to ensure you are not gobbled up by a big French bear. Have you told them of our friendship?"

She blushed. "I'm afraid they believe that ballet is a nice little way of passing the time for their daughter, but that it is no profession for a man. Neither of them *know* about the ballet. I inherited my love of dancing from my grandmother, who never danced again after she married."

"Your father does not dance?"

She giggled at the idea of her serious, well-built father in ballet tights and jerkin. "He is in business. A stockbroker."

"Nor your mother?"

"My mother sings."

"Ah. An opera singer? A Carmen?"

"No. She gives evening parties at which she sings." And how Arabella loathed them.

"So you have not told them anything about me."

"I have said that Madame Pavlova has introduced me to a very nice choreographer, and that sometimes, very rarely, I dance with him," she said miserably.

"And what did they say when you spoke of this nice fellow?"

"Nothing."

François smiled at the despair in her voice, pushed the hamper out of the way and put his arm around her shoulders. "That is good. If I do not exist, they will not object if I kiss their beautiful daughter."

"No," she whispered, wondering whether she meant that they would not object, or that he should not kiss her. It was immaterial anyway, for he drew her closer to him, and gently kissed her lips.

Arabella agonised over whether to wear her pink charmeuse evening gown or the blue satin, and decided on the pink. Its neckline was low, but not sufficiently so as to cause attention – save from Mama, and that was to be expected. All Arabella had to do was make it clear she had no intention of changing her mind, and eventually Mama would desist. It was well known that Madame Pavlova guarded the dress, deportment and reputation of her girls off stage as well as on, and therefore her mother fortunately reasoned that her daughter would not wear anything in public of which Pavlova might disapprove. Arabella had never corrected this misapprehension, since it suited her very well. The chances of information about a corsage an inch too low reaching Madame's ears were virtually nil and the pleasures of shocking Mama irresistible.

She refused to admit that the pleasure of François' approving eye was also a factor. On stage her bosom was frequently revealed more fully than in this evening gown, but in the roles they had danced together François had not yet been in a position to see it. In any case, the stage was a different world, where different attitudes prevailed. There one was not oneself, one was a character, and the dress part of it.

This afternoon she had visited Covent Garden with François to meet the great Monsieur Diaghilev. She had been nervous, for it was a great honour. Normally ballerinas at her level would have no opportunity at all of meeting him save at auditions, and here she was, being summoned.

He was a big man in every way, well built and tall, but his personality came over as the largest attribute of all. The whole room seemed to be full of this overpowering man with his sharp eyes and flamboyant gestures. He was said to be a man of sudden decisions, of irascible temper, and yet generous to those of whom he approved. And his gifts – François talked with breathless awe

of his genius in choosing programmes and dancers for his Ballets
Russes, of his introduction of splendid designers such as Bakst so
that costumes and stage settings combined with the choreography
in brilliant spectacle. Furthermore he realised the powers of
lighting on the final effect, and . . . but it never stopped. To
François, Diaghilev was *the* maître. There was no one like him.
And now Arabella had met him.

The meeting had been very brief, but François had seemed
delighted.

"Mademoiselle," Diaghilev had boomed, after she had withstood
silent scrutiny for some minutes. "I saw your *Rose Mourante*, and
your *pas de deux* from *Don Quixote*."

She waited in trepidation. The master had *seen* her? By chance,
of course.

"Your *pirouettes à battements* require attention." He was still
staring at her, judging her, and she had immediately been dashed.
"But overall, yes, they were well done."

"Thank you, monsieur." Oh, the relief, the pleasure.

"You are wearing a most delightful gown, Miss Peters," he
continued, to her surprise, "and, I observe, open-cut shoes. Again
delightful, but hardly suitable to display your virtuosity."

"Oh, but I—" Arabella stopped as he lifted his hand. She had
brought, just in case, her practice clothes with her.

"Fortunately, I have already seen your gift in that direction. I
should like to see something of the spirit of your dancing, the
emotion."

Her mind went blank. What did he mean? What could she
do?

He smiled gently, encouraging her. "Come, Miss Peters,
astound me! And, if you please, no Dying Swans."

She would not presume to attempt it; that role was Madame's
alone. But what could she do? She had no ballet shoes, no freedom
of movement. She closed her eyes, and immediately she was the
girl in *Le Spectre de la Rose*, dreamily smelling the rose she has
brought home from the ball, then being gradually drawn into the
dance of the rose's spirit, until her dream ends, and only the scent
of roses remains.

Diaghilev nodded thoughtfully. "You aim high, Miss Peters,
but not too high. You may astound me yet."

From him, she knew this was praise indeed.

Defiantly, as she dressed for this all-important evening, Arabella decided to leave off her stays. Someone who had received praise from Sergei Diaghilev did not need artificial boosting. Moreover, Madame Pavlova never wore them and encouraged her girls not to do so either. Their figures were firm enough, and stays could harm natural grace. Her mother had been horrified when she learned of this edict, for it smacked of Isadora Duncan and her shocking ideas of free-flowing Greek dress. Arabella had insisted that her career must come first, but this evening her mother had returned to the battle. Well, she would lose it.

It had not been easy to persuade her parents to accompany her to the ballet, although they would accept no other chaperone in their place, and so Arabella looked forward to the evening with mixed feelings. Diaghilev had a colourful personal reputation and was spoken of in the dressing rooms with hushed whispers, but she had never quite gathered why. It must be the exotic and sensuous themes of some of his ballets, and the wild modern music he commissioned for them, which would make this visit to Drury Lane a plunge into uncharted and highly murky waters so far as her parents were concerned, although it would be an evening of adventure for her. Arabella had announced her intention of going alone if they would not come, both to the theatre and to the proposed dinner afterwards.

"The dinner will be in a private room, Mama," Arabella had murmured, straight-faced. "And there are seldom white slavers to be found at Romanos."

At the dreaded mention of a private room, her parents informed her that they would be accepting Monsieur Santine's kind invitation.

François' ballet would last only forty minutes, appearing as a curtain-raiser for *Schéhérazade* and, to her pleasure, *Le Spectre de la Rose*. She was looking forward to seeing him dance with the Ballets Russes. Besides two short pieces for the two of them as partners, François had choreographed several short ballets for Madame Pavlova to dance at the Palace. Madame shone in such short pieces, like the famous "Dying Swan" which had been created for her by Fokine, and it was on similar pieces that Arabella's own career with Pavlova's company was based. One day she would be flying like a dragonfly, the next snapping like a firecracker. It was admirable experience, and yet every ballerina longed for a three-act ballet like *Lac des Cygnes* to develop her own ideas and emotions, to lend her own creativity to the dance.

Arabella wasn't sure what she expected of François' ballet, but to her surprise it was a comedy rather than a drama, and based on Grimm's fairy-tale. François was dancing the Frog (who was of course a prince under a spell cast by a wicked witch) and the Princess was danced by Rostovna, whom Arabella had seen in solo character parts in the Diaghilev's Russian Ballet seasons. She had also seen her at the Empire and the Coliseum, which, like the Palace, presented a variety of turns in the music-hall tradition. Arabella had never met Rostovna, however, and was looking forward to doing so this evening. She too would be at Romanos, as would the composer of the music, Arnold Prince. Arabella was relieved that he would be present, for this serious gentleman in his late thirties, who was an acquaintance of her parents, would offset the raffish behaviour her parents would most surely expect of what they termed "your theatre friends".

She caught her breath as the Frog came leaping on to the stage. To the ungainly froglike jumps he imparted a grace and control that were almost in the Nijinsky class. Later in the programme they would see Nijinsky in his famous role in *Le Spectre de la Rose*, which remained in her mind from the 1911 season when Madame Pavlova had escorted a few privileged ballerinas to the Ballets Russes. His leap through the window, his first appearance, had been in her mind that very afternoon. During his jump he had seemed to hover in the air. François had told her that Nijinsky could never explain the technique behind this achievement, for off stage he was inarticulate, but somehow François was achieving the same effect. Combined with the froglike movements, it was both charming and funny.

Rostovna too was dancing well. Comedy suited her. Her exasperation at the constant presence of the Frog grew delightfully, but excellent dancer though she was, she seemed to Arabella not quite right as François' partner. François believed, as did Arabella, in the technical execution of the dance taking shape from the dancer's idea of the whole. Unless one *lived* the experience, one could not dance it. Rostovna's dancing was more classical, with each step superb in its technique, and that,

Arabella decided, was the reason she danced character parts so well.

Arabella clapped enthusiastically at the end, but she was painfully aware that her parents were far less forthcoming. She had felt her mother stiffen in the scene where the Frog demands admission to the Princess's bed, a piece of high comedy that amused most of the audience, and she only hoped her mother would thaw by the end of the programme.

There was little chance of that, for the riot, colour and unorthodox music of *Schéhérazade* were hardly likely to relax her parents, though she regained hope when Nijinsky performed *Le Spectre de la Rose*. Arabella watched even this impatiently, anxious for it to end, so that she could tell François how wonderful his ballet had been.

He had told her he would meet them in the green room, and she hurried her parents there so quickly as the last curtain fell that they were in advance of François. Her father fidgeted disapprovingly, and conversation ceased. When at last François arrived, Rostovna was with him and also Mr Prince. Arabella rushed to greet him, earning herself another glance from her mother at this breach of etiquette. "It was splendid, François. You are a great choreographer and dancer. And Mr Prince," she added belatedly, remembering her manners, "what an excellent score. Like Rossini."

"I am honoured, Mademoiselle Petrovna."

She smiled at him, grateful to him for calling her by her professional name. She realised to her horror that she had also ignored Maria Rostovna and quickly introduced her parents to François who completed the formalities.

"Arabelle Petrovna. Of course," Maria smiled. "I saw your Butterfly. Most promising."

"You are kind, madame. Your performance tonight was excellent. Such grasp of the *rond de jambe relevé*."

Maria was pleased at the compliment, and linked her arm through Arabella's. "Now we approve of each other's dancing, we shall be friends, yes?"

It was hard to tell whether Maria was Russian or French, since her accent suggested both, and her classical features and dark hair made either possible. Arabella decided to ask her when they went to the ladies' cloakroom at Romanos.

"I can tell you trained in Russia," she added.

"The Imperial Ballet School," Maria confirmed. "My parents were French, however, and so François and I have much in common."

"You knew him before he joined Monsieur Diaghilev?"

"Oh yes. It was I who recommended François to Sergei."

"François has much to thank you for, then," Arabella said sincerely, impressed by the casual way in which Maria referred to the master.

"And I him. Someday soon I think he will write even more splendid ballets for me. We dance well together, yes?"

"Yes," Arabella replied, a little bleakly. François had obviously forgotten his casual comment that one day he would choreograph a ballet for her. Only a week ago he had said they would continue dancing together, but that was not quite the same thing. There had been no mention of her own ballet when he introduced her to Monsieur Diaghilev, and even though she had been asked to dance, nothing had been said about her joining the Ballets Russes. She put her disappointment aside, determined to enjoy the evening.

"The white slavers' parade," Arabella whispered to François as she rejoined him in the restaurant. Here was gathered the cream of theatrical society, most notably the Gaiety Girls and their aristocratic escorts, and she noticed her mother's shocked stare at the splendid but revealing gowns of the sparkling ladies of the chorus. And to think Arabella had worried about her pink charmeuse.

Fortunately by the time they were seated at table in their private room her father was showing distinct signs of thawing at Maria's chatter and obvious deference to him. Meanwhile Mr Prince was being subjected to her mother's views on the ethics of composing for the ballet as opposed to oratorios, requiems and symphonies.

"Yet I beg to suggest," François intervened eagerly, "that Sullivan's score for *The Yeoman of the Guard* will endure longer than his 'Lost Chord'."

Arabella's heart sank. François could not know that this was her mother's favourite ballad for evening recitals.

"They can hardly be compared," her mother replied, with a look that should surely freeze François to the marrow.

"I agree," Maria said gaily. "Such a dull old song."

"I have never found it so." Her mother's voice was glacial.

Even Maria realised she had put a foot wrong. "Pray forgive me. We are in bubbling spirits tonight, are we not? François, Arnold and I have much to celebrate in the success of our first ballet together."

"A toast," François cried, with no evidence of being frozen by her mother's icy glare.

"To the next ballet," Maria echoed. "Now that Monsieur Diaghilev's friendship with Nijinsky is so troubled, and you are so close to Monsieur, he will undoubtedly let you do more."

"Close?" her father asked sharply. Immediately, to Arabella's bewilderment, the atmosphere changed, as Arnold Prince too lifted his head to stare at François. "In what way?"

"François lives with the master now, don't you?" Maria explained. "It is a great privilege for a young choreographer to have his special patronage."

François flushed. "Monsieur Diaghilev has allowed me the use of his hotel suite until—"

Her father interrupted. "You need say no more, sir. There are ladies present. I understand completely."

"Miss Peters—" Arnold Prince tried to gain her attention, but Arabella ignored him in her puzzlement. Had she missed something? Why were her father – and François, come to that – so red with anger?

"When he and Mr Nijinsky are not there," François continued, with great emphasis on Nijinsky's name. "It is a large suite, with many rooms. If I might discuss this privately with you, sir—"

Her father rose. "I am not in the habit of discussing such issues, nor, sir, of dining with degenerates. We wish you goodnight. Come, Arabella."

*   *   *

Tara was glad she had not met Josh at his Blackheath flat as he'd suggested, for it would be far too intimate a setting to steer the evening the way she intended. Out here, sitting in a pub garden in Richmond, it was easier to speak objectively, as though Tara Maitland, tax lawyer, was with a client, and this beating heart and surging body were nothing to do with her.

49

"Well?" he demanded eagerly.

"My grandmother has the score – for the first two acts, anyway."

"Fantastic!" Josh banged the shandies down on the bench. "Sweet lass of Richmond Hill, say those magic words once more."

Tara laughed as she slowly repeated the words. She had known this evening wasn't going to be easy, but she hadn't counted on her own control showing such early signs of melting. If there had been no William, if she had been free to go to Josh – stupid to think so, for there was, and she couldn't. The Joshes of this world were summer evening dreams at Richmond pubs, not for every day. She was quite convinced of that now. With all his faults, she had been – *was* – happy with William.

"She has agreed to loan it to you, but she wants to meet you first," she continued briskly, as though his allotted ten-minute client interview was fast approaching its end.

He pulled a mock face. "To check my fingernails? Or my suitability for her granddaughter?"

"I suppose," Tara struggled to subdue the fluttering inside her, "she wants to assure herself you are serious about the ballet. Or perhaps she's curious to meet François Santine's descendant."

"Here I am." Josh smote his chest. "Behold one worthy of the family name. When do we leave?"

The flutter turned into a groan of horror. Why the hell hadn't she thought of this, and prepared a way out? The quick wits that served her so well in professional circles had unaccountably vanished. *"You,* Josh, not me." Her answer sounded curt, even to her.

He stared at her disbelievingly. "We're in this together, Tara, whether you sleep with me or not. This is something separate. We can sort the other out later."

"We are not in it together, Josh. Once and for all, I live with a man I—"

"Love?"

"Certainly," she retorted, trying to harden herself, as she saw the hurt in Josh's eyes. After all, she did love him, she assured herself. "And, irrespective of William, I have a job. I can't keep waltzing off with you whenever I feel like it."

"Waltzes are not in my repertoire. I had more the dance of life in mind. Look, Tara" – he leaned towards her over the table, taking her hand – "just answer me this. You owe me. Was it anything more than a one-night stand to you? I'd hate to think I was a mere mistake. I can't have been so wrong. Yet if you love this William so much—"

"That's not fair."

"Nor, my sweet nightingale, are you. I realise you can't rush off and leave him just like that. But please be sure it's not fear of flying, as they say, keeps you with him. After all, unicorns have four feet on the ground too. There *are* no dark valleys below; pretty Betty need not be scared. I seem to remember everything ends happily in the song."

"This isn't a song." But it should be, oh, it should be. Cling on, Tara, cling to the decision you've taken.

He let go her hand, and the fingers clenched into white knuckles round his glass. "Then ask yourself also whether it's not merely rational thinking keeps you with William." He pulled a face, defeated. "I can't fight reason any more than I could fight your genuine love for him. So if you'll give me your grandmother's telephone number, I'll be off."

Numbly Tara gave Josh the number and he strolled off, with a nonchalance his words had belied. He was going. She wouldn't see him again; she didn't even know where he lived in Blackheath, since he wasn't in the telephone book. Worse, she had not kept her promise to him. She had not told him everything she had learned in Brittany, as had been her intention despite his leaving the final decision about what she told him up to her. What she had omitted was so fundamental to *The Unicorn and the Nightingale* that she knew she would feel she had cheated him if she did not reveal it. Conscience struggled with common sense, and as her own desire weighed in on the side of the former, it was surely the more important? She picked up her bag and hurried after him, yelling, "Josh!"

He didn't turn round. Perhaps he didn't hear; perhaps he didn't want to. Tara broke into a run, which was none too easy in her tight skirt, and finally caught up with him. He looked tired, quite ordinary again, as he said quietly: "I can't take any more, Tara. I want you – well, want's a feeble word in the circumstances – but you have to see it for yourself."

She ignored this. She must. "I didn't tell you everything, Josh."

51

Even now she was conscious there was something she had no intention of revealing – her grandmother's parting words.

He shrugged. "Predictable. What is it?"

"Arabelle Petrovna was my great-grandmother."

His face sprang once more into life as he struggled to keep control. "I see why you wouldn't want to tell me. It's too much of a coincidence – for *you*," he said quietly. "Be blowed if I'm going to plead with you now, Tara. Even you can't be obstinate enough to think you can just walk out of my life after this." Excitement was winning over control as his voice rose.

"I'll come." The words were out before she'd thought them through, but she meant them.

Josh lifted an ironic eyebrow. "And what will dear William say to that?"

"He won't know."

"Oh yes he will." Josh's voice was very soft. "If you don't tell him, I most certainly will."

How were lions reputed to catch unicorns? By guile. They jumped behind a tree at the last moment and let the unicorn impale himself on the trunk by his horn. And that was just what had happened to her. What use was it for the unicorn to say savagely, "Keep out of my affairs," when it was caught fast?

To her horror she realised she had spoken the words out loud.

"You brought me into them, and we have to settle this one way or the other," Josh retorted. "Look, Tara, I'll compromise, much as I hate doing it. The company's off tomorrow for a week-long run in Sussex. I'll stifle my impatience to be off to Brittany; you can come down for a country weekend, see the show and give me your decision. We'll ring your grannie from there. You said your parents lived near Lewes, and Ashden House, where we're playing, isn't far from there. You can stay with them just in case the urge to sleep with me grows too great." Josh grinned. "We'll call the weekend Armageddon, shall we?"

"Of course I bloody mind. Are you nuts?" William roared indignantly. "We get little enough time together. I'm just back from Tokyo and you suddenly announce you want to swan off to Brittany with some chap I've never heard of, and furthermore you've promised to go and see him perform in Sussex this weekend. What kind of performance has he in mind?"

"Not that." It was true, after all.

"Come off it, Tara. I know you. We're not in the office now and I can read your face like a client brief. Your interest goes beyond a sudden notion to track down some ancient ancestor. A country weekend? You? You don't know a brogue from a ballet shoe."

"Ballet shoes are what it's all about," she replied evenly, on safe ground now. "My great-grandparents were heavily involved in a ballet choreographed by François Santine. As his descendant, Josh wants to revive the ballet and only I can help him. I told him I'd see if I could spare the time and tell him my decision this weekend. Brittany is a working trip for him."

"Then if it's business," William replied grimly, "you won't mind my coming with you this weekend."

"Music and Mime," William said, studying his programme. "Not usually your sort of thing."

"I explained: my great-grandmother was a ballet dancer, and danced for Josh's great-grandfather." Tara was tense in every muscle. Already William's hostility was showing. Hardly surprising, she was forced to admit, but it didn't make her own decision easier to stand by. It was difficult to feel emotionally involved with William – as she had to if she were to withstand Josh's attraction – while he remained as stiff and unapproachable as a hedgehog.

"Cosy," William commented shortly.

The performance was taking place in the Ashden House grounds, which were on the South Downs near Lewes. Outdoor performances were always a lottery, but tonight the weather gods had favoured them. Tara had packed a picnic, and as drink was available here, it could have boded well for an idyllic late-June evening. Unfortunately William's attitude was putting paid to that, and, even more unfortunately, Tara still hadn't reached her decision as to what to tell Josh. It had been a tough week, she excused herself, with several court cases.

"When does your working colleague appear?" William asked with studied patience.

"Josh doesn't appear. He designs and writes – or rather plots and choreographs – the mimes, and arranges the music."

"*The Frog Prince*," William read out. "Seems your colleague is as good at believing in fairy-tales as you."

"There's quite a variety of subjects." Tara managed to speak calmly.

"Here's another fairy-tale of yours," William retorted smugly, waving a slip of paper that had fallen from the programme. "The great Santine *is* appearing. It's a last-minute alteration to the programme. The item – a solo, no less – is called 'The Unicorn'. How sweet."

Tara's heart sank. How dare Josh do this to her? This was no coincidence. She had told him William was coming, and the unicorn dance was his way of staking out what he considered to be his territory. At least, it occurred to her, Josh wasn't popping her in a safe. He was declaring open battle. Mistake, for William had the tenacity of a Rottweiler.

"Unicorns were the subject of the ballet he is interested in reviving." Hold fast, Tara, and you'll be all right.

William stared at her, then to her amazement his lips began to twitch and he burst into laughter. "You mean I've been wasting my time agonising over losing you to a gay who chases unicorns?"

"He's not gay." The words were out before she could stop them, but William was carried away by his own mirth.

"Sure, how would you know? It would come as a big surprise to you that Quentin Crisp wasn't a stud. Bloody unicorns, eh? I can't wait to see it."

"Before you get completely fixated in prejudice," Tara reared up in defence – of what? Of Josh? Of unicorns? Or herself? – "could I point out that *ET*, in which you were so heavily involved on TV last week, is not based on fact either. The key issue is whether we can believe in it, knowing that. Do you think you could subdue your mirth long enough to judge this show objectively?"

"Certainly, ma'am." William gave her an apologetic grin. "I'm all attention. Roll on *The Frog Prince*."

It was the first item, based on the Grimm fairy-tale. Josh had turned it into a comic mime, with Sybille as the Princess, and someone called Michael Brown as the Frog. The music – chiefly from the classics – was provided by a quartet and fitted the subject perfectly. Tara knew little about mime, but she had

seen the Jean-Louis Barrault film *Les Enfants du Paradis* in which
it figured prominently, and so she was aware that it was a medium
that could portray emotions to perfection, whether they be comic
like this, sad, poignant, tragic, or joyful. What did surprise her
was that it had words, a poem or two, and narrations from the
story. She'd always thought of mime as silent. She'd ask Josh
about that.

Now William had at last calmed down she was able to
concentrate on the show and it was only as the end approached
that she realised her tension had returned in full measure.

Josh's unicorn dance looked completely different seen at a
distance, and with a setting of trees rather than the modernist
Pompidou Centre. It had acquired mystery, turning what had been
a dextrous dance of technique into an artistic creation. Now the
Unicorn had a soul: he lived, rejoiced, was hunted and captured.
As the light spotlighting the dying Unicorn faded, he stirred, horn
uplifted, leaving the audience in doubt whether he lived or died.
It was a moving moment, and Tara was lost in the beauty of it.

"Pig-sticking in India, eh?" William sarcastically ruined the
illusion. Her heart sank. He was still prickly about Josh, and
she thought with dread of the meeting ahead. What the hell was
she going to say? She comforted herself that even Josh wouldn't
expect her to chat about Brittany with William there.

When at last he came out to join them at the bar in the grounds,
she was even more relieved, for Sybille was with him.

They all shook hands like duellists and seconds. Thank goodness William had relaxed again, since he obviously saw scant
competition in the slightly built and shorter Josh. William was
a powerful six-footer, and all too clearly thought a "gay dancer"
no match for a partner of the mega accountant Willis-Brown.
Perhaps it was as well he didn't realise how mistaken his view
of Josh was.

"Most enjoyable show." William was into professional heartiness.
Very well, so would she be.

"I loved your Princess, Sybille," Tara said sincerely. "Do you
play comedy theatre too or just mime?"

"Like Josh, I wanted to be a ballet dancer, but he decided he
hadn't got it in him, and I decided I'd rather run my own show
than be a cog in a *corps de ballet*. That's why we started Music
and Mime, although I still keep up the ballet side."

Tara was about to put her question about voices in mime when Josh decided to play a part in the conversation. He, like William, was on his best behaviour. "I understand you're in company tax, William. It must be an interesting life."

"Not half so interesting as unicorns, I'm sure," William laughed, abandoning professionalism. "I gather you've heard of a few in Brittany?"

Sybille's eyebrows arched inquiringly. "What on earth's that about, Josh? You haven't mentioned it."

"It's not a firm fixture yet," Josh replied easily, to Tara's relief.

"We could all go as a foursome," William said mockingly. "I'll bring my unicorn-hunting gear."

"We could," Josh parried, "but it wouldn't be sensible. Not till I've received reports of a firm sighting."

Sybille giggled. "I can't go till the autumn anyway. Duty calls here."

"It doesn't seem to call loudly enough for Tara," William observed drily.

"You regard yourself as a duty, do you?" she flashed back.

"I was referring to your work. It contains elements rather more important than unicorns."

"And how can you judge that, William? Each to his or her own choice."

"Quite," Josh agreed.

"I never thought," William said slowly, "that I'd see you take leave of your five senses, Tara."

"Perhaps because I've found my sixth."

"And perhaps because you've developed a teenage fixation on Nijinsky here."

Josh laughed. "You're most flattering, sir."

"Have you, Tara?" Sybille asked interestedly. "Do forgive me, but this is all getting most exciting. What particular aspect of Nijinsky did you have in mind, William? Josh's artistry on stage or his predilections in bed? I can testify to both." She laughed as she saw Josh's face. "Only joking, but he asked for it, darling."

"I would suggest, Tara, this is better discussed between ourselves." William struggled for control.

"Why?" Josh's face was white with anger.

"And *I* would suggest," Tara replied heatedly, "discussions are pointless." Her decision had been made, and William could lump it. "I shall go to Brittany with Josh – if, after this fiasco, he still wishes to go." It was throwing the ball back to Josh, but he could cope with it. Whether it was in the interest of family unity, a reaction to William's interference, or just her own crazy determination to make amends to Josh, she was going.

Josh picked it up gratefully, and she realised that he had a quality William lacked: vulnerability. "Why not? It's a working trip, after all."

"Then I'll come too," William said quietly.

"No, William, you will not," Tara replied steadily. "Only those who believe in unicorns are welcome."

Sybille lightened the atmosphere. "You sound like the fairy Tinkerbell, Tara. Now, I do believe in unicorns, so bring me one back – alive, if you please."

Later that night Tara sank gratefully into the single bed she'd known all her life. The other bed, made up for William, was empty. He had elected, to her relief, to return straight to London to prepare for a two-day trip to Paris – and by the time she returned tomorrow night he would be gone. Oh, the bliss of an uncomplicated single bed! Tonight she would sleep, and no anxious dreams would trouble her. The decision was made. It was the first step along the path of discovery as to whether her grandmother's parting words made sense.

After leaving the unicorn studio for the last time, Tara had asked her curiously: "What are you keeping it all *for*, Gran?" Surely such a complete collection specifically displayed could not merely be for the sake of family record?

"For you, Tara. I was not the one; nor was your mother. But you, Tara, may be the one the unicorn chose."

Four

Tara glared at the leg of Josh's discarded jeans hanging limply down from the bunk above her, while their owner slumbered peacefully on. How – why – had she got into this? It had all seemed so simple in London: she had owed it to William to try to see things from his point of view. She had a temporary infatuation with Josh that wouldn't last, whereas on the other hand she and William had been living together happily for some time. William loved her; before this had happened she had believed that she loved him. Yet, with the shores of England well behind her, it was William, not Josh, who was taking on an unreal aspect.

There had been an inevitable showdown with William when he had returned from Paris. She had decided to move out of their flat, at least temporarily, but faced with the sight of an apologetic William – the William she *knew*, and not the stranger of that evening in Sussex – it had been much harder than she thought. Suddenly it was she who was being unreasonable.

"Look, Tara," William had suggested fairly, "go to Brittany with this fellow if you feel you must. We'll take a break ourselves later on." Then, just as her face had lit up at this unexpected escape route, he'd added: "Just one thing." His awkward self-deprecating grin that she knew so well had appeared. It meant there was a real stinger coming. And it came.

"Don't sleep with him, will you? You say it's business of a sort, so that seems fair enough."

She not only saw red, she was dizzy with rage that he should think she would do so – until she remembered that she had done precisely that in Paris. The biting reply that came to her mind was held back in guilt, especially after his face seemed to crumple and he added, "Please; I couldn't bear it."

For the first time ever, she saw tears in his eyes, and hugged him. "I won't, William. I promise."

58

Before she left to pick up Josh in her car, she had rehearsed her words carefully. Not that she would immediately plunge into this delicate subject, but the question was sure to arise. She needed to put on her own armour to convince herself as much as Josh. "After all, Josh," she would point out, "it will give us a breathing space. We can concentrate on the ballet and get to know each other—"

The speech always ended in this cliché. It sounded weak, and she knew it, but how else could she explain her promise to William? She and Josh *did* know each other, in a way she had never known William. She was aware of it, Josh was aware of it. Nevertheless, she had to put this out of her mind if she was to make her argument sound convincing.

There was only one problem. Somehow, as she rehearsed it, the person she had been addressing was the eager, "come-on" Josh of the first time they had met. This evening, however, even before they got on the boat, she had been thrown. That Josh had vanished. He was excited, but she was immediately aware it was not for her but for the hunt of the unicorns. It was the hunter that lay above her in the bunk, not the lover. In his attitude towards her he seemed to have taken two steps backwards. Was that good or bad? she wondered. She could not decide, but it was disconcerting.

OK, if that's the way you want it, she muttered to herself, and decided to fall back on formality. After all, there had been no need to make her speech tonight. These bunks were all too clearly made for one.

Josh had seemed to see nothing amiss in her remote briskness, but instead of being grateful, Tara was seething in frustration. By the morning, however, clad in jeans and a T-shirt and facing him across a ferry breakfast table, she felt calmer. It was time to take the initiative again, and, thank goodness, she'd brought her own car, which made it easier to do so.

"It's only about a hundred kilometres to Josselin," she said casually, as they headed for the open road. "How do you feel about a detour to see Mont St Michel?"

"Business trip?" he asked amiably.

Damn him, could he read her mind?

"No." She tried to keep the chill out of her voice, but failed. "I used to spend childhood holidays in Cornwall, and fell in love with St Michael's Mount. I've always been keen to see its big brother." Why now? she wondered, slightly surprised at her own suggestion, which seemed to have come from nowhere.

"Legends of two giants throwing stones at each other," Josh commented. "Now there's a theme for a ballet."

"You know Cornwall?"

"I used to go on digs there – prehistoric. You know Carn Euny, Chysauster? They're the famous ones, but there are many others."

"No." And that ended that conversation.

Even the fairy-tale magic of Mont St Michel with the morning mist still over it and the Breton villages through which they then passed failed to work any spells on either of them, and the edgy silence persisted all the way to Josselin. But what had she expected? That the detour would have resulted in a revived rapport, in which their situation could have been discussed without rancour? Huh. That too was a fairy-tale hope.

She would make one more attempt, Tara decided, uncomfortably aware that she was probably contributing at least 50 per cent to this disaster, if not more. She took a roundabout route into Josselin in order to approach it from the right direction for the best view of the famous de Rohan castle, or what had been left of it after Cardinal Richelieu had wreaked his vengeance on it. From the point at which she stopped, four of the original towers could still be seen soaring up to the sky and over the fortifying walls and battlements. Josh made no comment at all. All right, buster, she thought with gritted teeth, I'm not done yet, and she drove through the town to show Josh the old medieval square and the basilica of Our Lady of the Rosebush.

"There's a story that the basilica was built here after a peasant found a statue of the Virgin Mary among the undergrowth of a field," she informed him brightly, as they went into a café for a coffee. "He took it home, but it promptly returned here of its own accord. After several attempts he got the message. The Virgin Mary wanted a church built to her right *here*, and here it is, a legend for a fairy-tale town."

This time His Majesty condescended to speak. "Like unicorns," Josh observed. "I can see why your grandmother settled here; it's good unicorn country. I like it."

"I don't think that's the reason—" Tara broke off, realising she didn't know enough about her grandmother to be sure. Why *had* she come here? Tara had supposed it was Antoine's choice. Her grandmother was, after all, the child of Arabella and Arnold Prince, unless . . . She played with the fantasy that her grandmother's real father had been François, in which case she, Tara, would be some kind of cousin of Josh's. It was with relief that she realised her grandmother had not been born until 1920 and that François had died four years earlier.

"We'd be cousins of some sort if your great-grandfather was a Santine, not Arnold Prince. It would explain why we are on the same wavelength," Josh replied.

It seemed an idle comment, but it unnerved her for it was true. Since Josh presumably wasn't a mind-reader, it was uncanny the way they thought along the same lines.

"There's a different reason for that," she said dryly, then quickly regretted it, as he pounced.

"Sex?"

It was a gauntlet thrown before her, oh so nonchalantly, to see her reaction. If she agreed, the doors of the trap would snap behind her. If she disagreed, she'd be forced straight into making her declaration now, at exactly the wrong time.

"It's Arabella and François' story that's providing the wave-length," she parried.

He shrugged, adopting faint amusement as his own armour. "We don't know *what* Arabella and François' story is. Or even if they have one."

"My grandmother does." Dear God, why had she come? Straight into the next heffalump pit.

"Are you worried about what we may find out?"

"Of course not. Look, Josh, we're here for the *ballet*, not our family histories."

"Hasn't it struck you that they might be the same?"

Damn him. He may have stepped back two paces but he still threw a keen dart to the bull's-eye.

"We're here for the ballet *only*," she said obstinately. "I told William it was a working trip."

His eyes glittered. "Of course," he agreed. "Sybille wouldn't have it any other way."

"What the hell has Sybille got to do with it?" Was this some joker in the pack? She was aware she was trembling.

"As much as William. The unseen presences at our table."

The coffee was cold, and tasted bitter. Outside it was raining, and she longed for the security of her own home. Her *own*, not William's, not Josh's, not even her parents', but some blissful paradise where she need answer to nobody.

"You mean you and Sybille have been lovers all along, and you never told me?" She meant it to sound casual, but it came out as a croak.

"I hardly had time."

"You can't be serious." She hated him, sitting so smugly opposite her, casually overturning with a few words everything she'd thought there had been between them. It wasn't necessary, it wasn't fair! If Sybille had been in the picture throughout, nothing had been as she imagined. Appearance had not been reality. Odette had been Odile—

Where had that come from? What did it mean? A cold sickness crept up within her. "You mean," she continued, "the night I spent in your grandfather's house was merely your playtime while the cat was away?"

He actually laughed. "I don't think Sybille would like to hear herself described as a cat. I wouldn't put it quite as you have."

"I bet you wouldn't.

"Fortunately, since you are committed to William, it should cause you no concern."

It was out before she could stop herself. "I am, and just to avoid misunderstanding, I won't be sharing your bed here—"

"Nobody asked you, lady."

It wasn't two steps back they'd taken, it was yards, miles . . . There was no bridge over this gulf, even if she wanted to cross it – and she didn't. She was safe on her own side, and that's where she was staying. It was finished.

She should have been relieved, but instead the sickness crept higher. "Since there's no help, come let us kiss and part . . ." the sonnet began. No kisses here, or ever again. No matter that Josh looked as stricken as she felt. The gap was too wide now.

He was white-faced. "The ballet, Tara. Let's get it over with."

They drove in silence to her grandmother's house, and the nearer they came, the greater the ordeal ahead of her seemed. It was all very well to say "ballet only", but even that required common enthusiasm and goals. Tara struggled with the nausea inside her. She had to do her best to pretend nothing was wrong – but as soon as her grandmother opened the door, Tara realised it was a vain hope.

Her eyes went first to Tara, then immediately to Josh, as if she too had been anxious, but the mere sight of Josh seemed to reassure her. If Tara had been hoping for an ally, she had lost her.

"There is no need to introduce me, Tara. I can see Josh is a Santine."

Josh visibly relaxed, stepped in and kissed her grandmother's hand, a look passing between them that left Tara feeling excluded. Creep! The *creep*, she thought savagely, even as the rational Tara inside her (or what was left of her) whispered, You're jealous. Was she? If so, why? Because she was seeing the bond that had been between herself and Josh so soon transferred? Or was it simply that, willy-nilly, she might yet be pulled over the gulf and into unicorn land?

"You must have photographs of François if you recognised the likeness," Josh said politely, as they sat down to the buffet lunch her grandmother had prepared in the conservatory that ran the length of the old Breton house.

"Of course."

"Do you have any of him in *The Frog Prince*?"

He'd made a mistake, hadn't he? Tara was puzzled. He meant *The Unicorn and the Nightingale*, and instead had named the mime she'd seen in Sussex.

But her grandmother nodded. "I do. Even though Arabella did not dance in it, she kept photographs."

"I've recently staged a mime to the story," Josh said, oblivious to Tara's now evident bewilderment. "Not to the Prince score," he added hastily. "The copyright problems looked insoluble, even though the score's around."

"A pity. The music is magnificent. But the copyright situation does not seem to have deterred you from the hunt of the unicorn, Josh?" Her grandmother was smiling, but there was a steely edge of inquiry.

"That, Madame Lefevre, is a different quest, as you must know." Josh smiled too, just as determined.

What the blazes was going on here? Not only was Tara

excluded, but apparently invisible. How dare Josh not tell her about *The Frog Prince*, and why did he need to keep secrets from her? Her rational self pointed out that she had not told him everything either, but it was promptly quashed.

Josh had apparently passed another test, for her grandmother inclined her head gracefully to cede his point.

"I will show you the photographs, Josh, although the best is in my mind, not on film."

"You *met* François Santine?" Tara asked incredulously.

"No. My mother was the photographer of that mental picture. Now, some Breton cider, Josh?"

It was clear that this was not the time for questions about the past, for her grandmother changed the subject briskly – and embarrassingly.

"Tell me, are you both tired after the overnight crossing, or is there no peace between you?"

Tara might have known she couldn't keep anything from her, and was still searching for an answer, when Josh forestalled her. Damn him, he even laughed.

"The latter, Madame Lefevre."

"Ah." Her grandmother actually looked amused. How could she? Tara was already feeling an outsider, even if, she acknowledged, she had chosen to exclude herself. "Tell me, Josh, what it is you seek here, apart from the score of the first two acts of *The Unicorn and the Nightingale*."

Josh glanced at Tara, but she met his look with a stony face.

"That's all," she replied for him. "I would like Josh to see the unicorn room, as well as the photographs, if possible." *She* would play fair, even if he didn't.

"You agree the ballet is all that concerns you, Josh?"

Say yes, Josh, Tara was silently pleading, but he didn't. So much for what they had agreed. He saw his chance and took it. "In a way, for I've already told Tara that I believe the ballet and the story of Arabella and François to be one."

"What story?" her grandmother asked blandly.

"It exists. Of that I am sure," Josh said firmly. "But you may not wish to tell it to me, and that I understand. You don't know me well enough yet, but I hope you will."

"How could I know this *story*?" her grandmother countered. "My mother spoke of François as a dancer, it is true, but my father was Arnold Prince. It's hardly likely that any other sweethearts of my mother would be talked of in our house."

"But your name is Giselle. And you are the keeper of the unicorn room."

Again that look between them, transmitting some underlying dialogue which was not meant for Tara.

Her grandmother thought for a while, then said at last: "I will show you the unicorn room, Josh. Tara too, if she wishes to see it again. But there is one condition. I want you both to visit Carnac tomorrow."

"What for?" Tara was mystified. What on earth had her grandmother got up her sleeve now?

"Carnac is not far to drive in kilometres but in time it is, for you will travel thousands of years back to the soul of Brittany. That is where François Santine was born. Did you know that, Josh?"

"No." Josh's eyes glowed now. "Carnac is the big prehistoric site, isn't it?"

"Yes. He grew up near the thousands of megaliths that still stand there in testament to the old religions of the world. The desolate moors and crags of Brittany made a fitting place for him to ponder on the symbolism that underlay the medieval world, and its links to ancient times and fabulous beasts. It was easy for him to think there of the tales of one-horned creatures in ancient China, in India, in Russia, that were brought to the West by Greek writers and taken into the mysticism of European thinking. Go to François' birthplace – not the house where his parents lived, but the Ménec Lines and Locmariaquer – so that you sense what he sensed, and understand why he once took Arabella there. Then come back to the unicorn room. Do you agree?"

"Yes." Josh looked at Tara, who nodded, but only since she could hardly refuse.

"Marie will show you to your room, Josh," her grandmother said after lunch. "It is the room Antoine and I shared. Tara, I've given you the room you had before."

Josh disappeared in Marie's wake to cart up his luggage and as soon as she was alone with her grandmother, Tara found her voice again, albeit a wobbly one. "I'm sorry, Gran." She felt like a child again.

65

"This weekend, Tara," her grandmother said gently, "I should be Giselle, not Gran. We will forget family problems."

"Not just family ones," Tara said bitterly.

"Amongst Arabella's repertoire," her grandmother said reflectively, "was *La Rose Mourante*, and she used to tell me the scent of roses haunted her after François died. You remember that popular song some decades ago – 'I never promised you a rose garden'? What made you think, my love, that the path would be easy?"

"Because it *was*, with William." It sounded a stupid reply even to herself.

Giselle laughed. "Perhaps you are not on fire for William, body and soul together. Perhaps you never were."

"We're *happy*." Tara kicked herself for sounding so defensive.

"Then it does not matter that you and Josh are like two coiled cobras ready to strike?"

"It does. It seemed so easy at first. I thought . . . Oh, I can't explain."

"And so Arabella and François thought – must have thought," Giselle quickly corrected herself.

"So they *were* in love?"

"As much in love as you and Josh."

"That was just for one damned night," Tara burst out. "Oh, I'm sorry, Gran. Does that shock you?"

"I know all about 'one damned nights', Tara. And shock is irrelevant anyway. What *is* relevant is – if, as I believe, you are the one, Tara – that the path is long and bordered with thorns. As Arabella and François found."

"When will you tell us their story?"

"When it wishes itself told."

"Is this like Cornwall?" Tara decided to break the silence. Someone had to.

"The atmosphere is the same, but this is so immense. There must be six – no, more – of these avenues of standing stones. And look at those – they must be fifteen feet high at least."

"I see why Giselle wanted us to come here," Tara said stiltedly. "Out here it's easy to think of fabulous monsters."

"It makes," Josh paused, "the question of who's sleeping with whom look insignificant, doesn't it?"

66

"Yes." She accepted the olive branch gratefully.

"I'm sorry about yesterday, Tara." He stared at the lines of menhirs. "It tore me up when you went back to William. I suppose I wanted you to know what it felt like, but that seems petty now. I know you had no choice but to go back. I should have realised you needed time, and that you couldn't walk out on him just like that."

"Is what you told me about Sybille true?" Might as well have it out now, though she was puzzled as to why it should matter so much.

He grinned awkwardly. "Life's never easy. The answer's yes and no. We met at university and there's always been a bond between us, which has never quite come to anything, for we've never actually taken the plunge. It's as though we are always on the brink but never quite jumping in – emotionally, that is. The more we travel and work together, the less likely it becomes, I suppose. Do you know that poem by Robert Browning, 'The Statue and the Bust'? The knight rides by and sees his beautiful woman at the window. Love at first sight. They're always about to run away together but never quite find the right moment. As time goes by, their youth and looks pass, so the woman replaces herself with a bust of herself when young and the knight with a statue of him in his prime. Sybille's always *there*, a possibility."

"And how does she see it?" A possibility or a Sword of Damocles? Tara's throat was dry.

"The same way."

"Is that why she didn't tear my eyes out when she saw me leaving your grandfather's house early that morning?"

"Did she?"

"She didn't attack me; in fact, she smiled. I have to admit she's rather nice."

"Yes. Just like William."

"Josh," she said dangerously. "Take care."

"I wouldn't presume to tread on such sacred ground."

"Not here, Josh, not here," she pleaded. "This *is* sacred ground."

He took her hands. "Then tell me this. One can't be dishonest in these sacred avenues. You've made it very plain you don't want me to make love to you—"

"No, I *haven't*."

"Every inch of your body has said it, as well as your mouth."

"Only because I promised William," she cried, agonised. She wanted to throw herself into his arms, she wanted to run over the hills and far away – no, she wanted his arms, and *damn* common sense.

Josh stared at her, dumbfounded. One eyebrow lifted, then his mouth began to twitch. "Um – when *will* William sanction our relationship?"

Sense reared its ugly head again. "Look, Josh. I've lived with William for two years. As you said yourself, I can't just walk out. Besides, there's my job."

"You're sleeping with that too?"

"You more or less have to in my line of work," she answered seriously.

"Do you enjoy making love to it?"

Enjoy? "It's what I do," she answered stonily.

"And when, either with William or your job, did you last dance at midday round a standing stone?"

She was silenced, and he held out his hand. "Dance, lady, dance. How about in the middle of that semi-circle of stones?"

"No," she said firmly, but keeping tight hold of that hand. "Don't you remember the story of the Merry Maidens in Cornwall who were turned into stone for dancing on the Sabbath? There they still are to this day, a circle of merry stones – just like this."

"Then," Josh replied, "we shall dance outside the circle, even though it's not the Sabbath. I will turn you *out* of stone, Tara my love."

Any further demur whistled down the wind as he pulled her into his arms.

"Does my lady fancy a waltz?" he shouted over the wind, spinning her round.

"A tango," she yelled back, as he galloped her away.

"No way. All I know about that is that you do a quick glide, and I take you in my arms."

"Sounds good."

Dancing stopped as he promptly obeyed. "My nightingale." He held her close. "My nightingale of the far-off country."

That precious night in Neuilly was with her again: every nerve, every muscle responding to him, the touch of his lips exquisitely agonising, tempting and seducing her, first touching, then retreating, until she cried out for him again. But this time it could not, should not, *would* not end as it had in Neuilly, for the story of Tara and Josh would have its own pace, and the chains that bound her to her everyday life were too heavy to lift all at once. When the strength was given to her, then they could be broken, but only then.

"No longer," she assured him. "I've flown home."

"Mes enfants, it is time I think for the unicorn room." Giselle examined their faces anxiously when they returned. "Both of you," she added with obvious relief.

Seeing the room with Josh – when he wasn't darting from one side to another – made the visit entirely different to Tara's first. Then she had been impressed, overwhelmed even, but as an outsider. Now she was part of it; *they* were part of it. William and the tax world were far away; what was important now was Arnold Prince's and François Santine's ballet and the story behind it. Josh had said the ballet and the story could be one, but if so, what was it? Was François Sir Galymede, and Arabella Lilith? Or was Arabella Morgana? And *where*, she suddenly wondered, had the name Galymede sprung from? She was almost sure Josh hadn't named him. She must have seen it at Neuilly. Yes, of course. She must cling to reason, here most of all.

This time she was prepared for the unicorns; what she now took in with an increased awareness were the personal mementoes, the ballet shoes, odd pieces of costumes, programmes, all the paraphernalia of a dancer's life. The programmes were undated, but it was clear none had been collected after 1914. Hardly daring to look, conscious of Giselle's eyes on her, Tara looked at the last in the carefully kept file, that for the Drury Lane Season. It was an all-ballet evening, though the programmes had often been a mixture of ballet with opera; as Tara knew, Chaliapine was as beloved by the British public as Karsavina. It advertised *Papillons, La Légende de Joseph* and *Petrouchka*. The evening before had been *Boris Goudanov* and before that *Le Coq D'Or* and *Schéhérazade*. There was no mention of *The Unicorn and the Nightingale*.

"Is this what you're looking for, Tara?" Giselle had been watching her, and from a battered tin box she produced the

familiar cream-coloured programme with its black and red lettering: "Theatre Royal, Drury Lane. Sir Joseph Beecham's Grand
Season of Serge de Diaghilev's Russian Ballet." Inside, surrounded by the usual advertisements, was printed *"The Unicorn
and the Nightingale*, Choreographic Drama in three acts by
François Santine. Music by Arnold Prince, scenery and costumes
designed and executed by Léon Bakst." And in the cast list was
Mlle Petrovna.

Only one thing differentiated this programme from the others.
A thick green pencil line had been drawn across each page, and
one word added: "Armageddon".

Tara looked up and met Giselle's eye. Quietly she went to
show Josh, who was peering at a painting that she had not
noticed before, but vaguely recognised; a unicorn of course, in
a bush, and what must surely be a nightingale. "It's a detail from
'The Unicorn is Found' in the New York series," he said.

"My mother," Giselle explained, "took up painting after my
father died. Tapestry too."

"The needlecases," Tara said softly.

Giselle smiled. "And many other things. All unicorns. It's as
if—" She stopped, then went on, "it's as if she was driven to do
more and more."

That had not been what she had intended to say, Tara realised,
but here of all places she would not press her. There was time
enough.

"This is the other side of the pictures in my grandfather's
unicorn room," Josh said slowly. "Should you like to see it,
Giselle?"

"Perhaps one day. When it is over. Tell me what it is like."

"His room tells the story of the ballet – this one of something
more. This is the nightingale as well as the unicorn. A room
of love."

"Ah, but which love?" Giselle asked. "There are Arabella and
François – yes, they did love each other. Arnold and Arabella,
François' wife and her husband—"

"He was married when he knew Arabella?" Tara cried. "Giselle
– you must tell us. And was Arabella married to Arnold when she
fell in love with François?"

"No – to both. And I cannot tell you more, for the third act
was never staged."

"But that was the ballet, not what happened to Arabella and François."

It was Josh who answered. "The ballet and the love of Arabella and François are one, and you and I are part of it. Just as we thought. That's what you're telling us, aren't you, Giselle?"

"It is." Giselle looked suddenly tired. "And the third act is missing. It's for you and Tara to create. You must get it right, Josh. Both of you."

It was pointless for Tara to say she didn't understand, not here in this room, with its overpowering sense both of the past and of a present urgency. Josh had said "as *we* thought", and he was right. She and Josh were part of it, and she must dismantle the barriers inside her that were holding her back. If she did not, Josh would land up on the side of the path leading onwards and she would remain forever gazing into the far distance.

"Giselle, would you tell us what you do know about Arabella and François?" she asked quietly.

"I will tell you a little. It began in the summer of 1913. In July, Arabella took a decision that was to change her life . . ."

*   *   *

"François!" Arabella laid a hand on his arm. She had managed to charm her way through the Drury Lane stage door to waylay him as he came out from rehearsal. Tonight he would be dancing in Nijinsky's *Le Sacre du Printemps*, the unconventional choreography and strident rhythms of which had half captivated, half repelled its audiences. She was trembling, for it was the first time she had spoken to François since that terrible evening nearly a month earlier. Only once since then had she been able to dance with him at the Palace, an agonising ordeal, for how could she concentrate on dancing Columbine to his Harlequin when François himself occupied every thought? After that even the dancing had been taken from her. Her father met her at the theatre door each evening, and at weekends she was closely guarded. "For ever?" she had asked her father furiously.

"Until the end of the Drury Lane season," replied her father smugly. "There'll be no more opportunities for Monsieur Santine with Madame Pavlova. I've made it clear she must choose between you. She quite understood when she heard what had been going on. When the Russian Ballet leaves town, young Spaniel Santine will be following in his master's footsteps, and there'll be no more of this nonsense. You'll return to your senses."

Arabella still had all her senses, and needed them as never before. She knew that she must ignore her breaking heart, the unanswered questions, and her fury at her father's inexplicable attitude if she was ever to see François again. She was running out of time. Madame Pavlova had plans to take her company on tour to America in the autumn, and the Diaghilev Ballet would be leaving for South America after the company's two-week holiday at the beginning of August. It was already the twenty-third of July, and she did not know whether François would travel with the ballet or – as it was rumoured – with Monsieur Diaghilev to Europe.

Time was short for decisions to be made. The Palace season was at its end, and in two days' time the Drury Lane season would be over. Arabella was painfully aware that with her father watching her so closely, this was her one chance to see François. Only two weeks earlier she had danced with him the rapturous reunion of Swanilda and Franz in *Coppélia*. How could they communicate so well in dance that the difficult bluebird lift came easily to them, and yet find it so hard to understand each other?

François was hot, still perspiring from the dance, and the usual backstage smells of rosin, sweat and heat locked them into an embrace even without his arms enfolding her.

His haunted dark eyes looked into hers, agonised. "Have you come to find me, Arabella? I was told you did not wish to see me ever again."

One unanswered question rolled its terrible weight away. "My father is not speaking the truth," she said joyfully. She had thought François did not wish to see *her*.

"It was not your father. It was Mr Prince, the composer of *The Frog Prince*."

"He is a friend of my father's." She was dismayed, for he had seemed a pleasant man. How could he be so deceitful?

"He said you had agreed to marry him. I thought you no longer loved me."

Her head spun. "This is madness," she cried. "I hardly know

him. My father has put him up to this. He must believe it himself, but it does not matter now. In two days' time I will be twenty-one years old. My father cannot harm us after that, although he believes he can. I" – her life trembled on the abyss – "would like to come to you, François. If you still want me."

He kissed her hand, he kissed her lips, and there were tears in his eyes. "But I am leaving England in a few days' time, and you – you will be going with Madame Pavlova."

"You don't want me." A dark hole spread before her.

"Arabella," he whispered, "how can you doubt it? How can I convince you I want you, I love you, and that I will love you forever?"

"You are going to South America with the Ballets Russes?" she asked. She clung to his hand, longing to be in his arms, but that was not possible here, even though happiness was surging through her whole body.

"Yes. I am going to Brittany on holiday. To my home, and then" – he flushed – "to meet Monsieur Diaghilev briefly in Paris to discuss my new ballet. Then I travel with Monsieur Nijinsky to Cherbourg to take the ship to South America; it is a good opportunity. Diaghilev is to remain in Europe, and the Maryinsky may put on my ballet in St Petersburg. I may dance in it there on our return. And now that you have come to me, I know what the ballet will be. I had thought it impossible these last four weeks, but now I know that there is only one ballet I *can* write: *The Unicorn and the Nightingale.*"

"But me? What shall I do?" Arabella faltered. He said he loved her; she was to have danced in the ballet. Had Diaghilev thought her not good enough? "Could we live together?" she managed to say. "It is very common. The Russian dancers all live together."

She could see she had wounded him, perhaps even shocked him. Until she joined Madame's company she had had little idea of what married love was, but the dressing-room gossip had gradually enlightened her. She now knew that the feeling she had experienced on stage when she danced with François was as it would be in bed, once you were married. Only, she had realised by that time, it was not essential to be married to enjoy it, although it was usual since otherwise it was difficult to avoid having children.

Somehow, however, she could see how deeply she had hurt François without meaning to.

"Don't you want to marry me?" he asked, his face full of misery.

"Of course I do." She lifted an astonished, delighted face to his.

This time his arms went round her, and he pulled her into a prop room, closing the door, so that he could kiss her. Then his face clouded. "But there is no time – the papers, your passport—" he cried in dismay.

"I have a passport," she said eagerly. "Monsieur Dandré, Madame's manager, thought it best for our tours."

A new agony beset him. "If you leave your father's house he will not allow you back. You must be very sure, Arabella."

"I am."

"Then come, my love. In Brittany I stay with my parents, which is very proper for you. Then we will go to Paris where I meet Diaghilev, and I will arrange for you to travel with us to South America. We will plan to be married as soon as possible, so that your father cannot try to take you away, and until then you will be with the Ballet, again all very proper. Maria enjoyed meeting you. She will look after you."

"Father, I shall be going out today," Arabella announced. She sounded quite calm, although inside she was gripped with terror. "There is a meeting at Madame's home in Hampstead."

"You will not leave this house."

"Monsieur Diaghilev's company has already disbanded and left London for its holidays. After that they will go to South America. Monsieur Diaghilev himself is going to Baden-Baden. I will be but an hour or two. It is not long enough to reach Calais, if you suspect I have intentions of meeting François."

He looked at her suspiciously, but said no more, although he did not leave the house until after she had made her departure. Arabella had been prepared for this, and took only what she could cram in her rehearsal suitcase. She kissed her mother goodbye, and her ballet training kept her distress out of her calm face. Inside her heart was bleeding for her mother, and even for her father, who she knew loved her in his way. No doubts entered her mind as to what she was doing, however, as the railway train for Southampton steamed out of Waterloo.

Her heart was in her mouth as the ship docked at St Malo. Suppose he were not there? Suppose there had been some accident? But she saw him at the harbourside, waiting for her, and a rush of love overwhelmed her. She could hardly wait for the porter to take her one humble suitcase so that she could reach François.

"You are here." Tears of happiness were running down François' face when at last they were alone, and his arms were around her. "I thought you might not come."

"Oh, François, you doubt me still?" she asked happily, forgetting all her own anxiety.

He ushered her inside the cab waiting to take them to the railway station, but to her disappointment and surprise Maria Rostovna was inside. Arabella liked her – but why here, and why now?

"Darling Arabella, welcome," Maria cried. "François has told me all. Oh, we shall all have such fun, you and I, and François."

"What now, Tara?" Josh asked, on the drive back from Sussex.

It was a subject she had carefully been avoiding. She was still savouring the happiness of Brittany, and the question of what was to come had been postponed as long as possible.

"Tell me your plans for *The Unicorn and the Nightingale*."

"Here we go. Avoiding the issue again."

"*Resolving* it," she replied sweetly. "The ballet – as everyone keeps pointing out – *is* us."

"*Touché*. Well, the Music and Mime season ends here in early September, then we go abroad. France, Spain, Italy . . ."

"Oh." She savoured this unwelcome news, coming down to earth with a bump. "And I have to go to the States in September, and though I've two trips booked to Europe, I bet they won't coincide with yours."

"Ballet," he reminded her gently. "*Ballet* is us, tax is not. What are *your* plans, my lovely lady?"

"My turn for *touché*. But as I'm still employed by Pitkins, it still has to be thought of."

"And so does the ballet. Now Giselle has given me the score

to fit Santine's choreographic notes for the first two acts, I want to work on turning *The Unicorn and the Nightingale*, with her permission, into something suitable for Music and Mime."

"But how do you convert a ballet with what's probably a very romantic score into a trendy mime, which is silent, albeit with background music?"

Josh sighed. "In the first place, mime doesn't have to be silent. Marcel Marceau happens to be silent, but that was his choice. The tradition of mime goes back to the Greeks and Romans and nearly always involves the spoken word in some form – chorus, narrator, song, poem, what have you. *The Frog Prince* and my 'Unicorn' already have background music; adding dance, words or song is a small step, and, what's more, is dead centre of today's trends towards multi-media entertainment. See?"

"Yes, maestro, yes!"

"So, to answer your question – a highly reasonable one," Josh generously added, "perhaps I can't convert it. Perhaps I have to stick to the original and present it to a classical ballet company, or use my score and François' choreographic ideas as well as his actual steps, since his moves and dances were matched to the romantic mood. I had in mind using tap for the hunt."

"That sounds interesting." Tara could see that working. "Would you take it abroad to complete? Can I help?"

"Not if you're in New York climbing the greasy pole."

"Yours sounds even greasier."

He gave an exasperated sigh. "Tara, face the fact that sometime you have to make your bloody mind up, darling. Me or William? Ballet or tax? You can have as long as you need, but don't run away from the problem."

"You can't cut me out of the ballet now. I'm part of it." She was quite clear about that.

"Not heart and soul if you're still living with William. I don't want to pressurise you, but—"

"I'm going to move out." She'd said it, slightly to her own amazement. She'd been giving a lot of thought to it, and had realised that she couldn't, this time, even had she wanted to, return to William. She wasn't looking forward to telling him, but even he would see she needed some space. The moment she had come to this decision, the relief that had swept over her made her see that the niggles of discontent in her life with

William had been symptoms of something far deeper, and that, easy-going though he seemed to be, he had in fact held the iron grip of control. Never again. Next time she would walk into love on sure ground.

"Good. Are you moving in with me?"

Here came the crunch. Sure ground. "Josh, I want to. You know that. But while I'm in the tax world it isn't practical. I'd always be thinking of you, Arabella and François."

"Sounds OK to me."

She ploughed on doggedly. "I've decided I'm going to live with my parents for a month or two to adjust, and commute to London to work. It will let William down more gently if I ask for time to think things out."

A silence, while she held her breath. If she had secretly been imagining that Josh would plead for her to move in immediately, she was disappointed. When he did not reply at all, however, the niggle still nestling inside her burst out. "Why didn't you tell me *The Frog Prince* was an Arnold Prince score too?"

His shoulders shrugged as he watched the road ahead. "It wasn't part of us, I suppose. Never occurred to me."

And what else might not have occurred to him? Yes, she was right to focus on the need for space for a month or two. Just for a moment she doubted it, though. Was the butterfly magic of life slipping through her fingers? Was she dancing off the stage pointlessly? Tara banished the thought. She had made her decision and it was the right one.

Josh obviously agreed, for when he did speak again, he said practically: "Come and work for us. That way we'll be close without sex having to be on the agenda – I presume that's the hidden subtext of your decision. Depending on how you define sex, of course. If you include desire, I can't guarantee its non-appearance."

"Nor me," she replied huskily. "Do you mean it, Josh? Would it work?"

"I don't see why not. Music and Mime needs a manager. Sybille is terrific at casting, costumes and production, but where figures are concerned we're both babes in arms. Maybe you could even turn us into profit."

"I'm primarily a tax lawyer, not an accountant, although I'm trained in that too. Oh, Josh, I'd love to try, though."

"No more greasy poles?"

Tara took a deep breath. This was it. "No. I'll still have to give three months' notice, though."

"Have your bust ready, my lady."

"What—?" Then Tara remembered the Browning poem.

Five

"*Voilà!*" François threw open his arms, waving them wildly in the air in a way of which Monsieur Cecchetti would most strongly disapprove, and began to dance. Immediately Maria rushed to join him, and they began an intricate lively jig of their own.

Arabella watched them, feeling stiff and awkward, as though she were taking part in a drama she had not rehearsed. For once her body was refusing to obey her desire; it was dragging behind, although she longed to be dancing with François and Maria. She was out of place, an unwelcome stranger amid the avenues of these vast stones, which daunted her even more than Stonehenge. There were so many of them: hundreds, maybe thousands, and they stretched as far as she could see and beyond. To dance here would be not a tribute to life, but a propitiation to the past, to the people who placed them here, and to whatever gods they worshipped.

"It is a setting for Léon, is it not?" François shouted to her as they came near to her.

No, Arabella thought. Bakst's designs were full of colour and life, of vigour and warmth. This place of grey and green held menace. Perhaps, she thought, it was her own mood that made her feel this, for François was obviously enthusiastic.

"And it is the setting for *The Unicorn and the Nightingale.*" François let out a whoop of triumph as Maria pirouetted with some difficulty in her long green muslin skirt.

Everything in Arabella silently protested. François had told her the story of *The Unicorn and the Nightingale* and it had become rooted in her imagination in the forests and castles of a past, perhaps mythical, England, not in a present that was both mysterious and somehow sinister.

No, it *must* be her mood that was making her so unappreciative, she realised miserably, aware that she was resentful and bewildered mainly because she and François were never alone. Much as she liked Maria, she had expected it all to be so different. She tried to be fair, however. She was the interloper. Maria had been invited here by François when he had thought she, Arabella, had agreed to marry Arnold Prince, yet Maria displayed no annoyance at her arrival. Perhaps she had even been expecting to play the leading role in François' ballet. When this thought had first occurred to her, Arabella decided to ask Maria whether this was so, but to her relief Maria had merely laughed.

"*Chère* Arabella, I am a *demi-caractère*. I play whatever roles I am given, comic as in *The Frog Prince* or serious as in *The Unicorn*. So long as I dance, it matters not."

François' parents lived in a château that was small by Parisian standards, but large compared with what she had so far seen in Brittany. There was no great wealth here, this was no green and pleasant land; it was open moor and sky and houses that clung sturdily to the ground as if in fear of the elements above. François had been brought up here, though; he was part of it, and she must try, hard though it was, to see it through his eyes.

His father was an artist, a dreamer, but his mother was more practical – and cool. They were kind enough to her, but it puzzled Arabella that no word had been spoken about her becoming their daughter-in-law. To them, she realised with dismay, she was merely another *danseuse*, not even a member of Diaghilev's company – and that fact made her doubly insecure. She had left Madame Pavlova's prestigious company with no guarantee that she could join the Ballets Russes. Only a few days ago love had seemed enough – and so it was, she told herself. She trusted François, and she loved him. All would be well.

She had tried to explain to Maria last evening how she was feeling, when the older girl asked her why she was so silent. Maria had done her best to put Arabella's mind at rest.

"For you, *chérie*, and for me, this is a holiday. We are dancers; we must rest occasionally. It is different for François, for he is a choreographer as well as a dancer. These two weeks are his dreaming time. He dreams not only of you" – she brushed Arabella's cheek lightly with her hand – "but of ballet. Perhaps the two are always the same for him. Here in Brittany he can be inspired, and think of nothing but his work. In his mind, the nightingale and the unicorn dance day and night, and he hurries after them to record their God-given steps before they disappear into the harsh world. So he has brought his Morgana and his Lilith here, his Odile and his Odette, so that in his imagination we may dance into our roles. He sees us side by side with his images, and not as real people. Do you see? When we join the ship for South America it will be different."

Arabella did see. She was being selfish. The ballet was more important than all else for *both* of them at present. Even so, she could not help contemplating, as she watched them dance this morning, the fact that François had not even kissed her properly for some days; his kisses were loving, but somehow abstracted. With Maria and his parents so close, it was not the same, and sick terror still grasped her. What had she done? Her father would never allow her back if Monsieur Diaghilev did not want her for his company, and if François did not want to marry her. What would she do, homeless and alone? She looked at the stones, so majestically oblivious to time. They had strength, but it was not for her, and she knew she must find her own.

She remembered what François had told her about the strength of the unicorn, which was provided by God; the unicorn was the symbol for Christ, and for the path to salvation. Have faith, and nothing could stand in the path of the unicorn. Perhaps it would help her too? But how could it? It had been her own wish to come here; she had come of her own free will.

"The unicorn!" François cried out, throwing his hat in the air to the disapproval of other visitors to the Carnac menhirs. He and Maria came running back to her, their dance over. "And my nightingale," he added, kissing Arabella's cheek.

She glowed with love for him, and yet something in her held her from showing it. Perhaps it was Maria's presence; perhaps it was her own misgivings about her journey here, or was it, perhaps, that François himself seemed remote? She tried hard to see this place as François did, not colourless and bleak, but transmitting a vital power that Léon Bakst might bring to life in his designs and François in his choreography. With a great effort of will – or perhaps with the help of the unicorn, she laughed to herself – she began to see it so, and it seemed a smaller step from here to the forests and castles of Camelot.

That evening, after the formal dinner, which Arabella found

an ordeal with her less-than-perfect French, she, François and Maria sat on the terrace as the sun slowly disappeared. François obviously had something to tell them. Something must have happened while they were out, for he had completely changed from the dreamer of the day, and had been full of suppressed energy since their return, even while they had carried out their daily practice at the barre.

"Tell us, François," Maria said resignedly, as, bursting with excitement, he handed them both a fruit liqueur. Arabella sipped it very cautiously, for such drinks did not appear at her home, and were frowned upon by Madame Pavlova.

"It is to celebrate." He smiled at them, eyes alive and eager, and Arabella wanted to cry out loud how much she loved him, but she sat stiffly, as if frozen from words and movement. Oblivious, François continued importantly, "I have great news. A telegraph from Sergei." This puzzled Arabella for a moment until she realised he was referring to Monsieur Diaghilev. "He has telegraphed that he is to stay in Paris for a few days, and then go on to other cities. We will not go to South America either; we are to remain in Paris, while he makes his roundabout way to Venice, and then join him there."

Arabella was instantly both relieved and apprehensive. Much as she would like to have seen South America, the idea of going from Brittany to Paris and then travelling on board the ship had been daunting. For one thing, she had very few clothes, only those she had brought with her in her small suitcase, and a few she had bought in an attractive town called Josselin as they passed through on their way to Carnac. She had been relying on being able to buy more practise clothes and tights in Paris, and now she would have plenty of time to do so.

But what of her? Diaghilev had no knowledge of her presence yet. François was to tell him in Paris.

François must have guessed at her thoughts, for he came to kneel at the side of her chair. "All will be well, little nightingale. You shall come too, of course, for the master already knows my inspiration for the ballet."

She threw her arms around him, so full of emotion she could not speak. When she released him, she saw Maria watching them with amusement, however, and instantly regretted her action. François' and her love was between the two of them, not for outside eyes, and she realised that was what was inhibiting François as well as herself.

"Sergei is generous to allow his *pas de deux* with Monsieur Nijinsky to be disturbed by us," Maria laughed.

"No, you do not understand. Vaslav is still going to South America, and sails from Cherbourg as planned in six days' time, on the sixteenth of August, but Sergei has *asked* us to remain. He is waiting to hear from Monsieur Ravel as to whether he would orchestrate Scarlatti's music for a new ballet he is planning. He is anxious to have something completely different in style and mood to Nijinsky's own work."

Arabella knew that Vaslav Nijinsky was not only extraordinary and magnificent in his dancing, but in his choreography as well, especially after Fokine's departure from the Ballets Russes last year. Nijinsky's *L'Après-midi d'un Faune* had marked a complete departure from Fokine's style, and many thought his work ugly and ungraceful. At first taken aback, Arabella had come to appreciate as much beauty in its unorthodox naturalistic approach as François did in the stones of Carnac.

"Sergei will allow his precious Vaslav to travel without him?" Maria asked François.

"They are not so close as they once were," François said, and Arabella sensed that for some reason he was annoyed at her question. Nevertheless, Arabella once more felt excluded, and, perhaps realising this, he immediately began to explain his excitement to her.

"If Ravel does not agree to Sergei's proposal, the Ballets Russes will lack a new ballet for 1914 that would balance Nijinsky's work. That is why he is interested in *The Unicorn and the Nightingale*. It is not like Nijinsky's work, nor Fokine's either. It will combine the best of tradition and modernism too. Arabella, I already have our *pas de deux* of love at Camelot in my head. We can rehearse it here, if you wish."

If she wished! How foolish she had been to resent the closeness of François and Maria. After all, Arabella reasoned, if anyone had cause for resentment, it would be Maria.

"You are right, François," Maria said approvingly. "There is a good chance Sergei will take it. However, perhaps it is not for me to say, but I feel that Morgana should play a more active role. At the moment she casts the spell at the beginning and removes it at the end. In the middle, though she merely makes a passive appearance when Galymede discovers his mistake. Wouldn't it be more powerful if she presented a background menace throughout and then flashed into a solo followed by a *pas de deux* of triumph over Galymede? In that way a dark shadow would sharpen the attention on Arabella."

"I am not sure," François frowned, disconcerted. "The theme of the ballet is the power of love, and it is important to establish that from the beginning. To have too much presence of evil might imply that the unicorn is not all powerful. The last act is different, for that must be a mighty Armageddon between the forces of good and evil."

"The meaning is one thing," Maria objected, "but the story must come first. The more Morgana displays the threat, the greater the drama."

"That is not how I planned it," François said simply.

Arabella decided it was time to speak. "I believe Maria is right, François."

They both instantly turned to her, with surprise she noticed, as if they had forgotten her presence and that she might have views on the ballet.

"If you tell me so, Arabella," François said gently, "then it shall be so."

"No. Only if it is right for the ballet, François. Only you can decide that."

The Elysée Palace Hotel where Monsieur Diaghilev had arranged for them to stay, as well as himself, was a far cry from Brittany. Arabella felt on surer ground, as she had come here briefly last year with Madame Pavlova's company. Though she had not lived in such grandeur as this, she knew the Champs Elysées area, and the obstacles she had foreseen in Brittany began to vanish. François would see Monsieur Diaghilev, remind him of his approval of Arabella's dancing, and seek permission for her to come to Venice too. What could go wrong?

Nevertheless, on the railway journey to Paris, she *had* worried, especially when she saw how abstracted François was. Finally she had asked him, "What are you dreaming of?" He had a notebook in which he occasionally scribbled, but most of the time he looked with unseeing eyes at the passing scenery.

84

"I am making notes on the movements in my head."

"Can you do that without music?"

"Movements have their own music. You will see," he added happily.

They arrived in Paris on the sixteenth, but it was not until the morrow that François was allowed to see Diaghilev, much to his frustration. The master was even dining in the restaurant, but François said miserably that he knew better than to approach him without being asked. He must curb his impatience – and Arabella hers.

She waited on tenterhooks next morning, as the meeting took place, but when he returned, it was clear all was not well.

"What is the matter?" Arabella tried not to show her great alarm.

"He will not commit himself. I may dance for the 1914 season, I may go to St Petersburg with him this autumn, and you too, Maria. But, Arabella," François said, stamping round the room in vexation, "he has not decided about you. He wishes to see you before he leaves Paris. He tells me I may continue with *The Unicorn and the Nightingale*, if I wish, but he will not promise it a place next season. Nor will he pay me for it. It is too, *too* bad."

"He has not ruled it out, though," Arabella said stoutly, despite the turmoil inside her.

"What's his reason for this, François?" Maria asked abruptly. "Is he missing Nijinsky already?"

"Perhaps. But Sergei's mind is not on my ballet. He is still talking of Monsieur Ravel. He hopes he will hear before he leaves Paris tomorrow."

"Tomorrow?" Arabella cried in dismay. "He leaves so soon?" Suppose he went with the questions of François' ballet and of herself unsettled?

Maria laughed. "That is the way things go in the Ballets Russes, *chérie*. From one hotel to another, one city to another. Sergei is never stationary, and those who would work for him must travel like hat-boxes along with him."

"He is still motoring to Venice, but perhaps going to Baden-Baden and Salzburg on the way," François said gloomily. "If Ravel refuses him, he says he will commission a ballet to Bach's music. No doubt tomorrow he will forget Bach and demand one to the music of Mozart."

"Take no notice of François, Arabella," Maria said briskly. "He is always like this when he has a ballet in his mind. He just can't understand that no one else can peer inside him to watch it, so he gets upset when others are preoccupied with their own concerns and don't do what he wants them to."

"But what happens next?" Arabella asked shakily. What was to become of her if Diaghilev said he did not want her?

"We are still expected to travel to Venice early in September to meet him."

Such dictatorial behaviour had never been part of Madame Pavlova's methods. Everything was organised far in advance by Monsieur Dandré, and the welfare of her young ladies cared for. How different the Ballets Russes seemed to be.

"What if Monsieur Diaghilev does not wish me to come with you?" she managed to ask.

François was immediately alarmed. "But he will. He must."

"Perhaps if I say I am to marry you—" Arabella broke off as Maria and François spoke together.

"No!"

"Why not?" Arabella looked from one to the other. In her consternation, pride was forgotten. "Do you not wish to marry me now, François?"

He immediately came to her, and took her into his arms. "How can you think that?" he asked reproachfully. "I love you, and you will be my wife."

"Diaghilev does not always approve of marriages between members of his company," Maria explained casually.

Arabella saw the look of gratitude François gave Maria, but it was not for some time that she understood it.

There had been nothing sinister about her summons to Diaghilev's presence. Arabella had put on her practice clothes, presuming that he would wish to see her dance, and then felt somewhat foolish when he did not suggest it.

"What did he want, then?" Maria demanded.

"I'm not sure," she answered truthfully. "Just to see me again, I suppose. I may come with you, and that is all that matters."

It had been the most curious episode. Diaghilev had talked endlessly of his plans for the 1914 season, but made no mention of François's ballet or even of any role she might play in his company. Nor had he seemed to have his mind on what he was saying. It was almost, from the way he studied her, as though he was still assessing not her dancing, but her. He was not married, but she had never heard any rumours that he behaved improperly to the young ladies in his company, so this was puzzling indeed. However, she had permission to travel with François, and so, greatly relieved, she dismissed the problem.

The rest of their stay in Paris seemed an unreal period, as though they were marking time, warming up on stage while before the curtain they could hear the overture. In the mornings they practised, or sometimes rehearsed odd snatches of dance for François' ballet as they came into his head. So far he had not mentioned the *pas de deux* again, but yesterday they had experimented with a *pas de trois* that ended in the Nightingale's retreating to pine away to death. It hadn't worked, and François had been moody for the rest of the day.

In the afternoons they roamed Paris, and Arabella grew so used to the threesome that it ceased to trouble her. After all, it was in a way working time. However, this afternoon François was taking her to the Left Bank, and as Maria had chosen not to accompany them, Arabella was basking in the luxury of being alone with François.

"Where are we going?" she asked presently as he wove his way through the streets.

"Here," said François, pointing. "It's a museum."

"A *museum*?" she echoed, staring at the mellow grey stone. It was a beautiful medieval building in its own right.

"And also perhaps a little of my Camelot, which is as it should be, as you will see in Room Twenty."

The mysterious Room Twenty was on the first floor, and until they reached it Arabella saw little to differentiate the Cluny museum from others, fine though it was. Then they came to a long narrow room which ran almost the length of the building, and once she was inside she understood. Towering over her along the walls were six huge tapestries, six unicorns, six ladies, and a riot of colour and intricate detail. Entranced, she listened as François explained each one to her, but when she came to the last she needed no explanation.

"*A mon seul désir*," she read from the legend woven into the tapestry. "My only desire."

"My own desire," he said gently. "It means, I believe, the lady has free will to take or reject what is offered to her. This is where my ballet began, though it has travelled far in my head since then. My Unicorn has two ladies in whose lap he might lay his head, but Morgana is not what she seems – the hunt captures him, my poor little Unicorn. The other lady, the Nightingale, is the lady of these tapestries. I have discussed them with Bakst, who knows them well. He is to use this background colour, this rich red, for the ballet."

"Colour!" she exclaimed. "The grey of Carnac and red of Cluny. That's what you danced to in your head in Brittany."

"Oh, yes. It needed both inspirations. And it needs you." He took Arabella's hands in his. "We are one, *ma mie*. Very soon now."

She sighed with happiness. "I thought you were dancing away from me in Brittany, but now I see you were only dancing *to* me in your own way."

He gripped her hands, and she longed to be away from the gaze of incurious eyes so that she could feel his arms around her.

"And I have felt that you were my Lilith, drawing back from my love, regretting that you said you would marry me. But Lilith has vanished now, and my nightingale is with me. Always I am dancing *to* you, *ma mie*, only sometimes—"

"Tell me, François," she prompted him when he hesitated.

"I am in the dark forest fighting my way to you, and not finding you, although you are there all the time."

"Then remember only that, for that is the true path."

When she and François returned to the hotel, he went straight to his room, but Arabella caught sight of Maria waiting for her in the adjoining lounge and ran through to greet her. Too late, however, she realised Maria was not alone, and to her horror recognised Maria's companion.

"Mr Prince, you know Miss Peters, I believe," Maria smiled. "Did you enjoy the afternoon, Arabella?"

Arabella was too furious to reply to that. Arnold Prince *here*? There could only be one reason. Why could Maria not have warned her he was coming? How could she escape now?

"My father sent you?" she burst out angrily. "He has no hold over me; I am twenty-one."

Arnold Prince looked aghast. "No, Miss Peters, although he will be anxious to have news of you. Miss Rostovna tells me you are travelling together, which will be a great relief to him."

"Yes," Arabella answered more quietly. If Father had not employed him as messenger, what *was* Mr Prince doing here?

"And also that you plan to join Mr Diaghilev's company?"

"Yes, she replied, stonily this time. Mr Prince was a good-looking man, and she thought a kind one, but for her he would always be inextricably linked with her father, whether it was he who had asked him to come or not. Otherwise, she might have liked him, it occurred to her.

"Miss Rostovna also tells me you are not yet married to Mr Santine."

"That is no concern of yours." Arabella flashed an indignant look at Maria, who was immediately contrite.

"I am sorry, Arabella, but as we are together and it is all quite proper, I thought it might help you if Mr Prince told your parents that."

"You were wrong!" Arabella said simply, and turned back to Mr Prince. "Why *did* you come?"

Arnold Prince was taken aback at the vehemence in her tone. "Do you not know? Mr Diaghilev asked me to meet you here. I am to accompany you to Venice."

Arabella was outraged. How could this possibly be true? "I cannot believe it. This is my father's doing somehow."

"It has nothing to do with your father." Anxiously, he took a step towards her, perhaps intending to clasp her hand, but she drew away. "You must believe me, Miss Peters. I am to discuss the music with Monsieur Diaghilev in Venice."

This made no sense at all. "What music?" she asked slowly. Perhaps this was true, after all.

"Since the score for *The Frog Prince* was a success, I am to compose the music for *The Unicorn and the Nightingale*, or, if that does not go ahead, for another ballet for Monsieur Diaghilev."

"Does François know?" she asked, horrified, not knowing whether to be glad that he was here for such a straightforward reason or worried that a friend of her father's would be involved in the new ballet in which she hoped to dance.

"Of course. Did he not tell you?"

"He may have mentioned it," she said stiffly. "I do not recall it, though." Why should François have said anything? She hadn't asked, and as he was pleased with the earlier Prince score, it was natural he should be approached for the new one.

Maria giggled, to Arabella's fury. "I am *delighted* to have a companion," she said cheerfully. "I shall stop feeling like a large brick wall between you and François."

Arabella was surprised, and was about to reassure her there was no need, when François appeared, looking as astonished as she had been to see Mr Prince.

As he stepped forward to shake his hand, however, his face was wreathed in smiles. Arabella's heart sank. Was she alone in thinking his arrival here, rather than in Venice, strange? It would be another week before they left, during which time he would be their constant companion.

Arabella had never been to Venice and was bitterly disappointed that in such a romantic city they would now be four and not two, but cheered herself up by determining that somehow she and François would find time to be alone.

The Hotel Royal Danieli, where Monsieur Diaghilev's entourage was staying, was the most famous in Venice, and near the Palace of the Doges. She, François, Maria and Mr Prince were lodging at a smaller hotel nearby, but on the morrow they had an appointment to meet Monsieur Diaghilev at eleven a.m.. He was to hear a few motifs from Arnold Prince's score, which Prince had developed from François' scenario but which, François explained gloomily, could be switched to another project if the great Diaghilev so chose. Nevertheless, François would be present, and – as a great favour, Arabella gathered, since Diaghilev was in a good mood after his holiday – Arabella and Maria might also attend. Arabella was heartened by this, since it seemed to imply that in his mind she was still associated with the ballet.

"But say nothing," François warned her. "Not even I shall make a sound, or we will be thrown out. It is Mr Prince's music Sergei wishes to hear; and nothing else. As the music is played, he will see a ballet begin to form in his mind, and I hope it will be mine. Unlike me, Sergei sees *everything*, however: the décor, the lighting, the costumes, the whole spectacle."

There was an almost reverent note in his voice, and Arabella glanced at him curiously. It was she who now felt as though she were fighting through the forest to reach him. He had retreated once more, and Maria or Arnold Prince always seemed to be with him when they met. Arnold was a pleasant enough companion, but how she resented his constant presence!

At last, later that evening, she and François did escape, to her great pleasure. "A gondola is made for two," he said to her conspiratorially, as they stole away, and in the stillness of the twilight, words seemed as superfluous as they did in ballet. Sitting close beside him, she could feel the warmth of his body, hear his breathing, feel his hand around hers. They were as close as on stage, but here they were François and Arabella, and they were together as one. He turned her face to his, and the hand that had been holding hers enfolded her body as he drew her even closer to him.

"My Arabella, my love, for ever," he whispered, then his lips met hers and her body leapt for joy.

The evening ended all too quickly, but when Arabella went to bed that night, she hugged its memory to her as a warm blanket of happiness.

Maria, François and she arrived in the ante-room to the Diaghilev suite promptly at eleven the next morning. The door to his presence was opened by a lady in white muslin who, Maria had explained, was Madame Misia Edwards, a close friend of Sergei's. So perhaps, Arabella thought, worldly-wise, that explained Diaghilev's apparent lack of a private life. As soon as they entered, however, Arnold hurried towards them, looking very agitated, and quickly ushered Maria and Arabella outside again.

"I think you should wait here, ladies. Mr Diaghilev is not yet dressed."

Arabella had just had time to glimpse the maître's portly statuesque figure performing some sort of can-can in his night-shirt in the *salon*. She tried not to giggle, and gravely agreed with Arnold. How pompous and old-fashioned he could be at times.

"Does Mr Diaghilev usually receive in his night-shirt?" Arabella asked Maria when Arnold had disappeared once more. She had a vision of her father opening the front door of their Kensington home so clad, which was even funnier.

"Oh yes. Arnold is a gentleman, so he will pretend not to notice and of course François is used to it."

91

"Is he?" Arabella thought this even stranger, for François spoke little of Diaghilev as a person, only in relation to the ballet.

They sat down on the sofa once more to wait. Even though she was wearing her best linen costume with the Magyar sleeves, Arabella felt gauche compared with the smartly clad Maria, whose hobble skirt was no mere imitation of the great Poiret's designs. It did her confidence little good, and she was relieved that she would be bound to silence once they were received into the maître's presence.

A bellboy passed them bearing a salver with a letter or telegraph on it, and knocked at the door. Arabella fidgeted, for this meant more delay. The door was opened by the white muslin lady, who apparently did not need an Arnold Prince to look after her womanly sensibilities. Perhaps that was because she was married, Arabella speculated. It was not right that so much depended on marriage – and *why* did Monsieur Diaghilev not approve of it?

A silence fell as they waited for the door to open again to allow them in, or the sound of the piano to tell them they were being excluded. Neither happened, but after a few minutes came a howl of anguish – or indescribable rage – from inside.

Arabella jumped in shock at the sound, for it had been very loud even through the closed door. "That was Mr Diaghilev's voice!"

"Don't worry," Maria said airily. "It's always happening. Some trifling matter, no doubt."

They were soon to discover, however, that it wasn't in the least trifling. The sounds of sobs and screams of rage alternated for ten minutes, until suddenly the door was thrust open. Diaghilev, still in his night-shirt and slippers, filled the open doorway, his large body trembling with rage and his face bright red with anger. He shouted out to everyone and no one.

"Forbid the banns!"

Had François mentioned their plans? Arabella panicked, but in the commotion around them no one noticed. Misia Edwards rushed out to pull Diaghilev back into the room with Arnold Prince's help, and the two girls were left alone once more to listen, all agog, to the continued altercation. By now it seemed clear that whatever had happened had no direct connection with them.

"I've heard Sergei in a rage before," said Maria soberly, "but never this bad. Something's really wrong."

"Do you think he's heard about François and me?" Arabella asked, for the sake of reassurance.

Maria cast a cool look at her. "Possibly. He won't want to let François go – but this hullabaloo seems extreme for that."

More banging and shouting followed, and the bellboy rushed by to collect several telegraphs or letters from Misia.

It was not for another thirty minutes that Arnold Prince finally emerged.

"Where's François?" Arabella asked, unable to hold her anxiety back. "Is it he whom the Master is angry with?"

"No, no, my dear." Arnold's face was very pale. "He is comforting Monsieur Diaghilev, and has asked me to escort you downstairs to take coffee."

"*Dieu*, what has happened?" Maria cried. "Tell us, Arnold."

"A telegraph arrived from South America where the Ballets Russes company has just arrived. Vaslav Nijinsky is to be married in a few days' time."

"*Married?*" repeated Maria, dumbfounded. "He never even looked at a girl before he got on that ship. Who is it?"

"I do not know her. She is a new girl recommended for the *corps de ballet* by Cecchetti. Romola de Pulszky."

"I've never heard of her," Maria said blankly, and burst out laughing. "Who would have thought a girl from the *corps* could outwit Diaghilev? It's his own fault; he should never have let Vaslav off the leash."

"Maria, this is hardly the place for such talk," Arnold said hastily, although once at a table far removed from others in the hotel restaurant, he unbent a little. "Diaghilev is trying to stop the wedding. He is discussing the situation with Monsieur Sert and Bakst, and others have been summoned here immediately."

Arabella was reeling from shock, and in her agitation appealed to Arnold, as he had asked her to call him, although she still found it hard. "Is this how Monsieur Diaghilev always treats members of his company who marry?" She wondered wildly if this too could be by some contrivance of her father, but reason prevailed.

Maria shook her head. "Only his favourites, like Nijinsky. He doesn't like it, and rages about it, but nothing like this has ever happened before."

"You said François was a favourite too. Perhaps he will be able to console him."

It was an idle comment, but had an unexpected effect. Arnold and

Maria exchanged an odd look, although Arabella could see nothing strange about what she had said.

"François is not the same as Nijinsky," Arnold said after a moment.

"He could be," Maria added brightly.

Before Arabella could ask what she meant, François himself appeared. To her relief he was not just more relaxed but beaming with happiness. "You must return. All of you. *Now.* Monsieur Diaghilev wishes to speak to you."

Torn between apprehension, curiosity and excitement, Arabella followed him back to the suite. Catastrophe had apparently induced Diaghilev to greet the world in more conventional attire, although as yet no waistcoat and jacket had joined the trousers and braces.

He was slumped in an armchair when Misia Edwards ushered them in, but revived sufficiently to roar: "Mr Prince, the commission is yours. The music for a one-act ballet for the 1914 season, if you please."

A ballet? Why didn't he say *the* ballet if it was François'? It had already been discussed with Arnold. François' face was drained of all colour, as he too realised it might yet go wrong.

"*The Unicorn and the Nightingale,*" Diaghilev mused, pacing the room. "It will be new, it will astound; it must prove to *others* that there are great choreographers in the world apart from foolish boys who allow themselves to be entrapped by *poules de luxe.*" He was spitting with rage. "Monsieur Ravel will not deign to orchestrate Scarlatti for the Ballets Russes, Vaslav Nijinsky has traded his soul for his penis, but the Ballets Russes needs neither. The ballet, François. *Vitement.*"

"And the ballerinas, Monsieur Diaghilev? Who will dance Lilith and Morgana?" François asked firmly.

"Have you no eyes, François? Your Morgana and Lilith are here, as you well know. I know Maria's skills, and Petrovna has already promised to astound me." He fixed her with an eagle eye. "Have you not, Miss Peters?"

"Thank you, monsieur." Arabella dropped a curtsey of deep gratitude.

Diaghilev frowned. "It is a risk. But I," he reassured himself, "am *never* wrong."

Except over Vaslav Nijinsky. The thought was in all their minds, but remained unspoken.

"To work, Misia," Diaghilev roared. "This wedding is to be stopped. You understand? *Stopped!*"

Four days later, however, the news arrived that Nijinsky was already married, and any plans or wild hopes on Diaghilev's part that the wedding could be prevented were doomed. Shortly afterwards François reported to them that Sergei had announced that not only would Nijinsky never dance for the Ballets Russes again, but that no ballet choreographed by him would appear in his repertoire.

"But what will he do?" Maria was intrigued and somewhat concerned. "He has no other ballet-master. And what will there be new on the programme apart from your ballet, François?"

François shrugged. With Monsieur Sert and Léon Bakst here, he explained, that would all be discussed and settled, although first Diaghilev was going to Naples.

"What for?" Maria asked.

"To get drunk," François told them happily.

"Why in Naples?" It was a long way from Venice, Arabella thought.

Maria giggled. "They are handsome, the Neapolitans."

François looked black, and Maria said no more.

It took Arabella a long time to get to sleep that night. In her mind she turned the conversation over and over. At last she pinned down what was worrying her, trivial though it had been. It had reminded her of the terrible things her father had said at Romanos.

*   *   *

Tara found it strange to be living at home again, as though she were marking time in life. Indeed, she supposed she was, since she was most certainly marking time regarding Josh, if not William. That had been settled in an all-out dust-up.

She had thought it only fair to return to the flat to face William directly, and explained as best she could her need for space. He listened without interruption, his face so deadpan he hardly appeared to be listening. Some hopes! After she'd finished, he left a silence – carefully judged, it seemed – then let fly a dismissive broadside:

"That's codswallop, Tara. You've just got an itch for this

character, and you're rubbing away at it with baby talk of needing space and writing ballets. Grow up."

"I have." Tara had meant it. Growing up was to use her own free will, not to live according to William's views on life.

"Like hell you have. Look, Tara, I'm not going to weep and wail. You know I love you, even if I don't dance with unicorns to prove it. You'll get over this, and *then* we'll have a rational talk about our future. Yes?"

She shook her head. "I thought I loved you, William. And I still think so. But your way of living isn't always gong to be mine. I *do* want space to think, but if you push me to a decision right now, it will have to be goodbye. So *don't* push."

He gave a wry grin. "A little nudge from time to time?"

She laughed, relieved he was now making it easy. "If you like. The odd lunch sort of nudge."

"You'll be back, you know. I'm a great mender of broken pieces."

"Please don't bank on it, William," she pleaded.

His expression was unreadable, but his jaw was set in Rottweiler mode.

It was mainly to distance herself from William that she'd decided to move back to her parents' home for a while. Solo paradise could wait a little, while she sorted herself out. But the journey to Lewes, although that not long by train, was tiring to make every day, and her weekends were taken up with Josh, Music and Mime, and unicorns, which meant her evenings – or what was left of them after commuting – had to be devoted to her work.

She stuck it for two weeks before Sybille solved the problem. "Why don't you move in with me?" she asked casually. "There's plenty of room, so we don't have to live in one another's pockets. We're off to *le continent* in September anyway, and I gather you're away a lot too. It might work very well."

Tara was surprised and grateful. It would certainly be one answer. Was it a good idea, though, to be so close to Josh? It was much more difficult to put temporary stops on love if you were living with the loved one's business partner. Moreover, Sybille and Josh were, or had been, romantically linked. Sybille, Josh had said, was always a possibility. She supposed she should clear this up with Sybille, or it would lie between them.

In the event Sybille merely laughed. "I appreciate your asking,

Tara. Look, Josh and I have been on a back burner for a long time. It merely means the gas will be turned out. No problem. Besides, I have my beady eyes on a toyboy, Michael Brown."

"Really?" Tara had admired him on stage. He was a talented newcomer, straight from drama school. No dancer, but an excellent mime – and very good looking. She wouldn't have thought he was Sybille's type, though; not that she could judge from their brief acquaintance.

"Let's give it a whirl," Sybille suggested. "If it doesn't work, or if you move in with Josh or back to William, no bones will be broken – or hearts."

Apart from sharing the kitchen and bathroom, she rarely saw Sybille, though it was nice to know someone else was around. Tara had never shared a flat with a woman before and found the concept of companionship without responsibility (save for paying the rent) curiously comforting. Josh's reaction, on the other hand, was mixed – at least, it appeared so.

"Um," was all he said, when she carefully told him one weekend.

"You don't approve?" Tough, she thought. She'd made her decision and it was working.

He shrugged. "Might be difficult to prise you out of there, my winkle."

She couldn't see why, but dismissed it. As far as Tara could see, the only unsatisfactory part of living in Richmond was that it split her life exactly in two. It was odd leaving the house to work in the City, when increasingly she was thinking about Music and Mime's work. Josh and Sybille had exciting plans for its expansion, for they were hoping to dovetail their programmes with a small ballet company that was winning much critical acclaim. If the dovetailing worked, they might merge. With that in mind, Tara was already getting to grips with Music and Mime's finances and accounts – which bore no resemblance whatsoever to the accounts she was used to. In her tax job she rarely scrabbled on the floor for piles of old notebooks, foraged in garages for damp, ill-tied bundles of papers, or raced to the bank with life-saving injections of cheques.

It took longer now to get back into City mode, and one Monday morning she was hardly on line, either in fact or mentally, when the receptionist rang through to announce that William was waiting to see her.

What on earth was he doing here? She could hardly refuse to see him, for that would cause more rumpus than a brief meeting. She gritted her teeth, and announced she was free, but her heart was pounding by the time he marched in. Ridiculous. She knew him, she'd loved him, and she could *talk* to him. That was the good thing about William – and sometimes she missed it.

William looked curiously round her office. "Odd to see you at work."

"What do you want, William?" she asked evenly. "If it's to ask me to come back to you, this isn't the time or the place. I said the odd lunch, remember?"

"Good heavens, and there was I assuming you'd fall into my arms. How's the commuting?"

"It's not." She debated whether to tell him, and decided there was no harm in doing so. "I'm living with Sybille—"

Eyebrows raised. "Lover boy not up to scratch? I told you so."

"Strangely enough," she fought for control, "it was my decision."

"Quite right. When you have doubts . . ."

Tara knew it was her own fault for getting drawn in. "That's enough, William. What do you *want*?"

He put on a formal – if ironical – expression. "My firm, Miss Maitland, is mounting an international conference on planned giving in Washington in April. I've come to ask you if you would chair it."

She hadn't expected this, and the surprise took some time to assimilate. The offer was today's equivalent of the gold watch – except that this accolade meant she'd arrived, not that she was going.

"I'd give my front teeth to do it," she replied impulsively.

"You might not have the same compelling effect then," he laughed.

"Why, William?" she asked curiously, common sense coming to the fore. "Was this your idea?"

"No. I offered to ask you, that's all. It was Mark's brainwave." Mark was William's boss. "He's aware I know you, though not of the extent of our intimacy."

"This won't lead to my returning to you, you know."

"I'll take my chance with that, Tara. You know I want you back.

If this conference makes you see sense eventually, fine. If not, I'm no worse off."

She frowned. She wanted to do it, but it could be difficult if William were there. Moreover there was another problem. "I've given in my notice, William. I can't do a conference in April – or I could, but you may not want me to any more."

"I know that. Talk gets around. I also know you've said you might work part time till the summer. I thought you might like to go out with a bang not a whimper."

Damn him! Music and Mime started their season in May, and it made sense to keep her expertise polished until then – just in case. "Yes," she said curtly. "That's true. Thank you. The dates?" Her thoughts were already busy.

"First week of April, Monday to Wednesday."

"Do you want me to speak as well?"

"Yes, please. We'll get together over the programme, and agree the subject."

There'd be pitfalls ahead, but she could cope. It was true that there was little point – apparently – in climbing an enjoyable ladder upwards when she was about to abandon the City world. On the other hand, she had worked for this for four years. Planned giving was only now coming into its own in Britain and she deserved some recognition of her part in achieving this. Why not go?

Six

"How was it?" Tara did her best to sound bright, but it was a struggle she lost. She had not even seen Josh for three weeks. Music and Mime had been touring in Europe, and before that she had been in New York for a week. She had been briefly in Europe too, but in Rome when Josh was in Paris, and in Amsterdam when they left for Italy. She had not even been able to contact him by phone. There was a Paris hotel number of sorts, but it was seldom answered; when it was it appeared "monsieur" was always out. Now she had been caught on the hop, for she had staggered home to Richmond exhausted after work and had not expected to see Josh at all, or Sybille until much later in the evening. They must have caught an earlier train than they planned; whatever the reason, it was disconcerting, to put it mildly, to stagger home exhausted to find them drinking champagne (well, some kind of sparkling wine) and cavorting round the room in a close bear hug.

And to have her polite question ignored.

Josh did at least break free from the hug, and rushed to pour her a glass which he pushed into her hand. "Good news," he proclaimed with an elegant twirl, landing up on bended knee. Fun, but not the welcome she had planned.

"Not the notes for Act Three turned up at last?" This too was an effort to say. She didn't want to talk about the unicorn ballet in front of Sybille. It might be childish and illogical to think of it as a private bond between herself and Josh, but at the moment it seemed the *only* bond. She had to remind herself constantly that Josh *was* Music and Mime and so was Sybille, and that it was she, Tara, who was the outsider, even if she did have a vested interest in this particular ballet.

"No such luck." It was Sybille who answered. "But it's almost as good for our future."

Tara took a few sips of the wine to blur the sharp edges of irritation. She supposed, however, that her frustration was natural. They'd been working together for three weeks, and she had been deeply involved in a completely different world in New York. It was different, it was more like another planet, and coming back here was bound to be difficult.

"We've made a deal with the ABC," Sybille said triumphantly, but seeing Tara look blank she added, "The Albion Ballet Company."

"That's splendid," Tara said, genuinely thrilled for them. "For a merger or as partners?" It was good news indeed, for them all, herself included if this was to be her future.

Josh had been silent, although Tara was intensely aware that he was listening to every word, watching every movement she made. If only they'd been alone, they'd have been lying in each other's arms by this time. She could have cried with frustration at the thought.

In answer to her question, Josh explained. "One season of merged programmes to see how it works, and if it's a success, both companies look at the situation again late next summer to see what advantages could be gained from financial dovetailing."

"What does that mean in practice, for you?" And not only for Music and Mime; what about Josh's ballet? She was longing to ask Josh how he was getting on with sorting out the notebooks and how he thought he could use the Prince score.

During August the company had had so many engagements, often staying away two or three nights at a time, that he had made little progress beyond the initial excited reaction he'd generated when he played it. That had been a struggle, for Josh was hardly a great piano player, and in the end Music and Mime had had to pool its talent to gain an idea of the overall effect.

It hadn't been, as Josh had expected, another romantic *Swan Lake* or *Sleeping Beauty*; her great-grandfather's music had not reflected the grey of Carnac but, in Tara's mind at least, a vibrant red in its vitality, exuberance and drama. She realised she was thinking of the red of the Cluny tapestries, and wondered whether François too had seen them.

Presumably Josh would at least have begun to think how he would use the score in modern terms, and she wanted to *know* how it was going to work out. The Prince score was as much her concern as his, although that, Tara was ruefully aware, was only part of it. The other part was that it was at present the only lifeline between herself and Josh.

"We'll continue to carry on as we are," Josh answered her spoken question. If he guessed the unspoken ones, he ignored them. "Our mimes will be merged with short ballets, some old, some new – *L'Après-Midi du Faune* for example. After we've seen how that works, and if we merge, we can consider extending it to be more interactive, maybe to an overall theme. It's not even a new concept. After all, Pavlova used to work in a music hall venue at the Palace, with a similar sort of mixed programme. If it works, we could even draw in an opera company, or straight drama. The finances will be complicated, of course, whether we merge or not, but I told them you'd look after that for us."

Josh was right. It *was* good news. A tempting new horizon loomed, and she would be sailing towards it with them. Then a niggle pointed out to her that she had good news in her own career, albeit one from which she was gracefully bowing out. Was it a plus or a minus that her part in Music and Mime was already being taken for granted? She could, *should*, at least mention it.

"I've had some good—"

She didn't get very far, for Josh either didn't hear or couldn't wait to tell her more. "But the best news of all is this. The ABC are really interested in *The Unicorn and the Nightingale* – not in three-act form, at least not yet, but in my one-act adaptation of Prince's score. I modestly said I'd consider it, to whet their appetite. What do you think of that?" He was glowing in triumph. "It solves my main problem of whether to do it as a dance mime or ballet. It can be ballet, and Sybille's overjoyed."

"Oh Josh." Tara threw her arms round him. "That's marvellous. Congratulations – and I'm so thrilled for you, Sybille."

"Congratulations are due to you, too, Tara. We're all going to make this happen. I owe it to your grandmother. Do you think she'd come to the opening night?" Josh asked.

"She might." Tara was doubtful; she herself had never known her grandmother go anywhere.

"She will, if I have to fetch her myself. Now, you were about to say something—"

She'd almost forgotten, and now that she was reminded the

news had lost some of its lustre. "I've good news too. I've been invited to chair a conference on planned giving in Washington."

A short silence of bewilderment followed from which Sybille recovered first. "That's splendid, Tara. What is planned giving exactly?"

Tara explained the concept as simply as she could, aware that her words had little emotional meaning for her listeners, even though they took in the sense of what she was saying. Her enthusiasm of earlier in the day began to drain from her. This was all a mistake; her two worlds could never mix.

"When is it?" Josh asked. She could not tell his reaction from his tone.

"The first week of April, Monday to Wednesday."

He groaned. "That's the week the Albion have booked for the *Unicorn*."

"But you told me earlier that Music and Mime's season began in May," Tara cried in horror.

"That was before I knew about the Albion deal, and that they want to begin their season with a bang in the form of *Petrouchka*, two mimes and *The Unicorn and the Nightingale* – choreographed and adapted by Josh Santine from the original music by Arnold Prince," Josh explained.

"Which day do they open?" Tara was tense with dismay.

"Friday."

Oh, the relief. "I can get back for that easily. I won't have to miss the ballet." There was a dead silence.

"Do you mean, Tara," Josh asked disbelievingly, "that if this blessed conference had been, say, on the Thursday, you wouldn't have given it up for the *Unicorn*?"

"No – yes – Josh, I'm committed to Washington."

"I thought you'd given in your notice for the end of December."

"I have, but I've agreed to work part time till the summer. The conference is a natural – and, for me, excellent – ending. It establishes my position—"

She broke off, aware that in her agitation she had been about to say, "in case I need it in future". Nothing was settled; she needed to do this. Thoughts rushed through her mind in panic. It was only sensible to chair this conference.

Fortunately Josh did not pick up the implication.

"Beginnings are more important than endings."

"I can go to both." Tara glared at him.

"Of course," Josh said quietly. "You're already half-way between the two countries: the unknown country and nice safe terra firma. You've a foot delicately *en pointe* in each."

Unfair. How dare he refer to their private agenda before a clearly fascinated Sybille? "Be practical, Josh," Tara urged. "I need to be earning some money and until Music and Mime gets going next season, working part time is the way to achieve it."

"Do you get paid for this conference?"

"No."

One eyebrow was raised.

"Sometimes I do things for the honour and glory – just like you do, Josh," Tara said angrily. "It's like performing outside the Pompidou." Two could play the private-agenda game.

"Does William have a role in this?"

"Yes," she admitted unwillingly. "It's his firm co-sponsoring it, with a US university. But that's *not* why I'm going."

"You're a little further from the unknown far-off country than I thought." Josh seemed sad now rather than accusing.

"Now look," Sybille intervened brightly, to Tara's gratitude, "why don't you two take a break from snarling at each other, and we'll all go out for a meal to celebrate? Get that stuffy suit off, Tara, and put on your glad rags. And Josh, even if you're too mean to toast Tara's conference, we can drink to the future of Music and Mime. I'll give Michael a ring too."

Tara hastened to obey. Stripping off her City clothes and putting on a light skirt and blouse immediately helped her calm down. If only her two worlds could be switched so easily as her clothes.

"Are you still in love with Josh?" Sybille asked. "Forgive my asking, but drink makes brave heroes of us all. Talking of which, can I offer you one?"

"I think I've had enough," Tara declared. The evening had been an unexpected success, perhaps because Michael's presence had forced them away from the earlier tensions, and she had relaxed.

Sybille's Richmond home wasn't her style – it was too austere – although Tara had reacted against the clutter of her parents' way of living by veering towards the plain cook herself, even before she'd moved in with William. Now, living with Sybille's almost sterile décor, she found herself almost longing for a few piles of papers, books, *anything*. But, austere or not, the chairs were comfortable, and she had gratefully sprawled into one on their return from dinner.

"Cocoa, then."

"You sound just like my mother. Yes, please. I'll make it, shall I?"

Sybille's first question had revived the memory of her quarrel with Josh. Perhaps it was a good thing, for it forced Tara to confront the issue that had never really gone away. Was she or was she not "mid-Atlantic" over her commitment to Josh? As she went to make the cocoa she realised she hadn't yet answered the question, and as Sybille was padding after her into the kitchen, she would have to say something. *In vino veritas.*

"Am I still in love with Josh? Yes," Tara answered desolately. "Are you?"

"I am with Michael," Sybille said politely. "Josh and I are history, as I told you."

"I meant Michael," Tara apologised. "It's only the drink talking – or rather, *not* talking." She had seen Michael several times in Music and Mime performances, but she hadn't had a chance to get to know him, as she had this evening. He was a fresh-faced young man a year or two younger than herself, and he and Sybille seemed to get on so well together that it had surprised Tara that Sybille had come home alone. Michael and Josh had gone one way, they another, and cocoa, while consoling, seemed a poor substitute.

An uncomfortable thought occurred to Tara. "Do you want Michael to move in? Shall I leave?"

"Toyboys, my dear," Sybille announced with all the worldly wisdom of her three extra years, "must be handled gently; they are not for twenty-four seven, as you would say."

"*Would* I?" Tara was amazed. Could she really be picking up the jargon of a crazy life in which work meant all day, every day, and not even realise it?

"You do. Michael is for high days and holidays only."

"Like Josh."

"For different reasons, though. After all, you're still hankering a little for William, aren't you?"

Tara was about to deny this indignantly. She rarely thought of William, and rarely missed her former life – but could there be something in what Sybille said?

"It's only getting used to the situation," she replied at last. "William was – is – comfortable. Whatever Josh is, it isn't that."

"There's a lot to be said for comfort," Sybille observed. "I suppose that's why Josh and I never made it as an item. We're neither of us comfort people, and so when we're together there are too many sharp edges."

Sharp edges? But that was how *she* felt about Josh, Tara realised. Surely to be in love *meant* dealing with sharp edges. Did that mean she was in love with Josh, but did not love him? Tiredness and drink seemed to be making her mind fuzzy.

"*Do* I love him?" she asked out loud, by mistake.

"Ask the cocoa," Sybille replied briskly. "A lot of answers can be found within it."

Once they were back in their armchairs, Tara decided that as she had gone so far she might as well go further. "Did *you* love him? Josh, I mean."

"I'll have to consult my cocoa on that. Josh isn't an easy person to know, let alone love. He's got his own agenda, and if you're on it – as you are, Tara – that's fine. If you're not, then he sees you through a glass darkly, not even through a champagne glass. I suppose that's what got me in the end – or rather, didn't get me. What a confusing thing language is nowadays."

"You mean," Tara painfully continued, "he used you for his own ends? Like me and the ballet?" The minute the words were out she regretted them. She had thought that way of thinking had been closed up long ago. Fortunately Sybille did not pick up on it.

"Not consciously," Sybille said hastily. "Josh is a great guy to work with, a great guy to have as a friend, and a great guy anyway. He's a creature of impulse, though, and maybe that's what makes him so interesting."

Strange how all one's fears can come to roost together, even over a cup of cocoa. Without knowing it, Sybille was confirming what must have been uneasily lurking at the back of Tara's mind. Tara knew at present she was inextricably part of the ballet for Josh, but after it was staged, and they only had the memory of the unicorn to draw them together, what then? Did they have enough in common – apart from sex – to build a future?

"He's an independent spirit," Sybille continued. "He loves, but doesn't *need* women." Sybille was looking at her oddly, in a way that reminded Tara of somebody, although she could not think who.

Whoops. This was too much, even for late-night plain speaking, even for a well-wined dinner afterglow.

"You're not going to tell me Josh is gay, are you, Sybille?" she asked angrily. "You denied that yourself in Sussex when William was trying to cause problems."

Sybille had been joking then, but it had left an image of a Josh-Sybille relationship that, for all Sybille's assertions that it was past, and Josh's that it had never happened, could not be entirely eradicated. Perhaps this was merely a sign of how much Tara loved Josh, though. She struggled to think clearly. After all, William had had at least one serious relationship before he and Tara met, and she and Claire were now friends.

"No, he's not gay, but I still maintain he doesn't depend on women emotionally, to function. Perhaps you're an exception, though. I must admit I've been swayed since he met you. I've never seen him so hooked. The way he looks at you—"

"He never touches me, though." The *vino* was speaking with a vengeance, coming to the heart of her problem. Josh kissed her lightly when they were together, but the intimate touches of the hand, the quick embraces, had vanished since Brittany, despite their understanding. She had tried, oh so hard, to make a move herself, to give him a swift hug, or to kiss him and touch him in passing, as had come so naturally once, but somehow she could not do it. It was as if a level-crossing barrier swung down every time the thought occurred to her, and she had to watch the train of opportunity chugging by.

"But don't you see the way he looks? It's as if you're magnetised and he's holding himself just out of range. And whether you know it or not, you give the same impression yourself."

The rest of the autumn was hectic, both for Tara at work, as she tried to organise a smooth handover, and for Sybille and Josh, who were either travelling or had their heads down over the new programme. There were several weekends when Tara battled with the account books, and one blissful weekend with Josh when he talked to her endlessly about unicorns, symbolism, and his plans for the ballet. At other times an apparent camaraderie concealed – at least for her – an uneasy truce over their differences.

As Christmas approached, Tara saw little of either Josh or Sybille during the week, for rehearsals were in full swing for a pantomime to begin on Boxing Day. The story was basically that of *The Frog Prince*, but unlike the summer version this one had a narrator, less straight mime, a dramatic element, a dame, and much general mimed slapstick which changed it from Josh's earlier presentation. The music had changed too. Josh had permission from Giselle to use the original Prince score for it, which by "cutting and pasting" he had skilfully adapted to the pantomime. Sybille had the role of the Princess, and Josh the Frog, with Michael playing the wicked stepmother in drag. There seemed to be a dragon involved somewhere too; Tara couldn't recall this in the Grimm story, but it was certain to appeal to children.

With her work, and the ever-earlier Christmas parties and lunches it involved her in, Tara had given little thought to her own Christmas. When she did think of it, it yawned before her like a black hole. Neither Josh nor Sybille had mentioned this formidable date, there was no William, and no invitations from elsewhere – save one from her parents, which she accepted gratefully.

This arranged, Tara felt able to gather up her pride to ask Sybille her plans.

"It's a high day and holiday," Sybille replied, "so Michael's coming here. So's Josh. Do stay here if you like. Plenty of room."

Tara decided she didn't want to be an afterthought. "Thanks, but I'm going to Lewes for country fare. I'll be back for the panto, of course." And that was that. Subject closed.

Josh didn't even mention the word Christmas until the weekend before. When at last he did, it was a casual, "Where are you scoffing your Christmas turkey, Tara?"

Obviously Sybille hadn't told him what Tara meant to do, and it had taken Josh this long to ask her himself, such was his interest in the subject. No – that was unfair of her, for she knew full well that the panto was taking all his energy and thoughts.

"Home."

"William-type home or Lewes-type home?"

How could he manage to rile her so quickly? "The latter, and unaccompanied by any William type." Keep it brisk and unconcerned.

"Ah. I suppose—"

The brisk and unconcerned Tara suddenly vanished.

"Oh, *yes.*"

For once Josh was inside magnet range, and so was she. He pulled her into his arms and kissed her, not lightly as usual, but with the passion she feared had evaporated. Sybille had been right. "It's still there," he said huskily. "Despite all this, there's room on your horse for two. You can still read my mind."

"Of course. So we'll both go to William's, shall we?" She managed to laugh through her pleasure and relief.

"Be serious. Sure your parents won't mind? I'd like to meet them. I've been summoning up my courage to ask you for weeks, hoping against hope you'd ask me first."

Oh, the relief. A simple misunderstanding. But the worm of suspicion stirred. Of course he wanted to meet her parents. They were part of the unicorn story, albeit a lesser part than her grandmother. And then the worm fell asleep again, for how could she think that, with the warmth of Josh's arms round her?

"I know they won't." She did know it, for they'd suggested it. Her reply had been that Josh was too busy, but it could, thankfully, be reversed.

"I'll have to come back Christmas evening for the panto. I'll be looking forward to my Christmas stocking, though. Santa just might bring me a lovely honey-blonde."

Once they arrived, Tara felt jittery, since the happy glow of Josh's presence was tarnished by wondering if her parents were missing William, whom they had liked. She had never spelled out her relationship with Josh to them, but it couldn't have been hard to guess what it was after her earlier visit. Josh might be her grandmother's cup of tea, but was he theirs? And did it matter anyway? Why was it that friendships were so straightforward, and love affairs so frettingly complicated?

Josh had explained that his father had died some years ago and his mother had remarried and was living in the States, and that was the reason he had remained close to his grandfather. He was looking forward, he said, to Christmas with a bit of family. There were several ways to take that, and Tara decided not to enquire further.

Perhaps it had been unwise not to have been more forthcoming about Josh and her plans to her parents, since it immediately led to problems at dinner on Christmas Eve. She had been silently congratulating herself that all was going well, when her mother asked what his company was working on.

"A pantomime of *The Frog Prince*, the Grimm fairy-tale."

Her mother looked up sharply, and her father asked: "I thought you ran a mime company. How do you mime a panto?"

"It's not all mime. There are songs, narration, and all the usual ingredients. Anyway, you'd be amazed how receptive children are. It's only adults who are hooked to the stereotype of a division between music, words, song and dance."

"Dance?" Margaret picked up. "You're using the Prince score?"

"Yes, and for *The Unicorn and the Nightingale*. We're doing that in April, as Tara will have told you."

"No, Tara didn't tell us." Margaret, unusually for her, was growing frosty.

"She'll be heavily involved in it too, when she leaves the tax world behind next week," Josh continued.

Tara groaned inwardly. Why did he have to put his foot right in it? She'd been putting off telling them her plans, knowing they'd both disapprove – for different reasons.

"She didn't tell us that either," said her father, giving her a very old-fashioned look indeed.

"Thanks, Josh," she muttered. He looked concerned, but she had a suspicion that he had done it on purpose. "I was about to tell you," she said awkwardly to her parents, "but I knew you'd disapprove—"

"I might have done once," her father interrupted, to her astonishment. "Not now, though. It's all too easy to get caught up in one job and see the world through blinkered eyes. I'm a new fellow since I got my hand on the till of the garden centre. I can even tell a geranium from a rose now."

"That's different." Tara grinned, grateful for the reprieve. "You'd already established yourself both financially and in terms of prestige. You don't *have* to work if you don't want to."

"Nor do you," her father retorted, "according to what you told me in the summer."

She was bereft of words. She had never said anything of the sort to her father, and he knew it. It might have a grain of truth in it, but *only* a grain. Moreover her mother had a face like thunder, as if she thought Tara had sold out to the enemy. From Margaret's point of view, Tara supposed she had. She'd chosen the unicorn's path, not the sensible route.

Josh did not even comment, though she saw he had picked up on it. She was prepared for attack when he suggested they went for a walk after dinner "to see if Santa's coming".

"Look, Josh." She confronted him the minute they were out of the house. "It isn't *true* about the money. My father likes stirring things up."

"You don't need to sound so defensive. I said you could have all the time you needed, and I meant it." He put a casual arm round her shoulders, which was almost worse than no contact at all. *Did* he mean it? There was enough light to see even without the torch she had brought, but even so she could not read his expression in the distortion of the moonlight. "I like your parents," he added.

"Do you? I thought you would have nothing in common with them."

"Liking isn't a question of being the same. Your mother's quite something. She's not the least bit like your grandmother, and yet somehow you can see that she's her daughter. Something about their slightly scatty independence. What was her father – Giselle's husband – like?"

He *would* ask that. Should she give away the family secret or not? If she did she would feel she was in some way betraying her mother, and so she merely replied: "Rather staid, I gather."

Josh's lips twitched. "O buttoned-up lady of mine, your mother's already told me that Antoine was her father."

"I don't believe it!" Tara was outraged. "She's only met you for an hour or two and it took me twenty-five years to find that out. What the hell's going on here?" She tried to inject a note of mock indignation into her voice, but it failed, for she was genuinely bewildered. Her mother's frostiness must have been towards her, not Josh.

"It's my charm."

"What charm?" she answered crossly.

"The charm I once had for you, and no longer do apparently."

She was appalled. How could he think that? "You do, Josh, you do."

"Then why do we sleep in separate bedrooms, why aren't we loving and living together?"

Not again. She struggled to find the answer she had already tried to give in so many ways, but when it came it surprised even her. "Because of the unicorns."

Josh looked taken aback. "You're getting mixed up, beloved. Santa has reindeer, not unicorns, attached to his sleigh. So if you're waiting for them to arrive, you'll wait a long time. I must hand it to you; even Browning's lady didn't think of unicorns as an excuse. Maybe she remembered their horns are meant to be a love potion."

"Browning's lady had a knight who was similarly disposed to her," she pointed out.

"You don't get away with that one," he retorted. "I feel as I always have towards you. I want you, and I love you. It's you, my Lilith, who is refusing to travel to the unknown country, for which I have my visa ready – and as I told you, it has no expiry date. So what's all this about unicorns?"

"It's so mixed up, I can't see things clearly." She desperately tried to explain. "I want you too, and I love you. But somehow it's as if the path to you is so lined with blessed unicorns and nightingales that they're blocking the way. Does that make sense?"

"You think I love you only for the ballet, not for yourself alone," he said at last, shooting straight to the bull's eye.

She tried to answer honestly. "I think you're completely caught up in the ballet – and so would I be if I let myself. We could commit ourselves completely to each other – and to go to bed together again *would* mean that – but until it's over there's a danger of our lives and the ballet becoming irrevocably entwined."

"Too much thinking ruins the appetite."

"No danger of *that*."

In a moment his arm tightened round her, as he whirled her round and into his embrace. "Are you sure?"

"Yes."

"I love you, Tara. *Never* forget that, will you?"

His lips were on hers, her unloved body came to life and the ache began, but such a sweet ache, such sweet longing that she did not resist him. She felt his tongue gently exploring her mouth, his hands delving inside her coat to cup her breasts, and his lips on hers sending explosions of feeling rippling through her. Just when she felt she would burst with frustration, he drew back. "Hell," he said furiously, "I can't go on, I can't. How can I kiss you like this, when I know you'll be sleeping so close to me in one way, but miles apart in another? Maybe even dreaming of William's safe comfortable arms, wherever they may be."

"Don't mention William, please, Josh." She could not bear it. "That's over. Don't ever forget I love you too. The future is ours."

"Even though it's full of blasted unicorns prancing around?"

"Maybe they'll pack up and go home."

"My ballet won't just disappear after its first performance."

"But it will be out of your mind, Josh. That's where most unicorns are dancing at present, and I don't feel I can struggle through them."

She could see him trembling. "Remember we don't know what happens in the third act yet."

"We do, Josh, for it's our story too. And you must write it into the ballet."

"François may have said that to Arabella. Perhaps they were both beset by unicorns too. And look what happened."

"We don't *know* what happened. Josh, it's not like you to be pessimistic. Maybe that's our role: to rewrite their third act by getting it right ourselves." She spoke so vehemently, it wasn't until she'd finished that she understood what she had said. Perhaps understood was the wrong word, though, for surely it was nonsense? Or did she mean that it wasn't rational? Not everything had to be rational. The magic of Christmas as a child, the magic of her ballet days hadn't vanished, for they could be conjured up with all their potent evocative memories. And the enchantment of the Unicorn and of Arabella and François' story was lingering; more than lingering. It was demanding to be heard.

Josh grinned, perhaps convinced at last by her argument. "I think I see Santa's unicorns coming."

"Along with a honey-blonde for you."

"In spirit or flesh?"

"The first, but I wish, Josh, I wish."

Tara listened guiltily to her voicemail from an extremely cross William. "Tara? You may be working part time, but you should at least have the decency to keep up with your mail. I've tried three times already."

She had in fact heard the messages, and usually prided herself on returning all phone calls the day she received them or with an apology the next. Caught up in the pantomime, she had completely forgotten to call William back, assuming it was just a routine happy-new-year call. She hastened to make amends and invited him out to lunch.

"Good Christmas?" He glanced at her suspiciously over the rocket and parmesan salad when they met the next day.

"Splendid. And you?"

"First class. With my parents," he added.

"How are they?"

How long could she keep this up? she wondered, as he politely told her the news. She had lived with William, sharing all the intimacies of everyday life, as well as his bed. She knew him as a lover, she knew him as a companion, so why the hell could she find nothing to say to him? It wasn't as if he'd been disloyal to her; this situation was all of her making, not his. He merely wanted her back, though seeing his impassive face now, it was hard to believe. But then William was very good at keeping separate compartments in his life, hence his wish – surely outdated nowadays – that no one at conferences should know they were an item.

"What was so urgent?" she asked eventually, tired of formalities.

"Merely the programme, Tara. Remember the conference?"

"Naturally," she said stiffly.

"Good. This is the draft programme so far." He handed her a stapled set of pages while they were waiting for their main course, and she studied them eagerly. It looked good. He had John Hadlow for the British scene in tax and wealth management, and Petra Cone on tax and charities. The US speakers were good too, all of them at the top of their profession. There were also a number of European speakers, each covering his or her own country's perspective. Tara herself was down for the subject that she had requested, cross-border tax harmonisation, as well as sole chair for the three-day conference.

"When am I speaking?" she asked, since there were dates by the names.

"Provisionally Wednesday afternoon. You're the draw to ensure delegates don't sneak off early."

She laughed. "I'd prefer the morning."

"I'll see what I can do, ma'am."

"I really am grateful for this chance, William," Tara said sincerely. "It means a lot to me."

"It may mean a lot to me too. I'm hoping, of course" – he gave her a disarming grin – "that you'll get such a kick out of it, it will change your mind. All this capering about with pantomimes is rather juvenile for you. It's as if you're taking a holiday from yourself."

"Mime is part of pantomime," she pointed out icily, "and although the Christmas one is for children, it's serious business the rest of the year, and serious even when it's comic. And, William, so far as I'm concerned, this conference is business only. No pressure. OK?"

"Of course."

"There's a whole world out there, William," she said earnestly, suddenly feeling she wanted him to understand and stop being so *polite* about it, "that has nothing to do with tax. While we're beavering away at what we do, everyone else is just as involved in what they do. Yet how many people see the whole picture? Very few."

"So?"

"So there's no need to scoff at what Josh does. He's just as dismissive about what we do."

"*Did*, in your case, as I understand. You have thrown your lot in with this pantomime outfit."

"Yes."

"Not regretting your sudden loss of reason?"

"No. And that wasn't what it was."

115

"Then why stay on with Pitkins part time? Do forgive my curiosity."

"Because I owe something to my clients. Three months' notice isn't long enough to hand everything over to a newcomer. It's not fair on Janice" – her replacement – "or on the clients."

"I'm sure they're all grateful for your consideration."

"Dammit, William" – he'd got to her at last – "whether they're grateful or not is immaterial. It's what *I* think I ought to do, the way I think I want to live, the way I *know* I am that matters. I'm staying on part time of my own free will. That's what I told Josh, and that's what I'm telling you."

"Indeed," he murmured, obviously highly pleased at having stung her. "And did Josh sympathise with your determination to exercise free will?"

"He doesn't like it, but he understands it's what I choose to do."

William ignored this declaration of independence. "I thought he might object," he said smugly.

*　　*　　*

Arabella had visited St Petersburg before, when Pavlova had taken her company to the Maryinsky, but travelling with Diaghilev and with Pavlova were vastly different experiences. Madame Pavlova was temperamental, thoughtful and kind at one moment, irascible at others, but she allowed Victor Dandré to look after every detail of travel and programming.

Their journey to Russia in the tempestuous wake of Sergei Diaghilev, however, was far from organised. Diaghilev owned a small flat in St Petersburg, but had elected to stay with them at the Hôtel de l'Europe by the Nevsky Prospekt where he could hold a larger "court". It was uncertain when one arose in the morning whether he would still be there at night, and Maria had told her that had it not been for his problems regarding the 1914 programme he would have left within days.

Now that she understood that Diaghilev, like Madame Pavlova, frowned upon marriage between members of the same company, Arabella realised François could not tell him their plans at the moment especially with the uproar over Nijinsky's marriage still so recent. They had agreed they should wait to tell him openly until after the success of *The Unicorn and the Nightingale*, when, as François pointed out, "He will need *me* more than I need him." Diaghilev had scheduled it for early in the 1914 London season, which would open towards the end of May. But the waiting, oh, the waiting. Every kiss was both rapture and pain, as though they were dancing a ballet of their own in which at last a finale would be reached. Not a grand finale of *corps de ballet* and set dances of rejoicing, but the *pas de deux* of lovers.

More mundane matters bothered her too. Her lack of sufficient practice facilities – and lack of money. The money she had brought with her had all but vanished, and she had discovered that Diaghilev was notoriously slack about regular payments to his dancers. Moreover, she was not even officially employed by the Ballets Russes. Maria came to the rescue, realising her dilemma and her unwillingness to raise the matter with François, and offered to make loans to Arabella against such time as she could repay them out of her salary. Arabella was deeply grateful. Christmas would soon be here, and at least now she could buy some presents, even if it would be odd to buy a present to show her gratitude to Maria out of her own money.

She and Maria practised each day in an unused room in the hotel, but it was not the same as a proper rehearsal room, and proved even more difficult when François wanted them to try out his steps and movements for the ballet. For Arabella the sessions had personal difficulties, too.

"What's wrong?" Maria eventually asked, concerned. "You're not dancing your best."

"I know. But I was trained by Cecchetti and Madame Pavlova in the classical school. This is entirely different." She was glad of an opportunity to unburden herself. Just as Nijinsky had introduced unorthodox positions and movements in the three ballets he choreographed, so François too was moving outside the conventional. Cecchetti had ruled that in a high jump the soles of the feet should be drawn together in the air in order to land correctly in fifth position, but François was insistent that this destroyed the graceful line of the leg.

"François doesn't understand how difficult it is for me to both dance as I was taught and in the way in which he seems to work."

"Have you talked to him about it?"

117

"No. I'm worried it may affect his choreography."

"Nothing will do that, and no one," Maria said firmly. "And have you thought that some of it might be François' fault? Because of *The Unicorn and the Nightingale* he is not thinking of his own dancing. He lacks the practice that we do, and so he is getting remote from the practical realities of the stage. Here he is in St Petersburg waiting hand and foot on Sergei, while the Ballets Russes is touring Europe. He is like another Beppe to Sergei," she laughed. Beppe was a joke – to all but Diaghilev. He was his valet, a handsome young man whom he had met in Naples and befriended.

For the past month Arabella had seen little of François, for he and Arnold Prince had been working together on the score, fortunately harmoniously. Mr Prince had come to St Petersburg in November, and was working to François' scenario. François would impatiently await each new section of the score, while his mind was already half forming the steps and movements. After it had been played to Diaghilev, and herself and Maria as the other two principal dancers, endless experiments would take place as they tried out steps at François' orders in an attempt to achieve the magical effect he had in his mind. It was hard to see how it all fitted together and François was not good at explaining. She knew these awkward movements would sooner or later resolve themselves into a work of beauty, for she had faith in François, but nevertheless the small room they used for practice began to get claustrophobic.

At last, in mid-December, the music for most of the ballet was complete, and Arnold was leaving for England. Arabella felt a weight would be lifted from her. She had grudgingly come to like Arnold very much, but he still represented home, her father, and an indefinable and illogical black shadow over the future.

Just before he left, one major problem for the Ballets Russes was solved. François came bounding in to tell them the news as she and Maria were practising one morning.

"Sergei has won the battle," he cried happily, an arm round each of their waists.

"Which one?" Maria retorted.

"For a ballet-master. A chief choreographer. Monsieur Fokine has agreed to return to the Ballets Russes."

"That's wonderful." Arabella was relieved. François was obviously not senior enough for the position, but while the gap remained, not only had Sergei been moody, but a big question mark had hung over the whole 1914 season.

"Unbelievable," Maria said drily. "How on earth did Sergei manage it?"

"With difficulty," François laughed. "According to him, he spent five hours on the telephone before Fokine would even agree to see him, and he has only surrendered after much negotiation. Sergei insisted there must be other choreographers beside Fokine – *magnifique* – and Fokine insisted that Karsavina must not take all the leading roles, not because he does not admire her work – who would not? – but because he wishes his wife to dance too."

"And Monsieur Diaghilev agreed?" Maria was dumbfounded.

"He did. Oh, he was so clever. He agreed instantly and talked of the value of variety, and, when he had Fokine's full accord, he added, 'And that is why Monsieur Santine wishes Arabelle Petrovna to dance in his *Unicorn*.' There was nothing Fokine could say, but in any case, he is a generous man and a great artist. Once he has seen you dance, he will see why you inspire me."

"He wants to see me dance?" Arabella was overjoyed.

"Yes, and, *ma chérie*" – his arm was for her alone now – "Sergei made another deal. Fokine is ballet-master of the Maryinsky at present, and will allow us all to practise there at the Imperial Ballet School."

Arabella tried hard to take in all this good news at once, but François had not finished.

"And, finally," he crowed, climbing on to a chair so that they could appreciate his *attitude grecque* the better, "everything is changed. *The Unicorn and the Nightingale* is to be *three* acts, not one. Maria, you shall dance and menace me throughout as you wished; and Arabella, the world will sing like a nightingale at the beauty of your dancing."

Seven

"I cannot see the finale of Act Two."

Arabella looked up, startled at François' anguished howl. He was lying stretched out on the *chaise-longue* in her and Maria's sitting room and had not spoken for at least half an hour. It was becoming a routine. In the mornings they practised and rehearsed, in the afternoons François agonised over what he saw as the complete failure of his efforts, while she persuaded him that the situation was otherwise.

Despite his pleasure that *The Unicorn* was to become a three-act ballet, François had not found the transition easy. Nor had Arnold Prince, who had been highly annoyed to receive the news just as he left for England, although on receipt of François' extended scenario for Acts I and II he had agreed to revise his earlier work, and the score had arrived a week ago.

One major point remained unresolved in Arabella's mind: Act III. François had not even begun it.

"I shall bring the first two acts to perfection before I begin Act Three," was always his answer when she questioned him on it.

"But Arnold cannot compose the music until he has your scenario," was always hers.

"How can there be a scenario," he would cry, "until the beginning and the middle are perfect?"

Arabella would laugh, but she noticed that even Maria had stopped telling her not to worry. It was almost as if François *feared* writing the last act, yet to suggest this outright might be to drive him further away. All she could do was to encourage him.

"Describe it. Make me see Act Two." Arabella came to join him on the sofa, closer to the fire and to him. He promptly swung his legs down so that she could cuddle up against him.

January in Russia was quite unlike England's winters. Its temperature sank far below zero, and however much she muffled herself up the cold penetrated. No fire was warm enough and only the morning exercises at the Maryinsky Theatre helped. She thought longingly of the now unimaginable warmth of coming off stage at the Palace Theatre in London, her brow running with sweat, and having to put clothes on to maintain the heat and avoid chills. Here the snow lay in a thick layer, and ice clung immovably to the inside of the window panes, unthawed by the fire. "Jack Frost has visited us, I see," her mother used to say briskly, looking at the swirling patterns on her bedroom window at home. But Jack Frost quickly disappeared in England. Here he lay so thickly that even his delicate patterns were invisible.

At first, never having been part of a big company, she found the Maryinsky intimidating, but now, even though she was only practising there, either with the Imperial Ballet School or with François and Maria, she had grown accustomed to it. Fokine was temperamental, easily irritated, but it did not last long if he saw his inspiration fulfilled in one's dancing. She had seemed to please him, although with her strict classical training it took time for her to adapt to his and François' neo-romantic style.

"He likes your knees," François had joked, relieved after her first practice for the ballet-master, and when she giggled, he explained seriously, "They are *jarretés*, knock-kneed, good for the flowing movements we need."

She was even more delighted when Fokine promised her she could dance in two ensembles in his *Chopiniana* for four performances in February and March. He had asked Maria too, but she had declined, to Arabella's surprise. She explained that as a long-standing member of the Ballets Russes it was not proper for her to dance with another company, whereas Arabella was not yet a formal member of the company.

Arabella tried guile to solve François' current problem. "Perhaps if you worked on the scenario for Act Three, you might see the finale for Two."

Another howl.

"It is impossible, *ma belle*. How can I think of that while I am fighting my way through the jungle to the end of Act Two? If I try to think of Three, a dark cloud covers my mind. I see snatches of it, but then they are taken away from me, and I am plunged down in a bottomless pit of chaos."

"Would a muffin help?"

"Perhaps. But this hotel has no muffins. It is too bad."

"They have *pryanik* – honey-cake."

He groaned. "Very well."

"And then," Arabella said innocently, "you will see the ensemble for the Act Two finale."

"How?"

"Your stomach will churn so much that your mind will be full of foreboding and Morgana's evil followers. It will rise up as Galymede rushes towards the enchantress, and the nightingale, defeated, dances a lonely solo of death at the side of the stage while the evil spirits perform their lively ensemble of victory."

"What inspiration! Ring for *pryanik* immediately!"

It was not until he was half-way through the cake that he mentioned the ballet again. "I suppose Sergei is right."

"In what respect?" She had suspected François had been hiding something, and that his despondency had not been all for the finale.

"I meant about the programme for the coming season. He said it is the most exciting yet, despite the fact he has dropped Nijinsky's ballets. For opera-ballet he is planning Rimsky-Korsakov's *Le Coq D'Or*, and now he can add Stravinsky's opera *Le Rossignol*. And there is Strauss's *La Légende de Joseph*, though that is only partly ballet."

"Who is to dance Joseph? Nijinsky?" Arabella was torn between hope that François would get the role and hope that he wouldn't, for it would mean distraction from *The Unicorn and the Nightingale*.

"No, Nijinsky dances with the Ballets Russes no more. I heard he is forming his own company, and is going to the Palace in London this spring."

How strange. Madame Pavlova was in America, but Nijinsky would be at the Palace. It was like musical chairs – and no wonder, for the public, especially in England, was greedy for more and more Russian ballet at the moment.

"Will you be asked to dance Joseph?" she asked tentatively.

"Perhaps, but I do not think so, because I shall dance in *The Unicorn*. Nevertheless" – he hesitated – "Sergei feels that I should – *ma mie*, I have sad news."

She had been right. Her heart plummeted in dread of what was coming.

122

"We shall be parted for a month, perhaps more. Sergei wants me to join the Ballet on tour now. He feels I should be in daily contact with the company, and to dance with it, to feel part of it once more."

"But he wanted you to concentrate solely on *The Unicorn*." Her mind whirled in dismay. How were they to work on *The Unicorn* if she were to stay here?

"Unless I dance, how can I choreograph? That is his argument and it is a reasonable one."

"But the Maryinsky – could you not dance here, as I am?"

"I suggested it, but like Maria I am under contact for the Diaghilev Ballet, and Sergei requires my presence. My sweetheart, I must leave next week, to join the company in Germany."

"But when will I see you again?" All she could think of was that she was bound to stay here to dance in *Chopiniana*. What had been an exciting privilege now seemed an iron cage.

"In time for rehearsals for *The Unicorn* to begin with the company and for us to plan Act Three. Sergei knows we have worked together for the *soli* and *pas de deux* for the first two acts, and he is satisfied."

"But" – her head was still spinning – "the London season begins on May twentieth."

"Sergei plans to rejoin the Ballet in Cologne in March, which is when Monsieur Fokine says performances of *Chopiniana* finish. He will then leave St Petersburg for the Ballets Russes."

"But Act Three—" She broke off helplessly. It was impossible, quite impossible. And this was nearly two months, not one, that they would be separated. How could he have agreed to this? She sat upright again, appalled.

"You will be in my dreams," François said anxiously.

She wanted to cry out that being in his dreams was not enough. She wanted to be in his arms, as his lover, as his wife. Had his love for her changed? Was he seizing an excuse to flee from her? No, she could not believe that – but she was tired of being brave. The torment burst out. "*I* am in a jungle too, François, and it is closing around me. I'm not like your Nightingale: I can't find *my* way, let alone yours."

"You are crying, Arabella." He pulled her back into his arms, and they lay entwined beside each other on the *chaise-longue*. "Please, please, do not. Have faith. We *will* be together, the

123

ballet *will* happen, it is coming together already and so are we. We may be still stumbling through our forests, but I *know* how Act Three finishes now, thanks to you. We shall be free of this terrible jungle soon."

"François, I want you." Arabella spoke hopelessly into the thick wool jerkin to which she was clasped. Ahead lay barren weeks, and the undefined blackness of the future.

Fiercely he turned her face to his: "And do you not think I want you? I can only kiss your cold, cold face and hands, but do you not know how much I want to hold you so much closer, without this heavy wool dress, without the underclothes and chemises that imprison you? Then I would kiss your neck, your breasts, the whole body that I feel so close to me as we dance. It lights fires within me that taunt me now, but that one day will warm us both. Do you not know that?"

She did know it. All her doubts and uncertainties fled, for here was the François she had loved from the first moment she met him. However preoccupied François the choreographer seemed, however much he had to live within his own creative mind, the other François, the one she loved even more, was there, as firm and steadfast as she knew herself to be.

"Let's dance through every thicket of the forest," Arabella laughed through her tears. "Together we will strike down wicked witches, cast off magic spells, and reach the end of Act Three to live happily ever after. When *The Unicorn and the Nightingale* is a success, even Diaghilev will not mind us marrying. I will be an established member of the company, and you will be the ballet-master elect."

"We are a long way from that." Nevertheless he caught her mood, leapt off the *chaise-longue*, pulled her after him, and spun her around. "Monsieur Fokine is ballet-master and I am only twenty-five years old."

"But who knows what might happen, if Fokine falls out with Monsieur Diaghilev again?"

"Who knows what might happen anyway?" François said soberly. "If there is to be a war, as many believe there will be, everything might change . . . My darling, we go to Germany and then in early April, shortly after you join us, we go to Monte Carlo. Until you come, we shall both miss you so much, Maria and I."

"Maria?" Arabella repeated blankly.

"Did I not mention that Maria must come with me to Germany? Sergei has demanded that she take part in the Ballets Russes' repertoire there. She is very unhappy about leaving you, but she has no choice, as you are to dance in *Chopiniana* here."

All Arabella's joy vanished. There was nothing unusual about such conflicts of professional roles, but nevertheless she felt she had once again been thrown into a sea of confusion. She wanted to cry out: What shall I do here alone? Where shall I live? Who is my friend? but pride prevented her. François seemed to read her thoughts, however.

"Do not worry, *ma mie*. Monsieur Fokine will arrange somewhere for you to stay, and Maria and I have thought about this problem too." Maria and I? Arabella felt slightly sick. "And Arnold Prince still has the third act's music to compose."

"How can he if he doesn't know the story?" she asked dully, trying to think of the ballet, but failing. She was consumed with her own problems, and did not see what Arnold had to do with François' departure anyway.

"I have promised Sergei that when Act Two is finished – as, thanks to you, it will be tomorrow – I *will* write the scenario for Act three. I will complete it before I leave next week, and give it to Arnold."

"In Germany?"

"No." François grinned. "Here. He arrives tomorrow for two months to keep you company. He and I will study the scenario before I leave, and he has at least six weeks to compose the music, before coming with you to Berlin."

Here? This was the worst news of all. François and Maria gone, and she would be abandoned with Arnold *here*.

"He is more a friend of my father's than of mine," she cried in protest. How could François seem so pleased at this awful news?

He looked taken aback at her distress. "He is a friend to us both." There was some reproach in his voice. "His score is magical. He understands my needs exactly. He is always accommodating, always willing to change, to adapt, no matter how outrageous I am in my demands."

Arabella was forced to agree. The music had been both lyrical

125

and dramatic – but that, she thought miserably, did not make Arnold her friend. Who was her friend? Not even Maria, it seemed, for close though they were, she had given no hint of her departure. Perhaps, Arabella thought desolately, she believed it was François' duty to tell her, but this obvious explanation still left an uncomfortable taste in her mouth – and it had nothing to do with *pryanik*.

"Whatever you may think, Arnold has your good at heart, both for your career and for you yourself," François assured her earnestly. "He is fond of you, and I think now likes me also. He wishes to see us married."

She looked at him doubtfully. "But why not ask me first, before asking him to come? I do not *want* him here."

"It was his idea," François told her helplessly. "I wrote to him of my worry about you and he promptly said he'd come to work here on the third act. It seemed sensible, *ma chérie*," he pleaded.

Sensible? How could she convey to François how she felt when she could not put into words where her anxiety lay? Arnold might be an understanding and kind man, and he had a dry sense of humour, which made her laugh, but he was not yet a wholly trusted friend, although there was no sign that he was keeping her father informed of her whereabouts. He always had good advice about her dancing, and he was a pleasant companion. Yet still it seemed to her the forest had grown even thicker, and that although she and François would only be apart for six weeks, the separation held a deeper significance that she could not grasp.

To dance with François, whether on a stage or in a ballroom, was to float in a dream of inspiration. To dance the tango or waltz with Arnold, though enjoyable on one level, was a plodding earthbound experience. Nevertheless, Arabella was glad of his company when attending the Maryinsky performance, the theatre and the spectacular balls given by the St Petersburg hostesses, for they at least took her away from her lonely hotel room, as did her work at the ballet by day.

"I saw your *Chopiniana* last evening," Arnold said, whisking her expertly round the floor.

"My *Chopiniana*?" she laughed. "As a humble temporary member of the *corps de ballet*?"

Fokine's *Chopiniana* was known as *Les Sylphides* in the rest of Europe, but as it had first been performed in Russia, *Chopiniana* it remained when staged here again. The first version of it had been based on national dances, but the second, inspired by the first, was a mood ballet in purely romantic style. The costume for the *corps de ballet* in *Chopiniana* was the traditional one worn by Marie Taglioni with a three-quarter length skirt, which was essential for this atmospheric romantic ballet. It was giving her excellent experience, and she knew she was being carefully watched by Monsieur Fokine, who would report to Monsieur Diaghilev. To be in the *corps de ballet* was to walk on eggshells for a dancer with ambition. By its nature, one should conform, but unless one stood out from the others, one could have no hope of rising to greater heights.

"In the waltz particularly you shone out."

"I'm not supposed to shine in the *corps de ballet*, Arnold." All the same, she was pleased.

"But that is why Diaghilev has agreed to your joining his company. Do you think he would merely accept the whim of a choreographer, even François? Ah no; he made his own mind up that first time he saw you dance. As has Monsieur Fokine, I am sure."

"He has been very good to me."

"He is a great artiste, and will no doubt continue to be very good to you after *The Unicorn and the Nightingale* is staged, and you seek further roles. He is travelling with us to Germany, and no doubt his plans may emerge during the course of conversation."

Arabella turned this over in her mind, and wondered what disturbed her. "You will be coming to Berlin too, Arnold?"

"Of course. Didn't Maria tell you?" Now it was he who seemed uneasy. "By then I shall have the music for the third act ready, and I need to be on hand when rehearsals begin. Small problems always arise, and the music may need adjusting."

It occurred to Arabella that he might also wish to be where she was, for she was increasingly aware that his interest in her was not purely professional or even that of a disinterested friend.

Arnold smiled at her. "If you would like to take a glass of champagne with me in the conservatory, I can tell you about Act Three amid those beautiful surroundings."

He settled her in a wicker chair and despatched a footman for the champagne. Then he drew his chair closer to hers, and took her hands in his.

"If I were to tell you it is the best music I have ever written, that would not be boastful, Arabella. Firstly, it is true, and secondly, I have only been able to compose it because of you."

"Because I am to dance it." She tried to sound matter of fact, but sensed what was coming.

"No, Arabella, though that is a part of it. To have you at my side, to be able to watch you dance and practise, to be able to escort you, is inspiration enough, but it is Arabella I value most of all, not Arabelle the dancer."

She must make her position clear, gently and quickly. "Arnold, you realise François and I are still betrothed? We shall wed as soon as the ballet is performed."

"Of course," he said quietly.

To break the silence that followed, she asked: "Did you never wish to wed?"

"Oh yes. I was engaged once."

"And what happened?" She could not imagine Arnold passionately in love. He must be forty at least.

"Death snatched her away from me a few weeks before our wedding. That was many years ago," he continued briskly, "and my heart has remained my own since then – until now."

She scarcely caught the final words, but when she understood what he was telling her, she cried out: "Arnold – is it me? Oh please, I would not dream – I would not wish to mislead you."

Arnold flushed. "I have embarrassed you. I am sorry, Arabella. I realise you love François deeply, that you will marry him as soon as possible, and who is to say that you are wrong? I am much older than he, more staid; I can offer you much, but not what he can. I can only lay my heart and my hand at your feet, and say that if you need me, I am here. Always."

"Thank you." She struggled to feel *something*, anything, at this unselfish declaration, but words refused to flow. The situation felt unreal, sounded unreal. She had realised Arnold was fond of her, which was perhaps natural in view of the closeness of their association, but that he should wish to marry her had not entered her head. To her, he was of her father's generation.

He leaned forward and kissed her cheek. "And now, enough of

such things. Dinner and the tango await us, and two more weeks of pleasant comradeship. Would that please you?"

"Yes," she answered gratefully. The splendours of St Petersburg were beginning to pall on her; she longed only for François and to take up her role in his ballet. An undemanding Arnold – if he kept to his word – would help the days to pass more quickly.

"If you like Germany, wait until you see Monte Carlo," François said. "It is a most suitable place for unicorns. Full of white buildings and splendid soaring turrets."

She had disliked the journey to Berlin, which had seemed to last forever, while all she could think of was her reunion with François. Once she arrived, however, the city and the splendours of the Ballets Russes entranced her: the spectacular scenery, the vast company, and the way that apparent disorganisation and disharmony merged into a glorious triumph night after night. Seeing the ballet from the wings and realising what went on there gave her a different view indeed from her previous one as a member of the audience. Opera and ballet casts fought for the rehearsal rooms and German stage hands despaired at the complete lack of organisation as carpenters and painters struggled for priority. Fokine despaired of ever seeing his ballets on stage, meals were eaten on empty packing cases, and gossip, temperament and tears reigned supreme.

Outside, however, the magnificence of the Unter den Linden in spring entranced her, and it was here that she was strolling with François past the palace of the Kaiser's predecessor, Wilhelm I.

François had told her that Diaghilev had been delighted when Arnold had played the whole score to the company's artistic committee. Arabella had longed to hear it, but no one had suggested she or Maria should be present, although it was quite usual for principals to attend. François was eager to revise her *soli* and their *pas de deux* for the new first two acts, brushing aside any mention of the third act; she suspected something was wrong, but uneasily she struggled to retain her faith that all would be well.

Finally she struck, when he asked her to rehearse the steps for her final solo in Act Two as the Nightingale flutters away to die. "How can I," she demanded, "without knowing what comes next? I haven't even seen your scenario."

He avoided looking at her. "It's not necessary."

"To me it is, François. Why won't you show me? It exists; Diaghilev has passed it, Bakst is working on the design, Arnold has written the music. Aren't you satisfied with it? Is that the reason?"

"No."

"Then what is? You said the music was excellent."

"It is, but—"

"Please tell me," she urged him, when he hesitated.

"I do not think it follows my scenario."

"All of it?" Arabella was appalled.

"No. The ending of Act Three."

The worst. Despite their reunion, the dark forest had closed in once more. "You said it should have a happy ending," Arabella said painfully. It is our life too, François, she wanted to cry. We must fight for it. Yet how hard it was to fight when one could not see one's enemy, nor even be sure who or what that enemy was. Was it merely fate that threw so many obstacles in their path, or was there something more? If the unicorn could fight his way through to find his true love on stage, surely they could?

"My scenario does end happily. In Act Three the Unicorn is caught and bound fast by the hunters, but when he meets Morgana he still believes she is Lilith. Morgana transforms him back into Sir Galymede in preparation for their wedding, *mais*" – François' *port de bras* as he became carried away in his enthusiasm would have delighted Maître Cecchetti – "at the last stage of the transformation, the Unicorn remembers *la philomèle*, and rushes to find her. The Unicorn's power revives her, and, *alors*, he brings her to Camelot. There a final confrontation takes place between good and evil, and Galymede and the real Lilith are united. *Quelle joie*," he finished simply, arms uplifted in a *couronne*.

"Oh, François, but that's right. That's just what should happen." And it would, she vowed. It *would*.

"*Oui*. But Arnold's music does not fit that, and he confessed to me that the reason might be that he has always seen the story ending in the death of both Galymede and Lilith. They would be united in death, just as the seventh tapestry of the Hunt of the Unicorn shows the Unicorn in paradise."

"But Arnold's ending would be too much like *Swan Lake*," Arabella said immediately. François had once sketched this

130

second series of tapestries for her, for it was not in a museum but at the Château de Verteuil. It too depicted the Unicorn, he had explained, but only in the seventh did the Unicorn resemble the peaceful beast of the Cluny tapestries. In the other six, he was at bay, the hunters in full pursuit – but, trapped by guile, perhaps by the cunning of the woman, the last one showed him encaged and happy, and might symbolise paradise.

"Yes, but *malheureusement*, Arnold claims his music *will* work to my ending, that what I see as tragic passages are in fact the gentle triumph of good over evil. He will not rewrite." François stomped round the room in frustration. "Agreed, he is an artist too, but *mon dieu*, why *my* ballet?"

"What can you do?"

"Nothing. Sergei agrees with Arnold. He is sympathetic, though, and we have agreed to leave the choreography of the finale until the rest of the act is in place. Arabella, please, can you accept that?"

"Of course." It was not for herself Arabella was concerned, but for the ballet. If it was to end in a *pas de deux* she and François could practise it alone; what concerned her was that the ballet might slip from François' control, and into that of others.

The first night of *The Unicorn and the Nightingale* was now scheduled for mid-June, for Diaghilev wanted to programme it with other ballets, rather than have it mixed with opera, as would happen if it were performed before the ninth. Nevertheless it loomed close once they moved to Monte Carlo in early April. A few sporadic rehearsals were held, but no one save Arabella seemed concerned at the shortage of time. It was, she gathered, normal. It would all come right.

Unfortunately, Arabella had noticed, Diaghilev was no longer so personally involved in François' ballet. His interest was centred on *La Légende de Joseph*, which would open shortly in Paris. All the talk in the opera house was of the magnificence of the baroque design, how this would be a spectacle to outclass any others. There was little word of the dancing. The role of Potiphar's wife was even to be mimed, and Joseph was to be danced by a newcomer.

"Does that mean he's lost interest in *The Unicorn*?" Arabella asked Maria. They were not so close now as they had been in Russia, for Arabella was wary now of confidences. She had, thanks to payment for her Maryinsky performances, been able to repay the money she had borrowed.

"*Non,* but he has his eyes on Joseph, Léonide Miassin."

Arabella had almost forgotten the strikingly handsome young man whom Diaghilev had discovered in Moscow. "He must be good," she commented.

Maria laughed. "Must he? I've heard rumours all he had to do was prove he could jump over a chair to get the part. He was going to be an actor before Sergei picked him up. Fokine is cutting the part down, so that he can just stand there and look wonderful in a short tunic and flash those dark eyes."

"You sound as if you are in love with him," Arabella teased.

"I don't bang my heart against brick walls."

"How do you know it's a brick wall until you bang it?" Arabella asked idly, but Maria did not reply, and she thought no more of it.

She remembered the conversation, however, when she saw Miassin at practice, and again when she watched a rehearsal for *Joseph* one morning. In looks his dark hair and eyes resembled François', but where François was eager and impulsive for life, Miassin seemed reserved and enigmatic, despite his stage presence.

Maria joined her in the wings as the rehearsal progressed. "Look at those legs," she muttered admiringly.

"Sure you don't want to fall in love with him?"

"I don't want to find myself slung out on the street."

"You mean if you wanted to marry him, Diaghilev might not approve?"

Maria giggled. "I think we can take it he most certainly wouldn't."

"Why doesn't he?" Arabella asked curiously. "Does he fear his dancers would lose their sharp edge on stage?"

Maria shrugged. "It's nothing to do with ballet. He's in love with Miassin himself, of course. Exit Nijinsky *elevation* stage left, enter Miassin, hesitant plod plod, stage right. Stage centre is Beppe, dying swan, about to make a graceful exit."

"I don't understand."

Maria turned to her in amazement. "My dear girl, you can't have worked in the ballet world all these years without learning the facts of life and how they can be bent for those that have the fancy. Even with the way Pavlova looked after her little chicks, a few of them must have trickled through."

Maria looked highly amused, and Arabella suddenly disliked her, as all the sniggers and gossip in the dressing rooms began to come back to her.

"Perhaps I did. Anyway, tell me," she whipped back sharply.

"I'm sorry, Arabella." Maria was contrite. "I assumed you knew. Some men prefer to love other men rather than women, that's all."

"Like ancient Greek friendship?"

"Yes, but not just friendships. Did Diaghilev look as though he'd merely lost a good friend when Nijinsky got married?"

"You mean—" Arabella tried to take this in.

"*Mon dieu*, Arabella. They go to bed with one another, as most men do with women. Is that clear enough? So do some women with other women, for that matter. There's nothing wrong about it, it just happens. Didn't you even realise what your father was talking about last summer?"

A wave of nausea rose up in Arabella's stomach, so strong she could hardly speak. Her throat seemed to stiffen, making it hard even to croak words out. "You mean Father thought François was like that? That's ridiculous; he loves me."

Maria looked concerned. "It sometimes happens that way," she said gently. "After all, Nijinsky got married and his wife is already with child."

Dizziness enveloped her. "You can't mean that Father was right, that François – I don't believe it." She turned to run to the dressing room for refuge, but Maria followed her.

"True or not, when your father had heard that François was using Diaghilev's hotel suite, that was enough. Sergei is well known for his enormous appetite. He gobbles up young men like crazy, not just his prime favourites like Nijinsky, but anyone he meets to whom he takes a fancy. Do you think François would have escaped his notice, with his looks? Why do you think he's received all this special treatment? *That's* why it would wreck everything if you got married before the ballet, and why he's been putting it off."

Arabella threw off Maria's consoling arm, and rushed to the basin where she was violently sick. Maria dealt with it calmly and practically, and then came back to talk to her as she sat shivering and white in a chair. Get out, Arabella willed silently. Go away. She didn't want anyone around her, let alone Maria.

"Do you *know* this, Maria, or are you guessing?" she managed to croak, since Maria remained firmly there.

"Neither. I don't *know*, but I'm not just guessing. I'm presuming from the facts. But why should it worry you? François wants to marry you some time or other, and there's no reason he shouldn't."

Her stomach lurched again, and Arabella struggled to keep it under control. "Thank you, Maria," she said evenly. "I understand now."

Alone at last, Arabella wrestled with her new knowledge. There was no proof, she reasoned, so it should not influence her, particularly as she did not doubt that François loved her. Yet there had always been gossip, and the thought of Diaghilev's portly body embracing François' crept insidiously round and round her head, much as she fought to control it.

At last she thought she had mastered it. She sat at the window of her hotel room and looked out over the fairy-tale view of Monte Carlo. Glittering white buildings, the blue of the sea, and the Grimaldi Palace. But it wasn't fairy-tale, it was a Camelot, beautiful and real. That's why François had chosen it for his ballet. In its search for the Holy Grail, in its quests to do good, Camelot was the Armageddon for the forces of good and evil to meet.

"Save me from the lion's mouth," she prayed from the Psalm, "for thou hast heard me from the horns of the unicorn." The Unicorn's strength would win, for it was the strength of Christ. It *must* win, just as François had said.

Her rehearsals with François became her testing ground. She concentrated hard on becoming Lilith, not herself, in order to melt into François' body as Lilith must in Acts II and III. It was hard for her; whereas the Lilith of Act I, loving Galymede but shrinking from him, was easy for her to think herself into, the loving nightingale was much harder now, try as she did.

By the time they reached Paris for the opening of the season there, she thought she had overcome the problem, but she must have been wrong, since François asked during rehearsal one morning: "What's wrong, Arabella? Your wrists always seem stiff with tension."

"I'm tired, I expect." Please, please, François, don't look at me like that, your eyes so full of love. I can't bear it, unless I know—

No, she would not think that way. Arabella took deep breaths, expelling them slowly to calm herself.

François said nothing, but went on to talk of *La Légende de Joseph*. He had seen the final rehearsal last night. It was not really a ballet, he explained; there was far too much mime drama, and the ballet was confined to individual dances, often for spectacle rather than as part of the story. Much of the music was – he waved an expressive hand – *lourd*, heavy, save the scene of the clearing away of the feast.

"But the designs – ah, what colour, what magnificence," he enthused. "The blue-columned gold-bricked hall and overhead a vivid blue sky and palm trees. *Joseph* has blue, gold and green; the *Unicorn* will have red, gold and green. *Joseph* will be a big success for the Ballets Russes, but the *Unicorn* will be greater." His arm was round her.

"And what of Miassin?" She could not stop her words, and she could not stop the instinctive urge to shrink from his embrace.

"Ah, there will be talent."

"*Will* be?"

François shrugged. "He has but one dance as Joseph, the shepherd boy; he merely took a few steps in a circle. But his looks, his presence – oh yes, he will go far, and Miassin's success will please Diaghilev."

It came out of nowhere, certainly not her conscious mind. "Yes, we must be grateful that Sergei has found such talent, if talent it is. I know Monsieur Diaghilev has need of such handsome young men. He gathers them around him." The words were choking themselves out, and she was blinded with tears. "He needs them. Does he need you, François?"

She could not see his face through her tears, but she could sense his hurt, his wound, as he said in anguish: "You have been listening to gossip, Arabella. You are speaking with your father's voice."

"Tell me, *please*—"

"Arabella!"

"That you aren't his lover," she finished.

He said nothing, but stood at the barre, stricken, as she ran from the room.

*   *   *

"I'm sorry," Tara said patiently, when Josh strummed meaningfully on the piano. "It's not often I have to check a conference programme, but I do now, and in April it will all be over." Only a few weeks to go now, and the conference would be finished. Then she could concentrate on life number two.

Life number two had received a big boost a week ago, and this partly excused Josh's unusual impatience for her attention. Addressed to them both – though sent to Josh's flat, Tara noticed – was a parcel from Giselle. Inside had been the Prince score for Act III.

"My dears," she had written.

> Quite by chance I came across this in a box of my father's papers, not in the unicorn room where I found the score I gave you. As you will see from the pencilled notes and changes, it appears to be a draft only, and you should be aware of that. *Bon chance, mes enfants.*

Josh had already played it, and was eager to repeat it for them, but both Sybille and Tara had insisted on finishing their work first.

"Will it ever be over?" asked Josh. He crashed a few chords.

"For heaven's sake, Beethoven, some of us are trying to concentrate," Sybille complained.

"What do you mean?" Tara asked him warily.

"Are you sure there won't be another conference, and another? Wouldn't it be nice to carry on doing part-time work to keep your foot in the door? You manage to live in both camps so successfully you could do the splits."

"And what's wrong with that?" she countered.

"Nothing, if we're talking work only."

"Quiet, ladies and gentlemen," Sybille laughed. "Any moment now someone will mention the dreaded name William and the bulls will be running. I have work to do too. Designs don't create themselves."

"Quite right, Sybille," Josh said briskly. "Tara, why don't you go to William's flat to discuss jolly programmes while we get on with the trifling matter of *our* programme and ballet."

Tara wanted to retort that he was both petty and jealous, but she knew he had some right to be annoyed. It was her fault. Being in love took you back to childhood again; it stripped off the veneer of adult reason. She had been virtually sulking because Josh and Sybille had been deep in technicalities from which she was excluded, and supposed she was taking her revenge by making it clear she too had an Important and Interesting Job to do. That made her giggle, and Josh looked up at her curiously.

"I'm sorry," she said penitently. "I suddenly felt like Winnie-the-Pooh."

Josh's eyes gleamed with appreciation, though Sybille looked blank. "I'll restrain myself for fifteen minutes," he conceded.

It was a generous olive branch, and she ran through the rest of the schedule quickly. This was a draft of the programme she'd already seen but with a few changes she had to approve before William went ahead with the final one. She'd arranged to meet William for lunch tomorrow to hand it back.

Waiting for her too were Josh's account books. The outside auditor for Music and Mime had greeted her arrival like a rainbow after the storm, and Tara could see why. Everything was there – somewhere. The words "file" and "order" did not seem to enter into their "system". Large cardboard boxes did. Expense chits rubbed shoulders with VAT returns, tax demands with ticket sale records. Music and Mime was run in private partnership, and to dovetail that arrangement for the experimental season ahead with a company limited by guarantee was a problem anyway, without the cardboard-box syndrome.

"Did I tell you the ABC have become a charity now?" Josh suddenly volunteered.

"Oh bliss." Tara meant it. This apparently tiny detail brought great relief.

"Does that make it easier for you?" Sybille asked.

"No, but it's my field," Tara said gratefully. At last she might be able to contribute expertise if there were a merger. She rushed through the programme, the minutes ticking by. Her eyes read tax, but her thoughts were on the ballet.

Eight

Tara listened spellbound as Josh played the Prince score of Act Three through on the piano. He was not a brilliant player, but was good enough for the score to flow as Prince must have intended – and good enough for Tara, whose own musical ear was hardly professional. She could appreciate the lyrical qualities of his work, however. It flowed with some of the melodic romanticism of Tchaikovsky, but with a spark and fire that was all his own.

By now Tara had heard most of the first two acts in snatches and so could pick up here and there familiar motifs: the Unicorn, the Nightingale, the hunt. Even to her untutored ears, however, there was an increased menace, a foreboding of drama to come in his treatment of the last act, and the pace was quickening. Josh had been playing for nearly three-quarters of an hour now, and it was clear the finale was approaching, with music obviously meant for an ensemble crashing to a climax, followed by a quiet lyrical *adagio*.

"That's the end?" Sybille asked, surprised, as Josh stopped playing.

"It is. Pure Tchaikovsky, that ending." Josh frowned.

"It seems joyful music," Tara put in somewhat hesitantly, "but not joyful enough."

"You want a happy-ever-after finale? Unlikely," Sybille said. "Maybe it's only happy in the sense that the lovers are popping off to paradise together."

"They both die?" Why was Tara so disturbed by this, why had she been so sure that this ballet would have ended in Galymede and Lilith's reunion and marriage, and Morgana's downfall? "What do you think, Josh?"

"I think Sybille's right, and that's what the music implies." He was looking glum too.

"But that ending's too much like *Swan Lake*," Tara objected. "Arnold Prince would never have intended that, surely?"

"Good point." Josh frowned. "Yet to me there's no doubt that the finale is for an ensemble followed by a *pas de deux*. Satisfying – but not a good rousing marriage, and how many kids shall we have, darling?"

"Unless that isn't the finale," Tara asked hopefully. "Suppose the ending has gone astray?"

"Sorry, love. Your great-grandfather has written 'Fin' at the end, with several exclamation marks."

"Odd. So far he hasn't sounded an exclamation mark sort of man," Tara said.

"Perhaps there'd been ructions and he was sick of the whole thing." Sybille yawned. "Like me. We do have the rest of the programme to consider. Like which mimes we want for the opening night."

She was ignored. "I can't believe François Santine's scenario would have called for an ending like *Swan Lake*," Josh said crossly, "and that's what Prince would have worked to, if Diaghilev commissioned it specially for this ballet. You're right, Tara."

Tara had a sudden thought. "Aren't we all forgetting something?"

"What?" Sybille asked wearily.

"This is a draft score. There's no record of what the scenario called for, you don't have François' notes, and *that act was never performed*. How do we know that this score was the final one? He might have written another."

Josh frowned. "Then Giselle would have found it. Maybe François and Prince did work to a *Swan Lake* lookalike. After all, with all the modernism around in the Ballets Russes programmes at that time, maybe Diaghilev wanted a contrast."

"No." Tara was quite certain now. "Giselle told me Prince became well known as a composer for silent films after the war, and in the early part of the century he was writing music for musical comedies at the Gaiety and Daly's. Drama was his speciality. He would have appreciated François' wish for a happy ending in earthly terms, not heavenly."

"*If* François wished it that way," Sybille said coolly. "You're both too personally involved to see the wood for the trees. This music is in the same mood and ending as *Le Spectre de la Rose*, which satisfies without any need for the ghost of the rose to marry the girl."

Tara tried to laugh, though Sybille's negativity annoyed her. "François was a young choreographer," she persisted, "and wouldn't want to repeat either Petipa's or Fokine's style. Nor would Diaghilev have let him. He wanted *new* choreography, new music. He was captivated by Stravinsky and Rimsky-Korsakov. It was colour, excitement, and design he was after, not a row of white tutus floating into paradise."

"Wrong!" Sybille laughed now. "Diaghilev was probably in love with François and let him get away with anything. Why choose a mythological tale with unicorns, wicked witches and what not if he didn't want a classical approach?"

"Easy." Josh snappily demolished her argument. "Way back in the sixties John Cranko chose the theme for *The Prince of the Pagodas* precisely because it *was* a mythological fairy-tale. To take something so unrelated to modern life was, he thought, the only way he could create some modern choreography without repeating the past. It would provide a popular framework within which he could experiment all he liked."

"So," Tara asked eagerly, "François could have thought that way too? The unicorn-and-nightingale theme would give over-tones of Fokine and the past, while he created steps and groupings of his own . . ."

"Anyone fancy a Chinese take-away?" Sybille yawned. "I volunteer."

Tara nodded, but Josh didn't seem to hear. "His notations suggest that." He rushed to the desk to consult the papers. "There's an emphasis on turned-in movements that would have had even Nijinsky's eyebrows raised, let alone Fokine's, yet François managed to keep a romantic image throughout. By and large the principals – as usual – had the most romantic music, and the *caractères* like Galymede's father and the hunters were treated to the more modern approach where wit or humour was needed."

"How can you tell?"

"The notes suggest Arabella found some of the steps difficult at first. She was trained in the classical Cecchetti school, and even Fokine's neo-romantic style caused her problems at first. She

141

seems to have taken smaller parts in the other ballets presented in the 1914 season; *Les Papillons* was one of them."

"Who were the problems with?" Sybille asked drily. "Diaghilev?" She made no move to leave, and her dampening presence was beginning to irritate Tara. Someone had to keep them down to earth, she supposed, but not *all* the time. And not when her imagination was soaring so harmoniously after Josh's. Sybille seemed to think it was her job to carry a mental pin to puncture any balloon that floated by.

She struggled to keep to the subject. "Would François have written his first major ballet for Arabella with an ending that didn't end in the couple being united *on earth*?"

"Art demands more than heart," Sybille announced.

"I'm inclined to agree with Tara," Josh said. "If you take the situation—"

Sybille sighed. "But if you take the *music*," she interrupted, running to the piano to play the finale again. To Tara, it sounded quite different to Josh's interpretation of it: somehow it did not come over as his rendering had, although technically Sybille was a better piano player than Josh.

"Let's look at it from another angle," Josh suggested. "Let's think what might have happened in that act, assuming that we're right and François intended Galymede and Lilith to end up happily in each other's arms. At the end of Act Two we know that the Nightingale, Lilith, is defeated and sinks down to die as the hunt closes in, and Galymede is seduced by Morgana. So what happens next. Sybille?"

"Morgana bears her trophy off in pride, and they return to the palace to celebrate the marriage—"

"To a unicorn?" Tara couldn't resist it.

Sybille grinned. "All right. Big transformation scene. Morgana transforms him back into a handsome knight again, ready for her wedding orgies, but at the last minute the Nightingale totters in to die sweetly in Galymede's arms. Galymede then kills himself and they buzz off to paradise – if a unicorn does buzz."

"How can a nightingale die in someone's arms?" Tara enquired innocently, feeling definite spikes of resistance springing up between her and Sybille. "Or has she become human again, too?" Sybille's lack of passionate involvement in the ballet, which made her sound superciliously amused at the whole thing, was a good tonic, yet who wanted medicine at a time like this?

"But why," Tara continued doggedly, "should Morgana bother to transform her enemy Lilith back into a gorgeous girl?"

Sybille sighed. "OK, how about this? Morgana assumes the Nightingale is already dead, so doesn't bother to exclude her from the spell-lifting. So it's Lilith who totters in to interrupt the wedding, only she doesn't get lucky and expires on the spot. What do you think, Josh?"

Tara restrained herself with difficulty from giving her opinion: rubbish.

"No," Josh replied after a moment to her relief. "The music doesn't fit."

"Ah!" Sybille threw up her hands. "I surrender. All right, suppose the hunt closes in on Galymede and kills him this time."

"Nope." Josh turned this down too. "No room for the Nightingale. And what's the end jollification for if not a wedding of some sort?"

"Morgana's triumph or the hunt's."

Josh stared at her. "No," he said flatly. "No balance, and, even if you see Galymede and Lilith waltzing off to paradise, no satisfaction. It's Morgana you'd remember."

Josh was right. No way could that be allowed to happen. Then Tara had an idea. "Suppose Galymede, once transformed back, remembers the Nightingale, realises she was Lilith, goes in search of her?"

"Yes!" Josh punched the air in triumph. "We're forgetting he was transformed into a *unicorn*, not a lion or a scarecrow or a tin man, and one of many ideas for which unicorns are the symbol is unrestrainable power. Since he's allied to the Nightingale, who's symbolic of love, it *must* end in the defeat of Morgana."

"Galymede finds the Nightingale dying—" Tara continued excitedly.

"And revives her—"

"Or," Sybille put in her spoke, "the hunt, with Morgana at their head, is after them and kills them both in the forest."

"Then they wouldn't have Camelot music at the end – and that's clearly what it is. No, Josh and I are right, Sybille." It was time Sybille was stamped on, otherwise it would turn into Morgana's ballet. It occurred to Tara to wonder just which

143

part Sybille would be playing, but she decided she was being unnecessarily crabby. "Galymede brings Lilith back to Camelot again, there is a final confrontation with Morgana in which the Unicorn's power triumphs, and a happy ending."

"Fine, Tara." Unfortunately Josh as well as Sybille was looking unhappy. "I'm sure that's what François would have chosen too, but we're back where we started: the music doesn't fit. It probably ended in a *pas de deux*, but you can't tell me this music fits a rapturous honeymoon."

"Then you write it, Josh."

"No!" Sybille said sharply, but as Josh looked at her in surprise, she flushed in embarrassment. "I'm sorry – I can't think what made me say that. I've got stuck on paradise for the ending, I suppose. Take no notice. You're probably both right."

"What do we call it, if you write part of it?" Tara asked, tactfully changing the subject. "Can we call it Santine's ballet, if we don't know his ending, or Prince's ballet, with your music at the end?"

Josh hesitated. "I'm not happy either way. I *want* to call it an adaptation of Santine's ballet, but I'm not sure I can. Do you think it's too big a risk to leave the music for the ending to see how rehearsals go?"

Sybille's yes came in unison with Tara's no.

"There's only one problem with it," Josh added. "Rehearsals begin tomorrow, we've only two weeks, so leaving it till last really is one hell of a risk. I wouldn't normally mind that, but this time I do."

"Why?"

"Because you won't be here, Tara."

It hit her like a bucket of cold water. She'd forgotten. She would be away at the conference for the final weekend's rehearsals and following few days before the opening night.

"Forgive me for being obtuse, Josh," Sybille remarked, "but why does Tara have to be here, save to cheer you on?"

Josh shrugged, wearing the mutinous set expression Tara had come to know well. "I don't know. Because of her family connection, probably."

It sounded weak, and Tara was dismally aware that this wasn't the real reason. For all his protestations, Josh still couldn't help seeing her absence in those vital days as a betrayal, and perhaps he was right to do so.

"We can manage without her, though," Sybille pointed out somewhat acidly.

"I'm afraid you'll have to," Tara replied wretchedly. "I am committed now, but I'll be back on the Thursday for the dress rehearsal."

"The ending—" Josh began, before Sybille interrupted impatiently.

"For heaven's sake, Josh. Settle it before she goes, if you must have Tara around to inspire you."

"Don't you think François would have needed Arabella's presence?" he shot back at her.

"There's a slight difference, darling," Sybille retorted. "Arabella was in the ballet. I can't see François would have needed his accountant's help."

"What the hell's got into you?" Josh asked furiously.

"Bloody unicorns and nightingales, if you must know. Everything's going to pot while you prance around with mental horns on your head. And how applicable *that* is!" Sybille departed, with, "I'm off for the take-away. And I'll choose what *I* want."

After the door slammed there was a brief silence, then Josh remarked: "Sweet and sour?"

Immediately the tension evaporated. Tara began to laugh, and went over to hug him. She kissed him, holding him close – *not* a sensible idea in the circumstances – and then kissed him again, this time for longer.

"I suppose I'm getting too far into symbolism," he managed to say ruefully, when reluctantly they drew apart. "Unicorns and nightingales seem *us*, just as François must have seen the original as bound up with Arabella. My mental horns over William are another matter, though."

"How's the choreography going?" Tara asked hastily. "You're still using your own style?"

Josh had explained to her that there were two ways he could approach the choreography, given that the music was from an earlier period. Either he could use steps contemporary to the music, and recreate it as it would have been seen in 1914, or he could adapt the groupings and steps into his own style, which was what he'd chosen to do.

"Yes," he replied to her question. He was silent for a moment, then burst out: "I wish to God it was over, *all* of it. Your conference and this ballet. Then we could see the future. There's a chance for us, with Music and Mime's possible merger, and your leaving the City. Tara" – she knew what he was going to say, and trembled – "do you have to go to Washington?"

"It will be the last time," she replied, trying to keep her voice steady. "It's all announced; I can't pull out now. Besides, this planned giving conference could be helpful to us in the future if you become part of a registered charity. I'd need my foot in the door, and it would promptly be stamped on if I'd just let everyone down."

"I suppose so. It's just – I'm getting—"

"Sex-starved?" Take the problem head-on. After all, she was feeling the same.

"Not to mention love-starved."

"I've told William that this conference is strictly business, and after that I shall shake hands for ever—"

"Cancel all your vows?" He picked up the quotation. "How many did you make?"

Honesty was called for here. "I thought I loved him. Probably I did. But now I like him more than I ever loved him. I've no regrets over splitting up, though, if that's what you mean." She thought he would make some comment, but he didn't.

"So if William's no longer an issue, why do we still have to wait before we make love again? No pressure on commitment, or on moving in, but surely total abstinence isn't necessary? You don't want full sex, I don't want half-way houses, so I'm torn in two. I can't keep my hands off you, yet every time I touch you it means more frustration."

"Don't you realise it's the same for me?" Tara said in anguish.

"Then *why*?"

"I suppose I just don't feel I'm on safe ground yet. I used unconsciously to dance to William's tune, and so I've got to be very sure I'm dancing to my own before I listen to yours. Does that make sense?"

"Yes. But what's stopping you hearing this tune of yours? Is it my fault?"

"No – well, maybe, but you can't help it. We're both going to be too close to Sybille until this ballet is staged. I like living with her, but somehow it's blurred things. I don't know why, and I can't explain it. It's as if – you'll really think this stupid – I can't reach you while I'm living there. When I'm with you, everything is crystal clear, but with William or Sybille I feel I'm in a forest without any exit gates. I don't suppose it's their *fault*, it's just that they add a different dimension to our relationship – and at the moment moving out wouldn't help."

Josh grinned. "Not just held up on that trek to the unknown country, you've got lost in a jungle too."

"Don't laugh, Josh, please. I'm doing my best to tell you how I feel."

"Disenchanted with me," he joked, but with an anxious eye.

"No. *Enchanted*, in its true sense. So don't feel sorry for yourself."

"I'm not." He cheered up. "I do understand, because I feel the same for different reasons. François Santine has been inside me willing me to get this ballet choreographed and performed, maybe even eventually in a three-act version. It seems like a mission, and I'm not going to be free of it until the first night of the one-act version is over. François is ordering me to finish it, but I don't bloody well know how. Your suggestion's the best yet."

"Are you *sure* there's no clue in the notes as to what happened?"

"Quite sure, and that's what worries me. Something terrible, besides Arabella's broken ankle, must have happened for the ballet to be abandoned, not just postponed, before the first performance."

"It could be simply explained by the outbreak of the First World War a few days later."

"I don't think so. François didn't die until 1916, yet there's nothing in Giselle's papers or my grandfather's to show that he and Arabella were still in contact, or that he ever danced again, although he choreographed one or two minor ballets for Diaghilev in 1915. But effectively everything ended abruptly in July 1914."

"I can't believe the ballet was a flop, with Bakst's designs and that music."

"No. I've managed to find a press report from a critic present at the dress rehearsal, which said that the ballet, which had showed great promise, was abandoned through the indisposition of the prima ballerina."

"Even if it was a flop, does it matter, if you manage to adapt the ballet and get it produced?"

"Oh yes, my sweetheart. I think it matters to us very much indeed."

"When will you be arriving, William?" It occurred to Tara as she stared uninspired at the menu that she had sometimes used to call him Will when they lived together, but to call him William had now become quite natural.

"Not sure. On the Tuesday probably."

"You'll miss the first day of the conference?" It was true that William, like herself, wasn't speaking till the third and last day, but even so it was unusual for him not to be there from the beginning.

"You sound disappointed."

"Surprised." She smiled to take the sting out of it.

"Two clients of mine are flying in from Japan over the weekend, and I can't miss them. I'll get there earlier if I can, but I'm sure little you can manage quite capably while I'm absent."

"Thank you," she said sweetly, refusing to rise to the bait. "Do you have the printed programme yet?"

"No, but there are no changes to what you've already seen. I've decided to make the programme an easily removable pull-out from the main conference book, as the speakers haven't all sent in their outlines yet. It takes time. I'll probably have to get them couriered over or even printed over there."

Tara felt on home ground here. It was a familiar scenario. "Let me know if you need any chasing up done." Something unexpected always happened. Books went astray, slide projects and computer images failed to work, speakers had to cancel at the last moment. Tara was suddenly glad that she was nearly out of it all. Chair didn't usually get involved in that side, however. Her work would come during the conference itself, although since it was being planned by William there was hardly likely to be any major disaster.

"Any of the speakers I should contact before I go?" she asked.

"Not necessary, really. You've got a lot on your plate. How do you find working part time?"

148

"Like working full time but packed into fewer hours."

"Your pirouette with the arts isn't palling?"

"No, thank you, William. My pirouette, as you call it, is straight-forward accounting. Even if the full merger goes forward, it will be simple."

"Companies limited by guarantee are never simple. Nor are ballets, I suppose. How's Nureyev these days? More bounce in his feet than his—?"

"William," she said warningly.

He grinned. "Just prodding, and waiting for you to come down to earth."

"I won't."

"Time will tell. The curtain will fall sooner or later." He reached across and took her hand. "And I'll still be waiting, Tara. You know that."

She parted from him with some uneasiness. Pleading and waiting, had never been part of William's style. He went straight out for what he wanted, and didn't take kindly to not getting it. This was a new William, and she felt out of her depth – as, perhaps, he had intended.

She forgot her discomfiture in the excitement of returning to the ABC's theatre in Kensington to see the first rehearsal. Rehearsals for ballet, she knew, weren't like straight plays. They didn't begin at the beginning and end at the end, either in whole or within scenes, and this seemed just as well in view of Josh's indecision over the ending. At rehearsal, he seemed to work in brief snatches, but today he was concentrating on the hunt scene, since he had the entire cast present.

The hunt was composed of both men and women, the men to be costumed as hunters and the woman as the creatures of the forest: the squirrels, the weasels, and the foxes. Tara had been intrigued when Josh had mentioned using tap dancing for the hunt, having visions of Fred Astaire and Gene Kelly tip-tapping through the forests of Camelot. There was no Fred in this scene, however; the tap beat was menacing, and there were pirouettes, somersaults and turns in the air as one animal or hunter after another sprang from the wings to trap Galymede.

Tap was usually used to express joy in the old film musicals, Josh had explained. He had planned to use it differently. For brief intervals there would be no music, just the relentless shuffle-hop-stamp of the pursuing hunt. (Tap, like classical ballet, had its own terminology.) Whatever the steps were, they worked, and the hunt was an exhilarating triumph of the unexpected.

By the time she returned home to Richmond, Tara's head was still tapping to the beat, and it took an effort to concentrate on the long letter from the finance director of the Albion Ballet Company giving her the details she needed about its status as a company limited by guarantee.

That jogged her memory, and a question that had gone unanswered earlier that day reared its head. How had *William* known that the ABC was a company limited by guarantee? Had she mentioned it to him? She was almost sure she had not. Did it matter? No, it was of no importance, it was merely city gossip.

Arabella was living each day in a frozen dreamworld. Between herself and François there was a wall of ice, with no way of breaking through. It had been her own fault, for in her clumsiness and stupidity she had hurt him bitterly. Although he was polite to her, the light in his eyes that had shone only on her had gone out, and the ballet seemed his only concern.

Complete rehearsals would not begin until they reached London in two weeks' time, but she and Maria were constantly needed to experiment in their *soli, pas de deux*, and the *pas de trois* in Act II. Dancing with François was torment, for his body was so close, and yet the face she loved seemed carved of stone. Arabella felt as if she were smothering in clouds of gauze in her effort to reach him; no sooner did she sweep one away than another came down to envelop her. She danced her soul out for him, hoping that through her feet, her arms, her lips, she could make their love shine again even if words failed. But nothing worked, and now the gauze was gradually falling even between their bodies as they danced. It was torture to realise that she did not exist for him any more as his lover, only as a means of fulfilling his dream for the ballet.

Maria was sympathetic, but there was little she could do to help. "François feels embarrassed that you know," she explained practically. "You cannot doubt that he loves you, however. It will come right when the ballet is over."

"It must be before then, or I cannot dance." Arabella knew this was true. She would be leaden inside, so how could she feel the emotion of the ballet strongly enough to dance her best?

Maria did not understand. "Nonsense. You are a professional dancer. You can act, you can dance, and you must do so, no matter what happens between yourself and François."

Arabella tried her best, but it was not good enough, and by the time they reached London she was in despair. To the undiscerning eye there was no outward sign in her dancing that all was not well, but there would be eyes here that were far from undiscerning.

The London opera and ballet season had opened on the twentieth of May, while the Paris season was still in progress. François had travelled to London then, but she remained in Paris to dance in Fokine's *Le Coq D'Or* and so it was not until early June that she reached London. She arrived in time for the first all-ballet evening on the ninth, two weeks before the date for which the opening night of *The Unicorn and the Nightingale* had been scheduled. But *still* the end of Act III had not been resolved. Arnold was still refusing to change his score, still believing his ending for the ballet was the natural one. François was adamant that the whole ballet hinged on the Unicorn and the Nightingale being triumphant on earth. Otherwise the story had no point – the Unicorn's holy strength and the Nightingale's love would both have been vanquished by evil. The power of Christ *must* prove stronger in the final Armageddon between Morgana and Galymede. Still the battle raged on, with Arabella adding her unvoiced pleas to François' that Arnold would relent.

With only ten days to go, the inevitable happened: news of the problem reached Sergei Diaghilev. François and Arnold were both summoned, together with Maria and Arabella as principal dancers, to his suite in the Savoy to resolve the matter. Diaghilev hardly resembled a peace-making mediator, however; he had a face like thunder, and was quivering with fury as Arnold and François argued for an hour, with one or the other dashing to the piano intermittently to prove a point. Maria followed the argument with lively interest, but Arabella sat stunned, unable to believe that it had come to this.

Diaghilev finally exploded. "If you and Monsieur Prince cannot agree, François, the ballet is cancelled."

"No!" Arabella burst out, seeing François's look of agony. "Oh please, not that." She longed to rush to him to comfort him, but the barrier between them was as strong as ever. No kisses now, no embraces, nothing but formality, politeness – and the look of pain in his eyes.

"We have no other option," Diaghilev growled. "Tell me, Petrovna, what are your views on the finale?"

"It is unfair to ask Miss Peters," Arnold immediately protested. "Monsieur Santine and myself must settle it."

"But you're failing to do so!" Diaghilev's roar shook even Arnold. "Petrovna, I told you to *astound me* when you first danced for me. You're not doing so. Any competent ballerina could give your performance. I want *more*. Now, tell me how this ballet should end."

So he *had* noticed. Arabella was torn between admitting the truth, that her love for François might sway her judgement – in which case she might jeopardise their future – and casting her die to resolve the matter.

"The music pulls me one way and the steps another," she began truthfully. They had experimented with the Prince score, just to see if it would work with François' scenario, but it was hopeless.

"And which way would you move, Petrovna?" The growl might have been of pleasure or displeasure.

She cast the die. "A dancer is there to fulfil the choreographer's dream."

A shout from Diaghilev. "Gentlemen, you have it. The complete answer, though no answer at all. François, go ahead."

"Not to my music," Arnold said coolly.

"No; you'll rewrite the end," Diaghilev rumbled.

"I regret that is not possible."

Arabella's heart sank. Unbelievably, the compliant friend had turned into an intransigent stranger.

"Might I remind you, Mr Prince, that I commissioned this music, and that I approved the scenario?"

"And you may have it as I have written it. If you reject the ending, which I gather is not acceptable to Monsieur Santine, even though I understood it was to you on first hearing, I will not allow the rest of my music to be played."

"François?" Diaghilev was barely holding his temper in check now.

"For any other ballet, Monsieur Diaghilev, I would consider

altering my scenario, but for this one I *cannot*," François replied unsteadily.

It was up to her, Arabella realised. Diaghilev had failed, but there was a chance that she might, just might succeed. "Mr Prince," she began formally, "your music is splendid for this ballet. Although I believe that Monsieur Santine should have the last word on the ending, I would be heartbroken if your music was never heard by the public. Suppose we found other music just for the final scenes?"

"That's a good compromise," Diaghilev beamed. "I've no objection to that."

"I do not wish to compromise," Arnold replied icily, "although I am sorry to cause distress to Miss Peters. I would prefer to return your money to you, monsieur, in order that none of my music may be performed."

Diaghilev turned purple with rage. "Not so simple, Mr Prince. The copyright is mine by contract; if I choose to alter the last scene, I'll do so. We can put a note in the programme if you're worried."

"I shall not allow it," Arnold said quietly.

"You think you've got us nicely trapped, don't you?" Diaghilev snarled. "That it's too late for me to do anything but submit. I *never* submit, especially to blackmail."

"Though blackmail is not my intention, your private life makes you an easy target for it."

The calm words took a moment to sink in. Once they had done so, even Maria looked horrified. François was white with shock, but Diaghilev froze into icy stillness. No roars now, merely a concentrated venom.

"*The Unicorn and the Nightingale* is cancelled. I'll commission new music, and put it on next year. Your music remains my copyright, Prince. You'll not see it again, or hear it. I'll not tolerate insults from a puritanical bore like you."

Arnold said no more, merely picked up his hat and cane and left the suite. Arabella understood all too well now what this talk of blackmail had been about. Love between two men was illegal, at least in England. She sat quietly at Maria's side, not having been dismissed from the presence, while François talked with Diaghilev. She might have been invisible for all the notice they took of her. The master's tone was quite different now;

153

he talked to François gently as to a valued friend, not a junior member of the company. Arabella, torn in two, concentrated her thoughts on the ballet. She could hear Diaghilev talking of Strauss, or Rimsky-Korsakov, but she knew François would feel as she did.

There was no substitute for the Prince score.

Nine

The morning room, into which Arabella was shown by the butler, was full of sunshine on this June day, but to her it seemed cold. She had never visited Arnold's home in Hampstead before, and somehow its impersonal grandeur reminded her of her parents' taste. Since the terrible scene with Arnold, it was hard to think of him as a friend, but here in England she needed one. She had had no contact with her parents, nor did she wish to have any. Much as she loved her mother, it was better this way. She knew through Arnold that her mother had come to see *Les Papillons*, in which Arabella had a small role, but she also knew that it was not her father who had accompanied her. It was Arnold himself. She told herself that she merely pitied her father for his rigidity, but she was deeply wounded that he had withdrawn his love for her, and with that hurt had come a conviction that she and Arnold could never be completely clear of the past, however much she had thought him her friend. Now, however, she needed to forget that past in order to think of François' future. She had not announced her intention of coming this morning and she could hear her heart thumping as she waited for Arnold to join her.

Minutes marched by like hours and by the time he arrived she had lost whatever self-possession she had mustered to come here. "You don't look surprised to see me, Arnold," she blurted out, her carefully rehearsed words vanishing.

He smiled, which relaxed her. It was the Arnold she knew, not the stranger of that meeting in the Savoy.

"No, I had expected it. I will ring for coffee. It seems to me we may both need it. I take it" – he sat down opposite her – "that François is not progressing well with a new score."

There was no point in prevaricating. "No." The weekend had passed; there was only a week and a day left to go now if *The*

155

Unicorn was to be saved. Diaghilev had agreed to stay his hand until Wednesday before making a decision, and meanwhile rehearsals for *The Unicorn* continued in their usual disorganisation. A week from today the final rehearsal would take place, if the performance were to go ahead.

"It is never easy to use existing music, for it carries with it associations that cannot be erased from the composer's mind."

"Please, Arnold." Arabella was indignant. "Do not pretend to feel sympathy for François. Not to me."

Arnold looked appalled. He came to sit beside her, and took her hand. "You are wrong, Arabella. There is no pretence. In every composer and every choreographer, there is the private man and there is the artist, and it is wise to recognise the difference. Even Salieri knew the value of Mozart's music. That was his dilemma. You must believe me when I say it would be easier if I could *not* sympathise with François. He is no great musician, but I have seen enough of his choreography, not to mention his dancing, to recognise a fellow artist with whom I *can* sympathise. As a man" – he shrugged – "you know full well I cannot."

Here was her opportunity, and Arabella grasped it firmly. "Then it is to the artist in you, Arnold, that I appeal. Please will you not reconsider? The reason François cannot work to another score is because in his mind there is now nothing but yours. His head is full of dreams which you have helped create. Surely you cannot let such music be wasted?"

"I can, Arabella, I can. I would prefer to see it all go than to ruin it with music for an ending I consider to be wrong. But it is only the artist inside me that makes this decision – you must see that."

Arabella hesitated. "You said you loved me, Arnold. I am sure you *think* that your decision is merely artistic, but how can the artist and the man not influence each other?"

Arnold was silent for a moment. "You do me an injustice, my dear. I know how much this ballet means to you, and even though I also know you still wish to marry Santine, the lover in me would agree to his scenario for your sake. Yet I *cannot*, as an artist, because it is not the right ending. I can't write music for something I don't believe in – even for you, my greatest love. Will you believe me now?"

He was trembling, and she saw that he did indeed mean it.

"Yes, Arnold," she replied, rising to leave. "I will not tell François of this conversation, only Maria, but she will be greatly disappointed."

"Maria? She knows you have come here?" He grasped her arm, indicating that she should sit down once more. Hearing a puzzling sharpness in his voice, she did so.

"Of course. Morgana is her most challenging role yet, and she will be excellent in it. She is fond of François too, and she believes, as I do, that he has a great future ahead as a choreographer. I also believe that she will be a great dancer, and so she will be most unhappy if this ballet is cancelled."

"She has told you so?"

"I know it. Nevertheless, you have explained how you feel, Arnold. If Monsieur Diaghilev and François cannot persuade you to change your mind, how could Maria and I hope to?"

Arnold looked deeply unhappy. "Tell me, Arabella, are you still betrothed to François? I have assumed so, but it is nearly a year since you left home. Does he no longer wish to marry you? Maria is very worried."

She had to answer him, but every defensive hackle within her rose up in protest, especially at the thought that Arnold and Maria had been talking about her behind her back. "He is entirely preoccupied with the ballet at present. After its first performance is over—"

"But if there is no first performance?" he interrupted.

"Of course we will still marry," she replied quickly. In her mind, however, she could hear Maria's words: "You *are* the ballet for François." She ignored them. This had nothing to do with either Maria or Arnold. "This has been a difficult year for him."

"You make excuses. The fellow has betrayed you."

"No!" she cried in outrage. How could she explain to Arnold of all people that she had hurt François bitterly? Even if Maria was right about Diaghilev and François – and he had not denied it – she did not doubt his love for her. Perhaps it was quite natural for young men to have feelings towards both sexes, as Maria had said; perhaps she should not be concerned. But she was, she *was*.

Arnold watched her for a moment. "I cannot bear to see you so sad, Arabella. I understand now why this ballet means so much to you."

"Then change your mind."

He thought for a moment, then: "I will not presume to intrude further upon your private life, Arabella, save that to say it is obvious that something is wrong between yourself and François and that it may be past putting right. Even putting aside my own feelings for you, I cannot pretend that I think you would be happy married to Santine. This would not ordinarily be the time to speak of such things, but these are not ordinary times. We are at a crisis over this ballet. Think, Arabella, *think*. If your love for Santine is over, if his is for you, then remember my hand as well as my heart is yours. If you choose to come to me, for your sake I will rewrite the music for the final scene of *The Unicorn and the Nightingale* as François wishes."

In shock, Arabella tried to disentangle what Arnold was saying. "You mean," she said painfully, "that if I agree to marry you, you will let François have his way over the ballet?"

"That sounds uncommonly like blackmail. However, that is just what I mean."

Arabella stood up, her legs trembling. "I cannot, Arnold. *Ever*. I love François."

"And if he does not love you?" he asked gently. "I have watched you. You are much alone, often with Maria or others, and when François is present there is a barrier between you, even in your dancing. What will you do if you do not wed him? Will you remain single all your life? You are fond of me, I know. This is *your* opportunity for a glorious future on the stage. I could write such music for you, inspired by you, danced to by you. *The Unicorn* is only the beginning."

She could not think, she could not speak. All she wanted was to get away, to be on her own, to think about the enormity of what he was saying. She heard his final words as she made her way blindly to the door.

"I have sprung this on you, but I urge you to consider it. We could be happy, you and I."

Usually the atmosphere in the wings enveloped Arabella both with great excitement and the comfort of the familiar. Usually the moment she stepped on to the stage, whether she was dancing in the *corps de ballet* or as a second solo ballerina, she forgot all about Arabella Peters and even Arabelle Petrovna, for she *was* the ballet. Not tonight. The wings seemed to suffocate her as she nervously warmed up. Arabella Peters was still dancing within her, making her mentally leaden, and would inevitably dance on stage with her.

Tonight was the first night in London for *Le Coq D'Or*. It had been a sensation in Paris, and no doubt would be here also, even though it combined both singers and dancers. Monsieur Cecchetti himself was in it, as well as the great Karsavina as the Queen of Shemakhan. It had at first seemed odd to Arabella to have characters sung by one person and danced by another, but the strangeness had worn off, and usually Arabella enjoyed performing in it greatly. Fokine's dances were inspired and the décor of towers and trees, all in stark yellow, pink, green and white, was exciting, but tonight it served merely to remind her of the similar glorious designs for *The Unicorn and the Nightingale*, and therefore of her own dilemma.

Even Maria noticed that something was wrong, and asked anxiously as they went to the dressing room after the first act, "You have quarrelled with François again?"

"No," Arabella said shortly. She did not want to talk about what had happened. She wanted to forget it, push it from her, but that was impossible. Then she wondered if telling Maria about it before she spoke to François might help distance the problem slightly, and lift at least a little of her burden. "I went to see Arnold to plead for the ballet."

Maria gasped. "And did you win him round?"

"No."

"Then nothing has changed, so what's upsetting you?"

"He would agree to change his music, but his conditions are impossible to accept." Arabella hesitated. She did not want to tell Maria more, but the strain was too great. "The condition is that he wants me to marry him. *That's* why it's not possible."

"You don't like the idea?"

Arabella stared at her aghast. How could Maria treat it so nonchalantly? "Of course not."

"You should think about it."

"How can you say that?" Arabella was wretched. She should never have told Maria. She had been seeking comfort, not advice. Now look what had happened.

"It's the way of the world." Maria shrugged. "I'm older

than you. If Arnold Prince asked me to marry him, I'd accept immediately. You have to marry someone. Look what happens to ballet dancers as they grow older."

"They teach," Arabella said mutinously. She had thought this through long ago. "I'd open my own ballet school. I don't *have* to marry anybody, let alone Arnold."

Arabella found herself even more shaken by Maria's reaction than by her meeting with Arnold. That at least had been straightforward, whereas now she was left not only feeling that she was shut out from François' love, but that she was alone in a world in which she could not work out the rules.

It seemed strange to be living in a hotel room in the town where she had been brought up, but that night after the performance she was glad of its impersonality, and glad that she had the room to herself. She sat quietly, looking at the few photographs that she carried with her in their frames and put on the table in every hotel room she stayed in. Madame Pavlova with Mordkin in *Pas de Deux*, herself as a child with her parents, who for once were smiling with pleasure, one of Maître Cecchetti as Carabosse in *Sleeping Beauty*, and two of François – one of the dancer in *Swan Lake* and one of the man whom she loved.

These photographs must tell her what to do, and she stared at them for some time. They offered her a glittering career, for as Arnold's wife doors would be open that had been closed to her previously; the life of a society wife and mother; a career in the Ballets Russes if she refused Arnold's offer. Her eyes were always drawn, however, to the photograph of François on the picnic where they had fallen in love. She would not believe that their love had vanished; if she could it would be simpler. But she would marry Arnold, and her gift to François would be his perfect ballet, no matter if her heart were breaking.

Yet if his love was still there, despite the hurt she had inflicted on him, there must be some way to reach him. It was her future at stake. Her path immediately became simple, and she looked at the photograph again to give her inspiration. Then she closed her eyes. Tomorrow both the Nightingale's love and the Unicorn's strength must be with her.

"Why here, Arabella?" François looked around him at the stream, the fields, and the trees that shielded them from the world. "Why not in London?"

"I thought as it's a free day, I should drag you away from London, even though we see enough of trains in our travels. Besides, it's not a *real* picnic in London." She had had to plead with him to come, but he had reluctantly agreed at last.

"We had one once."

He remembered then, as she did, although his face gave no clue as to whether it had meant as much to him as to her.

"Do you not like it here?" she asked anxiously. She had given much thought to where this picnic should be, and had remembered a village she had visited with an aunt and uncle as a child in Kent.

"Yes, and I am glad we have come for now I can tell you what I have decided."

Arabella waited, heart in her mouth. If François had decided, there might be nothing she could do. Please, please, don't let it go wrong after all. She gathered her strength together again.

"I am going to tell Sergei that he must cancel the ballet," François said. "He must put it aside, for there is no other music that will fit. I will write another for him."

For *him*, not for her. Arabella tried hard to get over the hurt, for she had deserved it.

"But what would that mean to you, François?"

"It means my life. How could I stay in the Ballets Russes after this? I shall have to find another company – but *what* company?"

"And what of me?" Once Arabella would have said nothing, now she had the strength to fight.

He did not look at her as he replied: "You have great talent, Arabella, and you have done no wrong. Sergei would keep you on in the company – he still thinks of you only as a dancer. Maria was right to advise me to keep him in ignorance of our friendship."

"*Maria* suggested it?" It was her idea, not François"? She must think about the significance of this, but first she must struggle to ignore that dread word: friendship.

"Oh, yes." François seemed surprised at her concern. "She and Arnold urged me to leave all thoughts of marriage until after the ballet première."

"What concern was it of theirs?" Arabella fumed with rage. Arnold too? How could he? How dare he? How right she had been to be uneasy about their talking about her behind her back.

"They *are* concerned. Maria too has a leading role, and Arnold did not want – then – to see his music wasted. And also, Arabella, it is clear that Arnold loves you—"

She was about to interrupt but he continued, "And it was Maria who introduced me to Diaghilev. She feels protective towards me. We were at one time to be married, but that did not happen, so now we are friends."

"Why did you not tell me this before, François?" A thousand questions and suspicions were spinning through Arabella's mind. "You should not have listened to them without speaking to me." Did Maria *still* want to marry François? Had she been persuading Arnold to take the course he had?

"Maria said she *had* spoken to you." François did not seem concerned.

"Only to explain afterwards why you" – the words "would not marry me" stuck in her throat, so she compromised with – "were so distant towards me."

"But now they have been proved right. Sergei would not have kept us both in the company, you would have left. Instead I shall leave. It has all turned out for the best."

It was as though he did not hear her, as though he had already moved on, away from her. Arabella forced herself into the future. Once she had spoken she would not be able to retrieve the words, but they must be said. Please, please let me say the right thing. "I went yesterday to see Arnold to try to persuade him to accept your ending – for my sake. He is, as you say, very fond of me."

Sudden hope leapt into François' face until he saw her expression. "And he did not agree."

"No. Unless I marry him." It was out. The ballet had entered its third act.

A moment's stillness that would be etched upon her mind for ever. The water wagtail, the scarlet pimpernels in the grass, the uneaten picnic.

"And what was your reply?"

"I have not yet given it. I should consult you. It is – your ballet."

A tiny reaction that, had she not known every movement of

his muscles and nerves so well, would not have been noticeable. Did it mean relief or disappointment? It must be the latter, and so her last hope was gone.

"My ballet, yes."

In the back of her throat was a lump so large she could not swallow. She saw him through a blur of tears. "I do not know what I shall say," she cried. "I do not love him, but I like him, and now that you no longer love me—"

He turned on her a face so aghast with shock and grief she could no longer hold back the tears. "No longer love you? *Ma mie*, what can you mean?"

"We have been so apart. I hurt you by what I said."

"Yes. I thought you believed I was Sergei's lover. I thought you were so horrified that I had lost your love."

A ray of hope, a rainbow in the storm. "And you want it still?"

She was lying in his arms, he was caressing her body, kissing her lips, her throat, her breast. The sunshade had been tossed away so that she could feel the sun, although she was shielded by his body. He was muttering words of love, his hands caressing her ever more intimately. The feelings that shot through her body when they danced together were even stronger now, save that there were no steps to follow, only those that came naturally as he pulled at her clothes, as she longed for the simplicity of her stage dress.

"Please don't stop," she said in agony, as at last he tore himself away from her.

"I must," he choked. "If I do not stop now – I want you, but how can I love you as I want?"

"As *we* want. There is no one here save ourselves. Please, François, I cannot lose you again."

"You trust me? You do not believe that Diaghilev and I—"

"Never."

"I love you, for I heard the song of the sweetest nightingale," he whispered, as he took her into his arms once more.

"And now that I am your wife, François," Arabella said happily much later, "you must eat your picnic."

"Sandwiches? I hope so."

"Cold chicken salad, provided by the hotel. And strawberries."

"My favourite. Did you tell the hotel you were going to seduce a unicorn?"

"I told them it was a picnic for my maiden aunt."

"The maiden is a maiden no longer." He clasped her hand. "Does she mind?"

"The former maiden has never been more happy."

"Oh, but she will be, when she is my legal wife. We shall be married as soon as the season is over. That will be in just over a month's time, when the Ballets Russes disperses for holidays. I will get the licence. And we will never speak of what has happened between us in these last months again. Except" – he hesitated – "that I would like to explain more about Sergei, Arabella."

"Don't!" Nothing must spoil today, *nothing*, for nothing else mattered save herself and François.

"I must. He *was* attracted to me, he is attracted to many young men, and for that reason he watched me dance, but he would not have taken me for the Ballets Russes for that alone. I did not take advantage of the situation when I realised his motives after he allowed me to use the spare room in his suite. Vaslav was with him then, so I was placed in no false position, and as soon as Vaslav had gone, Sergei found Beppe."

"Then why," Arabella asked, determined to understand fully, as he obviously wished, "was it so important for him not to know that we were in love and planned to marry until after you had proved yourself with the ballet?"

"Because he is made jealous by all his protégés, whether they become his lovers or not. So Maria—"

Arabella did not want to hear about Maria. "And that is all?"

"Yes. And now, *mon amour*, what answer will you give poor Arnold?"

"That I will not marry him – because I am to marry you."

"*Magnifico, bravo!*" François pulled her to her feet and whirled her round in a pirouette. "I must take care," he laughed when he stopped. "My prima ballerina might sprain her ankle on a tree root."

That reminded her. "But the ballet, François," she asked, appalled. "He will not change the ending. Will you accept it as it is?"

His face clouded. "I cannot. Even more now that we have our own happiness. But I shall talk to Sergei and tell him I have found my own music for the ending, and that he must use Arnold's score apart from that. That is simple, for he can legally do so."

"He will fight it. He does not like being crossed."

"Sergei?"

"No, Arnold. He is kind, he is gentle, but he is adamant."

"And so, my beloved, am I. We will have our happy ending."

"But what is it? What music have you found?"

His face fell. "Nothing yet. But it will come. You will see."

Arabella spent much time in composing her letter to Arnold. She included no pleas for the ballet, for he had made his position quite clear; she spoke merely of her love for François, her friendship with Arnold, and her appreciation of his offer. She was dissatisfied with it, but could not see why, and so she decided to send it.

François had already come to her jubilant at Diaghilev's response. "Sergei will use the Prince score up to the final scenes, despite Arnold's threats, and, *chérie*, he has postponed the opening night. I think he guessed I had not actually found the music yet, but he believes in me. He is a wonderful man. The only date he can arrange is two days before the season's end, but what does that matter? There will be more seasons, more ballets, more dances. Ah, life is good, my Arabella." He performed a *grand jété* in triumph. "Arnold can go to as many solicitors as he likes, but he knows they can achieve nothing," he continued. "We will make it clear the music for the last scenes is not by him, and so he cannot complain – save at losing you, Arabella."

"He never had me to lose," she replied. "You know that."

Arabella had been worried about what to say to Maria, but in the end said nothing – at least for the moment. Maria seemed delighted that the ballet was going ahead, and Arabella had not the heart to scold her for interfering in her affairs. She decided to keep her plans for marriage from her, however, though she suspected that Maria might be able to read her happiness in her face.

Arabella hugged her secret to her. Although Maria had said that to François she, Arabella, and the ballet were one, François had chosen *her* over the ballet, and yet the ballet still flourished.

Joy unfolded inside her like a flower. She lived only for the rehearsals, the discussions, and her few private moments with François, even though he had said they should not make love again until they were man and wife.

"Why not?" she had asked. It seemed so long to wait.

"I think Sergei might not like it if we began a third member for his company ahead of our wedding."

She realised what he meant, laughed and agreed. "Have you found the music yet?" she asked him. The opening night, although in late July, was now only ten days away.

"I thought I had, but it won't come right. I need you to inspire me, Arabella. Here, if you please. At my feet."

In fact she sat on his knee, his arm round her, as they looked at his score notes together.

"I'll play it to you," he said at last, going to the piano. When she had heard it, she was forced to agree that, close though it was, it didn't work.

"How about Mozart?"

"Too well known."

"Handel?"

"Too stately."

Arabella thought for a while, then crowed in triumph. "I'm sure we've been thinking along the wrong lines, François. I don't believe we want conventional music at all. Camelot is about England, and that's why Arnold used some folk-dance music in his score. At our picnic" – she planted a quick kiss on his mouth – "you whispered something to me about a nightingale."

His arm went around her. "The song of the sweetest nightingale, my Arabella. It is from an ancient German folk song about the hunt of the Unicorn, the only one I have found that mentions the Nightingale too. I do not have the music, though."

"But there is an old English – or rather Cornish – song called 'Sweet Nightingale'." Arabella's words tumbled over themselves in her excitement. "No unicorn, but from what I remember the story would fit your ballet. *And*" – she paused impressively – "it finishes with—" She ran to the piano and played a few bars, singing along.

"The couple agreed.
To be married with speed.

166

And soon to the church they did go."

"Play me more!" François ordered peremptorily, striding round the room as she at first hesitantly, then more confidently picked out the music in her head on the piano keys. "Now sing it. All of it."

She obeyed, as best she could, for it was some years since she had learned the words in her youth.

> "You shall hear the fond tale.
> Of the sweet nightingale.
> As she sings in those valleys below."

François strode round the room saying nothing, so she played the melody again.

Another silence. Then: "Again!"

Arabella obeyed, and this time the pacing stopped, with a large sigh from François.

"That is our ending, *chérie*. It has charm, mystery and joy. You have found it for me."

Arabella went to bed that night full of happiness. All would be well now, now Act III could be finished.

The next morning she received a letter from Arnold, which she hastily scanned, impatient to leave for rehearsal.

> I have realised I was wrong to force such a decision on you. Please understand it was only my love for you that made me do so, Arabella, though I truly did not believe it at the time. You yourself know what force love has to set all other considerations aside.

She was about to put it aside to read later, until her eyes fell on the words: "I am willing to make amends by writing the ending to François' scenario as he wishes."

Arabella froze. This was the worst possible news. François was happy with his new ending, and here was Arnold offering his, which Diaghilev would most surely prefer in order to keep what goodwill of Arnold's he could. She hurried to tell François, only to find he had already left the hotel for Drury Lane. As soon as she arrived there, she handed him the letter in silence. There was no need for words, for her expression had forewarned him this was not good news.

To her surprise, he was not as alarmed as she; he shrugged, kissed her cheek and announced: "This is generous, but we have our own ending now. I will speak to Sergei, then write to thank Arnold, but, *ma chère*, decline his oh-so-kind offer."

It sounded so straightforward. After all, there was nothing else they could do at this late stage, and Arnold must surely see that. So why, Arabella wondered, did she feel so wretched?

*   *   *

Tara was counting the days to the next weekend, when she would be leaving on the Saturday evening for the Washington conference. She was still looking forward to it, but the performance of Josh's ballet on her return would be her real red-letter day. Besides fulfilling her own desire to see the ballet on stage, it would signify the end to this limbo in both love and work.

The ballet was still incomplete, however, for with under two weeks to go Josh was still worried about its ending. "I still can't see the Prince music fitting a happy ending and yet I'm damned if I'm going to choreograph an unhappy one."

"Change the music," Tara said promptly.

Josh laughed. "Who do you think I am? Lloyd Webber?"

"You're a one-man band, all miming, all dancing, all composing, aren't you? Yes. If you feel so strongly, you write the ending you want. Giselle won't mind, and even if she does, I can explain. I think she'll be all in favour of a happy ending. Not fashionable, but uplifting. And *I'm* most certainly in favour."

Tara was bursting with the conviction that had come so speedily to her. The happy ending seemed the passport to her new life with Josh and to the land of long ago which her seven-year-old legs had been unable to enter. The Pied Piper had led his troupe through the mountain into the magic land of faraway, but the door had slammed in her face because she did not have the ability to keep up with the rest of the children. Now, miraculously, it was opening for her again, and Josh was stretching out a hand to pull her in.

"I'll see what Sybille thinks."

"No," Tara objected. "*You* need to decide, not Sybille. Music and score are your department."

"And that of the ABC's artistic director."

"Do it first and show it to him afterwards."

"You're very dictatorial today. What's got into you?" He looked at her curiously.

"Arabella, perhaps." Tara laughed. "Anyway, I'm no musician, but I *know* that's the way to go."

"And do you also know – sorry, I'm not laughing at you, I'm taking you seriously – what kind of music it should be?"

"No."

"I thought not, my little nightingale."

"Why did you say that?" A sudden image, an idea half formed, came to her.

"What?"

"Nightingale. Josh, that's *it*!"

"What is?"

"That old Cornish song you talked about when we met, 'Sweet Nightingale'. It ends up happily with the couple agreeing to be married with speed, yet the music has a sort of mystic drama about it. 'No more is she afraid, for to sit in the shade or to walk in those valleys below' – where the nightingale sings. It's a theme of *The Unicorn and the Nightingale* and" – she added, unable to stop herself – "it's our theme too. You said so yourself when we met."

"So I did. The unknown country, the far-off valley of love. It might work," he said thoughtfully. "In fact, I think it will. By George, I think you've got it, to quote Professor Higgins. Thanks, my fair lady."

"I don't know where the idea came from," she answered truthfully.

"I'll work on the score this evening. You've no objections, have you?" They had planned to go out to a restaurant.

"No; I can do with the time."

She kissed him lightly, as she usually did, now that the door of the mountain was ajar, but Josh kept hold of her hand, pulled her to him again in a deep embrace.

"You've found that unknown country, haven't you," he said huskily. "I can tell, for I'm still living there. It's been hell without you. When you get back from Washington, move in with me. Please."

"Yes, oh yes."

"Shall we be married with speed?"

"Yes, oh yes, again." The far-off valley was not full of shade and mystery. It was glorious, glorious sunshine, and they would walk together in it for ever.

Tara returned home jubilant, floating over the stage of her life in sheer bliss, her head dizzy with what had happened. When she opened the front door, however, she heard familiar voices, and popped her head into the lounge in sheer curiosity. Surely it couldn't be whom she thought?

"William?" She had been right, but it was startling to find him here with Sybille. "What on earth are you doing here?" She toyed with a fantasy of William and Sybille being an item, but discarded it. No sofas for them; they were sitting opposite each other in armchairs.

"Waiting for you," he said easily. "I had a few questions about next week."

Sybille left them to it. "All yours, Tara. I'm off to meet Michael."

Still slightly puzzled, Tara sat down to discuss the conference, and planned giving in general, with William. It wasn't till after he had left she realised why she had been so surprised to find him here. She had told him she would be out this evening. He must have forgotten.

Ten

This was the *entrée*. It was almost time for the moment when Lady Lilith – not Petrovna – would take the stage with her simple *pas de bourrée couru*, running down the golden staircase of Camelot to meet Sir Galymede. The festive group dances at the court were almost over, and François – no, Sir Galymede – was already on stage dancing his longing for her in a solo of love. Arabella rubbed yet more rosin into her shoes, and nervously flexed her legs: *plié, dégagé*, and then briefly *en pointe. Now* came the beat for Lady Lilith to enter, and Petrovna was left behind. She was Sir Galymede's beloved, his chosen bride, even though still hesitant about the unknown country of love. Arabella took the music into her mind and her body, until there was nothing but the emotion and the need to dance out her story.

Maria had advised her to save something of her energy, reminding her that the final edge and polish should be reserved for the first performance tomorrow evening, but Arabella forgot this as deep within came the wish to dance with an intensity she had never experienced before. Although the audience for this rehearsal was small, she was aware of it, out there in the warm darkness. She must tell the story of Lilith and Galymede with such art that it would never be forgotten. Faultlessly she danced into Galymede's arms and felt them around her, holding her safe for ever, soothing her fears.

In the wings Maria would be waiting to cast her dark presence, as Morgana, over their love, but nothing could touch this moment of joy as François knelt for the bluebird lift, edging his shoulder beneath her ready for the moment when he must rise to lift her mid-jump. It had taken much rehearsal, but tonight she did not think of the difficulties, only of the supreme joy of seeming to float effortlessly above him.

From then on, there was no Arabella, only Lilith and her

happiness – until Morgana's appearance, and the change of music to the motif of the hunt, not yet obvious but quietly menacing in the background.

By the time the curtain fell at the end of the act, she knew it was a success. "François?" She gently touched his hand in the wings. How strange that on stage their bodies clung together for all to admire, but here convention ruled that no such intimacy could be shown.

By now Morgana's spell had turned Galymede into a unicorn and Lilith into a nightingale. François' costume was stark white, and the horn fixed to his head was also white. Her costume was brown of course: brown tights, head-dress and tutu. The lack of colour in both of them had worried her at first – until she saw the set designs. Such were the forest's brilliant colours that the effect of the white and brown of the costumes would be enhanced, not diminished, by the scenery.

François responded to her touch. He took her hand into his, intimately, lovingly. "My nightingale, my love, thank you. You have taken my ballet and given it wings."

Those wings sustained Arabella throughout the second act, as the lyrical motifs of the Nightingale contrasted with the Unicorn's ever-increasing desperation to find his way to the tower in which he believed Lilith was incarcerated. One tiny part of Arabella's mind registered that she was dancing extremely well, as the Nightingale tried her best to lead the Unicorn from the forest to safety. Maria as Morgana was also dancing superbly. Although her main appearance in this act was not until the end, throughout as Arabella knew, there were fleeting glimpses of her, hidden amongst the hunt, a sudden shape while the attention was on François and Arabella. Maria had been right, for the slow build-up of menace was powerful.

Never had the Nightingale felt Galymede's danger so strongly, never had she been so aware of the increasing menace in the music. Her feet warned her that some terrible fate was about to befall Galymede, and that the spell Morgana had thrown over them to prevent their love could never be lifted without her help.

A sharp intake of breath from the stalls made Arabella register that today she was excelling herself. Never had she danced so, never had she been so caught up emotionally, so that her body reflected every fear, every desperate hope. She could hear people moving in and out of the auditorium, but it was immaterial. Her world was here upon the stage, dancing out her life and love for Galymede, as she urged him to leave the forest with all the force of the Nightingale's voice; only for Arabella her voice lay in her feet, in her *batterie*, her *port de bras*, her *arabesques* and the poignancy that her steps *en pointe* could give.

Galymede did not heed her, enticed only momentarily by the sweet song of the Nightingale. All too soon the finale of the act arrived and the Nightingale sank down defeated as the Unicorn stormed the tower, oblivious of the hunt now closing in around him in triumph, only to find Morgana inside. Too late he recognised her, but by then her dance of seduction had lulled him into slumber, so that instead of fleeing he stayed, his head in the maiden's lap, as the hunters closed for the kill.

In legend, of course, the only way a unicorn could be vanquished was to be ensnared by a maiden. But what if that maiden wore two faces, and the beautiful face of the virgin girl could change into the darkness of treachery and betrayal? What then?

"You are crying," François said tenderly, as the curtain fell.

"I don't know why," Arabella said desperately, "for I know it all ends happily."

"It does. It will, just as I wrote it. My sweet nightingale will win in the end," he teased her. "In twenty minutes the third act will begin."

She ran happily back to the dressing room to check the sweat and touch up the paint on her face. She had scarcely begun, however, when Maria came in.

"Wasn't it wonderful?" Arabella greeted her joyfully before she registered that Maria was looking very anxious.

"Sergei has sent word he wants to see us immediately in his room."

"But why?" Arabella's excitement drained away immediately. "To congratulate us?" she asked hopefully. "He cannot think the rehearsal has gone badly." Her instincts could not have been that wrong.

"Perhaps. I do not know. Come, Arabella."

"But Act Three—"

"We will be back in time."

Had she not danced well enough? Arabella wondered anxiously, as she followed Maria up the stairs to the tucked-away room that Diaghilev had chosen for his "retreat". The moment they entered the room, however, she realised this was no mere discussion of the technical aspects of the performance, even had not the sound of angry voices already reached them.

Diaghilev broke off his tirade and paced round the room, as red-faced as she had seen him last September. Also present were not only François but Arnold and someone else whom she did not recognise.

Arabella could not keep back the question uppermost in her mind. "Are you not pleased, Monsieur Diaghilev?" She whisked round, full of indignation on François' behalf, as well as her own and Maria's. "And Arnold, were *you* not satisfied? The ballet seemed to me—"

Diaghilev waved this quickly aside. "*Oui*," he shouted at her, but with the nearest tone to kindness she had ever heard from him. "It was *too* good perhaps. I would like it to continue being excellent. François, my staff and my cast are superb. It is Mr Prince who has decided that he will not permit the third act to go ahead."

This made no sense, and Arabella turned in bewilderment to François. He did not move, but she sensed his longing to come to her. "Arnold has informed us that if we go ahead with my version—*our* version, Mademoiselle Petrovna – this evening, there will be no performance tomorrow night or ever," he confirmed, trembling.

It still made no sense. "Arnold," she began in bewilderment, but she was interrupted by the stranger.

"Permit me to introduce myself," he said smoothly. "My name is Lewis. I am Mr Prince's solicitor, and I have advised my client that he is within his rights to withdraw his consent, though he greatly regrets this late decision. It was only seeing Act One earlier this morning that made him realise he could not agree to the changes and he sent for me immediately."

"I hold the copyright to the music. It's all been discussed before," Diaghilev growled.

"It might well be your copyright, sir, had you ever signed an agreement to that effect. However, my client assures me he has signed nothing to that effect, nor have I ever been consulted on the matter."

"An oversight, but it's my standard practice, as Prince well knows."

"Immaterial." Lewis dismissed this with a wave of his hand that any *caractère* dancer would have been proud of.

"There is an understanding that the copyright passes with payment," Diaghilev shouted.

"Certainly, but unfortunately that too you have omitted to render to my client."

Arabella's heart sank. The Ballets Russes' usual tardiness over paying out money had now come home to roost.

"You can argue all you want after tomorrow night," Diaghilev retorted. "The season ends on Saturday. Plenty of time to sort it out then."

"Too late, I'm afraid. There will be no first performance tomorrow night. I am prepared to apply for an immediate injunction."

"Mr Lewis," Arabella intervened, for her head had cleared from the first shock now. "Did you know that Mr Prince wrote to me to tell me he had withdrawn his objections to François' ending? He can hardly object now. I still have his letter."

"Ha," roared Diaghilev triumphantly. "He wrote to you, did he? You didn't mention that, François."

"But now Mr Prince has changed his mind, Miss Peters," Mr Lewis came back immediately, "as he is fully at liberty to do."

"Arabella." Arnold turned to her gently, having remained silent in this battle. "I am truly sorry. I warned you that the artist in me was not as tolerant as the man. When I saw Act One this evening, I realised how wrong I had been to agree to change the ending, even for you."

"Nevertheless," Diaghilev said quickly, eyes darting from one to the other, "I hardly think the courts would rule in favour of an immediate injunction if they saw that letter. Take a cab to your hotel, Petrovna. Fetch it now."

"There is no need, Miss Peters," Lewis said swiftly. "I hardly think the court would be predisposed in favour of any plea by Monsieur Diaghilev. The fate of the late Oscar Wilde is still much in everyone's minds."

There was not even a shout of fury this time from Diaghilev, as though he expected the inevitability of this weapon. "I understood in this country a man was innocent till proved guilty."

"We're wasting time," Lewis answered coolly. "Mr Prince has

made his position clear, and he is legally in the right. I would like your written undertaking now that there will be no performance tomorrow, nor any third act rehearsal today, unless Mr Prince's music is used throughout."

To Arabella's horror, Maria burst out passionately: "Arnold is only doing this because he loves Arabella and does not want to see her marry François."

Why did Maria have to introduce this now of all times? Was she out of her mind? Instead of helping the situation, it might turn it irreversibly against them *and* the ballet.

Diaghilev nodded, as if all along he had suspected it. "I am surrounded by traitors," he moaned. "Why was I not kept informed of this, François? And Petrovna? I am wounded. I thought only of your future career and you repay me thus."

"There is no connection between the two," Arabella kept her voice steady, despite the churning turmoil inside her, in the hope that this new situation might yet be retrieved. "François and I had decided to delay any thoughts of marriage until after the ballet's first performance, in order for us to concentrate on that, rather than our private lives. That is why we have not told you of our plans."

"You were afraid I'd cancel the ballet, that's why." He yelled at her this time. "You thought only of yourselves. No one thinks of me. I *made* the Ballets Russes, I made both of *you* and this is how you repay me."

"We repaid you with a superb ballet," François cried. He was disregarded, however, for Diaghilev was concentrating on Arabella, waiting for her response.

"I am dancing for the ballet. I dance for you, Monsieur Diaghilev, as well as for François and Arnold. As does Maria," she replied vehemently.

"Maria?" Diaghilev laughed.

"We all do," Arabella swept on, not understanding his mirth. "We know you do not like marriages within your company in case they distract from the work of the Ballets Russes. But we have proved to you that that will not happen. You have no cause for annoyance."

"You are very clever, Mademoiselle Petrovna." The note of kindness had returned to Diaghilev's voice. "You have the makings of a brilliant dancer, for today you have proved that.

You have a great future ahead of you in the Ballets Russes. And," he barked, glaring, "so does Monsieur Santine. I've no intention of ruining his first ballet by submitting to your claims, Prince. Take your petty jealousy to the courts. The ballet continues in the form *I* decide. I commission music to fit the scenario, not the other way round. You have refused to follow the scenario. You've broken your contract – if you'd had one," he ended in a roar of self-confidence.

Arabella began to relax. The third act would be starting any moment, she must listen, prepare to hurry down for it.

"I had hoped not to use this weapon," Arnold replied, "particularly in front of two ladies. Unfortunately you have made it unavoidable, monsieur. The courts – and the whole of London – will be interested to know that the reason you are sanctioning Mr Santine's ending and not mine is that he is your lover."

"It's not true!" Arabella cried out. This couldn't be her friend. This Arnold had her father's intransigence and unscrupulousness. This room was fast becoming Morgana's tower, the end of the hunt for the Unicorn.

"Miss Peters is right. It is not true, it has never been true," François shouted.

"Why else would you have shared Diaghilev's hotel suite, ordered things on his account—" Arnold was not swayed.

"With his permission," François interrupted angrily.

"Precisely." Arnold smiled. "At a time when Monsieur Diaghilev needed friendship, when his – er – partnership with Nijinsky was failing, you were there to console him, and were rewarded for it. Most praiseworthy – but it is not a situation London society or the law would look on favourably. It could be misconstrued."

"Courts require proof," François hurled at him. "You have none, because there is none."

"Fortunately there is, and we have it," Lewis interrupted smoothly. "We have bills and witnesses from the hotels all over Europe, particularly Russia."

"You have achieved a great deal in the hour or so since Act One ended," Diaghilev snarled. He was ignored.

"I was in Russia, staying in the same hotel as Monsieur Santine," Arabella said steadily. "I would tell the court so."

"A dupe," Lewis said patronisingly. "Of course it looked better to have you and Miss Rostovna staying there with him. I think we have enough evidence for our purpose. After all, the penalty will be slight, Monsieur Diaghilev – merely the cancellation of this one ballet. You are leaving England at the beginning of August, I understand. I doubt if you will return speedily – whether there is war or not."

There had been increasing signs for the last week or two that war could erupt in Europe at any moment, but, caught up in her happiness, Arabella had not until now thought how this might affect François and herself.

To her horror, this time Diaghilev did not insist that the ballet would go on. If he would not speak, then she must, Arabella decided as the silence became obvious.

"Arnold, you cannot do this. You know your accusation is not true; and it is not the action of a friend, nor of a gentleman, to go back on your word."

François spoke bitterly. "He loves you, Arabella. We should have realised from the start that Mr Prince would not give up easily, even if it means wrecking your career along with mine."

"I refute that," Arnold replied coldly. "Indeed, I have already explained to Arabella that I am willing to *make* her career. What is there for her in the Ballets Russes? Karsavina is prima ballerina, Rostovna second, and there is Madame Fokine too. I've no doubt, you would throw Arabella the occasional titbit to keep her happy, Monsieur Diaghilev, but with me she would have Europe at her feet."

"In the music halls, perhaps? Or are you planning to begin Ballets Anglais?" Diaghilev jeered.

"There are other ballet companies than yours; indeed, some may think better ones, for most are less showy, and thus more suitable for a classical dancer who wishes to display her art. Many would be glad to acquire Arabelle Petrovna, for she established a reputation with Madame Pavlova on which she must build – not virtually rest, as she has been doing this last year, thanks to you two." Arnold glanced disparagingly at François.

"Tomorrow, Arnold, I have a wonderful chance to correct that," Arabella said pleadingly. "Will you not allow it to me?"

He sighed. "I have already explained. Perhaps I will give you one more chance—"

"Mr Prince," Lewis interrupted warningly.

Arnold lifted his hand. "I am not so obdurate as you think,

Arabella. One would not normally speak of love in business discussions, as this is, but here it is necessary. Arabella, I repeat what I said to you earlier: if you come to me, if you will be my wife, then for your sake the ballet may go ahead with the third act as François has written it, both for the rehearsal tonight and the ballet tomorrow."

Arabella felt faint. The room spun around her, and instinctively she moved to François' side for support.

"Blackmail again, Prince? I applaud your decision, but deplore the means," Diaghilev commented.

"I regret them myself. But a man in love – as you must know, Monsieur Diaghilev, in view of your behaviour over Mr Nijinsky – does not always follow an honourable course."

"You'll never write for me again," Diaghilev replied, with deadly calm.

"That does not concern me. What do you say, Arabella?"

François answered for her. "I have some say in this, I believe. It is my ballet and written for Arabella to dance in. *I* will ask the question, not you. Arabella, if there were no ballet, would you wish to marry Arnold, *ma mie*?"

"No." She looked gratefully up at him, the Unicorn who gave her strength.

"And would you wish to marry me?"

"I will love you always and forever, François, ballet or no ballet."

"Very touching," said Maria drily. "I hope you realise what you're doing to us all."

Arabella hardly heard her, so enveloped was she in her private *pas de deux* with François.

"You understand that you may be ruining François' career by this, Arabella?" Arnold did not sound so cold now. It was his turn to plead, to use every weapon at his disposal. "I hardly imagine that the ensuing gossip will do it much good. A cancelled ballet, for whatever reason, is hardly a fine start to a choreographer's career. Nor is being a rumoured nancy-boy a social asset. And the ballet *will* be cancelled if you refuse me, Arabella. We shall apply for the injunction immediately, and I imagine that even Mr Diaghilev will think twice about mounting the production with the Santine ending tomorrow night."

"You imagine too much," Diaghilev said almost gleefully. "François, do you choose to put the ballet or Arabella first?"

What was this? What terrible plan had he in mind? Arabella looked at François in terror, waiting for his reply.

"The ballet is Arabella," he said quietly. "Without the Nightingale the Unicorn will die."

Arabella clasped his hand to give him strength. She knew she should tell him to choose the ballet, but the words would not come.

"It's your choice, François!" Diaghilev roared. "Never mind your mumbo-jumbo about unicorns."

"I choose Arabella."

Arabella gave a small sigh, her hand clasped in his. She had not doubted it, but she realised that most present here had. Not only Arnold and Mr Lewis, but also Maria looked furious.

"You realise what this will mean for me, for the Ballets Russes?" Diaghilev demanded of François. "The ballet will be cancelled for good, of course. I don't trade with the likes of Prince."

"Yes. You have left me no choice."

"Have you thought what you may be putting Miss Peters through, if your name becomes linked with mine in unsavoury gossip?" Diaghilev continued grimly.

"Yes, but my Nightingale will triumph in the end," François said steadily.

He believed in her, he understood her, Arabella realised. At last she knew that nothing could part them.

"Arabella," Arnold said, "I give you one last chance. *You* too know what this would mean for everyone concerned. Are you still prepared to ruin his career?"

"It will not come to that," Arabella said. "The third act—"

"Will take place," interrupted Diaghilev in a roar of triumph this time. "Let the curtain rise. To the wings, *mes amis*."

Relief swept over Arabella as she realised he had been testing them.

"We will go straight to the courts," Lewis said.

"I serve a higher master than British law. I serve art! Monsieur Santine, Mademoiselle Petrovna, I believe you have roles to play; Maria too. The curtain is already late. *Go!*"

François shot out of the door with Arabella in his footsteps. She felt giddy with relief and happiness. Whatever struggles might lie ahead, the third act would be danced, and it would presage their own happiness. She ran quickly to the stairs leading to the wings, with Maria close behind her.

Already in Arabella's mind she was soaring into the air, even as her earthbound feet hurried down. This time it was not the *entrée* she was thinking of, but the dying Nightingale revived to life, her transformation back to Lady Lilith, and the *pas de deux* of joy at the end to the "Sweet Nightingale" music. They *would* be married with speed; no more was she afraid to walk in the shade, or to sing in those valleys below, for François would be with her for ever. The darkness of the valley floor beneath held no menace, for François was ahead of her. She was already being lifted by his strength and his arms high into the air.

But the arms were not there; instead she crashed down the remaining stairs to the dark valley below. Then there was pain, and more pain, and the murmuring sound of voices. In a ballet? Or had the voices begun before she lifted herself towards François? The pain spread and then there was nothing but the peace of oblivion as François slowly dissolved away from the stage.

*   *   *

Jet lag was surely one of the worst feelings one could have. Tara never got used to it, no matter how often she travelled or at what time of day. Countless remedies had failed, and she had finally accepted that she just had to put up with it. At least this time she would have the rest of Sunday to relax.

Once at the hotel she slept through the afternoon to get over the flight. By the time she awoke her watch said seven o'clock, though her internal clock pointed out that to her it was much later. After a quick shower she decided to contact one or two of the speakers who must surely be here by now, with a view to having dinner with them to discuss the general drift of the conference. William had told her they were checking in the day before the conference, and would be expecting to hear from her. She'd been grateful to him for that, for the last weeks had been hectic for her. She had felt she was being pulled in two directions at once. Josh was still muttering about the ending of his adaptation, still not satisfied. The music had worked, but the choreography

181

needed polishing and changing. That would be simple, however, he had told her confidently, because the music was so strong. Nevertheless she could not wait to get home on Thursday for the dress rehearsal. It was a milestone not only for the future of Music and Mime, but for her, and she had already told Sybille she would be moving out of her house and in with Josh after her return.

She rang reception for the room numbers of the two speakers she particularly wanted to talk to, but was surprised to find that not only had they not checked in, but that the hotel had no record of their being booked in for the night. She cursed herself for not having checked all these details for herself; they must be staying at another hotel, rather than this one, at which the conference was to be held, and William must have forgotten to tell her.

It occurred to her briefly that William was forgetting to tell her a lot of things nowadays, but she supposed she must share the blame for that. She no longer lived with him and she had had precious little time available to discuss all these routine matters. She tried one or two other hotels that she knew were popular for conferences, but without success. She left it another hour and tried again. Still nothing.

Eventually she made another call to her own hotel's reception desk. "Could you please check to see if they're booked in for tomorrow?" she asked. She had suddenly realised that they might be coming on one of the rare overnight Sunday flights, for if they were family men, they would naturally want the weekend at home. Odd, though, because although one of them wasn't speaking till the second day, the other was on the programme for the first day. Reception said they'd ring back, and, true to American hotel efficiency, they did so.

Or were they efficient? They seemed to have them booked in entirely for the wrong days. Both were booked in for arrival on Tuesday. A cold hand fastened over her heart. The speakers would have taken care of their own bookings, but it was a terrible mistake by someone. The hotel? For one, perhaps, but not both. Something was definitely wrong.

She began to feel somewhat nauseous, and all thoughts of a pleasant dinner vanished fast. What about the conference's delegates, and the other speakers? Had any of them checked in? She remembered that the conference programmes, which would include delegates' names, would have already been delivered to the hotel, and she quickly took the lift down to reception. Being Sunday evening, however, she had a difficult task in tracking the conference materials down, since the special conference staff were off duty for the weekend. Eventually one of the porters managed to track them down and, somewhat reproachfully, brought her one of the packages.

"They were marked for Wednesday, madam, not Monday as you said."

"*Wednesday?*"

The sickness in her stomach threatened to engulf her. What was going on here? She tore open the box and seized one of the programmes.

Her worst nightmare had come true. In large letters across the front of the conference book she read "Wednesday to Friday". And on Thursday Josh was relying on her to be in the Albion Theatre for his – *their* – dress rehearsal, on the day before Friday's first night.

Eleven

Telephones were torture. Tara sat on the edge of her hotel bed, clutching the only means she had had of explaining her predicament to Josh. They were supposed to be an aid to communication, not a weapon for the opposition. Were she face to face with Josh she could have explained it perfectly well, but separated by thousands of miles with only an impersonal telephone line to link them, it had been a hopeless task to convince that non-committal voice how devastated she felt at the inexplicable horror that had befallen her.

At first only Josh's answerphone had greeted her, although it was long past midnight by British time. She had tried a second time half an hour later, for what she had to say was too important for a recorded message, but again met with no success.

It wouldn't be sensible to wake him up in the middle of the night with such news, and so she had been forced to wait until morning in Britain before she could speak to him. By that time it was past two o'clock in Washington; she was dizzy with jet lag and shock and was forcing herself to stay awake, despite the fact that speaking to him in this muzzy state might be disastrous. She had to speak to him, she could not deal with this alone, but the warmth and pleasure in his voice as he realised who was calling had almost made her weep.

He was eager to tell her about the first rehearsal on the Albion theatre stage, and it was some minutes before she could speak herself, aware that the longer she left it the harder it was going to be.

It wasn't only hard, it was impossible. She explained what had happened, already aware that the wording she had rehearsed in her mind was failing miserably in practice.

"I *know* it was Monday to Wednesday," she finished. "I don't make mistakes like that."

184

The silence at the other end was more eloquent than fury. "What are you going to do?" Josh finally asked. It was impossible to tell his thoughts from the neutral tone of his voice.

"I have no choice. I have to stay on," she answered miserably. "But—"

"Of course you have a choice."

She hadn't, and she knew it. How could she put the whole conference in jeopardy by returning home in what would be seen to be a sulk at her own mistake? Not to mention the expense to her career if she didn't appear. Her name would not only be mud in her profession, but mud that wouldn't just be thrown aside and buried. Apart from her own feelings, that would not do Music and Mime any good either. She needed to be squeaky clean if she was going to carry clout in any merger. That was obvious to her; she should have been able to make it obvious to Josh too – but, thanks to the telephone, she clearly hadn't.

"Whose mistake was it, then?"

"I don't know. I'm going to find out."

"Immaterial either way. When will you be back?"

This she had thought out. "I might make the end of the first performance on Friday, depending on where *The Unicorn* is placed in the programme. If it's last—"

"That's good of you." No longer neutral.

"Sarcasm isn't usually your style, Josh."

"Whereas disloyalty is apparently yours."

She had retaliated, they had argued, and that was that. He hung up on her. She could try again, but what was the point? Her head was reeling. She seemed to be seeing everything as from a great distance, though that did not help. It made it worse, because she was wallowing in a quagmire she could not escape. If she lay down it would be worse, and so she went to fetch some water from the minibar. The one thing she was sure about was that she could not abandon the conference, and yet so many issues were fighting inside her mind. William, herself, Josh, the future, the past—

The lion and the Unicorn were fighting for the crown,
The lion beat the Unicorn all round the town . . .

Desperately Tara tried to pull herself together. She was going

185

crazy. The Unicorn *couldn't* be beaten. His strength was limitless, so how did the lion beat him? Anyway, it was Morgana's fault. She was the evil one, casting her evil spells over Galymede. It was she who had betrayed the Unicorn, in the guise of the virgin. And now the Unicorn had been beaten only the sad Nightingale remained to fight Morgana, but Arabella was drowning, losing the fight with no strength left. The Nightingale was dying.

Thoughts whirled, her stomach churned, and finally tension, fear and shock combined to make her physically sick. Once that was over, Tara staggered to bed, drained. She lay there, her head spinning, unable to control her thoughts, unable to help the Nightingale. When sleep came at last, its images were dark. The hunters were on their track, closing in upon the Unicorn and, near to death, she was powerless to prevent them. Just as the first spear was thrown, she awoke with a strangled cry, half of relief that she was alive, half still fear. She sat up to calm her beating heart, gulping deep breaths. There was nothing she could do, she decided wretchedly. She, and Arabella, must wait till the conference was over.

"How did it happen, William?" Tara demanded belligerently. She had had time to think more logically in the day and a half before he arrived, and had decided to challenge him as soon as he checked in so that this time it would be the hunter with the jet lag. Crazy thinking. She had been impatient with herself at not being able to control such rambling nonsense. William wasn't the hunter; he had done nothing save invite her to this conference. How could he have known it was going to clash so disastrously with Josh's ballet? That was what reason told her, and it had to be the remnants of her jet lag that were making her feel he was the enemy.

William had looked flabbergasted when she grimly told him she'd checked in for a Monday to Wednesday conference, but now he was laughing, which first irritated, then angered her.

"How did it happen?" she repeated.

"You always pride yourself on your organisational efficiency, yet you make a slip-up like this. How did *that* happen?"

"It didn't," she flashed back. "On the programme you showed me, it was Monday to Wednesday, not Wednesday to Friday."

William looked puzzled, then snapped his fingers in realisation.

"That, as I am sure I told you at the time, was the draft programme." The grin still lingered. "It was changed."

"Pity you didn't inform me," she said tartly.

"I did," William retorted. "I couldn't get you by phone; you were never there. I object to continually leaving voicemail for someone I've lived with for two years, so I sent a fax and confirmation by letter."

"Never arrived." Tara was suspicious.

He shrugged. "That's no fault of mine. It's a result of your only being part time in the office, I expect. Somebody must deal with your affairs while you're away. Have it out with them, not me."

She wasn't going to let him off so easily, even though she'd be doing some checking in the office when she was back. "Why not e-mail me?"

"Because I'd faxed you, dearest. Now, if you insist on a hotel lobby for our discussion, let's at least have a coffee and get down to business. That's if you're condescending to stay for our humble conference?"

"I have no choice, and you well know it." Tara was still smarting.

"All right, then we'll go halves on the extra accommodation," he offered generously. "Seriously, Tara, thanks for not rushing off and leaving us in the lurch."

"I still want to," she replied savagely. "It's highly inconvenient for me to stay."

"Ah. A touch of the old poetry, eh? I could not love thee, Josh, so much, loved I not honour more."

"I didn't say it was Josh—"

"I flatter myself he and his beloved ballet are the only reason you'd ever consider abandoning the conference and returning to England early."

Tara glared at him, still dissatisfied, but not knowing quite where to attack. He'd covered his flank – if there *was* anything to hide – very efficiently.

The conference went well, and after the first day's tensions and mini-crises had been dealt with Tara began to relax. She took the logical view that since there was nothing she could do to pacify Josh until she returned home, why not enjoy it? Telephone calls would merely invade Josh's final rehearsal time, and faxes and flowers to Sybille were all she could render in the way of immediate penance. She even found herself gaining her old enthusiasm for her profession, though at the same time she was aware that it was a swan-song. She had made her choice, and she was impatient to be flying home to ride out the undoubted storm that would greet her, so that, she could begin the next stage of her life.

Impatience turned into tension as at last she was able to board the airport bus for a very early flight on the Friday, having given her apologies to everyone at the conference personally during the evening drinks following the last session on Thursday. She heartily wished she could have taken an overnight flight but she had known that the drinks would go on too late, and that William's eye would be far too disapproving for her to sneak away before the end, even though she had a perfectly good substitute.

Some gave them white bread and some gave them brown.
Some gave them plum cake and drummed them out of town.

The lion and the Unicorn verse finished itself off neatly in her head. She'd had her plum cake at the conference, and now she was being drummed out of town. But which town – and who was the drummer? Surely not Josh in London? She had to be able to explain her predicament more clearly when she met him. But if the town was Washington, how could William be the drummer?

Such nonsensical thoughts ran through her head as she waited for the flight, until in desperation she picked up a magazine and tried to interest herself in flower arrangements. There were very few daytime flights to Britain, but by changing her ticket she had managed to find a route that would get her to Heathrow by mid-evening.

Or would have done, if there hadn't been an hour and a half delay. Wouldn't you just know? Tara groaned. That was her last chance of getting there in time to see at least most of the evening performance. She'd be lucky if she managed to see any of it now, even though a fax from Sybille had given her some relief, for the ballet was scheduled last in the programme.

The flight seemed more tedious than ever, and for once Tara was glad of the meals and drinks arriving at intervals and breaking up the monotony. She couldn't concentrate on her book, nor on the in-flight film, worried that she still had to get from Heathrow to the theatre. Taxis couldn't fly over the traffic, but the Underground might take even longer.

In the event Tara chose the taxi – which crawled through the traffic-laden roads so slowly that she regretted her decision. By the time she arrived at the theatre, she was not only tired and exhausted but gripped in a vice by tension. To her, it was beginning to feel like a ballet scenario of her own. She reasoned with herself that her presence was hardly vital, and so, even though Josh would be annoyed at her absence, she would be able to make him understand somehow. It was past eleven now, so the ballet must be nearly over . . .

She flung several notes at a surprised but delighted taxi driver and fled, not waiting to ask for a receipt. To hell with business travel. She hurried through into the back of the stalls, but saw to her dismay that she was too late. The curtain call was in progress, and it was obviously for the ballet from the look of the costumes and the fact that Sybille was taking an ovation as Morgana. So the house was enthusiastic. At least that was something.

Tara quickly made her way round to the stage entrance and into the wings. There she saw Sybille, rushing into Josh's embrace. Arms wrapped round each other's waists in triumph, they began to make their way to the dressing rooms. She didn't think. She couldn't. She rushed straight up to them.

"Josh, I'm so sorry – flight delay – but I can see it's gone well. That's wonderful." She knew she was burbling, but one look at Josh's stony expression had made her incapable of coherent speech.

"Thank you." He was trying to sound as though he meant it, but he might have been speaking to a member of the public.

Panic filled her. "Are we celebrating?" she asked uncertainly. "We?"

How could one word devastate her so much? Desperately, she tried again.

"Look, I'm really sorry, but it wasn't my fault."

"You weren't here, and that's what counts."

"But that's just childish," Tara burst out, frightened and tired.

"Don't I recall St Paul mentioning that children see face to face, not through a glass darkly, as you seem to, Tara?"

Sybille giggled uneasily. "Why don't you go home to get some sleep, Tara? You're obviously tired."

Tara had no choice but to follow Sybille's suggestion, for they walked away from her. Stunned and sick, she returned to the Richmond house and collapsed into a mercifully dreamless sleep. When she awoke, however, she was plunged back into the nightmare. The light of day brought not only the sharp stab of pain, but the knowledge that she had to deal with a situation she didn't fully understand, and which appeared to be leading straight to the door marked exit for her and Josh. "Never forget I love you," he'd once said. Where was that love now, when she most needed its reassurance?

She tried to think logically. Today was Saturday, and there would be a performance this evening. She would attend, see Josh to congratulate him, and all might yet be well.

Almost convinced, Tara put on her dressing gown and went to make tea in the kitchen, where she found a groaning Sybille half-way through a black coffee.

"Good celebration?" Tara asked brightly. She hadn't heard Sybille come in.

"Wonderful," Sybille said. "Late night, though. I went back to Josh's to carry on the victory parade. Look, Tara, I feel terrible about last night, but Josh was seriously unhappy about your not turning up. First-night nerves, probably. He'll be in a better mood today."

"I hope so," Tara had said quietly. The knife twisted in the wound. Sybille had been in her place at Josh's flat. She wondered – no, surely not. Then to her relief the question mark was cleared up.

"There's something else too," Sybille continued awkwardly. "It was a terrific celebration at the restaurant, and, so much so, I've got another shock for you. No rush, so don't panic."

It was hard not to. What on earth was coming now? Her imagination ran riot.

"Michael and I have decided to become an item – after the fourth glass of champagne I found myself asking him to move in. I don't know what made me do it, but once I had I saw it was a very good idea indeed. He was all for it. So—"

"I understand. You want me to move out." Oh, the relief that it was Michael, not Josh. "Anyway, I—" Tara stopped short. It wasn't the best of times to remind her that she and Josh were planning to become a formal item too. "It's time I removed myself from your hands and went independent," she finished. "It's been wonderful living here, but it's time to get my act together."

Where she would go was another matter, until she had sorted out the situation with Josh. Tara waited in all day but there was no word from him, nor any reply save the answerphone at his flat. Should she try to see him before the performance this evening or wait? Reluctantly, she decided to wait, hard though it was – and by the time she arrived at the theatre, it seemed even harder. There was the rest of the programme to endure before Josh's *The Unicorn and the Nightingale*. She watched *Petrouchka* with an enjoyable detachment, but the mimes – in which Josh appeared – were painful reminders that shortly she must face him once more.

At last his ballet began. It was strange seeing it as an outsider; she could see it was magnificent, but she seemed to have played no part in it. Josh did not perform in it, but to watch Sybille was fascinating, for even she could see that Sybille had gifts as a dancer that weren't being sufficiently exploited in Music and Mime. The role of Morgana suited her to perfection.

Tara waited impatiently for the last scene, for in view of her *impasse* with Josh, it seemed even more important to know how the ballet ended. Had he kept the "Sweet Nightingale" music, or reverted to the Prince score? When she heard the strains of the Nightingale song, she felt an enormous relief, for this must surely have significance for them, as well as the ballet.

She found Josh in the green room, still flushed and sweaty after the ballet, and laughing and joking with cast and visitors. Instantly she was the outsider once again. This was natural enough, she tried to convince herself, for she was not known to most people here, and the closeness of performance was still gluing the cast together.

Her voice sounded artificial, when she at last managed to detach him from the group. "It was superb, Josh."

She meant it, but it went for nothing. "The ending was wrong," was all he said. No hostility at least, just a great weariness. It was almost worse.

Tara tried fiercely to contradict him. "It wasn't. The dancing and the music were *right*!"

"No one noticed, of course," he continued, as though he had not heard her, "it's too short a scene for that, but it didn't fit. It jerked, it didn't flow. They should have died."

"No." Tara's lips were dry.

"I've been talking to John Haycroft, the ballet critic. He agrees with me."

"It doesn't matter a damn what he thinks, only that you should think it."

"When I develop it into three acts, I'll change it."

"Is this new?" The "when" had sounded very definite.

"Oh yes." He sounded almost indifferent. "The ABC are quite sure they want it for next year. It could be a real winner, they think, as a mix of ballet, voiced mime, and song."

"The Nightingale's song? Do they want this ending?" She held her breath. Surely this would sway him.

"It's for me to decide."

Her heart sank. "Don't I have a say? Oh, Josh, I want one."

"Giselle told us to make our own ending," Josh said flatly. "And whether you meant to do so or not, I think you've decided it."

"But you know my not being here was by accident," she replied hopelessly, with a sudden doubt whether this was so. Could William have engineered it? No – how could he have known the date of the ballet's première?

"Perhaps, but you've explained often enough that you wouldn't forsake your career easily. You tried an experiment to combine it with us, but it's failed. That seems fairly conclusive. We could give it a whirl, I suppose, at being a two-career partnership, but this time I think it's I who needs space before we leap."

"But, Josh—" She broke off, for pride would not let her cry out, "What about our love?" Where had it gone? What would she do if there was no Josh? Instead, she blurted out: "I'm leaving Sybille's."

She waited for Josh to say she'd misunderstood, that he still wanted her to come to him, but there was a terrible silence which he broke with an awkward: "I'm sorry about yesterday. I was pretty mad."

There was nothing to say but the ridiculous: "What about the company accounts?"

He smiled at that. "Businesslike to the last. If you could see them through, I'd be grateful. We'd pay you, of course. And I won't do anything about *The Unicorn* till I've cleared it with Giselle."

A small concession. Where be your fine hopes now? she asked herself, as she returned desolately to Richmond. "I'll pay you, of course." What words to end an affair that hadn't even fully begun. It had still been waiting for its spring, and now the frost had come to kill the tender shoots. Arabella, what did *you* do? she cried silently. Where did you find your strength? This happened to you too. It must have done. How did you survive?

*   *   *

"You're very kind."

Arabella meant it. Gwendolen Prince, Arnold's elder sister, was nearer her parents' age than her own, but nevertheless in the few days Arabella had been here she had come to seem more like a friend than the voice of authority.

Gwendolen's anxious face looked gratified. "We must get you well again, Arabella."

"Yes." Arabella looked at the plasterbound ankle peeping out from beneath her long skirt as she lay on the sofa. Her sprained wrist was bandaged too, but the pain from both and from the bruises that seemed to cover her entire body was diminishing. It left a worse pain inside her, though, and even the knowledge that she was in such good care in the Prince family home in Kent where Gwendolen lived could not assuage it. Arabella felt a caged nightingale, unable to fly and only able to look out upon the gardens and the distant woods of freedom. She supposed she should be grateful to Arnold too for bringing her here, for Gwendolen had told her that her parents had wanted her to go to them, and that she could not yet have borne. On that terrible evening, Arabella had been conscious of nothing save pain, faces she could not properly see, and voices whose words she could not distinguish.

Arnold had apparently insisted she come here, since he blamed his own intransigence for Arabella's accident. She had been so distraught at what had happened in Diaghilev's room that she had not taken sufficient care on the steps.

"I am grateful, Arnold, but could I not have remained in the hotel, near my friends?" she had asked wearily, when he visited her yesterday.

"The season has finished. After the two-week holiday period, I understand Diaghilev is taking the Ballets Russes to the Continent. That's if war does not break out and interfere with his plans."

She had been here for five days, the Bank Holiday weekend would soon be here, and she should have been going to Brittany with François.

"Arnold, I was to go to France," she had been forced to ask. "What is to happen?"

"I do not know. I would tell you if I knew anything, but I do not. Maria is coming to visit you this afternoon; she will know more."

Maria – she clutched at this straw. Surely Maria would not be so unkind as to forsake her now? She would help. "But the ballet, Arnold? What happened to the first night?"

"Postponed," he answered gently. "No one but you could dance the Nightingale. Diaghilev presented *Le Coq D'Or* instead with *Schéhérazade*."

Arabella could hold back no longer, but she asked her question of Gwendolen, not Arnold: "Are there no letters for me, no word, no telephone message from—"

"François?" Arnold looked genuinely sympathetic, as he answered for his sister. "No, my dear. Perhaps he is too appalled at what happened. Maria may know more."

Too appalled? What did he mean? It made no sense. Surely he would be at her side all the more, not stay away. The obvious answer then occurred to her. How would François know where she was? Arnold would not have told him; and although Monsieur Diaghilev had sent flowers to this house, there was every chance he would not have passed the address to François. After all, he wanted François with him in the coming weeks, not sitting at Arabella's side. She was not happy with this explanation, however, and continued to puzzle over it deeply, thankful that Maria was coming today.

Now that the physical pain was abating, fear was taking its place. How long would it be before she could dance again and be free? When François knew where she was, once she could at least walk again, they could be married, and live together.

194

Arnold was not an ogre: he loved her, he was not her gaoler, even though she knew he would wish her to stay here as long as possible in the hope that she might forget François. She must take care in what she said to him.

When Maria arrived, Gwen tactfully left them alone, to Arabella's relief, as she could hardly question Maria about François with Arnold's sister present.

"Oh, Maria, I'm so pleased to see you." To see her vigorous lively face and smart London clothes was a tonic.

"And I to see you, *chérie*," Maria said fondly. "How is the ankle?"

"The doctor says it will take several weeks to heal. It is not a straightforward break."

"But it will heal eventually?"

"Of course," Arabella answered with some surprise.

"*Bien.*" Maria dismissed the subject airily, but it left Arabella with the uneasy impression that Maria might have been implying that it *would* never heal – or never heal well enough for her to dance again. She struggled to put this new nightmare aside.

"What happened, Maria? How did I come to fall? Did I slip?" She had no clear memory of it, only of François ahead of her, and of something that stopped her – a shape, an image that would not clarify.

"No one knows exactly." Maria's voice was grave. "François is blaming himself, of course."

"Why?" Arabella was bewildered. Arnold might justly blame himself, but not François.

"Oh," Maria paused, "because he was hurrying to rush you to the stage for the third act." She smiled so brightly, however, that Arabella knew there was something she was holding back.

"Is that why he has not written? Or does he not know where I am? Tell me," she cried in anguish, as Maria did not reply.

"He does know where you are, so it must be because of his guilt." Maria frowned. "It's been a busy time, of course. He has had endless discussions with Sergei and Fokine about his future, and next year's programme."

"What about the future?" Arabella asked this with dread. The newspapers had been increasingly full of reports that Europe was on the brink of war, and Arnold was convinced that England might be drawn in. The death of the Austrian archduke in Sarajevo at the end of June might prove the tinderbox for war. The Ballets Russes had commitments after the holiday period on the Continent, and were to meet in Berlin on the first of October, but if Germany was at war by that time then everything would be in doubt. If François went to Italy with Diaghilev after the Breton holiday, he might not be able to return to England, or she be able to join him when she was fit.

"Sergei sees no reason why a war should interfere with his plans." Maria meant to be comforting, but it was making things worse.

"François was going to Brittany. Will he still do so?" Even as Arabella spoke, she guessed what was coming.

"Yes," Maria said gently, "and because of your accident, François has asked me to go with him to discuss a new ballet."

"But what about me?" Arabella knew her pitiful cry sounded childish, but she could not help it. Something was wrong. Something they were keeping from her. A *new* ballet? Discussing it with *Maria*? All her suspicions flooded back, but even if Maria was seizing the chance of furthering her own career, it didn't explain why François had not come to see her or written.

"Darling, your ankle keeps you here for a while. François is heartbroken, but he has to go."

"Does he *really* know where I am?"

"He knows you are here with Arnold's sister."

"But not of my free will, and only for a few more days. You must tell him that, Maria, you must. Oh please, take me with you today."

"Oh Arabella, if I could I would, but your ankle won't permit travel."

"Then ask François to come here!" She was in agony.

Maria sighed. "He sends his love. Oh, Arabella, I suppose I should tell you. It *is* guilt keeps him from you. He believes your foot tripped over his, and that is how you came to fall. He cannot be sure because it happened so quickly. Do you recall anything?"

"I felt something." Arabella replied miserably, "but what I do not know."

"Then it could have been François," Maria said quietly.

"But I will write to him, and tell him nothing matters save that we should be together."

Arabella immediately seized her writing paper and began to scribble a note. "François, my love, please, *please* come to me," she began. When she had dashed it off, she put it in an envelope and gave it to Maria.

"Remember he is very busy." Maria gently kissed her cheek. "Get well soon, Arabella, for François' sake. He needs you, for the ballet."

"I should like to see the doctor again, if you please, Arnold." Arabella spoke as firmly as she dared when Arnold paid his next visit a week later. He had been planning to come on the Bank Holiday, but the war situation had made it impossible. Now the worst had happened, for war had not only broken out between Austria, Germany, Russia and France, but England too had entered after Germany had invaded neutral Belgium. Gwendolen was agog with gossip about how the village was emptying of menfolk as reservists were called up and other men volunteered. This set up a new worry. What if François had to join the French army?

Dr Hastings arrived from London two days later but, eminent though he was, Arabella wasn't sure she liked him. Arnold assured her she was receiving the best advice, however, and Sergei Diaghilev had apparently insisted on paying all the bills. He had chosen Dr Hastings himself.

She ignored the doctor's pleasantries, for there was too much on her mind. "I know Mr Diaghilev will have asked you this question, and I wish to ask it too. How bad is my ankle? When shall I dance again? I mean really dance, not just hobble."

"We do not know as yet, young lady. Everything depends on how well it mends." He was too soothing for her taste.

"But you must be able to compare it with other breaks. You must have attended other ballet dancers, if Mr Diaghilev asked you to look after me. Have others danced after such a break as mine?"

"In *caractère* parts, sometimes."

"But as prima ballerinas?" Arabella faltered, horrified at the implications of what he said.

"Everything is possible, for those who have hope." He spoke cheerily, as though this was his usual reassurance of patients in her position.

197

She controlled her anger. "How much hope shall I need to have, doctor? Tell me, if you please."

He sighed. "A great deal, my dear. It was a bad break; the bone was shattered. It is, I fear, probable that you will never dance again."

Twelve

I will dance again, I *will* . . . Arabella limped round the room, trying not to reveal how painful it was, even with a stick. She did not speak her determination aloud, for Gwen was watching anxiously. Too anxiously, and Arabella was beginning to feel like an over-cosseted kitten.

"Not too soon, Arabella, please," Gwen pleaded. "Arnold tells me of so many dancers in your position who return too early to the stage."

"It is not too soon, Gwen." Arabella tried to smile, for she was truly grateful for Gwen's care. She tried a simple first position with her feet, and then cautiously took her right leg forward for a fourth. Even though she kept the weight of her body on the left foot, the right still objected strongly at being turned, and this time she did wince, giving up the attempt. She felt as though she were a six-year-old again, going for her first lesson with Miss Ermyntrude Pictson; and Miss Pictson's stern eye would certainly not have approved of her present fourth position.

What would she do if she could not return to the stage for some time? She refused even to contemplate the possibility that Dr Hastings was right and that it might never happen. If only François would come to her, or she could reach him, they could still marry; she could work with him on his choreography until she was fit again. But she had heard nothing since he and Maria left for France, and it was already late in August. Diaghilev would still be in Italy with Léonide Miassin and Maître Cecchetti, and François, she presumed, was probably with them.

It was scarcely surprising that she had heard nothing, now that war had broken out. Since the beginning of August England had gone mad with patriotic fervour and righteous indignation over Belgium's plight. Sometimes Gwen took her to the village in the governess cart, and Arabella could hear and see war fever

199

for herself. The only talk was of war, of who had gone and who had stayed; of the hardship it was already causing for families suddenly deprived of their menfolk's wages, with no arrangements made for their womenfolk to receive an allowance; and of the ever-soaring price of food. It wasn't only the men who were eager to help in the war effort, either, for women too were beginning to organise their own services in the nursing field, since there was sure to be need of them, even if, as expected, the war turned out to be a short one.

It would be over by Christmas, or so they were all saying, yet *The Times* had published reports today of a battle near Mons, which meant the Germans had advanced a long way. Though the report claimed it had gone well for the British Expeditionary Force, she had noticed there was no mention of the German armies retreating.

It seemed very unlikely now that the Ballets Russes would be reassembling in Berlin as planned. Russia after all was France's ally, not Germany's. Perhaps Diaghilev would return to St Petersburg instead? It seemed the obvious solution. Monsieur Fokine had already done so, according to Arnold, and in his view was unlikely to work with Diaghilev much longer. Arnold had also told her that Diaghilev had been on the verge of reconciliation with Nijinsky in July, but that it had had to be postponed since Fokine was still his ballet-master.

Now war had come, everything might change. Art, like everything else, had to bow to the restrictions of war. But if, Arabella reasoned, Nijinsky could not join Diaghilev, he would be left without a choreographer which made it all the more probable that he had summoned François to join him in Italy. His new protégé Miassin was to have lessons to improve his dancing, but he could not fill the gap left by Fokine's departure. And where was Maria? Presumably, like Fokine, she must have returned to Russia after the Breton holiday, although travel was not easy. Arnold had told Arabella that Karsavina, who had delayed her journey back, had not yet arrived there. In fact she had just been forced to return to England to try yet another route home.

She herself must join François in Italy, Arabella decided, immediately her ankle was fit enough to begin practice again. The battle had been in the north of France and Belgium, not Italy, and so she must be able to travel there somehow. She was quite sure Sergei would think of some way for the Ballets Russes to continue performing, if the planned German tour did not go ahead.

Arabella was aware that letters were still coming through from the Continent, and yet she had received none. She knew François must be very busy, and was probably expecting her to join him at any moment, but the coldness of her solitude began to bite increasingly into her. The only solution was to get her ankle strong as soon as possible.

As the weeks went by, it gained strength, and Dr Hastings seemed pleased with her progress when he came on his monthly visit in mid-September. The plaster had gone by that time, and a supporting bandage bound it. Eager as she was to believe him, however, the over-enthusiasm of his voice made her fear it was still false cheer.

She persevered, however, and by October was able to show her prowess proudly to Arnold. "Look, my first *jété!*"

No matter that she hit the floor awkwardly, so much so that Gwen cried out in alarm. She had done it, and, excited, she looked to them for approval.

"Bravo," Gwen said heartily. *Too* heartily.

"Take care, my dear, not too fast," was Arnold's warning. This annoyed her, for he should be encouraging her.

"Will you play for me, Arnold? I am ready to try to dance to music now." Arabella had been practising hard at an improvised barre, often when Gwen took her afternoon rest so that the older woman should not know how many hours she put in. "I shall dance a solo from Act One of *The Unicorn*," she added. It might seem tactless, but she must make her position clear. This fall had changed nothing. And seeing his anxious face, she added firmly, "I can do it, Arnold."

She had become increasingly anxious both at the lack of news from François, and about the fact that the news from the war front was not good. The Germans had been turned back before Paris fell, but with winter fast approaching there was little sign of any resolution to the conflict. On the contrary, more and more men were leaving to fight, and the prices of food were increasingly higher still despite the Government's strict measures to control them. Gwen was constantly in discussion with her housekeeper. Hoarding was unpatriotic, but tempting in these times with the seaways threatened by the German fleet, and Arabella suspected the housekeeper was quietly tucking things away.

In addition, she was worried that she was beginning to feel as though she were part of this household. Gwen would like nothing more, she realised, but Arabella knew her life did not belong here. Her life and her art were bound up with François', and she must reach Italy. How this was to be managed, since she still did not know where he was, occupied all her thoughts now. Three weeks ago she had written a careful letter to François' parents, but there had been no reply. She told herself that they would have sent it on to him, but her frustration grew.

As she danced the solo from *The Unicorn*, Arabella knew she had to remember that Arnold and even Gwen were biased. Arnold loved her, and would not easily relinquish her to François, and Gwen, apart from doing everything Arnold asked of her, also had her reasons for wanting her to stay. Arabella had to be firm. "I want the *artist* in you, Arnold, to tell me how good I am. Is Petrovna still in me, or merely a cart-horse? You will know."

He kissed her cheek. "The man is banished. The artist will tell you the truth, Arabella."

He laid down a rough carpet on the drawing-room floor to minimise the risk if she fell again, which she did not like, although she knew it was sensible. Then she closed her eyes as the music began. Arnold's playing lacked the heart and emotion that François had put into it, but nevertheless the music caught her by the throat, chokingly, with its sensuous familiarity. It was a short solo, and not technically difficult, since Lilith had to convey simplicity. She closed her eyes, and let the Nightingale speak to her. When Arnold stopped playing, Arabella knew she had done well, and waited for their verdict.

Gwen clapped, and Arnold rose quickly to come to her. "No cart-horse, my love; not even a fine thoroughbred. Petrovna is still in you, but—" He hesitated, and her hopes crashed. "So far to go," he finished briskly.

"I will practise. I heard Cecchetti was going to Italy to give Miassin lessons. I plan to go to join them."

"Arabella!" he exclaimed. "Dr Hastings would never allow it. It was a bad break, and you are not yet ready for the stage. And even Diaghilev would not want you there in time of war. You would be a liability."

"A liability?" Despite her intention to take his verdict objectively, she found herself stiffening. "You mean you still believe I shall not dance again, Arnold, that I shall never be good enough?"

"My love, I do believe that, but with all my heart I wish I didn't."

Only the thought of François kept Arabella's resolution aflame now. Over the following weeks she practised even harder, determined to prove Arnold wrong, although she was careful to avoid Gwen's accusing eye. Still she heard nothing from François, nor even Maria. Surely in all this time they could have managed to get some message to her? It was December; four whole months had passed without a word, and even though the war was far from reaching a conclusion, they should have been able to contact her somehow. What was she to do? Even in the torture of her position, she knew she had to solve this for herself, for Arnold was not her friend in this.

She was not a prisoner in this house, Arabella reasoned; she had money of her own. She had received some money from Diaghilev, enough to save. First, then, came the question of her dancing. Arnold might not think he was biased, but he was, and therefore she must take a second opinion. She would go to London and without his or Gwen's knowledge.

The theatres in London had been closed for a time after the outbreak of war, and although they had reopened, Covent Garden was no longer mounting ballet and opera productions. Indeed, it was said it was to be a government store. She ruminated for a while, then remembered a school of dancing in Mecklenburg Street near Russell Square, which was not intended for classical ballet studies but for musical comedy. Nevertheless its principal, Miss Payne, whom she had met, knew a great deal about ballet. Miss Payne would tell her the truth, perhaps even coach her back to fitness. One morning, therefore, Arabella crept from the house early, leaving a note for Gwen telling her she would return by evening, and, stung by the brisk morning air, walked to the railway station.

She drew deep breaths of fresh air, feeling free for the first time in months. She must dance again, she *must*, for François and for herself. The train crawled to London with a pace that had become usual since war broke out, for in Kent especially many trains were used for troops. When eventually she arrived it was to a London she hardly recognised. Gone were the smart ladies and gentlemen of town; instead there were uniforms everywhere, and an air of brisk business. Charing Cross was crowded with families in the midst of farewells or reunions.

Miss Payne put her through a rigorous test, at the end of which Arabella danced a solo to the music of *Swan Lake*, aware of the teacher's non-committal face. After Miss Payne stopped playing, however, she nodded slowly. "Were I George Edwardes or Robert Courtneidge, Miss Peters, I would employ you immediately."

"But," Arabella asked, heart in mouth, "if you were Monsieur Fokine, or Sergei Diaghilev, what then?"

"You have not been practising as well as you should, you tell me, since it is not possible where you are living. However, I saw you dance at the Palace with Pavlova, and at Drury Lane in *Le Coq d'Or*, and it seems to me – though I am not sure – that your style is still there. Indeed, why should it not be? Style comes from the heart, not the feet, and from what I see of the technical ability in your feet I believe that it will improve to match your style, given time and practice."

"Miss Payne, I could kiss you." Arabella was in tears with relief.

"Please do," Miss Payne graciously suggested.

It was the encouragement Arabella needed, and in the train going home she immediately began to make plans. She would write to Monsieur Fokine at the Maryinsky, since he would know where Diaghilev was, as well as to Diaghilev's favourite hotel in Florence. Or should she just go there? No; that would be too foolish, even in her enthusiasm to join François, for travelling alone in time of war, was not sensible, and she knew Monsieur Fokine would give her what help he could.

Full of excitement, she hurried back along the lanes to Gwen's home, although her ankle was beginning to ache now. No longer did it seem as though it were a prison, for the caged bird was choosing to return after its taste of freedom. There was hope now, for Dr Hastings had been wrong. Arnold had been wrong, too: she *would* dance again. The music was already bubbling inside her, waiting to explode into movement. Just a little more patience . . .

As she rang the bell, Arabella nerved herself to apologise to

Gwen, who would be annoyed at her surreptitious departure. It would not be hard, for she felt she could cope with anything now. When the maid opened the door, however, the first person she saw was Arnold coming into the entrance hall to meet her. Excellent, she thought; she could tell them both her plans, and this time she would not be swayed from them.

"What are you doing here, Arnold?" she cried gaily. It was not his usual visiting day. "I am sorry not to have been here, but, oh, Arnold, I have been to London. I must tell you and Gwen about it." She hurried into the drawing room where she knew Gwen would be taking tea, and Arnold followed.

"I shall dance again," she cried triumphantly, doing a *pirouette* for their benefit. "I have been to London and taken an expert opinion. Miss Payne believes with time and practice I will dance as well as ever. Isn't that splendid?"

To her dismay, they did not seem to think so. Gwen promptly burst into tears, and Arnold looked very grave. Surely they could not be that offended at her behaviour?

"I am sorry,' she said uncertainly, remembering she hadn't yet apologised to Gwen, "for not telling you of my plans. I feared—"

Arnold lifted his hand to stop her, though he was looking at her kindly. "We are not annoyed, Arabella, quite the contrary. I'm delighted, and I'm sure Gwen is too, that you have such good news to sustain you."

Sustain? What did he mean? A lurch of doubt – or was it fear? – seized her.

"I too have news," Arnold continued, "and I am afraid – my dearest, please sit, for this will be a terrible shock for you."

"What will? Tell me!' she cried. "My parents?"

It was Gwen who told her. "No. It's François, Arabella. He is married."

Married? *Married?* Arabella stared at her, waiting for her to correct her mistake. Gwen did not; she did nothing but give hiccuping sobs.

"This is some misunderstanding," Arabella said uncertainly. "How can he be married? He is to marry me."

"He married in Italy a month ago."

"No." Arabella felt very faint. "Either this is a malicious

rumour or your information is wrong. I am the one he loves. I am to marry him. It is arranged."

"I am afraid there is no mistake, Arabella." Arnold came to sit by her, putting his arm round her, and she did not resist it. For the moment, it was giving her comfort.

"But whom has he married?" The dark shadows of Morgana closed in on her in triumph. François, she and the ballet had been one, but now they were split in two for ever.

"He has married Maria."

*   *   *

Tara was becoming used to the commuting life, which was more bearable now that it was only for three days a week. Where better to mark time than her parents' home? She could keep up her work in the office, and still call in for the occasional evening at Music and Mime to do the books, even though it was an ordeal. Did she hope or dread she would see Josh on these occasions? Usually it proved a mixture of the two. When she saw him, an invisible mask would slip over his face, although he was always polite and helpful – disastrously so, in fact, for nothing could have underlined their separation more vividly.

She spent the other two weekdays and the weekends helping in the garden centre and, to her surprise, found herself enjoying it. Broken hearts could find welcome poultices in messing around with muddy earth. It also gave her opportunities to talk to her parents at length, which at first she did not welcome, but that too changed.

"To what do we owe this undoubted pleasure?" her father had asked mildly, at dinner, when she had announced her intention of moving back again.

"Love," inserted her mother, dishing out some concoction that looked like left-over vegetable pie.

"Partly," Tara amended stiffly.

That interchange had later led to a mother-daughter talk, though with Margaret this was less of a tea-and-sympathy chat, and more of a follow-me-round-the-greenhouse talk on the trot.

"Is this love problem due to those awful unicorns?" Margaret asked.

Tara gave her the logical answer. "I can't see how my affair with Josh could be influenced by something that happened donkey's years ago to two different people."

"Don't kid me, Tara. I've had enough of unicorns from my mother to recognise them baring their horns a mile off."

"I thought you and Giselle never talked about it."

"She tried to, oh, she tried. I was dragged off to ballet lessons at five, and I hated them. I only wanted to be messing around with flowers, but I had to gallop around *jétéing* and *pliéing* until I was seven before she'd believe me. She was disappointed in me. Not fair when I took after my father as well as my mother, and when even *she* hadn't inherited Arabella's gifts."

"Your father?" Tara queried tentatively, wondering whether her mother was at long last going to admit the truth.

No, she wasn't. "Peter Thompkins was solidly attached to terra firma. That's why I loved him."

So this was still a no-go area, Tara quickly realised. Well, she would not intrude. Unicorns were a different matter, however, for they concerned *her*. Increasingly she knew that the earlier answer she had given her mother wasn't true. The affair between herself and Josh *was* being influenced by Arabella and François. In the superficial sense, it had begun with Josh's unicorn dance, and had centred on that ever since. There was a deeper sense in which they were connected, however, and one which up till now she had been unwilling to fully acknowledge. She had become so involved with her ancestress's story that she now felt it deep inside her as though it had its own existence. It was a big step, however, to acknowledge that there really was a force motivated by someone or something other than herself. Scary. Even now she couldn't do it, though just in case, her thoughts added a mental apology. "I'm sorry, Arabella."

Tara decided to compromise. She had realised that as yet she and Josh – if there were still such a couple – had no idea how the love of Arabella for François Santine had ended. "I'll find out," she vowed, although with her mother she would have to tread carefully, and without Josh the whole subject was painful.

"Why did you try so hard to keep unicorns in any shape or form away from me when I was young?" she asked lightly.

"Really want to know?"

"Yes."

"I didn't want you to be influenced, as I had been. If there was anything in the rubbish that my mother believed, I reasoned it would come out sooner or later of its own accord, without my having to shove those blessed unicorns under your nose all the time. Even so, I was seriously alarmed when you used to endlessly recite 'The Lion and the Unicorn'. That was when you were about eight. You even wrote it out and pinned it on your wall."

Had she? Tara had completely forgotten, but something must have jolted the image back to life for it to have returned to haunt her so recently.

"Then you forgot it, and I relaxed," her mother continued. "I thought I was safe once you reached your twenties and took up tax work. And now this happens. Great!"

"You realise now I've no option. I have to know more."

"Why?" Her mother presented a stone wall.

"Because Josh is mixed up with it, and ghastly though the situation is between us, my only hope of sorting things out is through what you call those blessed unicorns. And I want Josh."

"Sure?"

"Oh yes."

Margaret sighed. "OK. Overtures and beginners please."

"Did you ever meet Arabella?"

"I was only six when my mother left home and me, and went with Arabella to her Brittany home to live."

"But I thought—"

"There was a third in the happy party," Margaret interrupted, "but it's Arabella you want to know about."

Of course there had been a third: Antoine, who apparently still must not be mentioned by name. But Arabella's story was beginning to make sense. She owned the house in Brittany, and Giselle had gone there to live with her and Antoine.

"Arabella died in the fifties, and I only saw her once after my mother left. I've vague memories of having liked her, but being nervous of her too. Even at my young age I could sense that she was hoping for something from me too. I remember being forced to show off my ghastly ballet steps before her, and though she cuddled me afterwards, I knew I'd disappointed her too. Come to think of it, I believe Arabella recited 'The Lion and the Unicorn' to me. In her London house she had a special room full of ballet and unicorn pictures, and it didn't take long before I loathed unicorns as much as ballet. When I went to see her in

Brittany that once, the first thing she took me to see was another boring unicorn room. Can you blame me for not wanting to foist the same ordeal on you, once you'd shown no aptitude for ballet either?"

"Inside I did." Tara laughed. "Inside, I was Fonteyn, Karsavina, Markova, all in one."

"And Petrovna?" her mother asked quietly. "Is she inside?"

"Yes." Tara half choked on the word, through the sheer unexpectedness of her mother's understanding of what she was going through.

"Then go to my mother, and *tell* her that. Only she can help you, Tara, not me."

"Does she know the story's end?"

"Oh yes, but she'll only tell you when she's ready."

"Why don't you see her more?" Tara plunged awkwardly into alien territory, but after a moment her mother replied:

"It was sad really. It was beastly ballet again. She asked me if I wanted to leave Papa and come to Brittany, but I reasoned that if I went with her I'd be stuck with ballet and unicorns and the memory of my disappointing her for the rest of my life. If I stayed with my father, I wouldn't have to do ballet ever again. Moreover, my father thought everything I did was wonderful. He had no expectations, no false hopes. That's why I stayed. Quite logical for a six-year-old."

"But why not see Giselle now?"

"My dear, you should know enough about families by now to know I would *still* disappoint her. I, as she would put it so sweetly, so lethally, am not the one."

*   *   *

She must have fainted. Arabella opened her eyes to find that she was in bed and that Arnold was sitting in the chair at her side. The nightmare consumed her again, and she struggled to sit up. Pride would not let her consciously reveal how deep her wound was. Like the Nightingale in François' ballet, she would perish alone. Only in the ballet had she been brought to life again, but there was no hope of that for her now. She might live on physically, but the song inside her was silenced for ever.

Arnold must have seen the misery on her face, however, for

209

he said gently, "You know now you may dance again. Is that not some compensation?"

His words made no sense. "What has dancing to do with it?"

"Art is *always* consolation. As I know myself."

She was immediately contrite. "I am sorry, Arnold. It is the shock. If you would leave me for a while, I shall decide what to do."

"Very well, but let me first repeat what I said to you once. I will write for you such music as I can to take away your grief: ballet, musical comedy, whatever you desire, and—"

"Later, Arnold. It is too soon."

He flushed, kissed her hand, and left her, to her great relief. After he had gone, she managed to propel what now seemed a leaden body out of bed to sit in the armchair by the window looking out over the grounds. It was already dark, but she drew the curtains back. Out there were the twinkling stars like the hush of an audience waiting for the ballet to begin. Her ballet was over. She could dance if she wished, life had ordained, but not have François.

Perhaps the news was not true? Arabella grasped this straw for a moment. After all, Arnold had believed Dr Hastings' false verdict, so perhaps this gossip too was distorted through the difficulty of obtaining news from war-torn Europe. Perhaps François and Maria were merely partnering each other in the Ballets Russes company. In her heart, however, Arabella knew it was a vain hope. For whatever reason, François had married. It explained so many things: his silence and lack of contact, the compassion with which people spoke to her – and Maria.

She remembered that François had once told her he and Maria had almost become lovers. Had that "almost" been a strong enough possibility that merely her own absence and Maria's presence had wrought such a change in him? No, she could not believe it; she would not. This was like some spell of Morgana's to take Galymede for herself. Could Maria, like Morgana, have wanted this all along, pretending to be her friend so that she could remain close to François? This terrible thought crossed Arabella's mind, and would not go. After all, it had been Maria who warned her that François might be in love not with Arabella herself, but with a heroine for the dreams in his head. After her accident, perhaps he too had realised that, and married Maria, so that she might provide a different inspiration. It had been Maria, too, who had hinted there might be some truth in the story of Diaghilev's love for François. And Maria who held secret discussions with Arnold. Arabella was appalled at the way her thoughts were running. Surely they were ridiculous. But something had happened since her accident, something had made François turn from her. Perhaps it was just his guilt at believing himself responsible for it, a guilt he could not face. Just as she had been guilty of wounding him so deeply over the slurs about his friendship with Diaghilev.

It was the only explanation that made sense. This was no spell cast by others. Arabella could not blame Arnold, nor could she blame Maria; only herself and François were involved. She had been blinded with love and so had he. Both of them had believed the chains of love so strong that nothing could break them. Now François, of his own volition, had destroyed his own, yet left hers intact for ever.

                    *   *   *

How could Josh do this to her? He must have known how Tara would feel, arriving at the theatre for a business session only to be told by the caretaker that it had been switched to Josh's flat in Blackheath. The change had been made for the best of reasons, no doubt, but how did he think she'd feel sitting there like a fish out of water?

Tara did her best to pull herself together once on the train. She couldn't follow her instincts and not go, for she was a linchpin of this meeting about joint finances. It had been agreed that Music and Mime and the ABC should merge in time for the autumn programme, which meant some swift work, so surely she could manage to put a professional mask over her private feelings for a couple of hours . . . Who was she kidding? The mask didn't seem to fit too well nowadays.

In the event, she managed to slip it into place quite effectively, chiefly because she was so busy looking at the books that David, the ABC's finance director, had brought with him that there was no time for much else. Josh didn't appear to have put his stone-wall mask on either, and was as animated and enthusiastic as she had ever seen him. Damn him, a little

211

voice said inside her, couldn't he even look a *little* sad? Sybille was glowing as well, so her new relationship with Michael must be prospering.

"The September finances will take some working out, with the new three-acter," David pointed out.

"What new three-acter?" Tara asked casually.

It was he who replied, not Josh, and no wonder. "*The Unicorn and the Nightingale*. It's an expansion of the one-act ballet Josh wrote in April. You'll like it. Come and watch a rehearsal."

He had spoken innocently; it was Josh who looked guilty. And he damned well should, too. After all, she was involved with this.

When he remained silent, she said coolly: "I'm sure you've cleared the copyright situation, as you said you would, Josh."

David looked surprised. "Have you, Josh?"

Embarrassment was written all over his face. "I was given the score by Prince's daughter, who was pleased to have it revived. Anyway, he's been dead over fifty years, which is the normal term."

Tara donned a look of anxiety. It was petty, but oh how she enjoyed it. "No longer, I'm afraid. The current legal position is that as Arnold died in 1939, copyright wouldn't expire until 2009."

"I'll get written permission," Josh answered curtly. "You know as well as I do that Giselle would never refuse—"

Now was her big moment, for he was clearly expecting her to take revenge by blocking copyright. She cut him short. "No, Josh. *I* will get the clearance for you. You can depend on me."

He did not reply. David was looking slightly mystified, and Sybille was clearly keeping well out of it.

Tara rose to slip into the bathroom as the meeting ended, complacently happy that she had scored one tiny point. How dare Josh not tell her his plans had been brought forward? Did he no longer have any feelings for her? She was still smouldering as she washed her hands.

Suddenly her eye fell on two electric toothbrushes standing side by side. *Two?* And then she saw a hairbrush and other items which she recognised all too easily, and of which there were enough to make clear this was no one-night convenient stopover in a second bedroom.

They were Sybille's.

*   *   *

"Nurse Peters!"

Arabella eased her aching back as Sister approached. She had been a VAD now for six months, and did not regret her decision to take up hospital work, even though there was far less soothing of wounded brows than of scrubbing endless floors and wheeling trolleys. She welcomed her exhaustion like a friend, however, for it kept her mind off her own heartbreak.

She had had two choices: to dance, either on Arnold's terms or her own, or to turn her back on the stage by following the example of so many and training as a VAD. The course had been short and skimpy, and so she was learning on the job at Shooters Hill hospital, a major centre for wounded soldiers. There were many, for the war, far from ending at Christmas, had broken out with renewed ferocity in the spring in an effort to break the deadlock.

Her coming here had solved decision number two: where to live. She knew she could have remained with Gwen, or returned to her parents, with whom she was partially reconciled, although on her own terms: she would lead her own life. She had decided against both options, however. At Shooters Hill she could live in lodgings with the other VADs, and lose herself in physical work until she was so tired that she no longer thought of dance. Every step would have led her thoughts to François had she chosen to return to ballet, whereas now it was dulled by the plight of the wounded men she was helping to care for.

Arnold had been annoyed at her decision, pointing out that she could not hope to dance in classical ballet again without practice, and that she was ruining her strength. Arabella thanked him, but ignored his strictures.

She had plucked up courage to ask him, however, where François and Maria were, but he had claimed he did not know. Reluctantly she believed him, for all her own enquiries in London had proved fruitless. There was talk that Diaghilev was in Switzerland, of trips to Paris and plans for an American

213

tour, but no word of François. Such personal talk as there was of the Ballets Russes centred on Diaghilev's developing relationship with Léonide Miassin, who, it was said, was not only developing into a fine dancer, but was being encouraged by Sergei to take up choreography. There had been no word of François in regard to that either.

The work in the hospital had opened her eyes to the horrors of war, to which the terrible wounds of the soldiers bore witness. The sight of amputated limbs was commonplace, and it was sometimes one of her tasks to remove them from the room afterwards. At first she had been sick, then she had steeled herself. Those who had lost legs moved her greatly. She was conscious that she still had both of hers, and yet she had chosen not to use them to the full. She decided that she must do more than the minimum practice she allowed herself, that she should use her talent for the good of others, and so, to Sister's disapproval – which was overruled by Matron – she would sometimes give a performance of *The Dying Swan*, or, in lighter vein, *Coquetterie de Columbine*. Her favourite was *La Rose Mourante*, however. No one could match Pavlova's performance, but her audience here was starved of diversions from their injuries. If that audience wanted to admire her body as well as her artistry, she saw no harm in it.

When the news filtered through in the autumn of 1915 about the disaster at Loos, however, Arabella knew her time at Shooters Hill was over. She wanted to be nearer the war, far away from the painful memories of England and closer to the battlefields. She would apply to the Red Cross for an immediate transfer to France.

*   *   *

"I think I'll go to France earlier than I planned." Tara tried to sound casual on her return to Lewes after that terrible evening at Josh's flat. "Maybe next week." She would see Giselle, get her written consent for the ballet, and, more importantly, carry out her own agenda. She had another responsibility: to Arabella. She felt she was abandoning her, had disappointed her in having parted, even involuntarily, from Josh – and it had, she acknowledged, been at least partly her fault. She had tried to live in both camps at once, had been afraid to take the plunge. If ever amends were to be made to Arabella (she dared not even think of Josh) then she should know what she was dealing with. So far she knew little of Arabella's story, and Giselle was the only person who could tell her more.

"Tell me what's wrong, Tara. *Please.*" Her mother had ignored the casual note in Tara's voice, and picked up the underlying anxiety.

Rather to her own amazement, Tara did. "Another slight reverse in the love department. I think Sybille has moved in with Josh. He's replaced me very quickly, hasn't he?"

"I don't understand." Margaret frowned. "You told me Sybille had moved one of the other members of Music and Mime in with her."

"It must have gone wrong."

"What about William? Will you go back to him?"

"Absolutely not."

"Understood. Very well, tell me about this Sybille, then. I can't say I took to her much from what you told me, though she was very pleasant on the one occasion I met her."

"Josh once said that he and she had had an affair that didn't quite happen. Now it appears to have done so," Tara said bitterly.

"Did she object to Josh falling for you?"

"She never did seem to." Tara considered this carefully. Maybe her mother had got to the heart of it. Or maybe not. "After all, she asked me to move in with her, we liked each other, and there was never any trouble."

"Odd."

Tara stared at her mother. "Unusual," she amended, "but she was intending to move Michael in with her, not Josh. Or so she said." But then Sybille had said a lot of things. And Sybille had been found closeted with William – who had met her in Sussex last summer.

William and the conference – that was how he could have known the ballet dates in advance. William the Rottweiler, who never let go. Tara felt sick; she was sure she had the truth of it now. Michael was a blind; Josh was Sybille's chief objective. "Anyway, it's blown up," Tara continued carefully, "because Josh has thoughtfully arranged to put on his full version of the Unicorn ballet much earlier than planned. I gave in to temptation and implied I could stop the whole thing through copyright refusal for the score."

"And would you?"

"No. It gave me great pleasure to go on to say I'd help all I could. For one thing, Giselle would murder me if I didn't, and second—"

"What?" her mother asked when Tara broke off.

"It would seem like murdering Arabella."

"Then," her mother replied slowly, "you *must* get Giselle to tell you what she knows."

"And if she won't?"

"She will. I'm coming with you to make sure she does."

Thirteen

How could he look just the same, strolling casually towards her, just as if nothing had happened? What was Josh doing here, anyway? Even as hope refused to be crushed, Tara felt her hackles rising. The garden centre, if nowhere else, was *her* territory, yet here he was sauntering along the path between the pots of overgrown lavender and the last of the roses. His demeanour allowed her to harbour a sudden fantasy that nothing *had* happened, that he had come to apologise, to tell her he had come to his senses, that he needed her and loved her. Some hopes.

She and her mother were in the throes of preparing the garden centre to be left in the hands of her father while they went to France. Her mother was continuously on the go, potting up, planting, trimming, sowing, simultaneously getting ready for the autumn season while tenderly nursing the last of the summer flowers, shrubs and herbs. The last person Tara had expected to interrupt the turmoil was Josh.

She straightened up warily. She was hardly going to throw herself into his arms, whatever his mission here was. She would let him do the running.

"Do you have a few moments to talk?" he asked, as casually as though he had found himself passing the door and dropped in for a chat with an old acquaintance.

"Certainly." She nearly added, "Romantic bowery nook or in the office?" but bit it back, puzzled that her hackles seemed to be growing into a protective hedge. She led the way to the small coffee shop, run by dozy Tricia, who wouldn't notice anything odd, whether she and Josh made love on the floor or fought each other all around the town like the lion and the—

She stopped herself instantly. *No* unicorns. Not till Josh had explained why he had come. All the same, she admitted to

217

herself, their relationship *was* turning into a battle. Sometimes, even today, it was hard to remember their earlier passion, and that frightened her.

She bought two coffees and a sticky bun for Josh, and sat down, pretending a nonchalance she did not feel.

"I thought I should come before you left for Brittany."

So he knew – had guessed? – about her planned visit. She wasn't going to ask which.

"You could have telephoned first," she pointed out.

Josh was taken aback. "I could, but I felt I should explain—"

That was too much. "Yes, why don't you try that," she whipped back.

"If you'll give me a chance. The ballet—"

"The ballet?" she echoed stupidly. Seeing Josh here, all she could now think of was his duplicity over Sybille – and he was *still* only interested in the ballet.

"You seem surprised," he said drily. "Sorry it's left so little impression on you. I wanted to tell you there's no need for you to go to Brittany. I've already explained to Giselle."

"No need?" Tara seemed incapable of anything but repeating his words. So much for keeping the upper hand. The defensive hedge inside her rapidly made way for an offensive. How dared he speak to Giselle before her? That explained his knowledge of her plans – but, her mind suddenly cleared, how odd it was of Giselle not to have mentioned it to her. Tara had spoken to her on the phone only last night. Although it wasn't so odd, she supposed, if Josh had given her the impression all was well between them – the snake!

"The board's decided it would better not to use any of the Arnold Prince music."

"What on earth do you mean?" This didn't make any sense at all. "You mean you're scrapping the ballet?"

"No. We're not using the Arnold Prince score, that's all."

"You're dancing around to silence?" she flared out.

"Grow up, Tara."

Fool, she told herself, to have been tempted by the cheap comeback. There was a certain amount of cunning involved in trapping unicorns. Either the lion leapt behind a tree at the last moment so that the unicorn impaled himself with his horn chasing after him, or one provided a chaste virgin for him in whose lap to lay his head. Or not so chaste. She remembered the sly look in the said maiden's face in the New York tapestries of the hunt of the unicorn. Sybille to a tee. She'd twisted Josh round her little finger, and fooled her, Tara.

"Though in a way you're right," Josh conceded. "We've decided to do it as a voice mime, with occasional music and dance to established tunes. It's a great idea. The story will be the same, and the dancing won't be inhibited by the period score."

"When you say the board, you mean *you've* decided, with their approval."

"Yes."

"How could you, Josh? Abandon the ballet if you must, but to do it on your own, without me, after all our work on it, is a betrayal – of me, of Arabella, of François." It was a sad statement rather than a plea.

He stared at her, and for a moment she thought that if only she made the slightest movement towards him, he would be in her arms. But if he had any intention of coming to her, the moment quickly passed. "The copyright for the choreography, or what I'm using of the original, is mine remember? I am François' descendant. Nothing else is relevant now," he said flatly.

"His notes were in my grandmother's possession."

"Not all of them, and in any case that has nothing to do with copyright, unless she has documentation conveying it to Arabella or her family."

"What's happened, Josh?" Tara felt near to tears, the hedge trampled down with a few brief words. "It began so well. What's happened?"

"I don't know, Tara." Josh looked at her for a moment with the familiar eyes of the Josh who loved her. "I wish I did. Perhaps the lady and the statue just waited too long."

He was carved of stone, and she would grow grey and old without knowing his love again, without feeling his arms around her.

"Then I might as well return to William." What on earth was she saying? She had no intention of ever going back to him, but pride stopped her saying so, after her flat statement.

When he said nothing, Tara continued, "After all, you have Sybille. I gather she's moved in with you." She was devoid of pride now. She had conquered it sufficiently to ask Michael, when she saw him at a meeting, whether it was true that Sybille had moved in with Josh, or whether after all it was only a simple overnight stop. It was a delicate question, but he'd answered readily enough. "We didn't get anywhere," he'd told her ruefully. "Sybille's let me stay on in the house while she cavorts with Josh. Big deal."

Josh paused, then replied to her at last: "Yes; after all, I have Sybille."

No Josh, no ballet? Tara sat stunned. She supposed she must have subconsciously have been seeing the ballet as a last tenuous thread between herself and Josh, and now even that had been broken. Even if the ballet went ahead, it would no longer bear much relation to the Unicorn and the Nightingale of François and Arabella. Did that matter very much, now she and Josh had split up for good? Yes. There was still the unresolved story of long ago. She supposed she must fight for it, even if there seemed little hope for the ballet and none for her and Josh.

What shall I do, Arabella, what shall I say? Tara silently pleaded. If there's any hope, *tell* me. "The ending, Josh; what will you do about that in your voice mime?" Her question seemed to come from nowhere, taking her by surprise. Perhaps Arabella hadn't quite given up on her.

Josh looked uncertain for the first time. "I haven't got that far; this is all fairly new."

"Then I suggest you think about it," she suggested. "There's not much time, and François would hardly have wanted you to put on his ballet, even in your own adapted form, without the ending he envisaged."

"We don't know what that was." Now it was Josh on the defensive.

"I thought we agreed we did."

"That was in an unknown country, Tara, as you well know. The unhappy ending is much more in keeping with the mood of the story. We're all agreed on that."

"Not me. I don't agree."

"You're hardly involved."

"Oh, but I am. I'm still the Nightingale to your Unicorn." What the hell was she babbling? It wasn't usually her style to burst out with sentimental rubbish, even if she did harbour more than a suspicion it was true. As she glared at him in hostility, she felt she was speaking words to a script she hadn't written, and that Josh was quite right to stare at her in amazement.

"Very poetic, Tara, but unfortunately this unicorn has to get on with life."

"One with Sybille?" Now Tara was creeping back into the usual script. Arabella wouldn't have been so petty.

Hardly to her surprise, he did not answer that, and left her after formal goodbyes. Fighting on hardly seemed worthwhile now. What was the use of going to Brittany? There was no chance of Arabella's ballet being staged as she would have wanted it, and Tara had scored an own goal by raising queries over copyright. She didn't care any more, though. Josh had smashed any last remnants of fantasy that they had a future together, and she was by no means sure that she wanted one anyway. Perhaps at long last she was coming down to earth again, and beginning to see things clearly for the first time in sixteen months. It was William who represented happiness and security, and had done so for several years before Josh intervened. It was blindingly obvious that she should return to him, and she would speak to him now.

When his familiar voice answered on his office line, it sounded so right that she quelled a moment's doubt.

"William," she asked softly, "can we talk?"

He must have picked up the change of voice immediately. "Lunch?"

"I'm in Sussex."

"Ah, of course. The Josh and Sybille show. I'm sorry, Tara."

"Only a few bruises," she replied lightly, almost choking as the sympathy in his voice got to her. "Tomorrow?"

It was agreed, and only after she'd rung off did she remember that she now had to ring Giselle and tell her mother the visit was off. They had been due to leave tomorrow.

Margaret listened in silence to Tara's explanations. "You always liked William, and you were quite right. I'm a chip off your old block," Tara explained, certain of her ground. "No more of this ballet stuff. It's over, finished. You're happy here, and I shall be happy doing what I'm good at in the City. No need for us to beard Giselle now."

"Aren't you forgetting something?"

"What?"

"Me, daughter dear. *I* still need to get the ballet out of my

221

system. You may be able to shrug it off, but we're going as planned to see Giselle – the mad old cow," Margaret added to lighten the atmosphere. "You got me into this, Tara, and we're going to finish it together."

*   *   *

Arabella had known that her work in the General Hospital in Rouen would be even more demanding and emotionally draining than it had been at Shooters Hill. The men in Kent had been well enough to ship home, but most of the patients here were not up to the journey back to England.

She had arrived in the autumn of 1915, when in addition to the mutilations caused by shells and guns, there had been a new, unexpected enemy to fight: gas. Gas had first been used by the Germans in April at Ypres, and the resulting blue faces and rasping choking coughs had been at first horrific, as was the gangrene that the gas could cause. In the interests of the patients she and the other nurses had had to come to terms with it, though they never became used to the appalling waste of human life. The Battle of Loos had produced fearful casualty rolls, and still little ground was gained or lost. Once again the men had settled into the trenches while winter mud and cold made major offensives unlikely, though the skirmishing continued unabated. With the approaching spring it would all begin again as both sides strove to resolve the deadlock.

They were now nearing the end of February, and news had come yesterday of the German attack at Verdun, the stronghold in the east of France which the French were determined to hold at all costs. With it had come an urgent request for volunteer nurses to help out in the French hospitals near the battlefield, which were overwhelmed with casualties. The field ambulances run by volunteer Americans were arranging to fetch them over, and, listening to the drivers' graphic accounts of the appalling conditions, Arabella had requested permission to go. It seemed to her that in some small way she would be helping François by nursing his countrymen. Some of the friends of his youth might be amongst the victims and, although she knew that being surrounded by French voices and customs would take her right back to the days of Monte Carlo and Paris, she steeled herself to do it.

They had travelled on the rough roads all night; the jolting made it impossible to sleep, and Arabella rubbed bleary eyes as they arrived at a fine-looking château near Verdun. The outside appearance was deceptive, however, and inside were not the fine appurtenances of a country house, but the smell of ether and the stench of decay and death. She quickly discovered that the numbers of wounded were so huge and supplies so limited that scant help could be given to any of them. Even ambulances lacked priority on the one narrow road to and from Verdun, for reinforcements were more important than caring for the wounded. Most of them died, the transport driver had told her laconically, and there were few doctors. Arabella nerved herself to face sights far worse than ever before. She determinedly put her heart and stomach at an ice-cold distance in order that she could do her best to help, and her good command of French promptly ensured she was in constant demand.

Closing her eyes in the nurses' room, trying to gain strength after she had been there a week, Arabella let the chatter flow around her, making no effort to understand the French or take part in the English conversation. She needed to conserve what energy she had left. Nevertheless her thoughts drifted back to the past as she picked out the word "ballet". She automatically snapped back to attention to hear: "*Un danseur, le pauvre.* Death is near."

The ice in her heart cracked. There were thousands of dancers, she reminded herself, yet her stomach churned so fiercely and she was shivering so much that she could not hold the cup.

"What's his name?" she asked, but already she knew.

"François Santine. He must have been so handsome – so sad—"

"And his injuries?" Arabella could scarcely choke the words out.

"He has lost a leg, and has gangrene, of course. He will not live, that is plain, but he must have always had sad eyes, that one."

François laughing with his sandwich in his mouth? François twinkling at her, kissing her? No, his eyes had not always been sad.

"It is war," Arabella said painfully. "It does that to all of them. Where is he, Jeanne? I know François. I must see him."

"He may already have gone to the railway," Jeanne warned her.

223

Many patients were shipped on straightaway. "But if he remains, I will take you, if you wish."

Arabella walked in a dream into the past she had been convinced was dead. And so it shortly would be. He was not expected to live, and the nurses always knew. How could she presume to think François would want to see her again? It would be different if she were Maria, who was his wife, but Arabella had long ago faced the fact that François' love for her had been forgotten. Yet how could she not go? Every inch in her cried out to rush straight to him; fate could surely not be so cruel as to deny her this.

He did not even have a bed, only a thin mattress on the floor amid twenty such others. Arabella saw him immediately, his black hair against the one thin pillow, the white gaunt face, the sickness it revealed. Even the blanket over him could not disguise the now deformed body beneath. The dancer who had danced out the magic of his art could now do so only in his mind.

His face, despite the unshaven growth and suffering, was so little changed. Why had not the years marked him, made him a different François whom she could greet as a friend? This one was still her lover, and tore Arabella's heart apart.

His eyes were closed, and she hesitated to wake him lest the shock was too great. Or was she afraid that he might not recognise her, or look at her with indifference? The question was settled for her, for as she hesitantly approached, his eyes opened and looked straight at her.

"I knew it was you, *ma mie*. My dreams told me so."

The love in his rasping voice, the look on his face dissolved the long, anguished months of separation. She had been wrong. This was no lover of the past. He was here with her now, his love unchanged, yet all else so terrifyingly different. She still needed reassurance, however, to be quite certain that it was her François and not Maria's husband, albeit with fond memories.

"I thought I should come. I have just arrived here by chance." She sat down at his side on the floor, and took the hand that lay over the blanket.

He looked puzzled. "But I knew you would come someday. I could not believe that you no longer loved me, even though you fled from me."

Fled from him? She stared at him, not understanding. Was his sickness making him lose touch with reality?

"I never fled from you, my love."

"I was told you were married to Arnold, yet God has sent you to my side in France. Are you real?" Doubt filled his eyes. "I have strange nightmares."

"I am real, I am here at your side. I am married to no one, save to you in my heart." How could he have imagined she would have married Arnold?

"Take my hand, Arabella, and then I shall know that to be true."

His eyes closed, and she felt the tremors running through his hand. The hand seemed to be dancing in hers, full of artistry and love, over the battlefield of life.

"Sleep now," she whispered. "I will return." But his hand would not let her, and his eyes opened again.

"No. I shall die – I know it. You must stay."

"But Maria should know. She is your wife. Cannot I—?"

"Maria?" he interrupted bitterly. "I do not know or care about her. She may be with our son, or with her parents. I left the Ballets Russes, I left her and came to defend France, for France was all I had left after you had gone."

"You have a son?" Arabella's voice broke. It might – it *should* – have been hers. And what did he mean by "gone"?

"She took him from me, as was natural."

"Why did you marry her, François?" She tried to keep her voice steady. "Was it that you thought our love was only a dream that was shattered by my accident?"

"What else could I do? You had been taken from me."

"*Taken* from you? How?" she cried, tears of frustration overwhelming her decision not to speak of such unhappy times. "I spent months waiting for you, but you did not write, you did not call on me. At first I told myself we were separated by war, but then I knew it was more than that. At last I heard you had married Maria and I understood that you no longer loved me."

His eyes grew fierce. "You understood nothing, Arabella. Not write? Not call? I wrote every day, but heard nothing. I called on Arnold's London home each day until I found out where you were. Then I called on you in Kent, but was turned from the door. You blamed me for your accident, Maria said."

"*Maria* said that?" Arabella moaned in growing horror. "Oh, my love, she is Morgana. She deceived us both, but she was too

225

close for us to recognise that. I had no letters from you, nothing. I did not know where you were, whether you were in Italy, Russia, France, America even. I was told you thought yourself responsible for my accident. I believed guilt had made you forget me."

"But I even came to England again before I married, but again the lady said you did not wish to see me."

"*Gwen* said that?"

"Arnold's sister, yes."

So many traitors.

"*Ma mie.*" He painfully turned to her. "I shall not live much longer."

"You must, François; oh, now you must live for me," she cried in agony.

"For you, I will try." His voice was already weaker. "I suffered no guilt over it, save in hurrying myself to the stage. I believe" – he hesitated, then continued – "it was Maria who tripped you up. I thought it an accident all this while and that she was not aware of it. Now I see that she planned it all along. She had never forgotten that once, briefly, we believed ourselves in love. She believed her career depended on me. She saw you were my inspiration, but thought with you gone, I would be inspired by her. First Maria cheated me of you, and now death will do the same."

"No," she cried. "I will not have it. You shall recover. We shall dance again."

He smiled slightly. "Do you know what happened when I left? No – how could you? Maria and I went to Florence, where Diaghilev was delighted to see me. He asked me to choreograph for him again, for although Miassin was learning, he was not yet ready. Maria was constantly urging me to write a ballet for her, but I managed only by dreaming of you. When this war is over you may still hear of *Lancelot and Guinevere;* that and *The Faerie Queen* both are mine. They are good, because your memory inspired me, but I could stand no more. My country needed soldiers, not dancers, and even though I knew I would die, I did not care. If the Unicorn was to die after being betrayed by a maiden, then at least it would be a death that was of service to someone. I had thought the maiden you, but it was Maria, always Maria. When I reached the trenches I saw what war is. Death is not glorious, and the service of one man's death is lost amidst the slaughter . . ."

He began to ramble, and Arabella lulled him into sleep. This time his hand fell from hers, and she ran for the doctor. He looked at her as if she were mad to call him for one dying man when so many had to be attended to, and turned away. Panic-stricken, she returned to François' side, and once more his eyes flew open as she approached.

"Come here," he said hoarsely, "come close." She knelt to bend over him. "Arabella," he continued urgently, "I am dying now."

"No." The agony pierced her. "Please, François, fight. I love you as I've always loved you."

"I have not the strength."

"Then tell the Unicorn to fight for you."

He managed to smile. "When unicorns die they go to paradise, but I have my paradise already now you are here."

She tried again. "The Nightingale *doesn't* die, not as we wrote it. But I will, dear love, if you leave me now. You revived the Nightingale, and you have brought me back to life. Together we will live!"

He was only half listening to her. "My love, do you truly believe that all unicorns go to paradise?"

"Yes." Tears blinded her eyes.

"Then we shall be together one day. The Unicorn is the power of God, and it cannot be His plan that our love should die."

"No, you must live!"

"I cannot, but you must see that our love will come to happiness. Now, *chérie*, Arnold is a good man. If he listened to Maria's scheme, if he succumbed to deceiving you, I know it was because he loves you. Marry Arnold, please, for my sake."

"I cannot," she choked. "How can you ask me to marry him after what he has done?"

"Because I know that you are fond of him, and that he did what he did because he believed, however wrongly, it was right for you. He loves you. Have the children with him that we have not had, bear them as I have fathered my son, and let them know our story. Somehow, if you have faith, it will be fulfilled, for the power of dreams is stronger than that of one generation. The Unicorn shall still have his sweet Nightingale . . ."

The hand in hers was limp now, but Arabella sat there together with him, willing herself into the future for his sake. Then she bent over him, kissed his eyes, his cheek, his loving mouth, gently closed his eyes, and rose to return to her duties.

Fourteen

In England the bells, so long muffled, would be ringing. Here in France the end of the war heaved into being with a great sigh. No one could quite believe it, even when the hour of eleven o'clock had struck here in Rouen. Then, slowly, the atmosphere had begun to change. The unbelievable had actually happened. The war which most people had expected to drag on into 1919 was over, an armistice signed on this eleventh day of the eleventh month. No matter that the guns had been booming death right up till the last moment, no matter that another enemy, the Spanish flu, was laying its deadly hand upon them; over four years of war had ended, and this kind of slaughter would surely never happen again.

Arabella and the other nurses had gone round the wards telling the patients of the good news. Those who would recover and those near to death greeted it with equal relief. It seemed to Arabella the whole world must be giving out a great sigh of exhaustion. There could be little joy, for too many had suffered and died.

"You'll be able to go home to your sweetheart now," joked one soldier.

"Yes," she smilingly answered.

He was perceptive, however. "Sorry, ducks. He'd want you to find someone else, though; that's what I'd feel."

"Perhaps." It was over two years, and still nothing had changed. She had closed off her heart when François died, save for her patients. When she looked at each young face, she saw a François; each note she helped them write home was for her. Soon, however, her work here must be over. The hospital would not close just because the war had ended, but as patients gradually left there would be little need for VADs. Then would come the need for choice. She could train further and stay in nursing, she could return to her parents, or she could do as François had suggested: marry Arnold.

She had delayed the decision too long, and now Arabella was suddenly frightened because she could not see her path ahead. How could she marry Arnold in her present state of merciful suspension from any other issues of life save the ones before her: illness, death and hope? How could she return to the life of a wife, and perhaps mother, without wearing a hypocritical mask for ever? It wouldn't be fair on Arnold. Somewhere there must be a path back, but where could it be found?

In her free time she strolled into Rouen, where the streets were by now full of revellers. She pushed her way through, for it was not here that help could be found. She went instead into the Gothic magnificence of Rouen Cathedral. This too was crowded with worshippers giving thanks for the ending of the war. She sat down in a pew, but her prayers seemed empty and she felt as alone here as in the streets.

Then something made her glance towards the windows. And there she saw it: a unicorn, sitting serene amid his enemies, untouchable through his faith, the light shining on him through the blue, green and beige colourings of the stained glass. How had she never noticed him before? It must always have been there, but she had not had the eyes to see. *This* was the way, François' way.

"Give me your strength, Lord. Give me your unicorn's strength."

A great peace, a great light, consumed Arabella as she prayed, and she felt the strength within her building up. The light would be before her on the path for the rest of her life; its burning clarity would be there to be called upon, and never forgotten. The Unicorn had infinite strength, and would be with her for ever.

With the first signs of spring Arabella's war work came to an end, and she returned to London. She had not seen Arnold for three years, and when he came to greet her as she was ushered into his Hampstead drawing room, she saw that he had aged, and that anxiety had etched itself on his face. She had maintained her correspondence with him through the war, but with never a word of François. She had written instead of the hospital, of the patients, of her fellow nurses, and of the war; he of Gwen, of London in time of war, of his own concerns – and of the London musical scene. Well aware that such references were far from casual, she never commented on them.

She felt a sudden rush of affection as she saw him, realising that he too had suffered, and that he was cautious, waiting for her to speak. That was right, for she had much to say, and it would be hard for him. She put her arms round him and kissed him on the cheek.

"A good friend's embrace to show how pleased she is to be back," she declared.

"And that is all?" he asked stiltedly. "Arabella—"

"I know what you are going to say, Arnold, but I have to talk to you first. Do you still feel as you did about me?"

"Can you doubt it?"

"Then I must tell you, Arnold, why my heart is weeping. I saw François. I was with him when he died. He was terribly wounded at Verdun; his leg was amputated, but he died of infection."

The colour drained from Arnold's face. "Why did you not write to me of this? I could have helped you in your grief. You should not have borne it alone."

Arabella took no notice. She *had* been alone, but was so no longer, thanks to François. "We both learned then what Maria and you had done to us, particularly Maria. Her poison dripped in my ear little by little, while you kept François' letters from me, you barred the door to him, you tried to persuade me I should never dance again in classical ballet, but only to your tune. I have even discovered it was not Diaghilev who paid for Dr Hastings, but you, Arnold. And, worst, I know too that Maria caused me to fall on the stairs in her last desperate attempt to stop the third act."

Arnold cried out, obviously genuinely shocked. "Arabella, *no*. It was an accident."

"Can you be sure of that?"

He was silent. "I did not know, Arabella. I swear to God I did not know. I believed Maria when she told me you had tripped against François' foot. She was there, and I was not."

"And now what do you believe?"

He sighed. "It is true that Maria and I often discussed your best interests, thinking them not to lie with François and the Ballets Russes, and it is true I agreed with her we should not encourage your marriage, especially when she brought to me such firm proof, as it seemed then, of François' relationship with Diaghilev. And it is true she sympathised with my plight over the ending of the third act, and urged me to maintain my objections. François, she assured me, would come round to my point of view; he had told her he was almost persuaded. How could I have imagined she would want to stop the ballet so desperately that she would hurt you, with her own role so prominent?"

"But when she married François did you not realise then how eaten up with jealousy she had been, so that rather than see me shine, she would ensure the ballet never took place? There would be other ballets for her to shine in, if only she could rid François of me. Tell me, Arnold, make me understand what made you Maria's accomplice. Please."

He flushed, and put his head in his hands. When he lifted it again, his eyes were swimming with tears. "Because she told me what I wanted to hear, that you would never be happy with François. Can you forgive me, Arabella? I ask for nothing more than that. I knew when you learned you would be able to dance again that I had lost you. It was genuinely Hastings' opinion that you would not dance again. I had hoped merely to delay you from rushing to the Continent to rejoin François, and allowed myself to agree with Maria it was best to keep you away from François' letters and presence. Never, *never* would I have conspired with Maria to trip you, however."

"I believe you, Arnold."

"I loved you then, I love you now, Arabella. Never would I have done anything to hurt you so terribly."

"Save to help take François from me."

He bowed his head. "I still believe that to have been in your best interests. Santine was a genius, but his head was in the clouds; he could not give you what I could. Love, yes, but in marriage one needs more than that."

"I did not ask for more."

"And so you have come to tell me that you will not marry me. I understand. I hope at least you will be my friend, that we may forget the past."

"No, Arnold, I have not come to tell you that." Arabella came to him, "I am here to tell you that I will marry you, that I will be your loving wife, that I will bear your children, and that we shall be happy, you and I."

His immediate look of astonished joy vanished as he saw her expression. "There's something more, isn't there, my love, something you have to tell me? I know your face; I can read it like a painter. Tell me what it is."

"I have never written to you of my dancing, Arnold, and when you mentioned it in your letters I ignored it. While I was nursing, I had little energy to spare to dance. Practice was hard, nor was music easily come by. I practised only to the music in my head, and although my ankle is strong again now, I am too old to re-enter classical ballet. Nor would I wish to."

"There are other ways of dancing. I can write—"

"No, Arnold, that is not possible. I will be your loving wife, but I will not dance for you. Or," as she saw his expression change, "for anyone in public. My dancing is for me alone. Do you understand?" she asked gently, as she saw the deep unhappiness in his face.

"I understand for myself, Arabella; it must be your choice. But that your gifts should be so wasted . . . I cannot bear it."

"But I can." Music and dance would remain trapped inside her, the music that was François, that was ballet. One day, however, it would live again.

*   *   *

"Tell me, Tara," Giselle said, pouring the tea, her hand not quite steady, the gaiety in her voice unsuppressible, "how did you manage to persuade Margaret to come with you?"

Such a question seemed calculated to send her mother completely up the wall before they even began. To Tara's surprise, however, Margaret herself answered. "She didn't, Mother. Believe it or not, I dragged Tara here, and a hard job it was."

Giselle looked sharply from one to the other. "So, this is bad news. Not that I am not delighted to see you, Margaret." She reached out a hand and patted her daughter's, a more informal gesture than the ritual double kiss at the door. "What had happened, *ma petite* Tara, that made you not wish to come?"

Thanks, Mother. Tara gritted her teeth. "There seemed no point," she answered. "Things are tough at work, and I was just postponing the visit. That's all. There's no mystery."

"No truth, either," Giselle retorted, as Margaret laughed. "Who's going to tell me? You, Tara, or will you, Margaret?"

"Me," Margaret said promptly. "It's all the fault of your blessed unicorns, Mother."

"Naturally," murmured Giselle.

"Tara has got in too deep both with the ballet and young Josh Santine, and now it's all gone wrong with both. She's throwing in the sponge. You began it all, you should be able to understand what's going on. I certainly can't."

"*Ma petite*" – Giselle turned gravely to Tara – "I told you and Josh to find your own ending. Have you done so? Is *this* the one you choose?"

"I have no choice," Tara cried fiercely. "Josh more or less walked out on me, so I've decided to go back to live with William – and don't look at me like that, Giselle. I was happy with him before all this started, and this ending is Josh's doing, not mine. And now Josh is redoing *The Unicorn* ballet into three acts—"

"But this is splendid."

"Not so splendid. He wants to drop the Prince score. *And* he's living with Sybille—"

"Answer my question," Giselle interrupted sharply. "*Is this the ending you choose?*"

Tara looked at her mother for help, but found none. Nor was Giselle going to relent. This choice, she realised with sickening clarity, had to be of her own free will. *A mon seul désir.* And so the struggle began again. Oh, how easy it would be to go back to William and her old life. She had not cancelled her lunch with him, merely postponed it. With William, she had a past and a future. Even if by some miracle things could be sorted out with Josh, what kind of life might lie ahead of her? An uncertain one, for sure. They had so little in common, love alone would have to carry them through – and since Josh's love had vanished and hers was fast following, that was that.

And yet what did she want? The easiest path, or the path her five-year-old self had longed for, dancing in her ballet shoes, the moment when she was allowed to try her points at last, discovering the world of music and magic that it created? In her nostrils a familiar smell came back: the scent of roses. The rose that she had left on Josh's pillow had been artificial, but the love it had conveyed was not; and its scent was with her now, Arabella's gift, to tell her that the colours, the hopes, and the dreams could be hers again if she danced on the stage of life instead of sitting in the audience. Who would be her partner, however, lifting her, inspiring her, always there and never still, reaching for the same grails as she sought?

"I choose *Josh*." It was a cry of triumph. "I choose Josh," Tara repeated to herself more quietly, savouring the import of those amazing three words.

"Splendid, *ma petite*," Giselle relaxed happily. "And now we must see how this can be achieved. Margaret" – she turned innocently to her daughter – "I fear there may be talk of unicorns. Do you wish to leave the room, my dear?"

"No." It came out as a growl, but it was said.

"Even more splendid. But now we must all leave the room together, for I wish to take you to the Unicorn room."

"I knew it," said Margaret in resignation. "I suppose I asked for it."

It was strange to be in the Unicorn room with her mother, who at home controlled the household with her impetuous dash at organisation; here she was quiet, maybe disapproving, or maybe looking at the room with new eyes. Whichever it was, she left the floor to Giselle, and wandered around studying photographs and tapestries.

"As Margaret is with us, we won't dwell too long on unicorns, if I can help it," Giselle smiled at Tara. "I would like to show you some pictures of the *real* Unicorn and his Nightingale." She produced an ornate Victorian-style album, very old, with worn leather. It had been lovingly kept and cherished, and the photographs were all of François and Arabella. Some were professional studies, more of them informal snapshots. François doing a handstand against a tree, François holding a sandwich aloft, and one, the only one, of them both together, in what looked like Kensington Gardens, perhaps taken by a roving photographer. Their young faces, full of hope and excitement, gazed out at them over the years.

"But how did she manage to keep this, while she was married to Arnold?" Tara asked. "Suppose he had seen it?"

"The Unicorn room was not my idea," Giselle answered, "though you may well have thought so, Margaret. It was my mother's. She had one at her home in London, into which Arnold never went; nor did he wish to. It was understood. When she moved into this house after Arnold's death, she brought it all with her and asked me to keep it intact. I imagine that François' son did the same, though with more difficulty since he could not have known his father. François died in 1916."

"What happened to them both?" Tara asked. "I think I can guess, but I'd like you to tell us."

"The story of *The Unicorn and the Nightingale* tells you. Arabella and François too were under a spell, though they never realised it. The Morgana in their case was Maria Rostovna. It was she, my mother told me, who caused her accident. Maria conspired – she did not say how, but I guessed my father had been involved – to keep François away from Arabella, for she was jealous both of François' love for Arabella and of Arabella's career. Then war broke out a few days after Arabella's accident, and believing she did not love him, François married Maria. My father was greatly in love with Arabella and tried to dissuade her from going back to classical ballet. She decided not to return of her own volition, however, and became a VAD in France. It was there she met François again, after he was seriously wounded at Verdun in February 1916. My mother, by some miracle, some might say the power of the Unicorn, volunteered for work at the hospital where he was taken, and they were reunited."

"But then he died," Tara whispered, agonised at what Arabella had suffered. "It was an unhappy ending after all."

"Not altogether. He gave my mother his blessing to marry Arnold, and when the war was over she did so. I was born in 1920, when François' son was five years old."

"She was able to dance again?" Margaret asked.

"She chose not to. In public, that is. She danced at home for me, and only for me, never for my father. She hoped I might have inherited her gifts, I suppose, but I had not. I could dance, and I have danced, but I did not have sufficient talent for classical ballet."

"So you tried to nag me into it," Margaret threw at her.

Giselle smiled cherubically. "Yes, but you, my love, were even more untalented than I was."

"No, Giselle." Tara cried out in horror at this worst of all gibes. "Mother *was* talented. You just never saw it. She has so many gifts: she can create beauty in a garden, in a home, she can give love, she can . . ."

Mother and daughter looked at each other, and it was Giselle's eyes that dropped first. "Tara is quite right, Margaret," she said quietly. "I never saw that. I was so obsessed with the need to find the one who would carry on the flame, I never saw the warmth around me."

"Anyway" – Tara was still furious – "you said I was the one, but I'm probably a slightly worse dancer than Mother would have been."

"Even Arabella could not hope for everything. I still believe you are the one, Tara. You can make music happen, even if you do not dance to it."

"How much did Arabella brainwash you with unicorns?" Margaret asked abruptly.

"She tried not to," Giselle answered defensively. "I knew nothing save that she took me into the Unicorn room every now and then, and was always weaving or painting unicorns, as if she could make things happen the harder she tried. She gave me ballet lessons, which I loved, but I never met her hopes. I never knew how much I had disappointed her till many years later."

Margaret's eyes were full of tears, which she struggled to hide. Never could Tara remember her crying before. Giselle noticed, and immediately was full of remorse. "But I told you too soon, Margaret. I am sorry, *ma petite*."

"I *can* grow things," Margaret cried out fiercely. "Tara's right. I have a home, I have a husband—"

"And you have a mother," Giselle said gravely.

Margaret began to cry in earnest, and Tara crept out of the room. She wasn't needed here. Instead she wandered around the garden, thinking of life's oddities. How strange that unicorns, having once divided Giselle and her daughter, now appeared to be reuniting them. Perhaps, even yet, the same could happen between her and Josh, though it was hard to see how. There was no more she could do, and the path back was definitely muddied by his having moved Sybille in.

Giselle and Margaret reappeared in the garden arm in arm half an hour later.

"We've agreed an armistice," Margaret said cheerfully.

"What are the terms?" Tara asked guardedly.

"We're going to sort you out, my girl."

Tara laughed. "Tall order. Too much baggage."

"Baggage can be shed, and any that can't belongs to this whole blessed unicorn-obsessed family. If you ask me, it's our role to sort Arabella out first," Margaret replied. "Mother is quite convinced she has it all worked out, and Arabella's unicorn is hard at work trying for her happy ending."

"Is it true, Giselle?" Tara asked.

"Yes. Not long before my father died in early 1939 Arabella told me the whole story of her love for François. I'd always known a little about it, though I hadn't taken it too seriously, but it was then that she impressed on me that it wasn't just another unhappy love affair. Her love was going to be fulfilled in some future generation, through the power of the Unicorn. I thought she was gaga, but the more she talked, I began to see some point in it. After all, I had just met Antoine – don't stiffen up so, Margaret. It's time you listened to that story too. I was eighteen, I'd met a gorgeous painter, what could I think but that Arabella or her Unicorn had sent me this fantastic Frenchman, just as François had come to her? I would have fallen in love with Antoine anyway, but not perhaps so quickly. That was in late 1938, the year Hitler had marched into Austria, the year of Munich, and the year all rational people realised war was coming. In 1939 it came. In those days one thought carefully about making love, but it seemed to me that Arabella's story was being played out again, particularly when I found that Antoine drew unicorns."

"You're joking," Tara exploded.

"Not a bit. He drew pictures for children as a sideline, and unicorns in particular. I asked him why, and he told me that as a child he had been fascinated by a unicorn in the stained glass of Rouen Cathedral. He *was* your father, Margaret," she said sadly.

Margaret said nothing.

"And my grandfather," Tara added stoutly.

"Yes. Antoine loved you, Tara."

Margaret swallowed painfully. "It will take time, Mother. Leave it, can we?"

Giselle bowed her head in acquiescence.

"But the ending of the ballet" – Tara tried to divert attention from Margaret by switching subjects – "was to be an unhappy one, so far as we could judge by the score. Josh decided to change it for his one-acter, but Arabella's story ended thus, and now so has mine. It's all very well for me to say I choose Josh, but there are two in this equation, and so far as I know Josh is rushing straight ahead to do his three-acter but not to Prince's score. It won't even be a ballet."

"I said you should make your own ending, Tara. Did you? You did not. You let events dictate to you. Arabella told me that one's decision for happiness had to be of one's own free will, and I chose Antoine. That was the commission Arabella laid on me – not to ram unicorns down your throat at every point, or to force you into ballet shoes that would not fit. I was to try to see which way the Unicorn would leap."

"Or the Nightingale fly," Tara added savagely. "I understand now."

"And so, I think, can I," Margaret muttered. "But—"

"The problem with you, Margaret, is that there's *always* a but," Giselle said.

"And the problem with you," Margaret snarled cheerfully, "is that there never is."

"To go back to the ending, Giselle," Tara said. She was now impatient to get the whole truth. "If it was always unhappy, as in the score, how can I suddenly change it for Josh and myself?"

"I didn't tell you it was unhappy. You told me Josh had a set of choreographic notes for the first acts and then a blank over which François had written "And the third act was Armageddon". What Josh could not know was that François, my father Arnold Prince, and Diaghilev argued about that ending for months. It's what brought about the final catastrophe. My father refused to write music for the happy ending François required – well, he would, wouldn't he? François was adamant that it should end happily, and as the score was commissioned for his scenario he was in the right. My father brought matters to a head, however, by refusing to allow his music to be used at all, on the very morning of the dress rehearsal, after the first two acts. He had written to Arabella to say he would alter his music for her sake, but then changed his mind when he found out François had written his own. It was based on—"

"I think I can tell you," Tara interrupted. She knew what was

239

coming, for it hadn't been her idea but Arabella's. "'Sweet Nightingale', the old Cornish folk song."

"Yes. And, Tara, if anything was needed to convince me Arabella's Unicorn is still around, your knowing that fact would be it," Giselle answered.

"Nevertheless, you're now telling me that all the while Josh struggled to complete his adaptation of the ballet, you *knew* the original had a happy ending?"

"More than that. I have the score, for Arabella gave it me with François' scribbled notes. She went to see Diaghilev in the twenties to see if anything of François' remained in the Ballets Russes archives. They were a mess, but this turned up."

"Then why didn't you give it to us?" Tara howled. "If you knew the trouble it has caused—"

"Because Arabella forbade it," Giselle replied patiently. "You and Josh were to have free choice over the ballet – as they did. All she wanted the Unicorn to do was to give you a little encouragement now and then."

"And now what happens?" Tara demanded belligerently. "Any encouragement now?"

Giselle's expression was grave. "You have made your choice and the unicorns should do the rest with your help. My only advice is to think about Maria Rostovna. Is there a Maria in your life? Is there an Arnold Prince, come to that?"

"Both," Tara replied hollowly. She remembered who the sly and furtive lady in the New York tapestry had reminded her of. It was Arabella's Maria, and her own—

The ringing of the doorbell inside the house startled them.

"I'll go," Tara offered, knowing that Marie, Giselle's maid-cum-companion, was out shopping. She ran quickly through the house to open the door. On the doorstep was Sybille.

*   *   *

Arabella watched her daughter carefully, as she struggled at the *barre* in the room she used for dancing. She was graceful, she had a dancer's body and style, but she would not be a classical ballet dancer. It didn't matter. Arabella knew she had been lucky in her daughter, and in her marriage. Perhaps Giselle would be the one to unite herself and François, perhaps not. That too did not matter,

To My Own Desire

for the future was infinite and she could wait. The Unicorn's power would go on, François had said so, and she knew he was right. But she and François were the ballet too, so that must be resolved first. Somehow it must be played, and the third act end with its "Sweet Nightingale". Then she and François could be at peace.

*   *   *

"What are you doing here?

Tara was as taken aback as if Morgana herself had appeared in all her Camelot glory, and it made her brusque. There was no point in beating about the bush, after all, it was obvious now that Sybille and William had been in cahoots all along. That was why Sybille had been keen for Tara to move in with her, and like a dope she'd gone.

"Is Josh here?' Sybille's face was expressionless, devoid of its usual good humour.

Take it easy, Tara, she warned herself. *Where was this heading?*

"No." For the moment truth would suffice. When Sybille did not budge, she said unwillingly, "You'd better come in." She could hardly do anything else, since Sybille had been at such pains to call here. *Why?* Had Josh been intending to come? Was he still coming and, if so, why?

She led the way through to the garden where Giselle and Margaret promptly stopped talking to greet the newcomer.

"Sybille wants to know where Josh is," Tara explained warily, after the introductions were complete.

A quick glance between her mother and grandmother. "We can't help, I'm afraid." Giselle rose. "Margaret, I need you in the kitchen, if you please."

Tara was to be left alone with Sybille – that was the message, endorsed by her mother's whisper in her ear as she left: "Armageddon?"

"Why should Josh be here?" Tara asked as soon as they were alone. She tried to retain at least something of their earlier friendly relationship – for the moment.

"Not to see you. To see your grandmother."

Right. Gloves off, Tara. "You should know where he is; you live with him. Or has he thrown you out?"

241

Sybille's eyes flickered. "No. But I still don't know where he is." She hesitated. "Do you have any ideas? I'm not asking for myself; it's for the ballet."

"Josh told me he was redoing it as a voice mime without the Prince score." Tara kept her voice non-committal. "What's that to do with my grandmother?"

"He couldn't get going with it. There was an argument, and the ABC threatened to pull out of the whole merger. They've given him a week to get his act together, but the next meeting's in three days' time. I thought he'd come here to get permission to use the Prince score again."

Tara thought quickly. This wasn't for Sybille, but for Josh. "I've got the Santine notes and score for his Act Three now."

"What you haven't got, unfortunately, is Josh."

"You'd better tell me everything, Sybille." There was obviously more to this than she'd heard yet.

"He's gone AWOL. No one knows where he is. He's a temperamental sort of cuss sometimes, as you well know, and he just walked out. No one's heard from him or seen him; he hasn't been back to the flat."

"Someone must know where he is."

"No one in the company. I've tried his parents, who swear blind they don't know, and that's all too likely to be true. I've even been through his address book. My last hope was that he'd come to you in Brittany. We've got to find him, Tara."

"We?" Her mother was right. This had to be Armageddon. "There *is* no we, Sybille, as you well know. Your 'we' was with William, when you both so successfully stitched me up."

Sybille actually had the nerve to laugh. "It was a pleasure, believe me."

Tara did, fuming with fury but determined to keep her temper.

"Personally," Sybille continued, "I can't see why on earth you'd want to leave William. Did you know he'd gone back to Claire? It didn't take long. Last Christmas, it was. He's a really nice chap. Unlike Josh."

"Your lover," Tara whipped back, grappling with this news. Was this another Sybille try-on? If so, it was an own goal. Tara's reaction was immense relief. After all, she should have expected it. William, the Rottweiler in business, was hardly likely to change breed in his personal affairs.

242

"And why not? My God, I was there for him years before you danced on to the stage. We started Music and Mime, we ran it together. We had plans for ballets long before you came along. My sort of ballets, not romantic slush like *The Unicorn and the Nightingale*. We're talking my life here, Tara."

Tara steadied herself – or was it Arabella doing it for her? "I notice," she replied quietly, "you weren't above taking a role in the romantic slush."

Sybille shrugged. "I have to support Josh, whatever my private feelings."

Tara longed to wipe that supercilious smirk from Sybille's face. And why shouldn't she? She'd go out into the battlefield and fight.

"Which do you want, Sybille? Career or Josh?"

The dark eyes narrowed. "Both."

"I can't guarantee that, I'm afraid. However, there's no problem, my grandmother says, about using the Prince score with François' own ending for the ballet, so that's your career nicely taken care of."

"Too good of you."

Tara ignored the sneer. "*And* I'll find Josh."

"So you do know where he is, you bitch."

"No, but I'll find out. When I do, though, that will be the end of your hold over him. You'll be out of his flat and private life, lock, stock and toilet bag."

"Josh has some say in this." Sybille's face was as hard as granite. "He wants me, not some frigid lawyer who thinks sex has to be authorised by an act of parliament before she'll indulge."

"Oh, Sybille," Tara said fervently, "how wrong can you be?"

In a moment she was back in Neuilly, in her lover's arms. The night was sweet, and birdsong filled the dawn. It was still there, waiting for her; she had only to step on stage, take her part in this ballet, and she would be there again. This time the door would not close in her face, as it had when she was seven. This time she was opening the door of her own free will, at her own desire, and inside was the land of colour, scents and sweetness she had sought for so long.

If – no, *when* – she could find the Pied Piper.

*   *   *

Suppose it went wrong again? Suppose the ballet never happened? So much could go wrong. Arabella was in agony, knowing she should trust the Unicorn to take over when she died, and not quite daring to. Alone in her dancing room she shut her eyes and listened to the music inside her. Not that of Arnold's lovely score, but that of François' "Sweet Nightingale" ending. She was an old lady now, but she could still dance the Nightingale's last solo of joy here in this room. And surely if she danced it, she could make it happen despite all the evil spells in the world.

*   *   *

Where would Josh have gone? Tara sat alone in Giselle's garden, thinking furiously. Neither her mother nor grandmother would, or even could, help now. Arabella, tell me where he is, she pleaded, but there was no apparent answer. He lives in London – where would he go? she asked herself. She had looked again at the photograph in Arabella's album of François and Arabella in Kensington Gardens, from which their faces stared out at her in blissful hopefulness, but still nothing occurred to her.

Then the thought of Kensington reminded her of Music and Mime, and so she came back to Sybille and a shattering thought. How did she know Sybille had been telling her the truth? Tara quickly ran through her contacts and decided there was only one person as likely as she to be feeling narked at Sybille's behaviour: Michael Brown. There was no reply from his old telephone number, however. Without much hope, she tried Sybille's Kensington home, and there to her surprise she struck gold.

Caution, Tara. He's in love with that woman – or was. "Is Sybille there? It's Tara."

"No. I thought she was off to see you."

"She arrived. I just thought it odd, as she's living with Josh, that she didn't know where he was."

"Ah."

"That tells me a lot, Michael. Thanks," she said cheerfully.

"In fact – look, Tara, I love Sybille, that's why I went along with it when she asked me to tell you she was living with Josh if you ever enquired. I've changed my mind, though. If anyone can find Josh, you can."

"Do you mean she's *not* living with him? Her gear was in his flat."

"Planted deliberately for the evening."

Blissful hope began to spring up but was promptly quenched. "No way, Michael. Josh *told* me she was living there."

"Did he? That's odd. Had you upset him?"

Tara tried to remember, and then groaned. "Yes; I said I was moving back to William."

"Ah. Not Josh's usual style, but nothing is nowadays."

Tara put the telephone down and returned to thought. Yesterday, she'd rung William to cancel lunch, congratulating him on having the sense to take up with Claire again.

He'd merely laughed. "I told Sybille not to tell you. Pity. It would have given me immense pleasure to have that lunch with you, listen to your telling me you'd graciously come back to me, and then tell you to push off."

"Is your face *worth* saving, William?" she joked back. Another own goal, this time William's. He'd let her off the hook of guilt without meaning to. Oh, his arrogance. How could she not have seen it? She was free at last. Free to find Josh – if only she knew where. It was time to consult the Unicorn.

She went back to the Unicorn room and stared once more at the photograph of Arabella and François. Kensington Gardens: the Princess of Wales, the Round Pond, and Peter Pan. That was all it said to her. The faces gazed back at her, as if willing her on. All very well, but where to? She wasn't Peter Pan; she couldn't fly through the air to Never-Never Land, though she could ask Tinkerbell what she thought of it all. Tara didn't need fairies, though; she needed a miracle. Perhaps she should clap? There was nothing to be lost by doing so – only it was not Tinkerbell, but Arabella for whom she did it. Nothing happened, however, which was hardly surprising. That's what came of stupid, childish notions like clapping.

Clapping? She remembered a crowd clapping, remembered herself clapping, on a spring day outside the Pompidou as a dark-haired student type danced a quaint unicorn dance. Where would Josh go if he went AWOL? *There*! She opened her eyes joyfully, convinced she had solved the problem, but such light of day as percolated the Unicorn room poured cold water on her idea. It was crazy to go to Paris on a mere whim. What were the chances of meeting him? Even if he were there, she might miss him by a hair's breadth for a million reasons.

Shut your eyes again, Tara, Arabella pleaded.

Slowly Tara closed her eyes again. It wasn't just Sybille and William's fault that she'd lost Josh, she knew now; it was her own. The something in herself that had made her hold back, however, had vanished now.

Keep your eyes shut, Tara. Keep thinking.

She was at the door of the mountain; her hand was about to push the door open, and still she hesitated. So far, for maybe nothing?

He's there, Tara. You know it, don't you?

Tara opened her eyes. She did know it, and this time the magic stayed, for it was within her. She was Arabella's great-grand-daughter, and the world should dance because of it.

It was a sunny summer's day when she reached the Pompidou. Crowds of tourists and schoolchildren had flocked there, watching the performers outside and melting away as the hat came round. There was an especially large crowd round the flying figure of a dark-haired student type, dancing to the music of a cassette player. It was playing the Arnold Prince score of the solo when the Unicorn believes Lilith dead. Tara watched for a few moments. What should she say? What to do to make it come right?

The ballet's nearing its end; play "Sweet Nightingale".

"Play 'Sweet Nightingale'," Tara cried of her own free will.

The dark head flew up, his astonished eyes met hers, and still the mask came down. Pray let me alone, was the message it sent from the song, but the song was past that stage now. She *knew* it was. The couple were sitting on the bank "where the primroses grow", to "hear the fond tale of the sweet Nightingale". All was well for them, and would be for her and Josh, for the Nightingale, though it sang in dark valleys, was love. François and Arabella had listened to its song, and so must she and Josh.

"Play it," she cried again triumphantly, ignoring the puzzled faces around her.

Still he hesitated, and the crowd dispersed, assuming the show over, until only Josh and herself remained.

"Play it," she insisted. She had to walk up to him, for he did not move.

"No. Suppose it isn't true?"

"It *is* true. Play it and dance it. You must have it on tape. We haven't much time."

She watched calmly as he changed cassettes. As the familiar strains began, Josh began to dance, not with the technique of Santine or Arabella, but in his own idiosyncratic way.

"Well," he came back to her as he finished, with a sort of hope in his eyes, "do you have a penny for the old man's hat?" He thrust out the same battered old hat towards her.

"I've the golden apples of paradise to offer," she said softly, as she dropped Santine's score for the ending into it. The panama looked so old, it could perhaps have been François' own. And maybe it was. "Josh, much of this has been Sybille and William's doing, but Morgana's spell is broken now. We're free."

"Not of you and I ourselves, Tara," he replied soberly. "Think about it. I listened to Sybille, you listened to William, both of us because we wanted to."

"Do you still love me Josh?"

"I never stopped."

Tara threw her arms around him. "Will you love me for ever, until we eat the golden apples up there with Arabella and François?"

"If you'll take the time to tell me what the hell you're on about, yes."

"Now who's being logical and sensible?"

With a whoop he swept her off her feet and into the air. "You'll never make a dancer," he jeered.

"No, but I can make music happen."

"What about magic?"

"That too."

247